Unhappy Camper

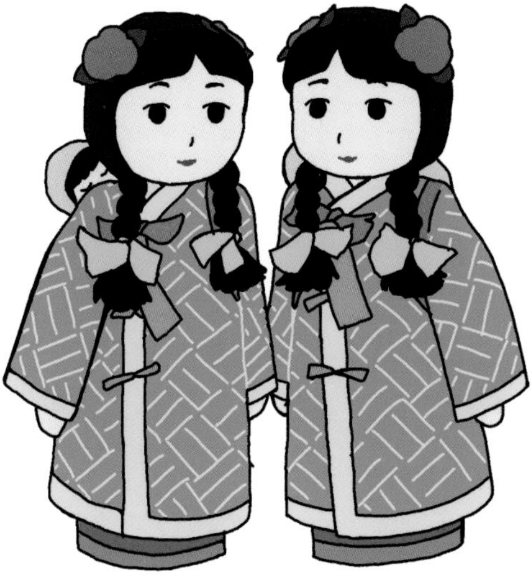

Lily LaMotte

Unhappy

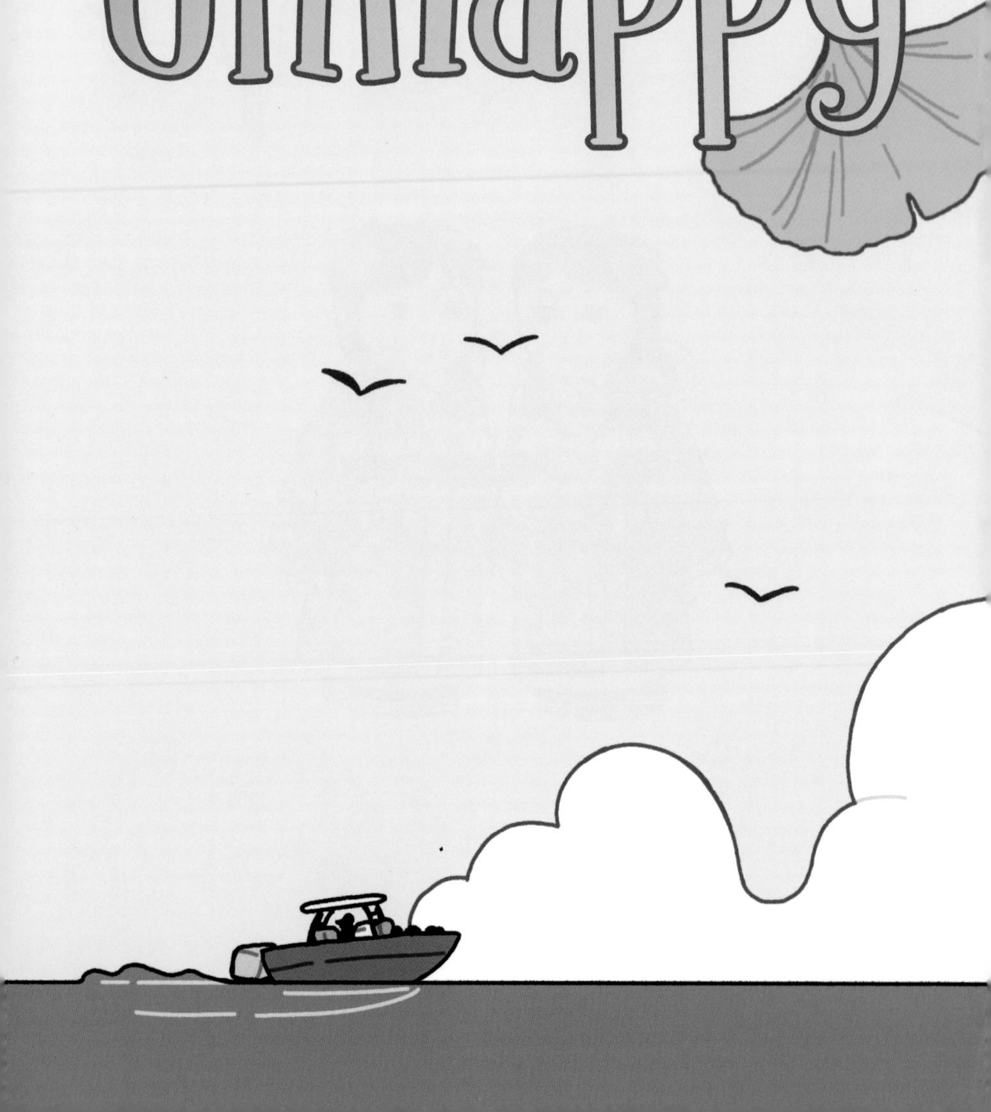

Camper

Ann Xu
and Sunmi

HARPER
alley

An Imprint of HarperCollinsPublishers

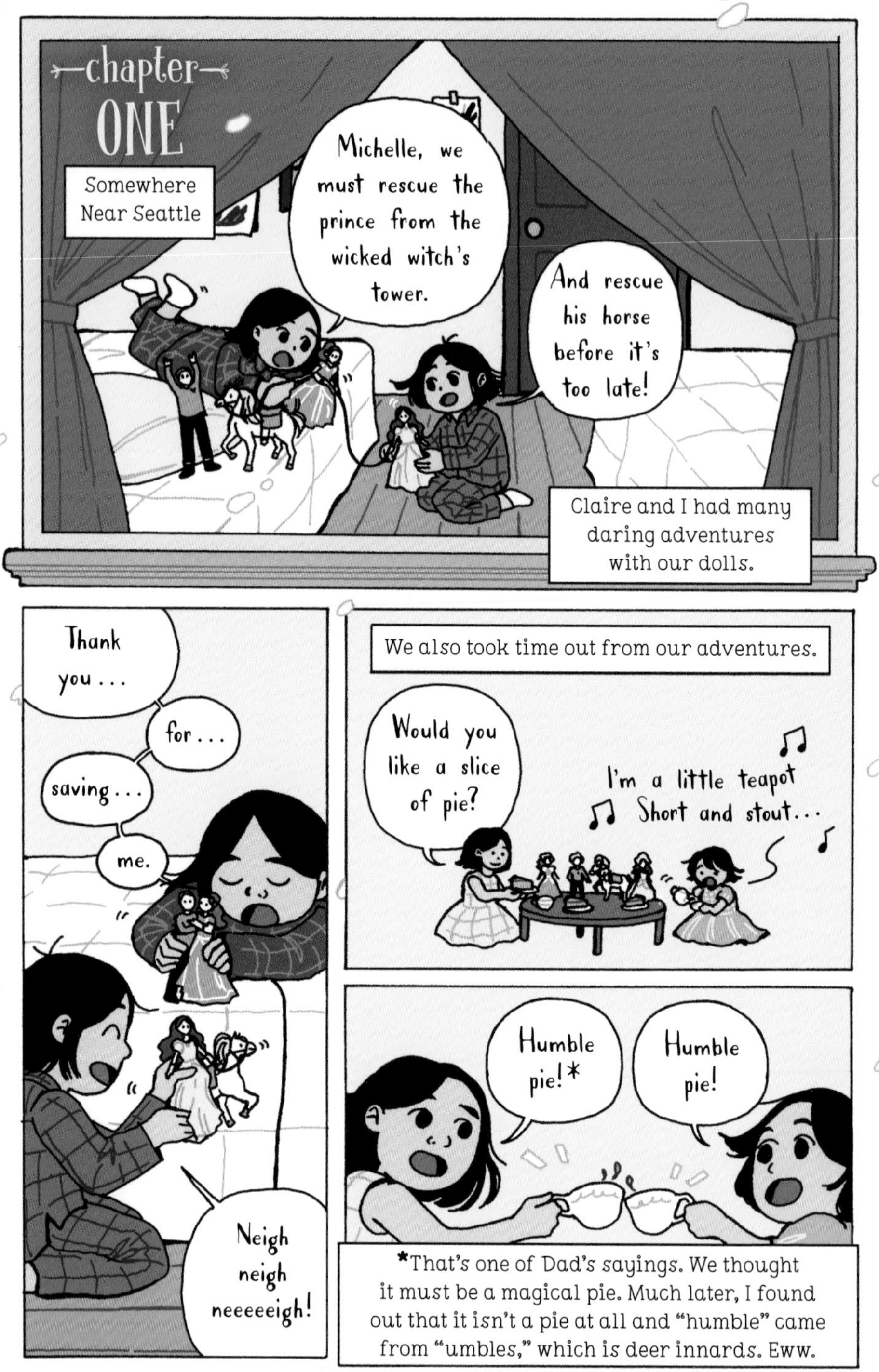

chapter
ONE
Somewhere Near Seattle
Michelle, we must rescue the prince from the wicked witch's tower.
And rescue his horse before it's too late!
Claire and I had many daring adventures with our dolls.
Thank you . . .
for . . .
saving . . .
me.
Neigh neigh neeeeeigh!
We also took time out from our adventures.
Would you like a slice of pie?
I'm a little teapot Short and stout . . .
Humble pie!*
Humble pie!
*That's one of Dad's sayings. We thought it must be a magical pie. Much later, I found out that it isn't a pie at all and "humble" came from "umbles," which is deer innards. Eww.

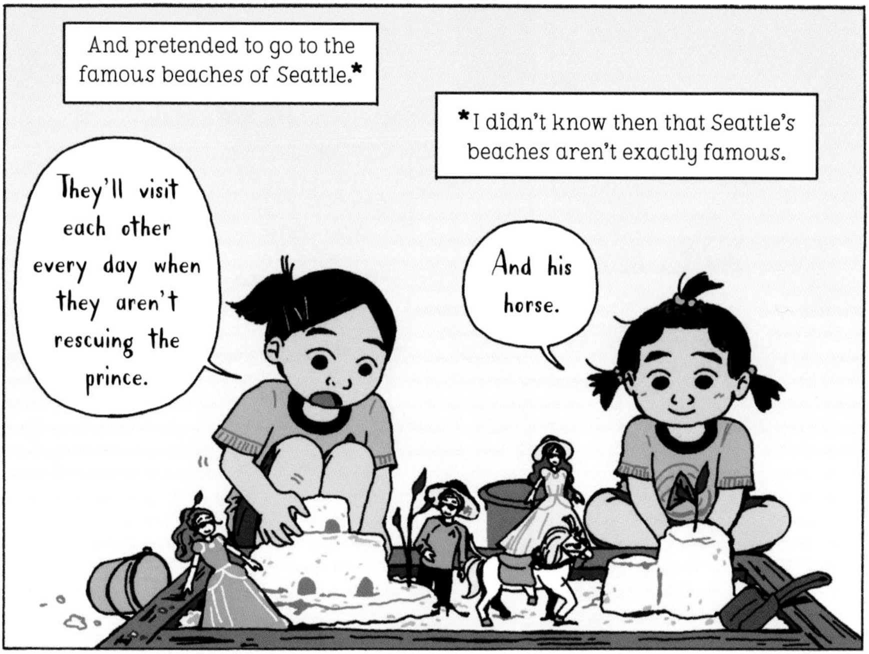
And pretended to go to the famous beaches of Seattle.*
*I didn't know then that Seattle's beaches aren't exactly famous.
They'll visit each other every day when they aren't rescuing the prince.
And his horse.

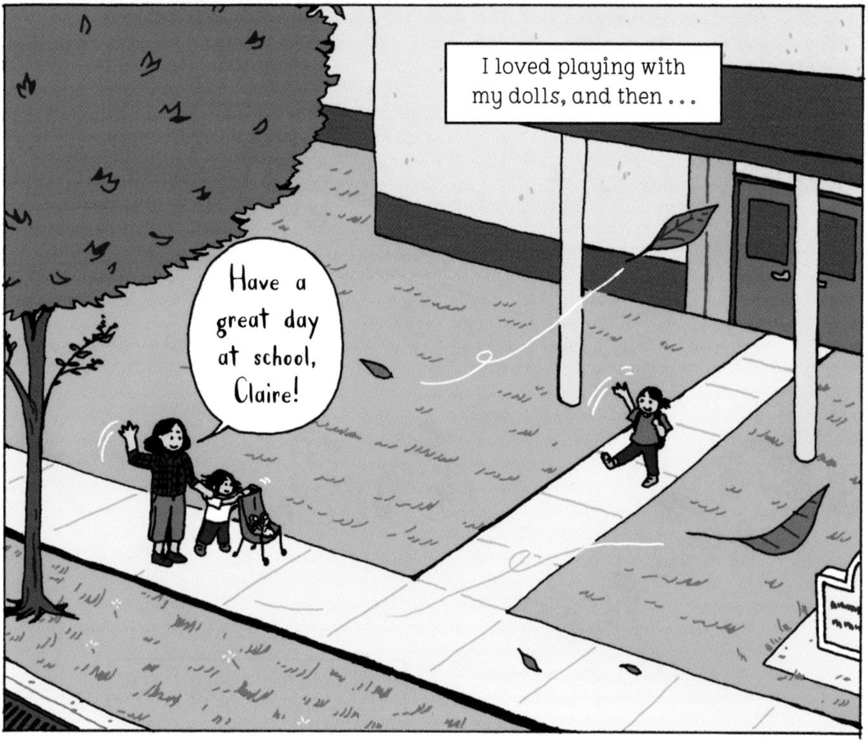
I loved playing with my dolls, and then . . .
Have a great day at school, Claire!

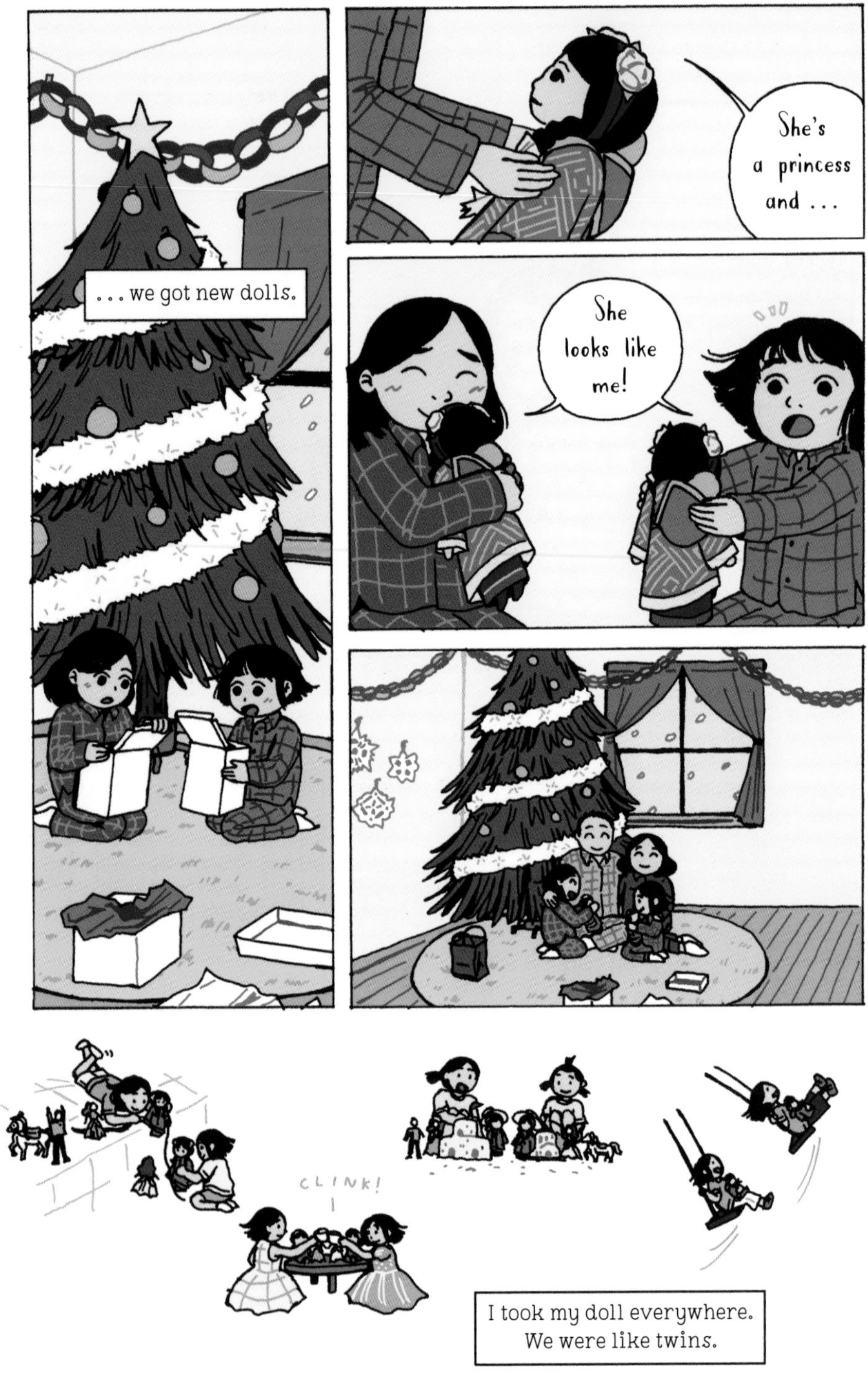

. . . we got new dolls.
She's a princess and . . .
She looks like me!
CLINK!
I took my doll everywhere. We were like twins.

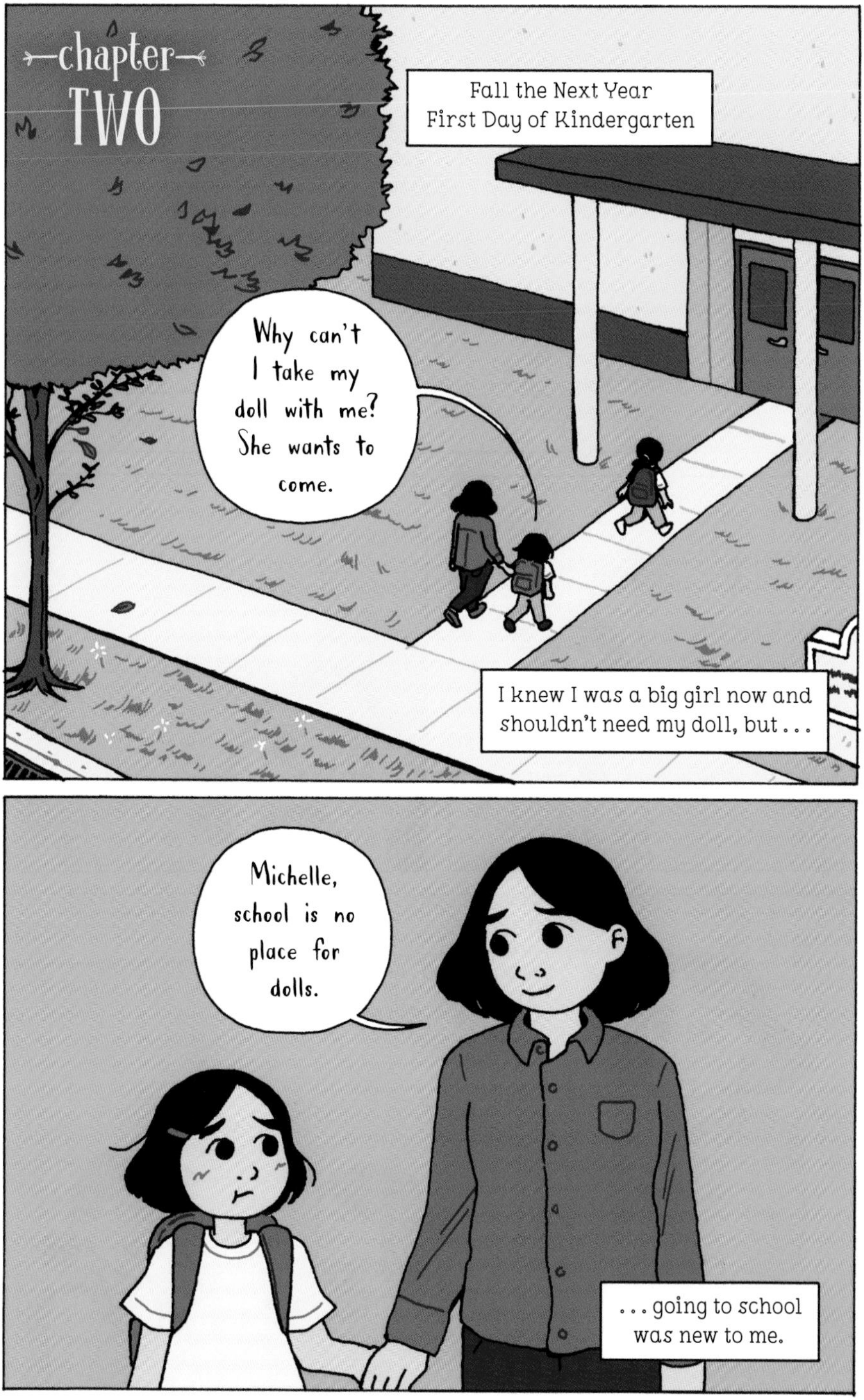

chapter TWO
Fall the Next Year First Day of Kindergarten
Why can't I take my doll with me? She wants to come.
I knew I was a big girl now and shouldn't need my doll, but . . .
Michelle, school is no place for dolls.
. . . going to school was new to me.

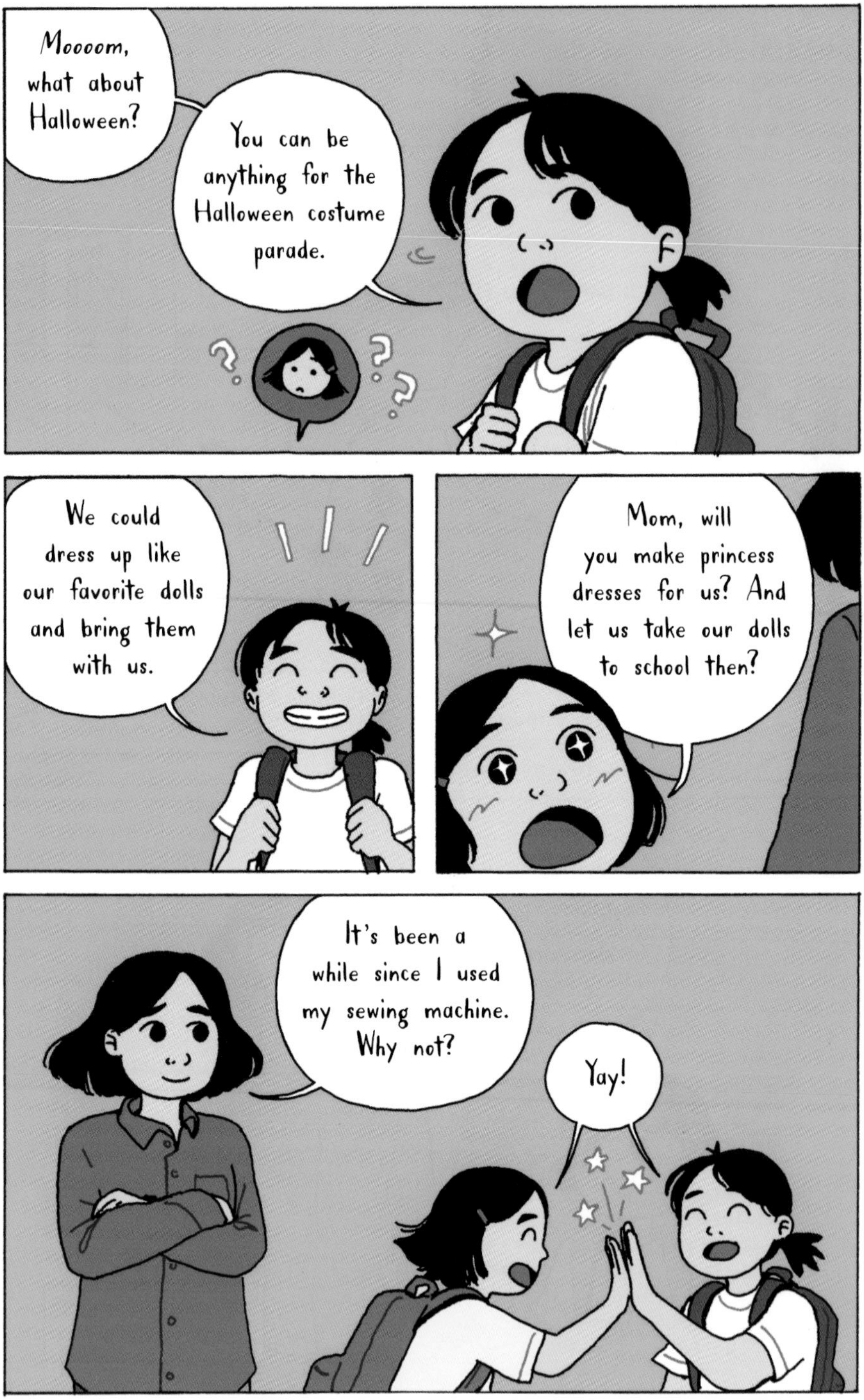

Moooom, what about Halloween?
You can be anything for the Halloween costume parade.
We could dress up like our favorite dolls and bring them with us.
Mom, will you make princess dresses for us? And let us take our dolls to school then?
It's been a while since I used my sewing machine. Why not?
Yay!

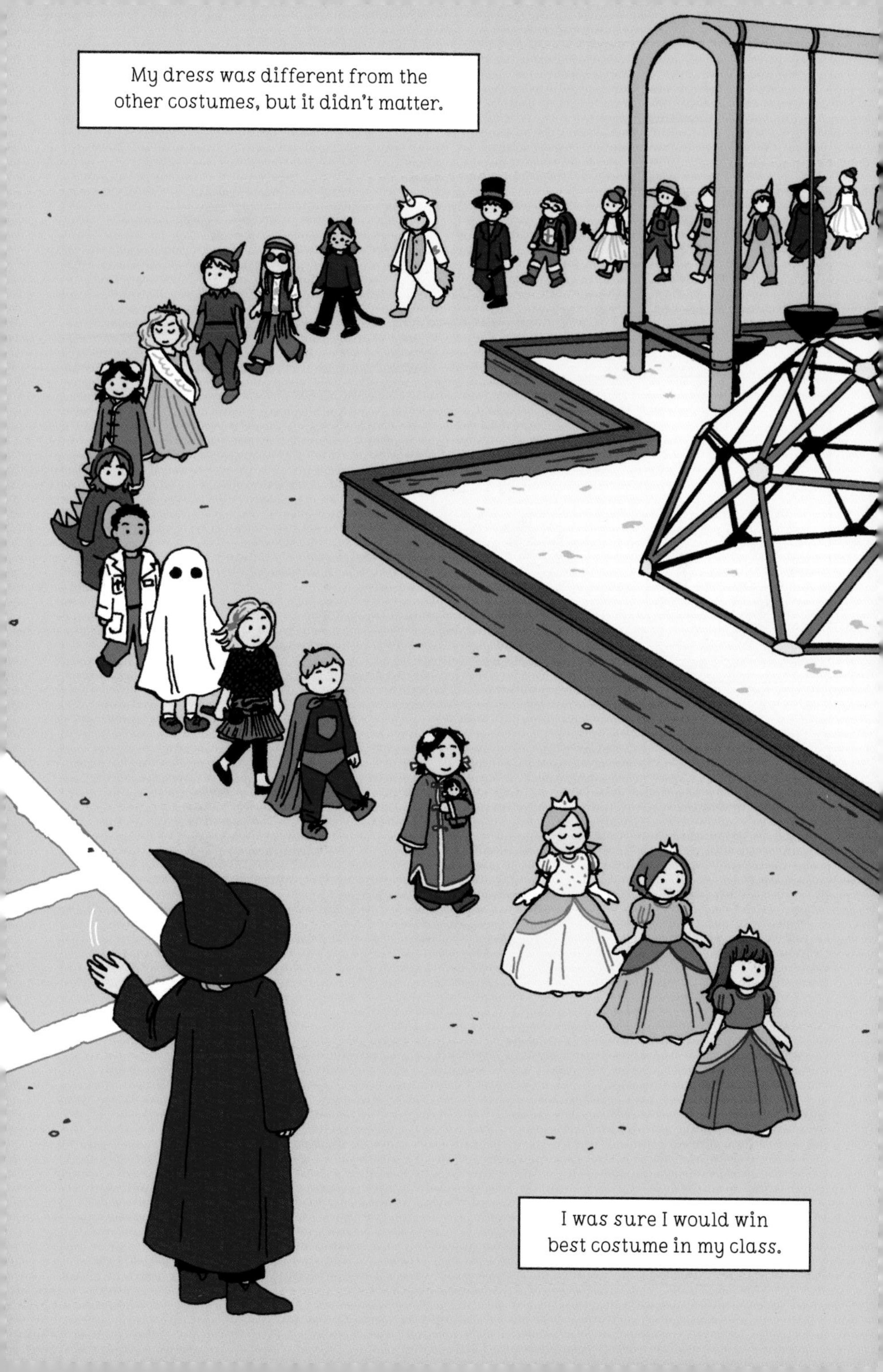
My dress was different from the other costumes, but it didn't matter.
I was sure I would win best costume in my class.

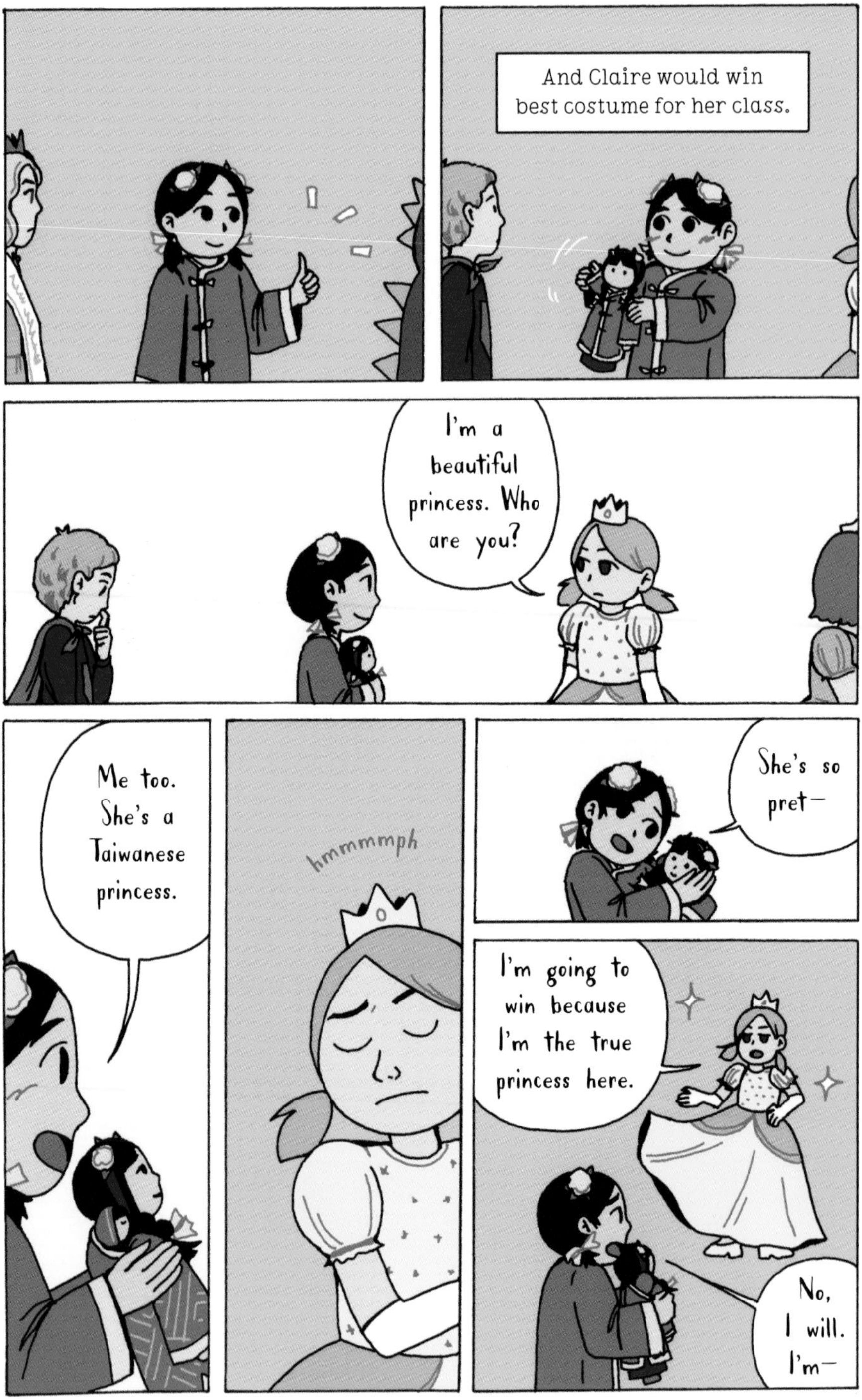
And Claire would win best costume for her class.
I'm a beautiful princess. Who are you?
Me too. She's a Taiwanese princess.
hmmmmph
She's so pret—
I'm going to win because I'm the true princess here.
No, I will. I'm—

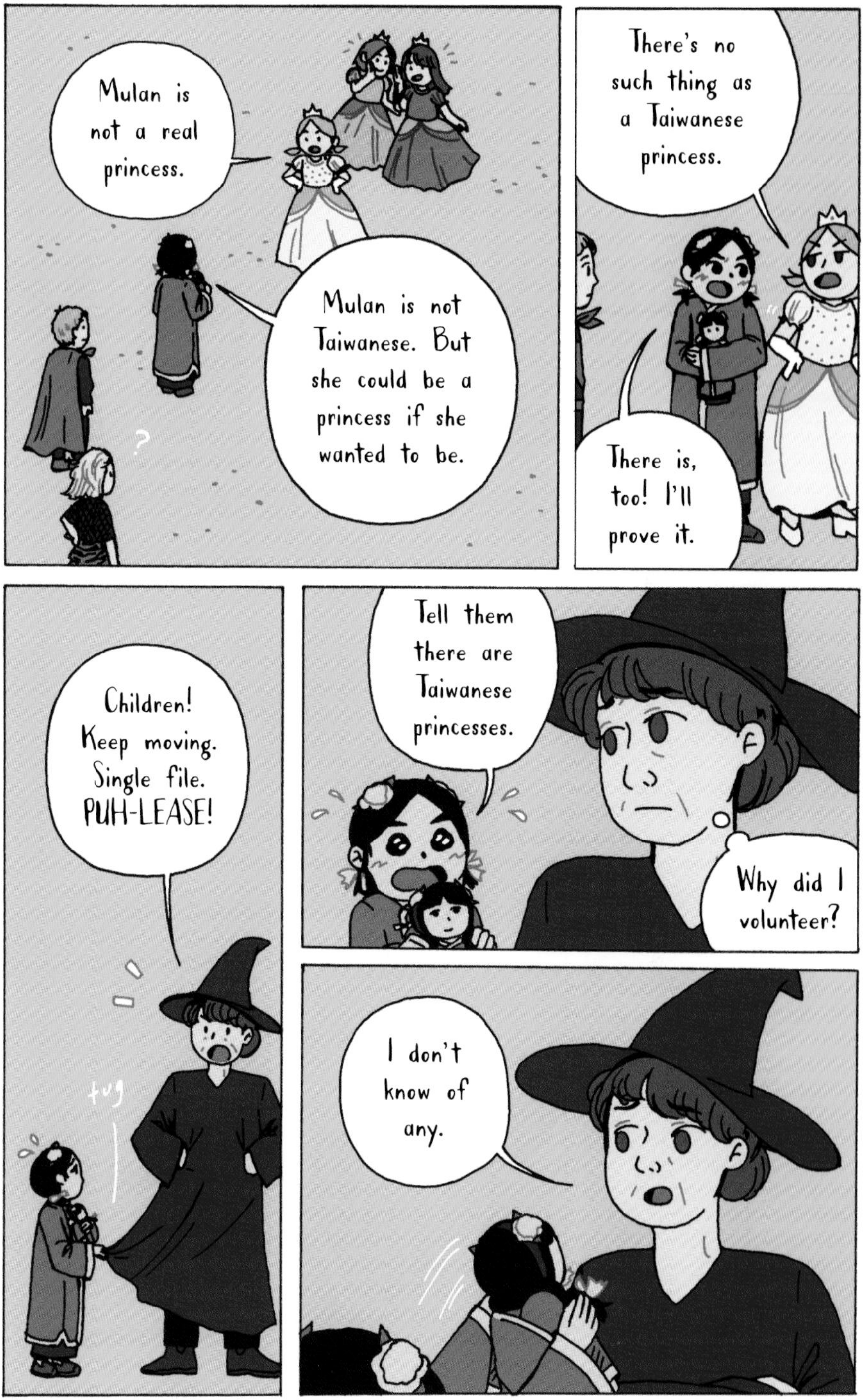
Mulan is not a real princess.
Mulan is not Taiwanese. But she could be a princess if she wanted to be.
There's no such thing as a Taiwanese princess.
There is, too! I'll prove it.
Children! Keep moving. Single file. PUH-LEASE!
tug
Tell them there are Taiwanese princesses.
Why did I volunteer?
I don't know of any.

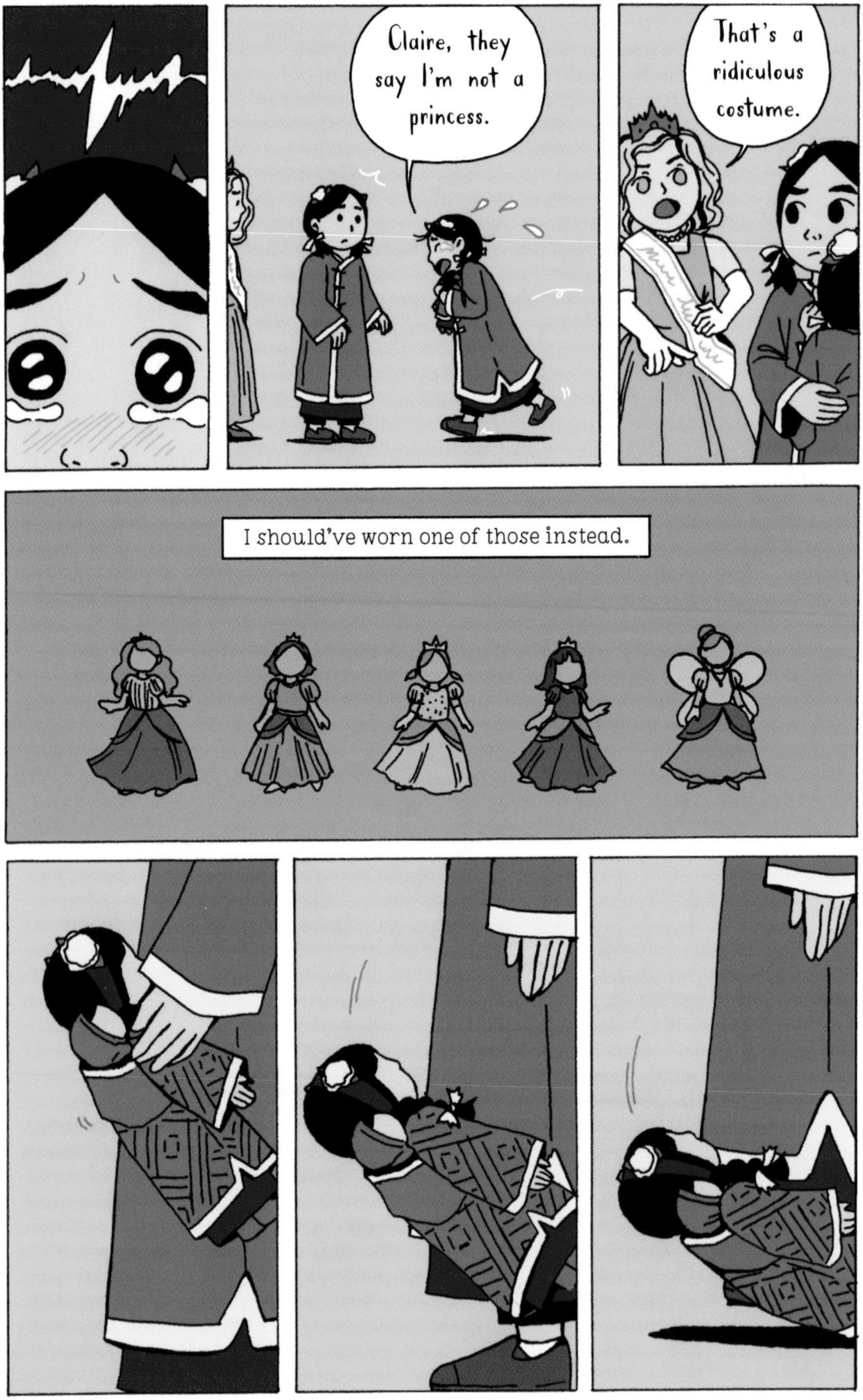
Claire, they say I'm not a princess.
That's a ridiculous costume.
I should've worn one of those instead.

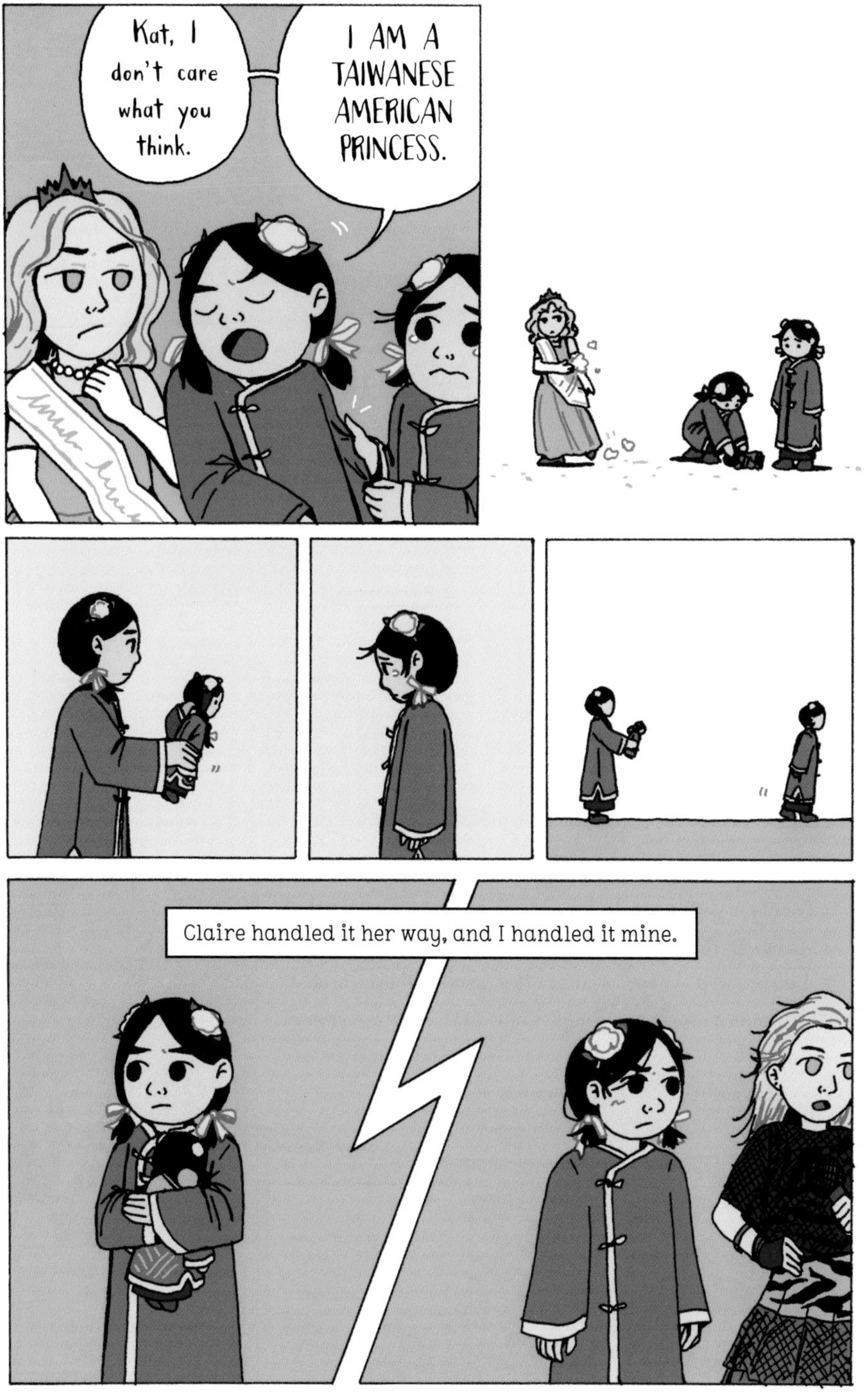
Kat, I don't care what you think.
I AM A TAIWANESE AMERICAN PRINCESS.
Claire handled it her way, and I handled it mine.

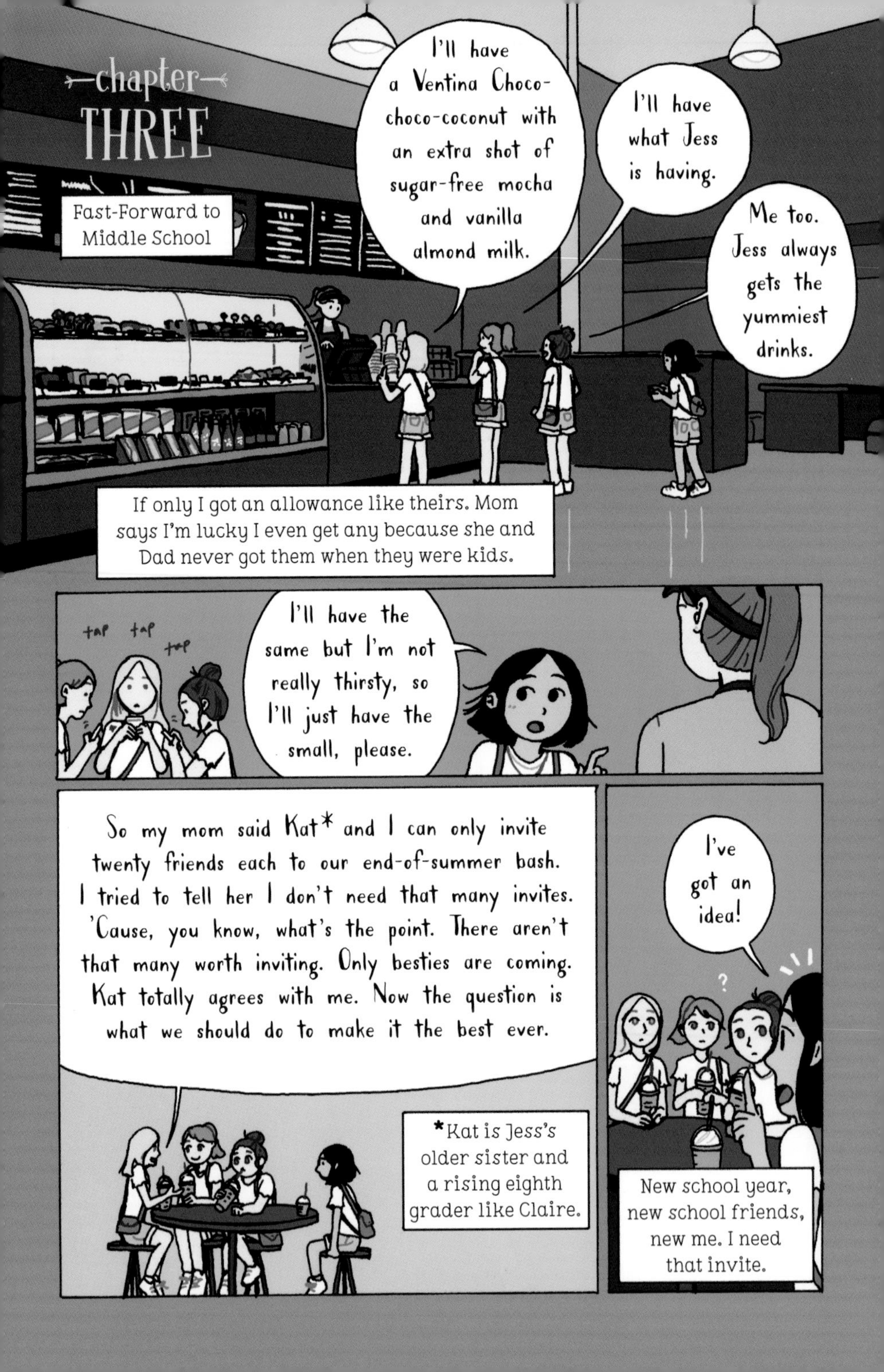
chapter THREE
Fast-Forward to Middle School
I'll have a Ventina Choco-choco-coconut with an extra shot of sugar-free mocha and vanilla almond milk.
I'll have what Jess is having.
Me too. Jess always gets the yummiest drinks.
If only I got an allowance like theirs. Mom says I'm lucky I even get any because she and Dad never got them when they were kids.
tap tap tap
I'll have the same but I'm not really thirsty, so I'll just have the small, please.
So my mom said Kat* and I can only invite twenty friends each to our end-of-summer bash. I tried to tell her I don't need that many invites. 'Cause, you know, what's the point. There aren't that many worth inviting. Only besties are coming. Kat totally agrees with me. Now the question is what we should do to make it the best ever.
*Kat is Jess's older sister and a rising eighth grader like Claire.
I've got an idea!
?
New school year, new school friends, new me. I need that invite.

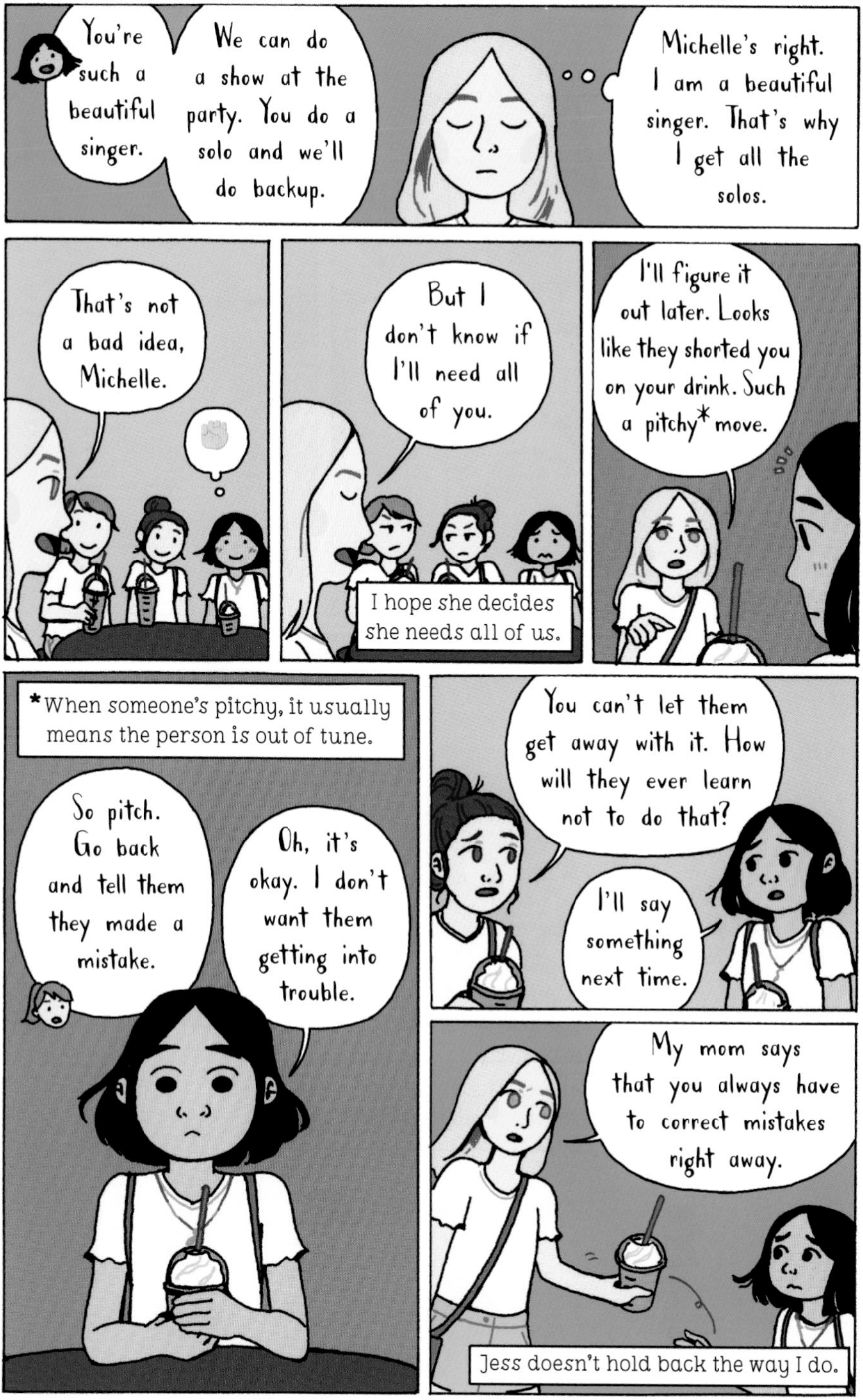
You're such a beautiful singer.
We can do a show at the party. You do a solo and we'll do backup.
Michelle's right. I am a beautiful singer. That's why I get all the solos.
That's not a bad idea, Michelle.
But I don't know if I'll need all of you.
I hope she decides she needs all of us.
I'll figure it out later. Looks like they shorted you on your drink. Such a pitchy* move.
*When someone's pitchy, it usually means the person is out of tune.
So pitch. Go back and tell them they made a mistake.
Oh, it's okay. I don't want them getting into trouble.
You can't let them get away with it. How will they ever learn not to do that?
I'll say something next time.
My mom says that you always have to correct mistakes right away.
Jess doesn't hold back the way I do.

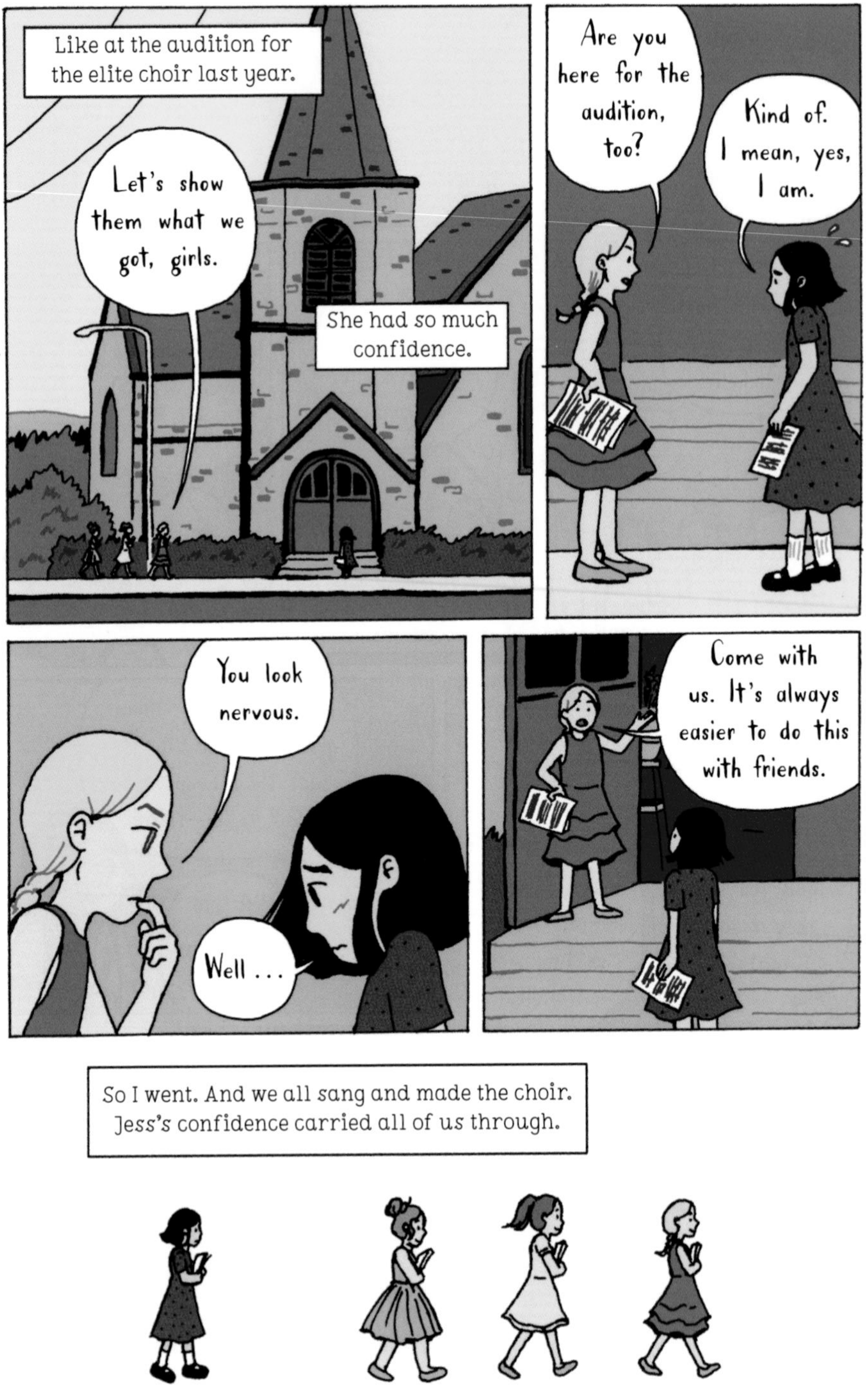
Like at the audition for the elite choir last year.
Let's show them what we got, girls.
She had so much confidence.
Are you here for the audition, too?
Kind of. I mean, yes, I am.
You look nervous.
Well . . .
Come with us. It's always easier to do this with friends.
So I went. And we all sang and made the choir. Jess's confidence carried all of us through.

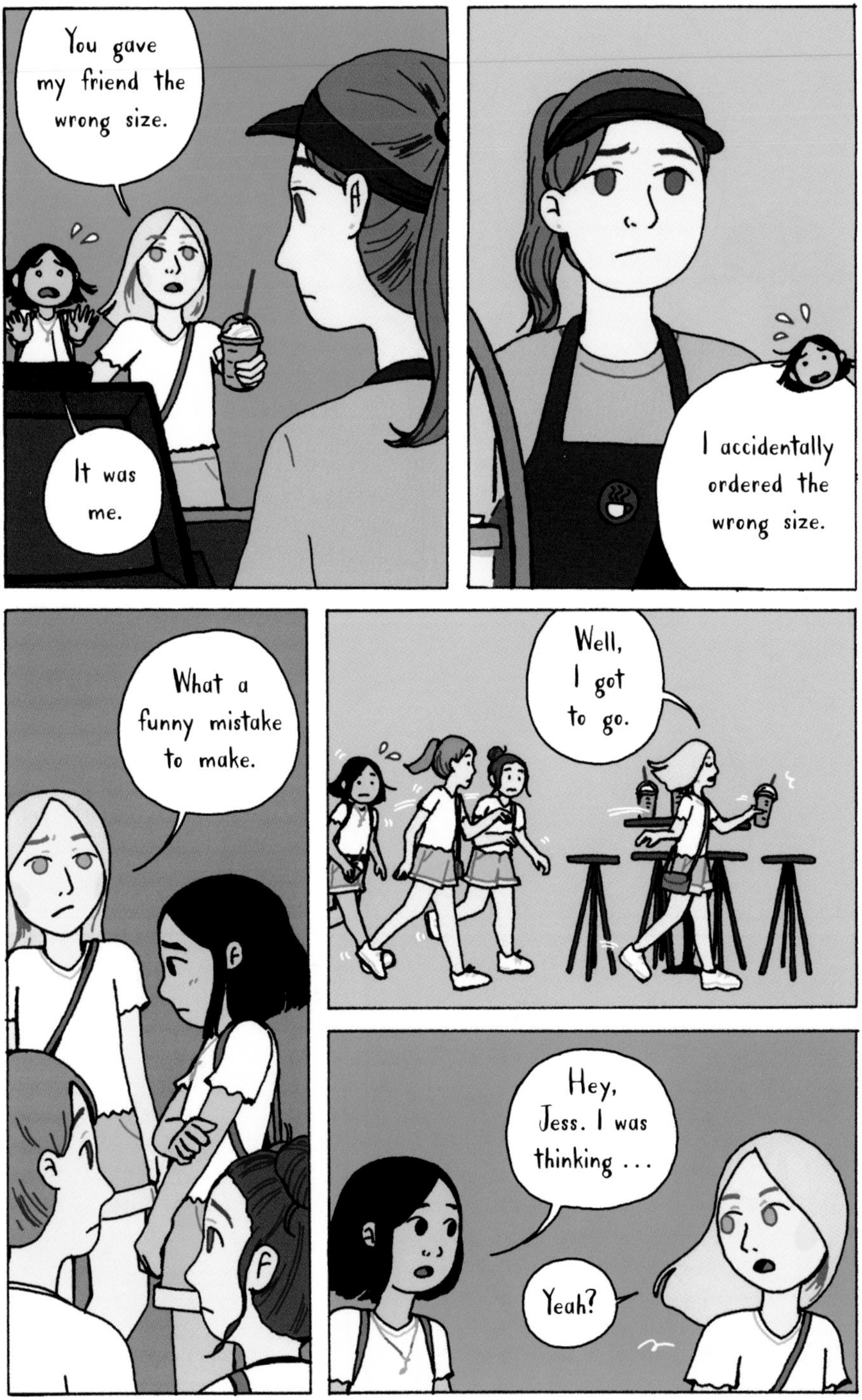
You gave my friend the wrong size.
It was me.
I accidentally ordered the wrong size.
What a funny mistake to make.
Well, I got to go.
Hey, Jess. I was thinking . . .
Yeah?

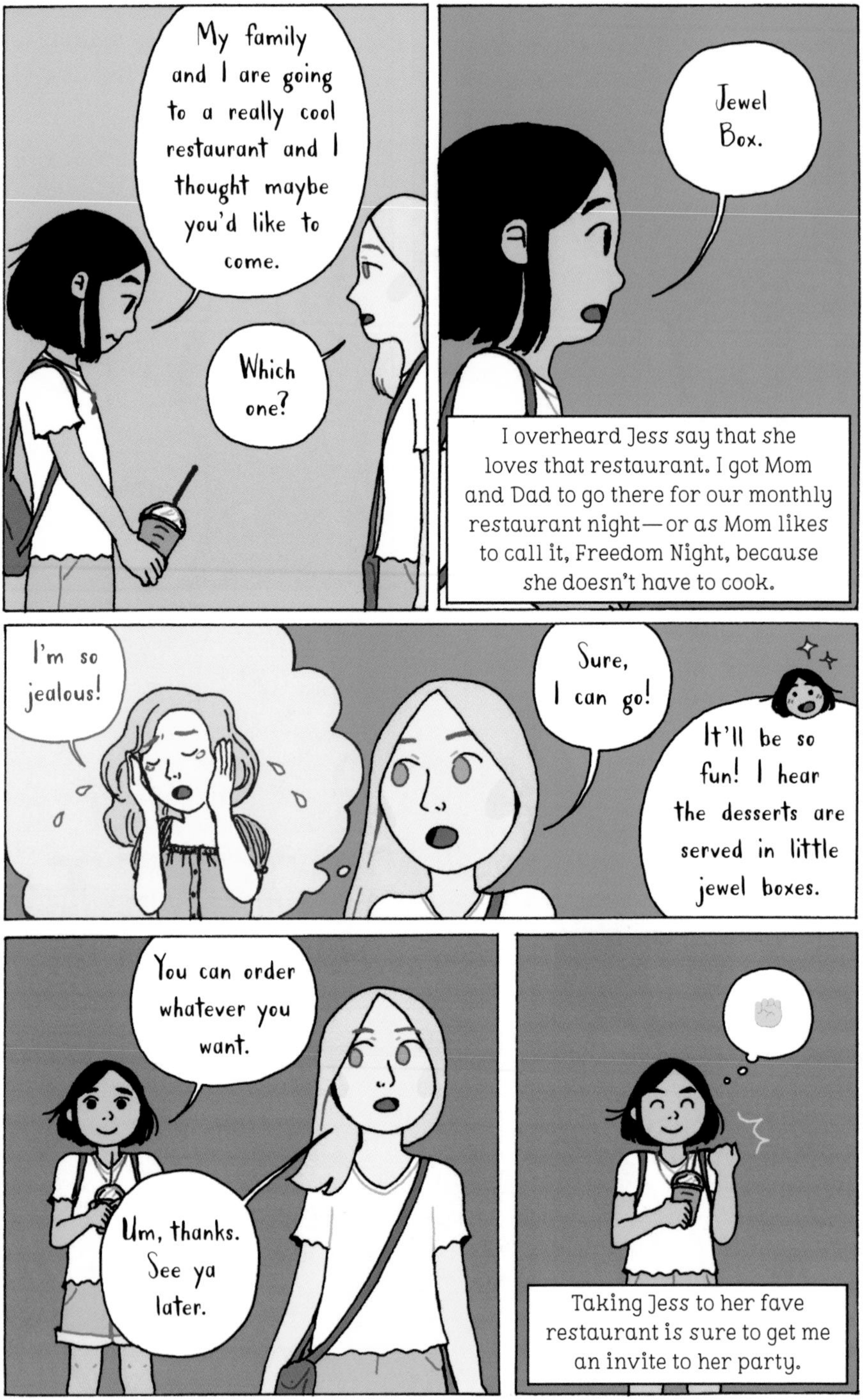

My family and I are going to a really cool restaurant and I thought maybe you'd like to come.
Which one?
Jewel Box.
I overheard Jess say that she loves that restaurant. I got Mom and Dad to go there for our monthly restaurant night—or as Mom likes to call it, Freedom Night, because she doesn't have to cook.
I'm so jealous!
Sure, I can go!
It'll be so fun! I hear the desserts are served in little jewel boxes.
You can order whatever you want.
Um, thanks. See ya later.
Taking Jess to her fave restaurant is sure to get me an invite to her party.

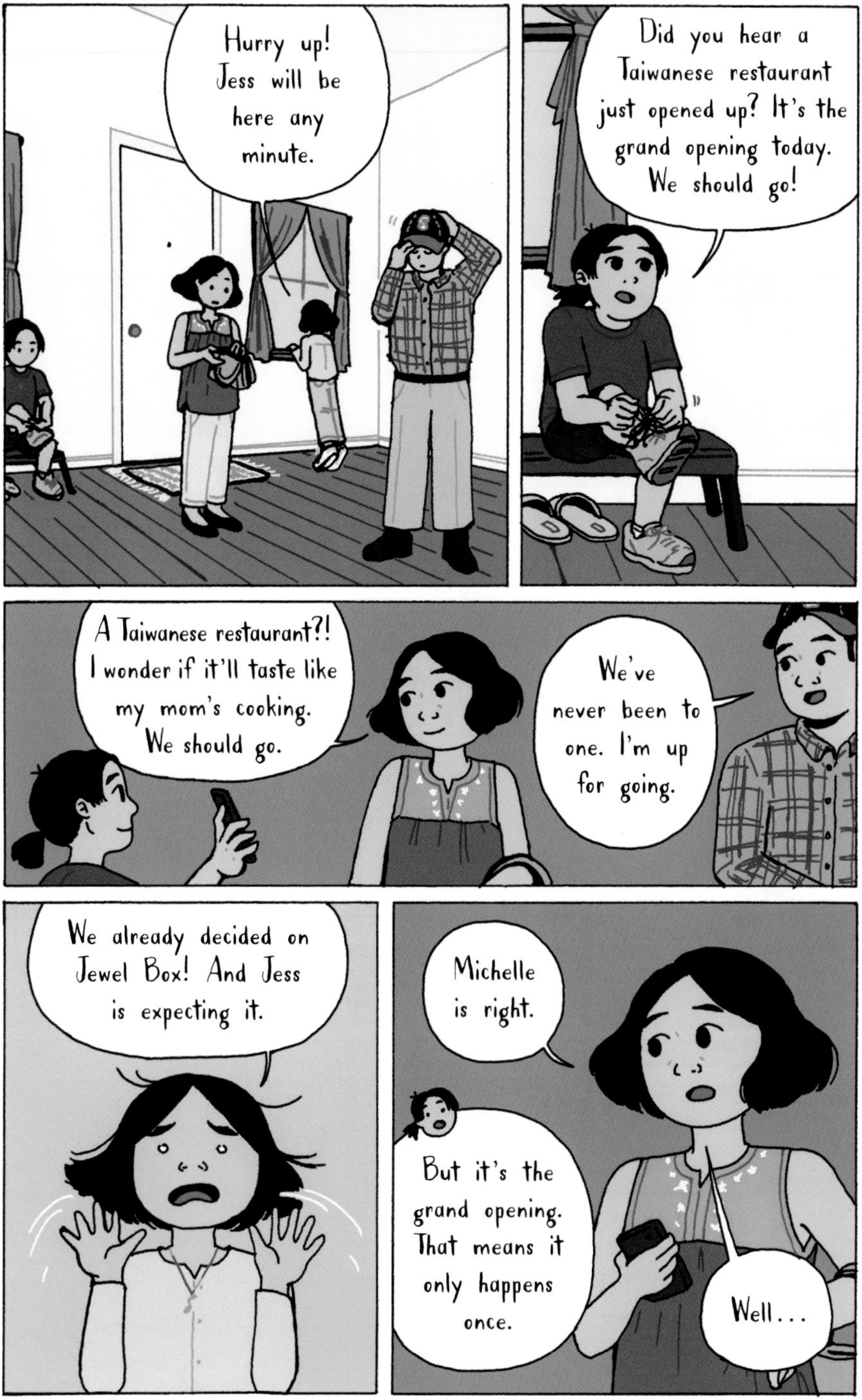
Hurry up! Jess will be here any minute.
Did you hear a Taiwanese restaurant just opened up? It's the grand opening today. We should go!
A Taiwanese restaurant?! I wonder if it'll taste like my mom's cooking. We should go.
We've never been to one. I'm up for going.
We already decided on Jewel Box! And Jess is expecting it.
Michelle is right.
But it's the grand opening. That means it only happens once.
Well...

You're ruining my life, Claire!

Changing restaurants isn't going to ruin it.

Girls, please.

If you're going to fight, then Mom and I will decide.

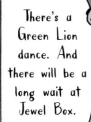

There's a Green Lion dance. And there will be a long wait at Jewel Box.

Lion dance or—

Long wait?

Let's go to Green Lion, ya sure, ya betcha.*

This is so unfair.

*Dad could've just said "for sure," but he likes his sayings. This one is from Ballard, Seattle's Scandinavian stronghold where he grew up.

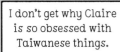

I don't get why Claire is so obsessed with Taiwanese things.

She even got Mom and Dad to send her to Taiwanese American camp two summers in a row.

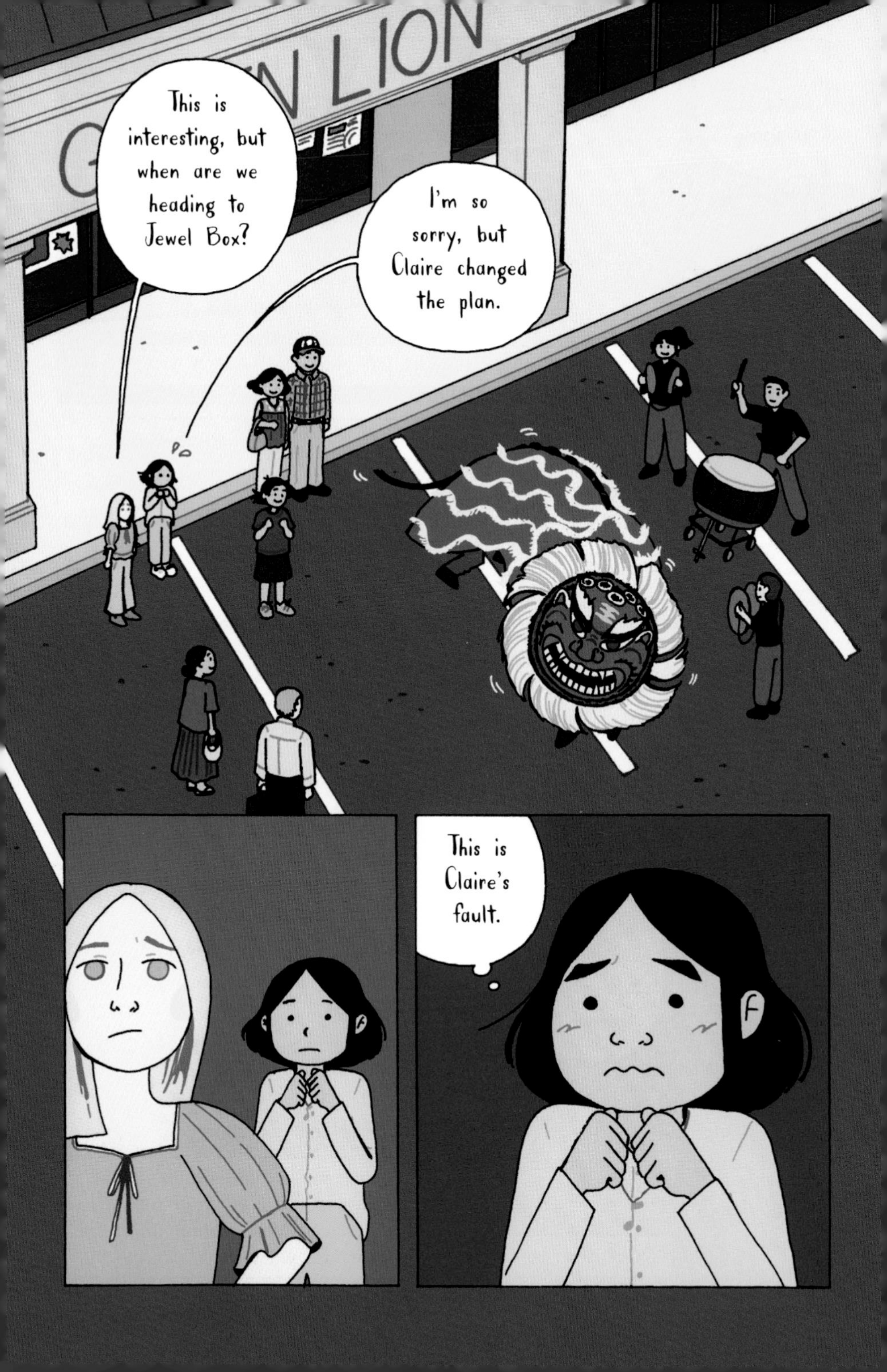

GOLDEN LION
This is interesting, but when are we heading to Jewel Box?
I'm so sorry, but Claire changed the plan.
This is Claire's fault.

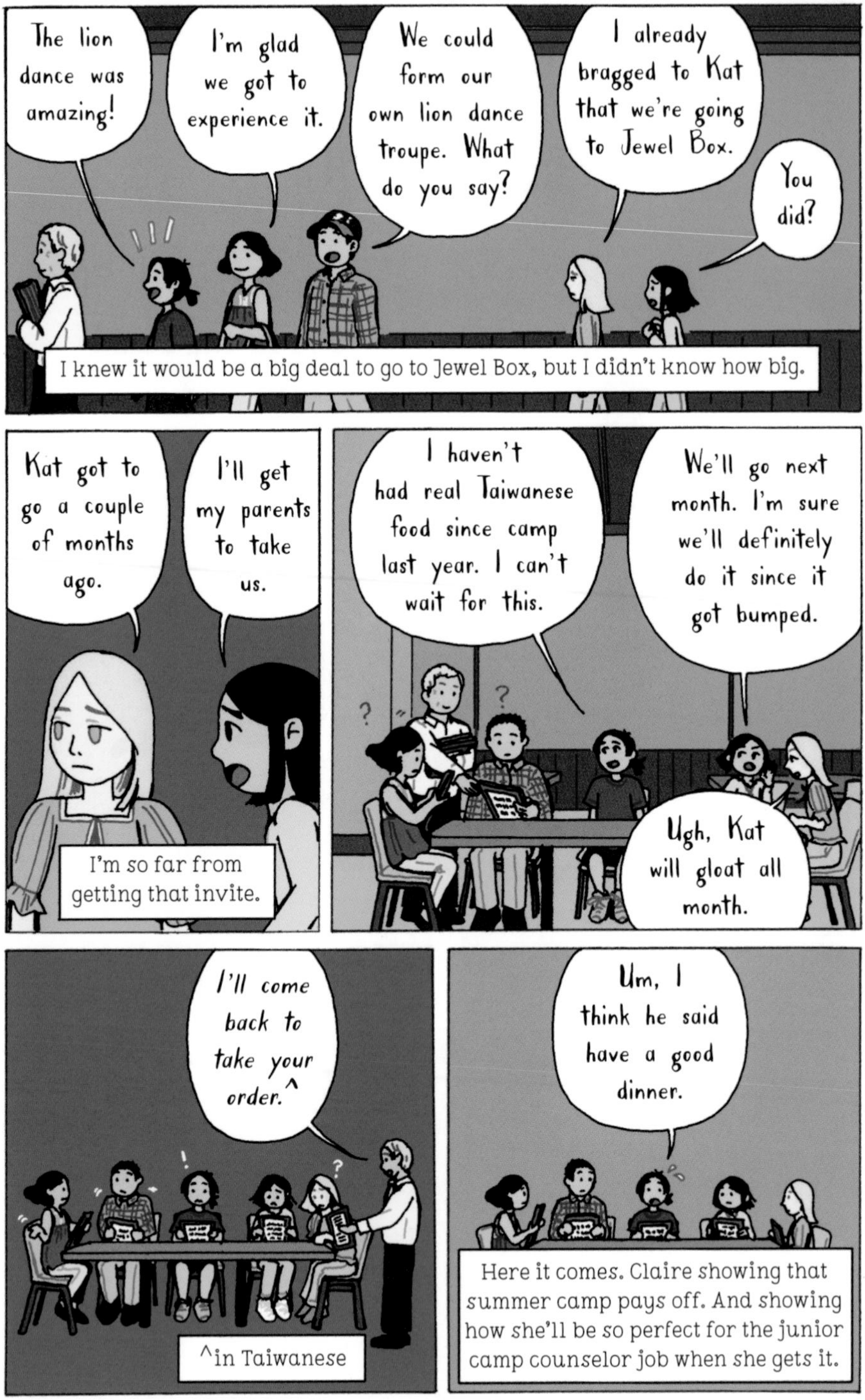
The lion dance was amazing!
I'm glad we got to experience it.
We could form our own lion dance troupe. What do you say?
I already bragged to Kat that we're going to Jewel Box.
You did?
I knew it would be a big deal to go to Jewel Box, but I didn't know how big.
Kat got to go a couple of months ago.
I'll get my parents to take us.
I'm so far from getting that invite.
I haven't had real Taiwanese food since camp last year. I can't wait for this.
We'll go next month. I'm sure we'll definitely do it since it got bumped.
Ugh, Kat will gloat all month.
I'll come back to take your order.^
^in Taiwanese
Um, I think he said have a good dinner.
Here it comes. Claire showing that summer camp pays off. And showing how she'll be so perfect for the junior camp counselor job when she gets it.

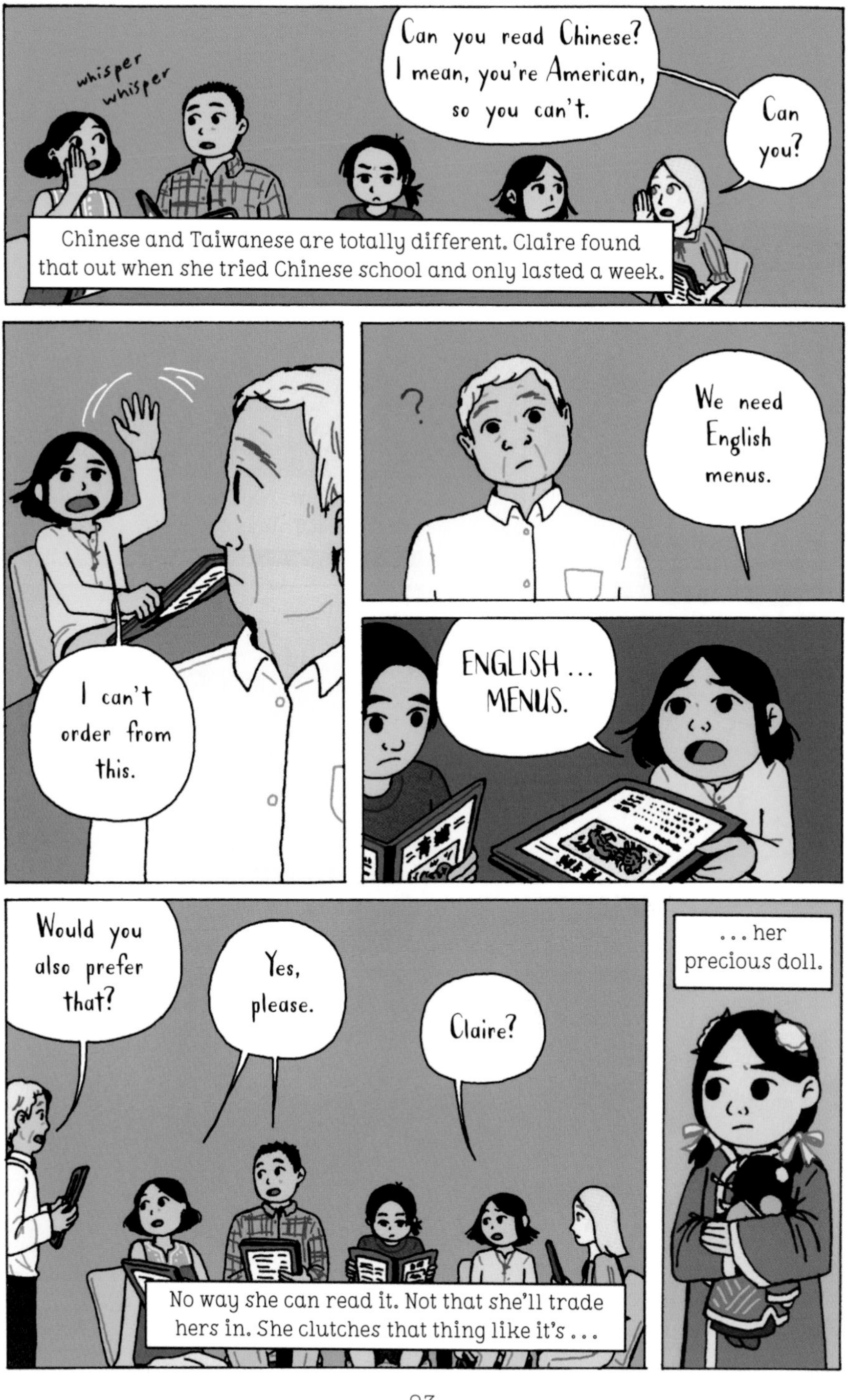
whisper whisper
Can you read Chinese? I mean, you're American, so you can't.
Can you?
Chinese and Taiwanese are totally different. Claire found that out when she tried Chinese school and only lasted a week.
I can't order from this.
?
We need English menus.
ENGLISH ... MENUS.
Would you also prefer that?
Yes, please.
Claire?
No way she can read it. Not that she'll trade hers in. She clutches that thing like it's ...
... her precious doll.

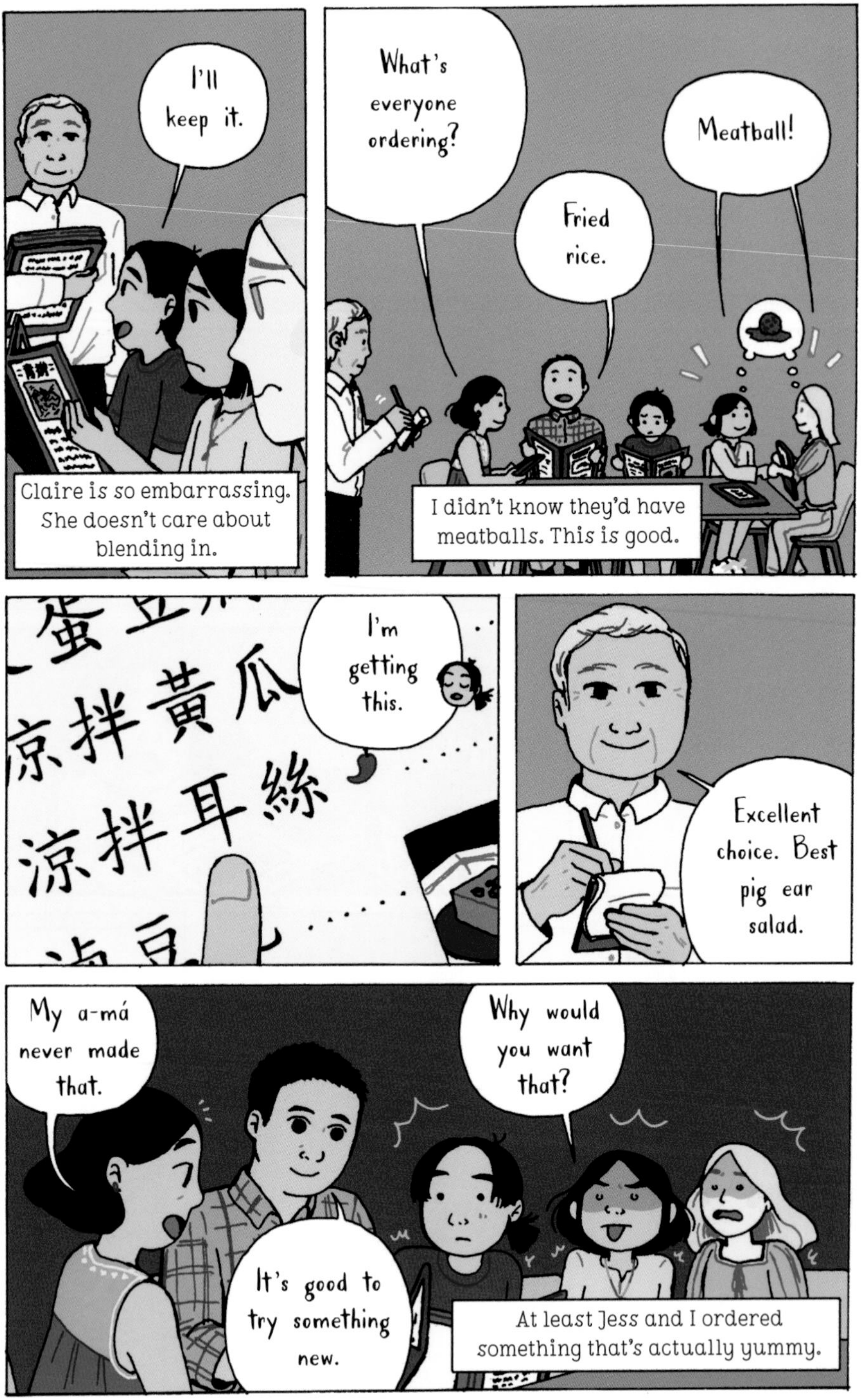

I'll keep it.
Claire is so embarrassing. She doesn't care about blending in.
What's everyone ordering?
Fried rice.
Meatball!
I didn't know they'd have meatballs. This is good.
涼拌黃瓜
涼拌耳絲
I'm getting this.
Excellent choice. Best pig ear salad.
My a-má never made that.
It's good to try something new.
Why would you want that?
At least Jess and I ordered something that's actually yummy.

What is that?
That is sooo not a meatball.
Yum, I can't wait to dig in.
Claire is such a show-off.
POKE
BLOB
BLOB

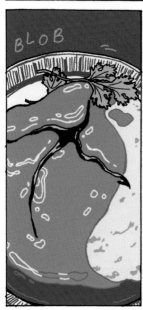

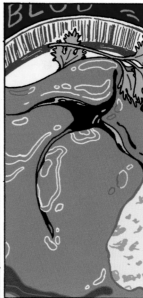

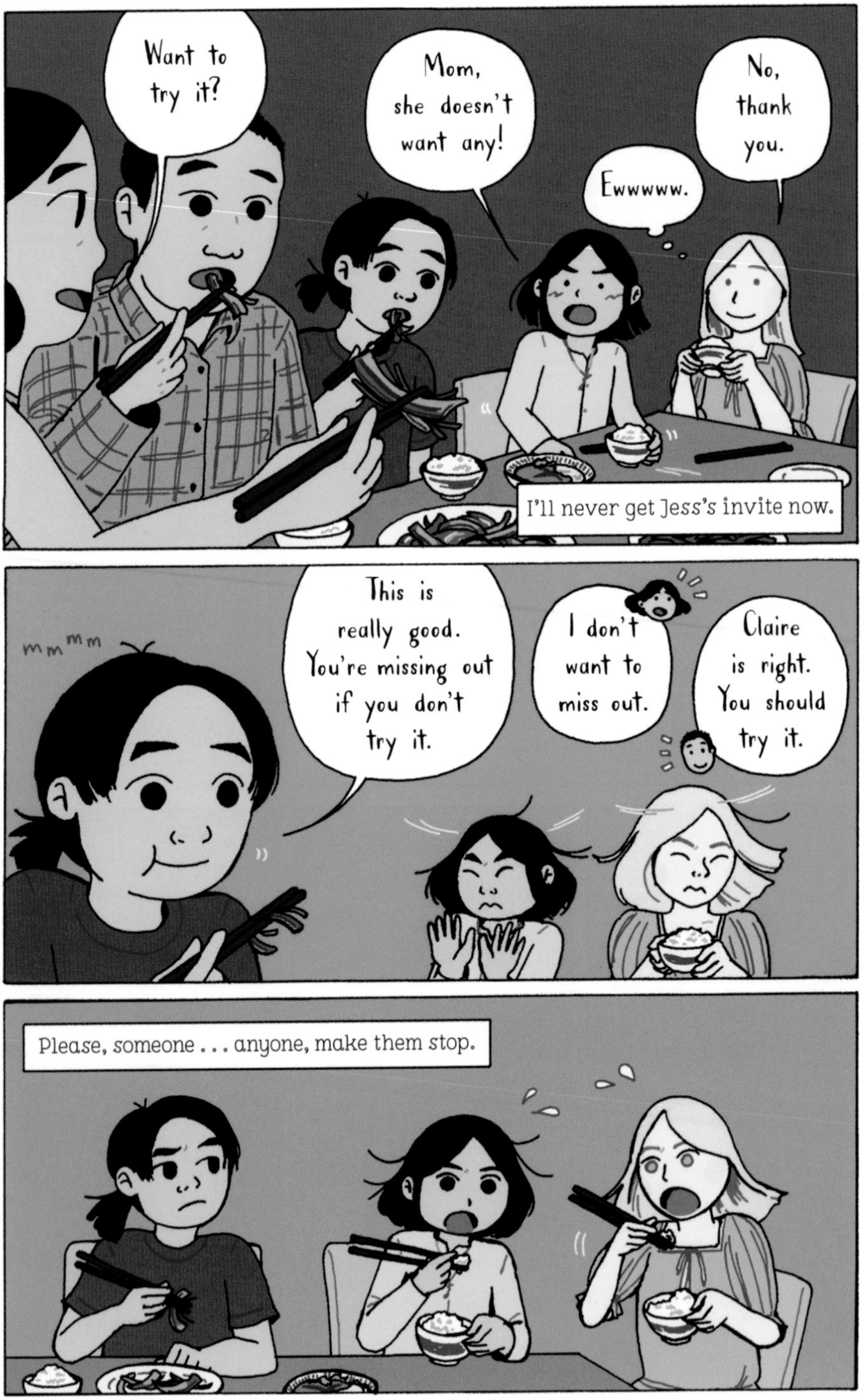

Want to try it?
Mom, she doesn't want any!
Ewwwww.
No, thank you.
I'll never get Jess's invite now.
mmmm
This is really good. You're missing out if you don't try it.
I don't want to miss out.
Claire is right. You should try it.
Please, someone . . . anyone, make them stop.

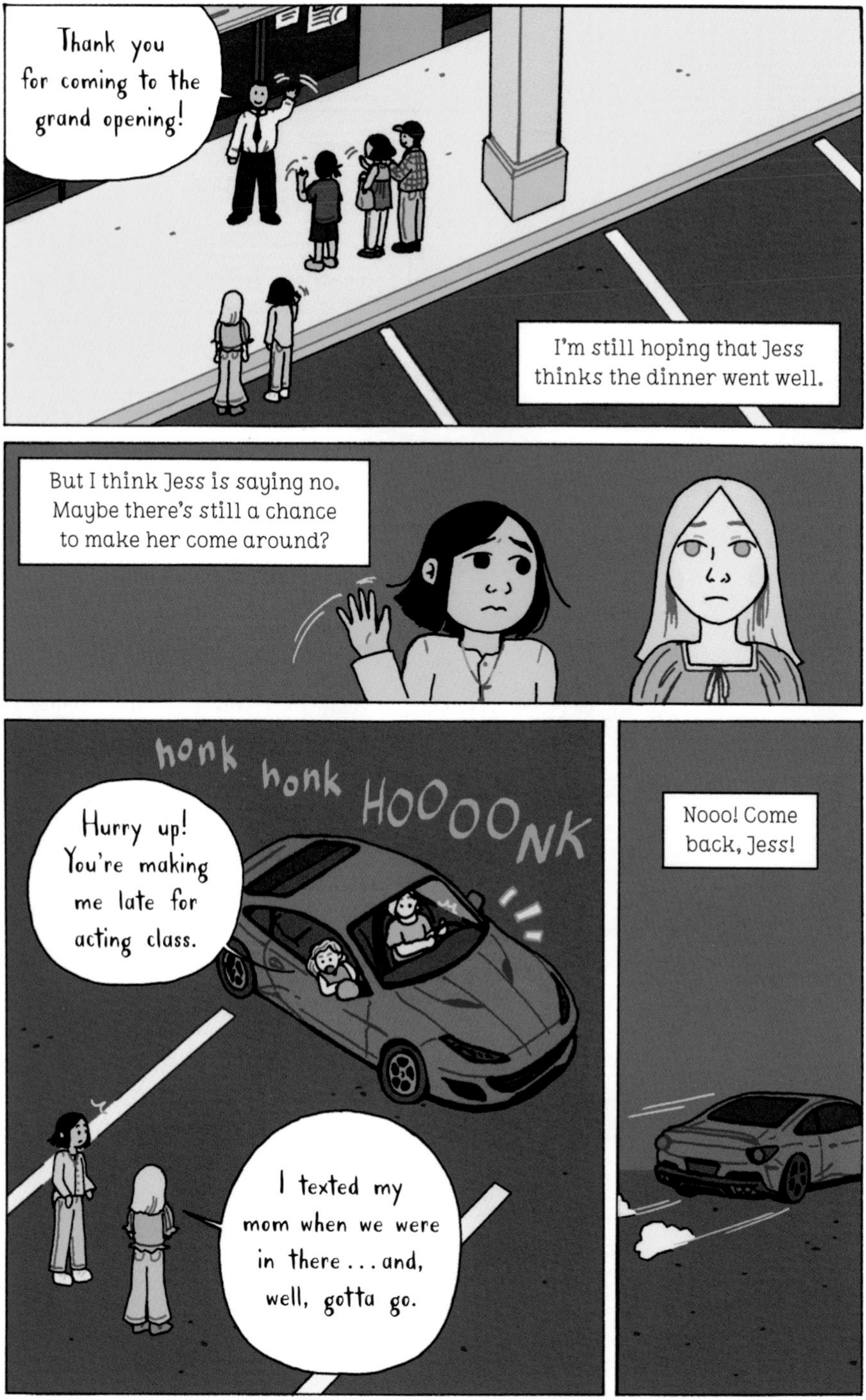
Thank you for coming to the grand opening!
I'm still hoping that Jess thinks the dinner went well.
But I think Jess is saying no. Maybe there's still a chance to make her come around?
honk honk HOOOONK
Hurry up! You're making me late for acting class.
I texted my mom when we were in there . . . and, well, gotta go.
Nooo! Come back, Jess!

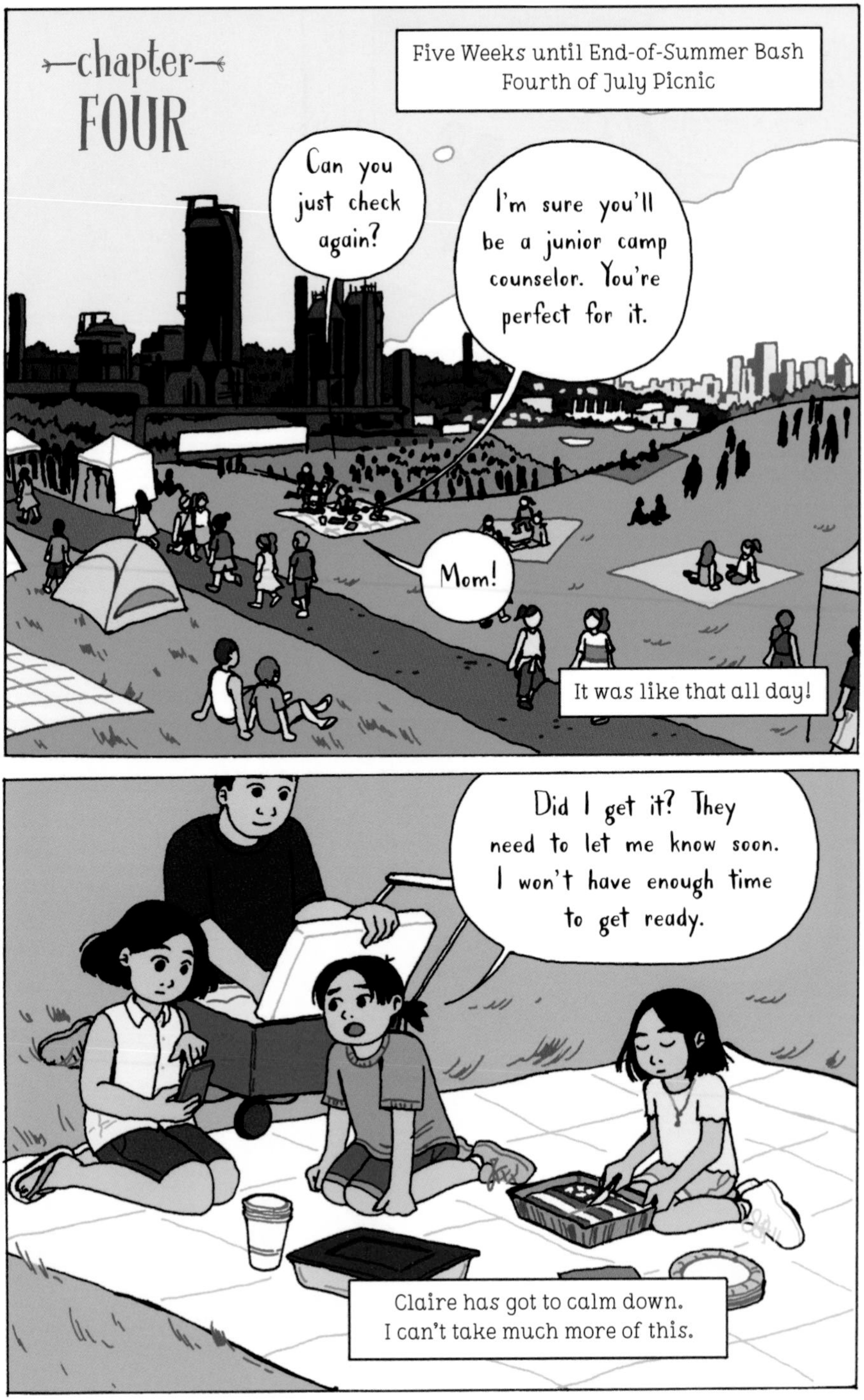
chapter
FOUR
Five Weeks until End-of-Summer Bash
Fourth of July Picnic
Can you just check again?
I'm sure you'll be a junior camp counselor. You're perfect for it.
Mom!
It was like that all day!
Did I get it? They need to let me know soon. I won't have enough time to get ready.
Claire has got to calm down.
I can't take much more of this.

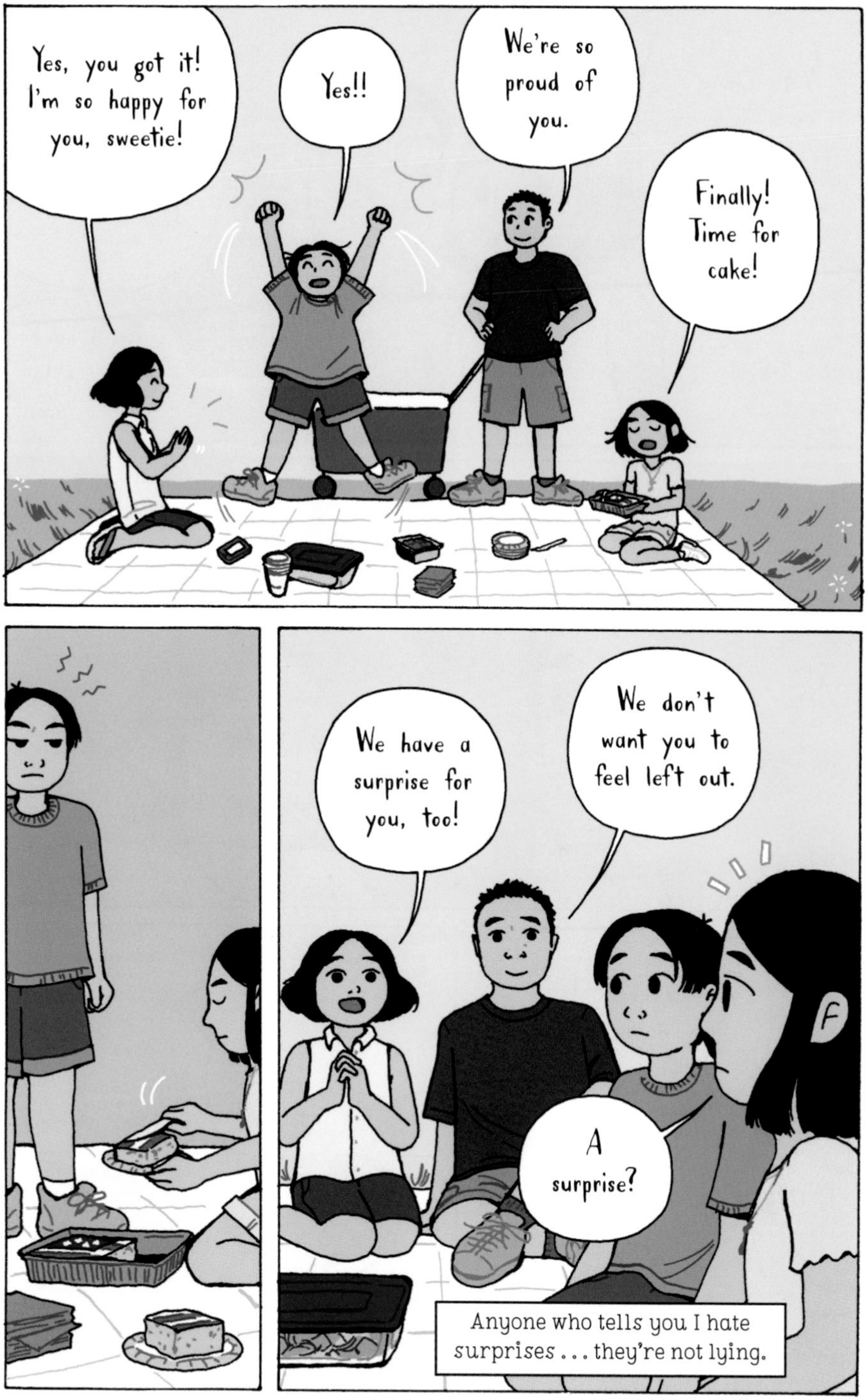
Yes, you got it! I'm so happy for you, sweetie!
Yes!!
We're so proud of you.
Finally! Time for cake!
We have a surprise for you, too!
We don't want you to feel left out.
A surprise?
Anyone who tells you I hate surprises . . . they're not lying.

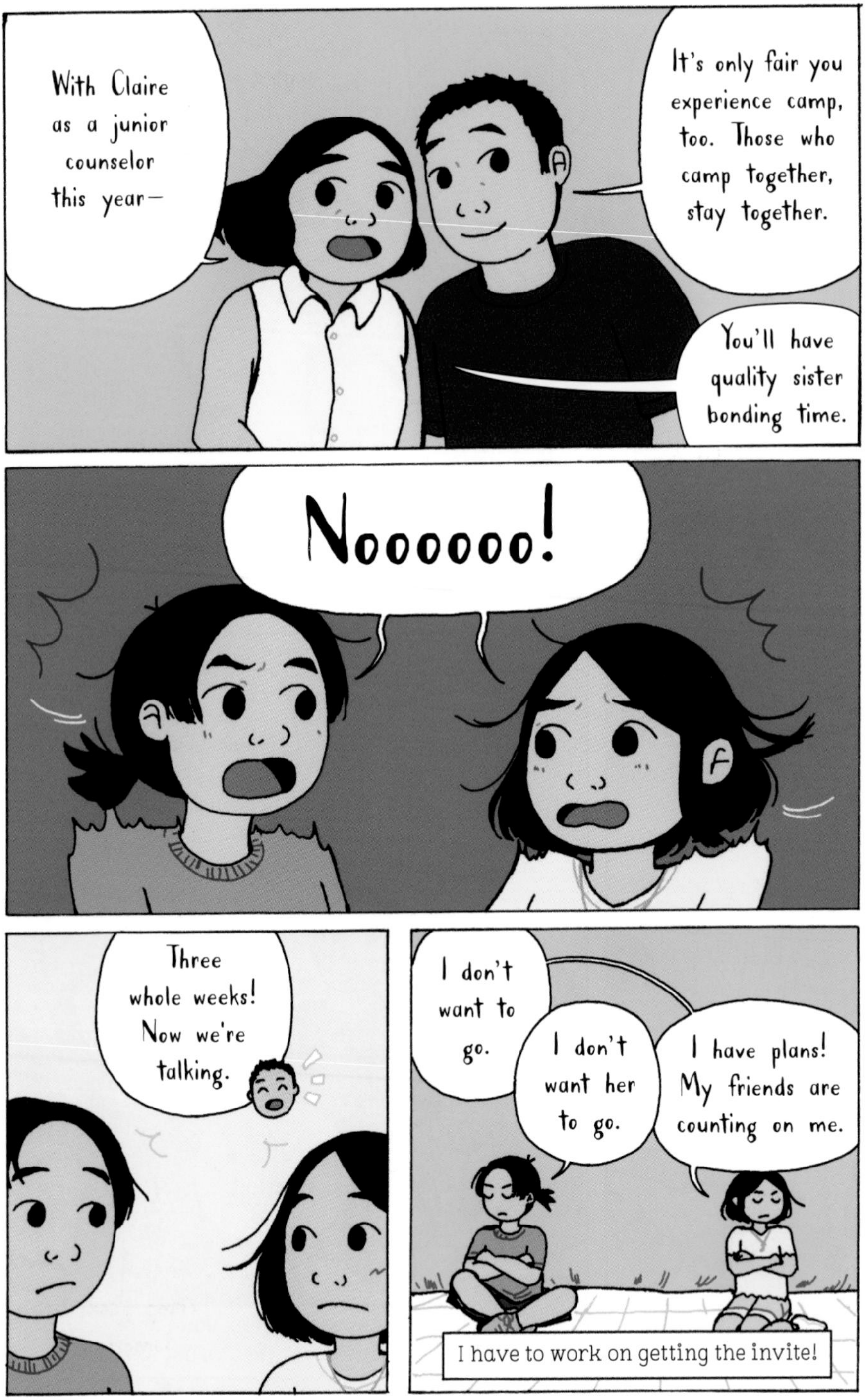
With Claire as a junior counselor this year—
It's only fair you experience camp, too. Those who camp together, stay together.
You'll have quality sister bonding time.
Noooooo!
Three whole weeks! Now we're talking.
I don't want to go.
I don't want her to go.
I have plans! My friends are counting on me.
I have to work on getting the invite!

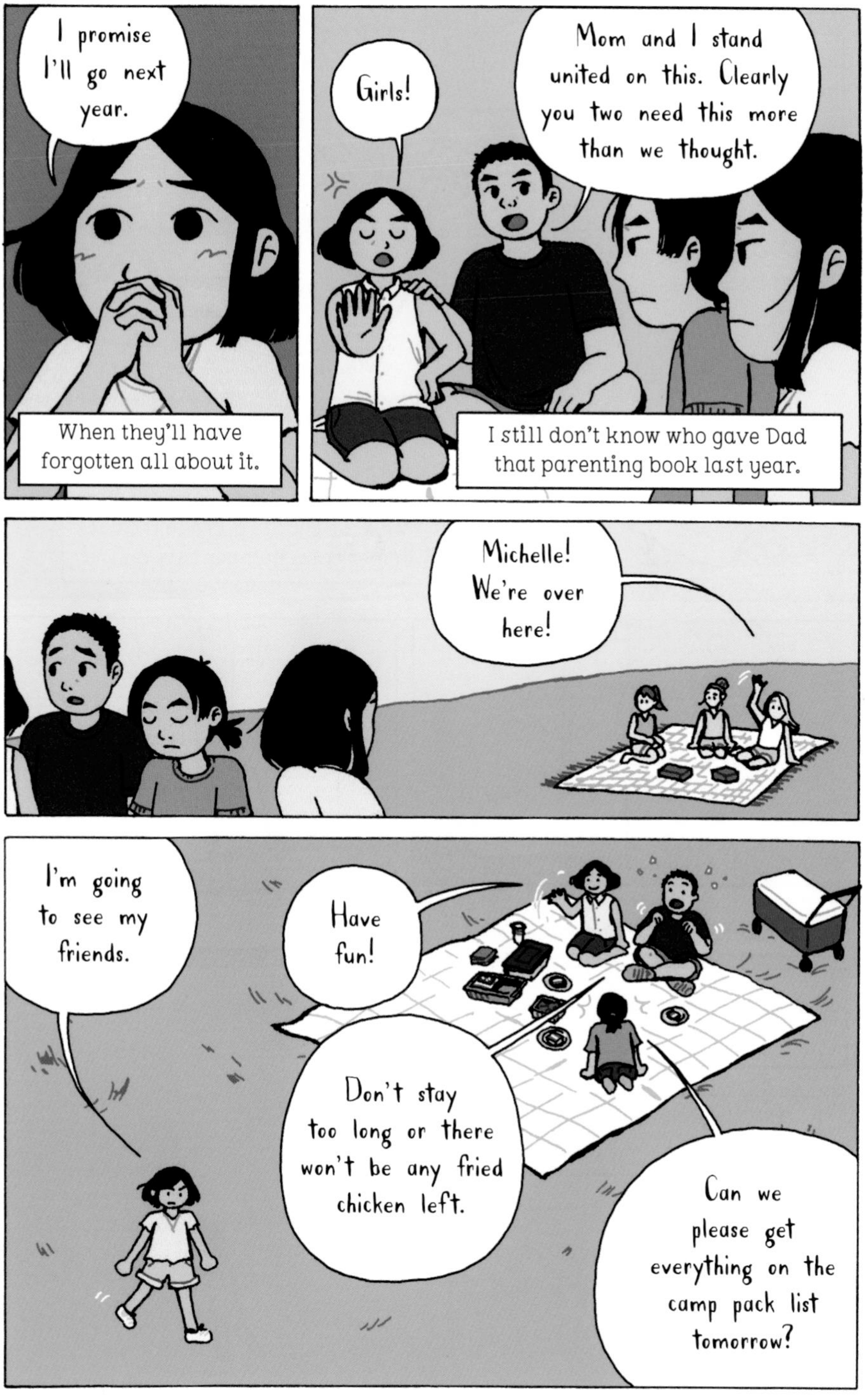
I promise I'll go next year.
When they'll have forgotten all about it.
Girls!
Mom and I stand united on this. Clearly you two need this more than we thought.
I still don't know who gave Dad that parenting book last year.
Michelle! We're over here!
I'm going to see my friends.
Have fun!
Don't stay too long or there won't be any fried chicken left.
Can we please get everything on the camp pack list tomorrow?

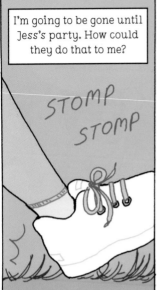

I'm going to be gone until Jess's party. How could they do that to me?

STOMP
STOMP

STOMP STOMP

What if Jess hates me for messing up our summer plans? No more tubing down the Wenatchee River. And we were finally going to try out ice bumper cars. Bumper cars on ice!

If I tell them I'm going to Taiwanese American summer camp ...

... they'll chill me out.

I'm doomed to be a middle school tacet.*

*During a tacet, I don't sing for a long time. Just silence—sometimes until the end.

drag
drag

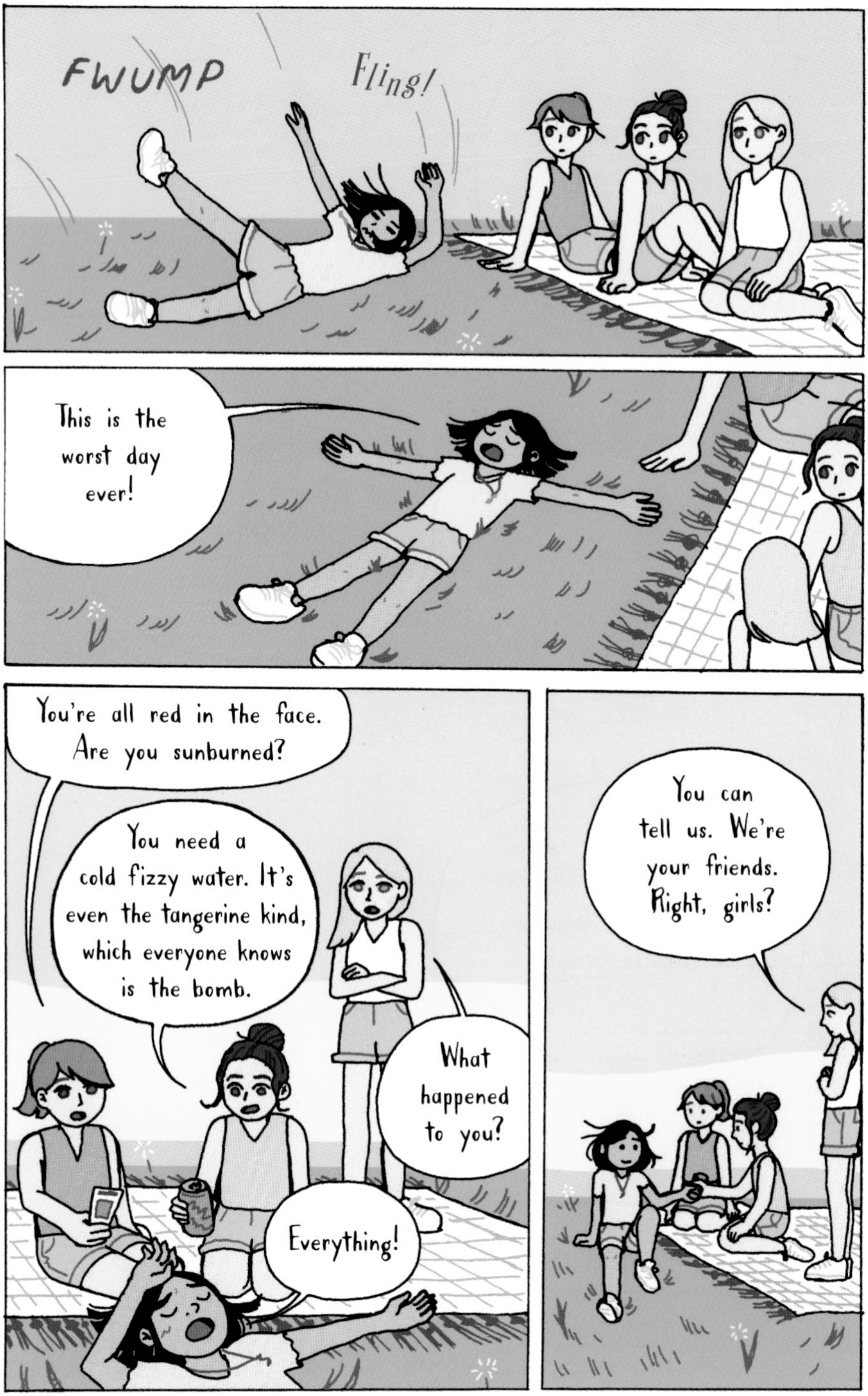
FWUMP
Fling!
This is the worst day ever!
You're all red in the face. Are you sunburned?
You need a cold fizzy water. It's even the tangerine kind, which everyone knows is the bomb.
What happened to you?
Everything!
You can tell us. We're your friends. Right, girls?

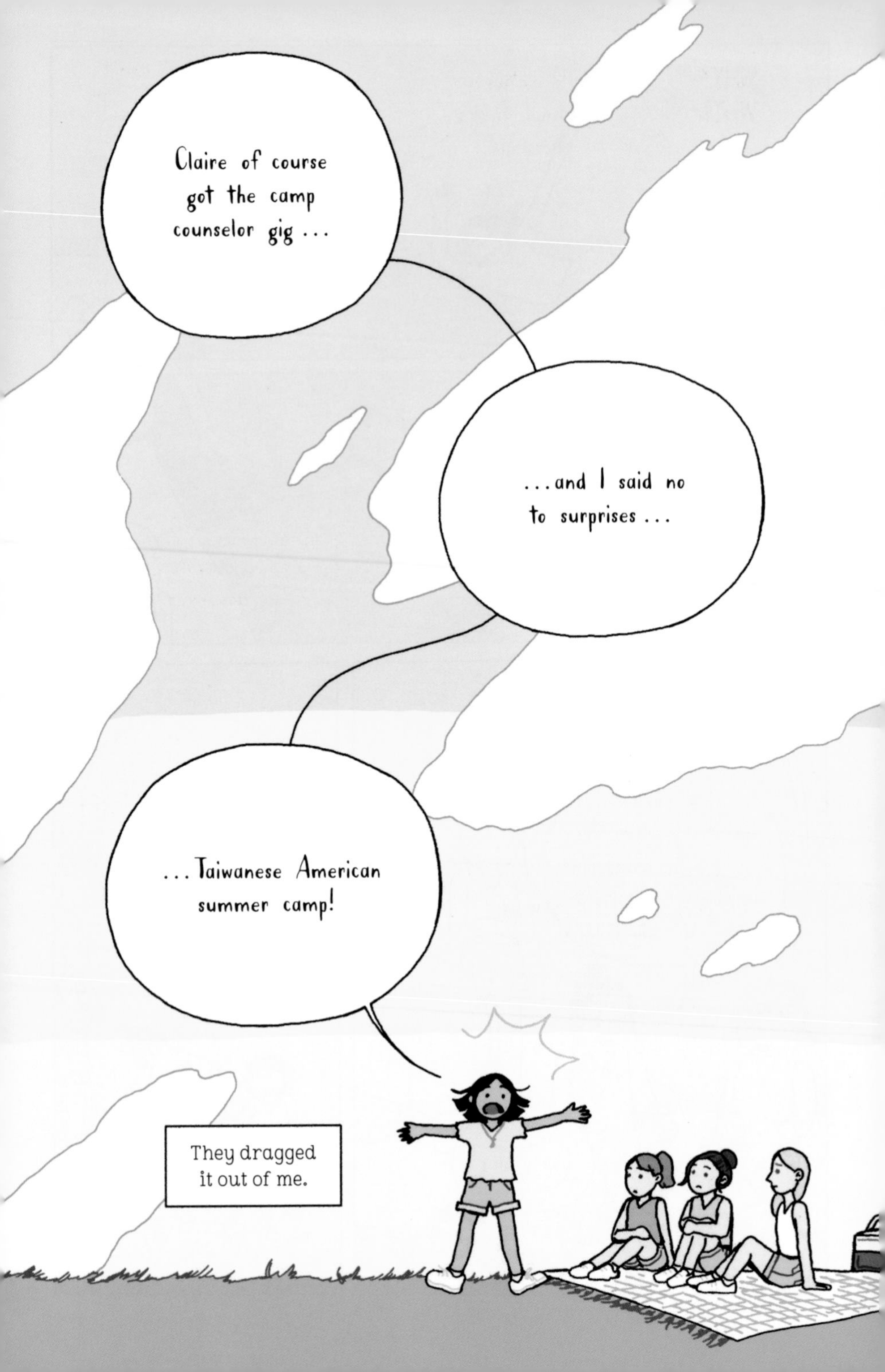
Claire of course got the camp counselor gig . . .
. . . and I said no to surprises . . .
. . . Taiwanese American summer camp!
They dragged it out of me.

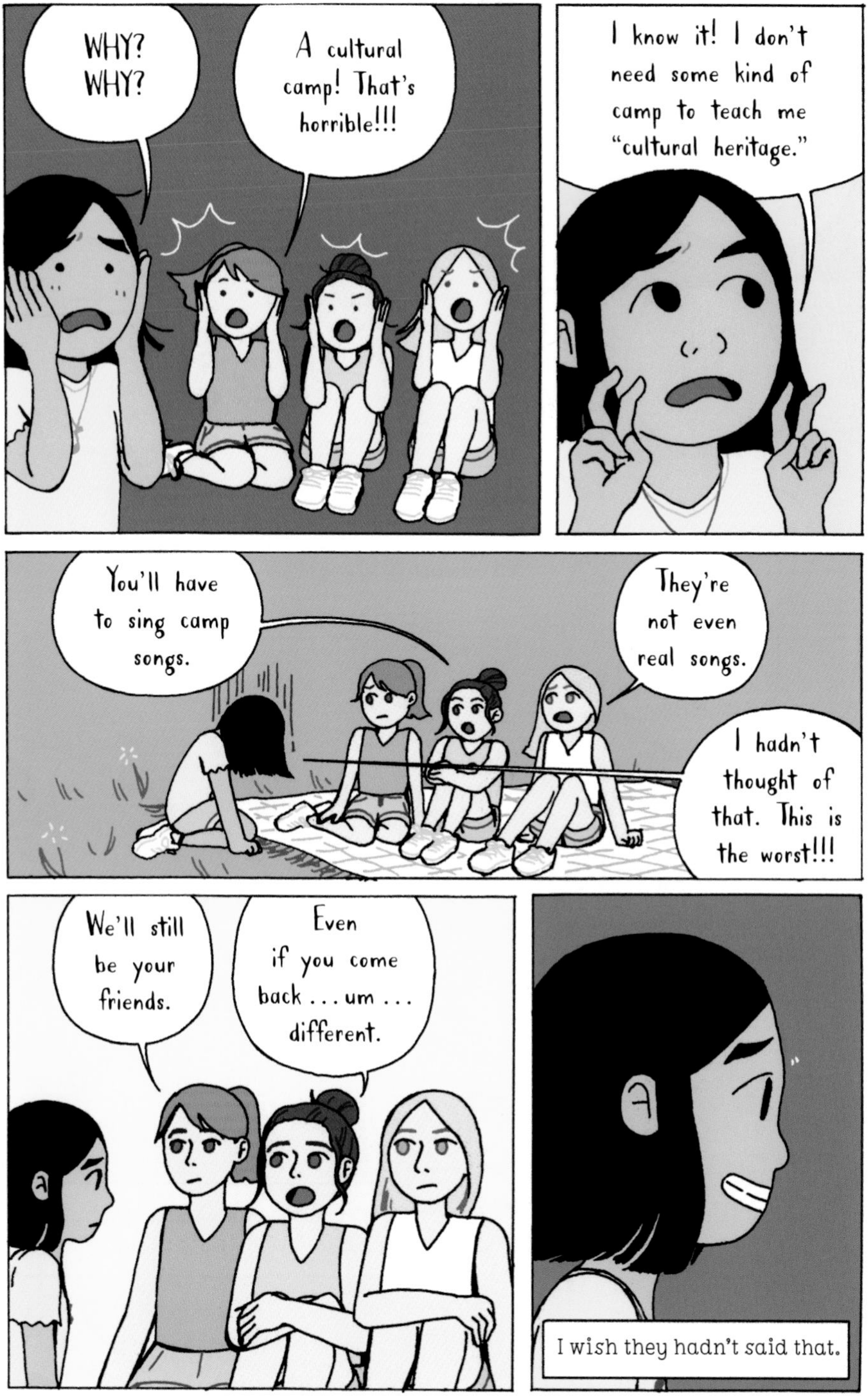
WHY? WHY?
A cultural camp! That's horrible!!!
I know it! I don't need some kind of camp to teach me "cultural heritage."
You'll have to sing camp songs.
They're not even real songs.
I hadn't thought of that. This is the worst!!!
We'll still be your friends.
Even if you come back . . . um . . . different.
I wish they hadn't said that.

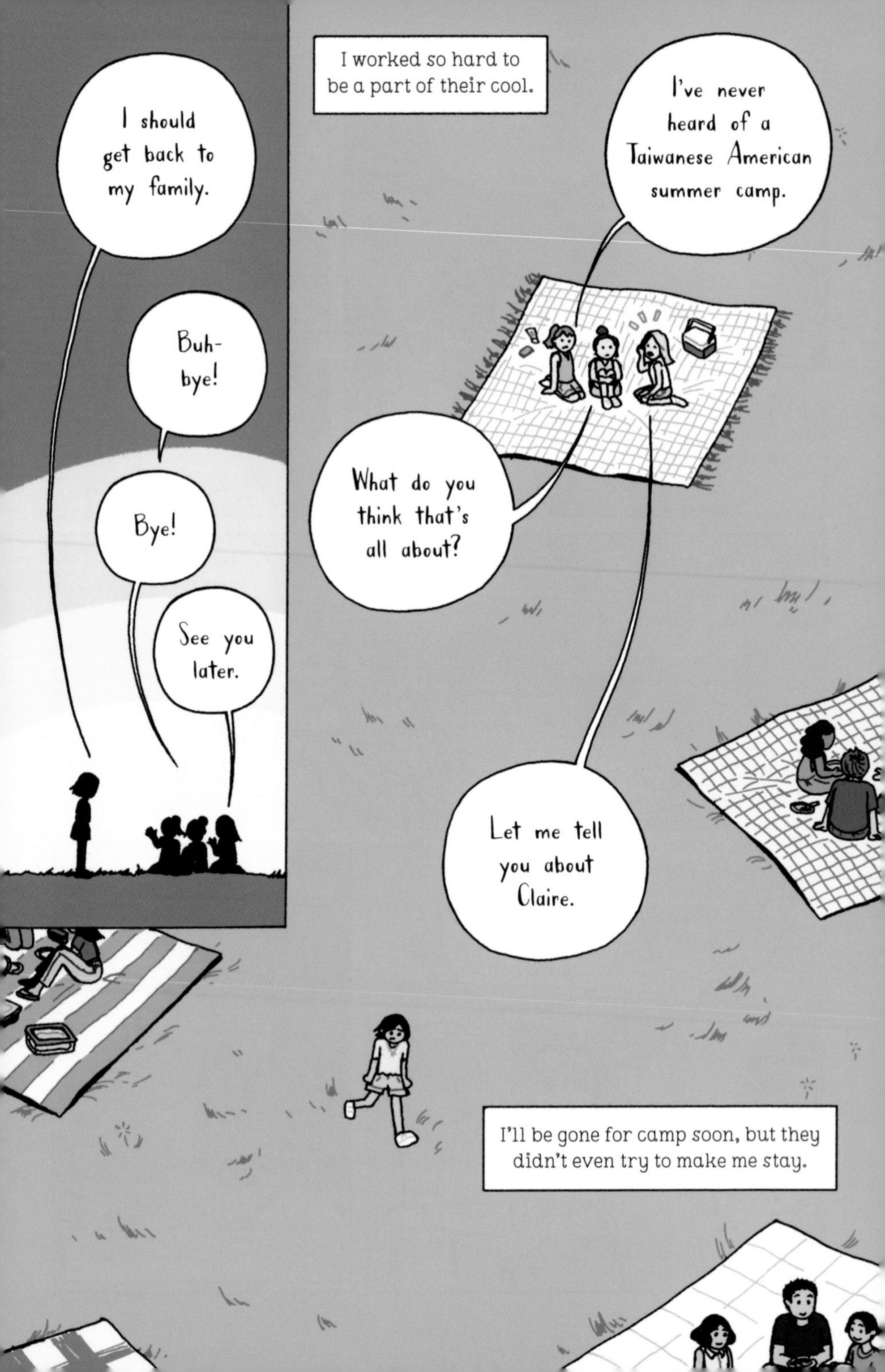
I should get back to my family.
Buh-bye!
Bye!
See you later.
I worked so hard to be a part of their cool.
I've never heard of a Taiwanese American summer camp.
What do you think that's all about?
Let me tell you about Claire.
I'll be gone for camp soon, but they didn't even try to make me stay.

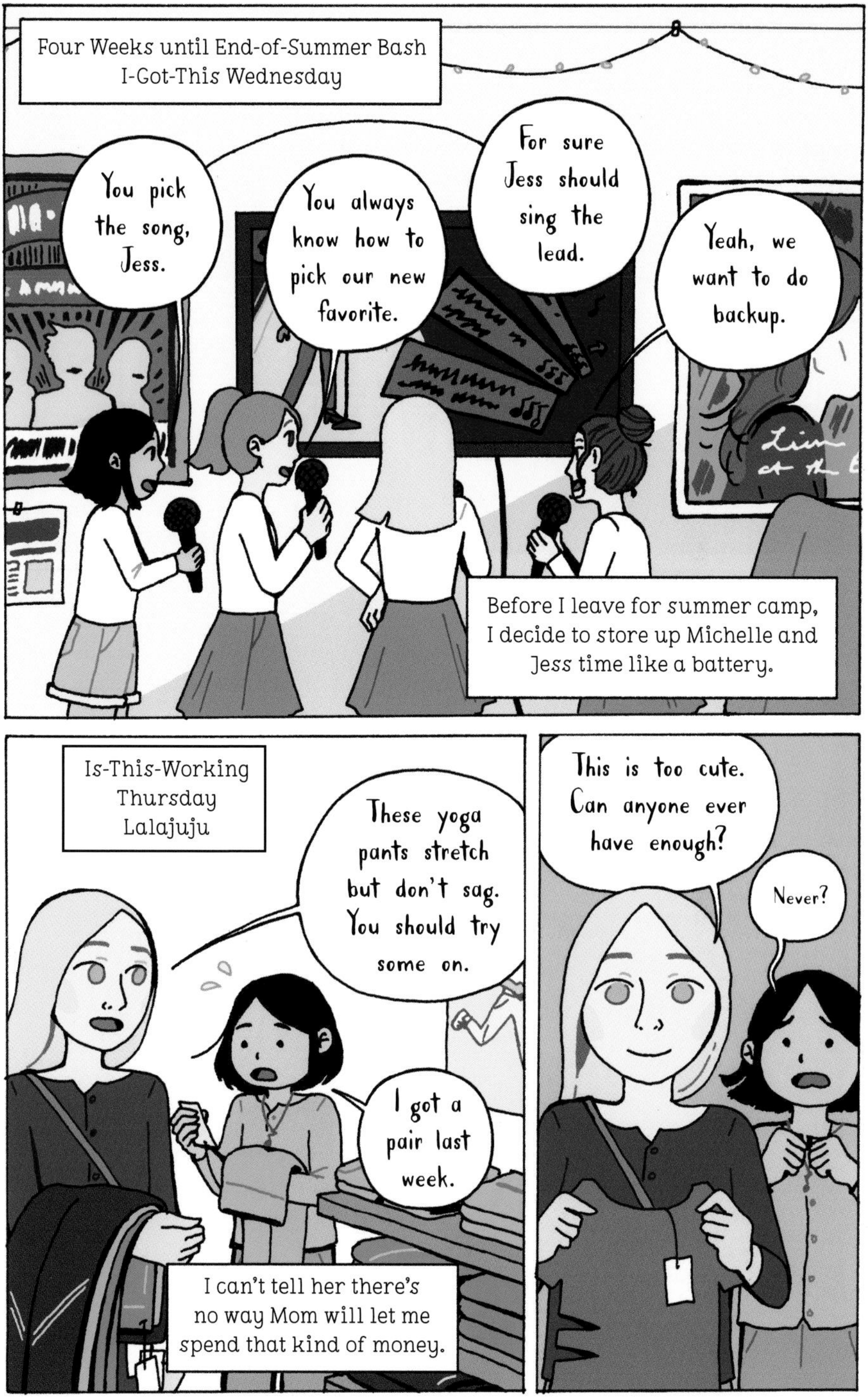

Four Weeks until End-of-Summer Bash
I-Got-This Wednesday
You pick the song, Jess.
You always know how to pick our new favorite.
For sure Jess should sing the lead.
Yeah, we want to do backup.
Before I leave for summer camp, I decide to store up Michelle and Jess time like a battery.
Is-This-Working Thursday
Lalajuju
These yoga pants stretch but don't sag. You should try some on.
I got a pair last week.
I can't tell her there's no way Mom will let me spend that kind of money.
This is too cute. Can anyone ever have enough?
Never?

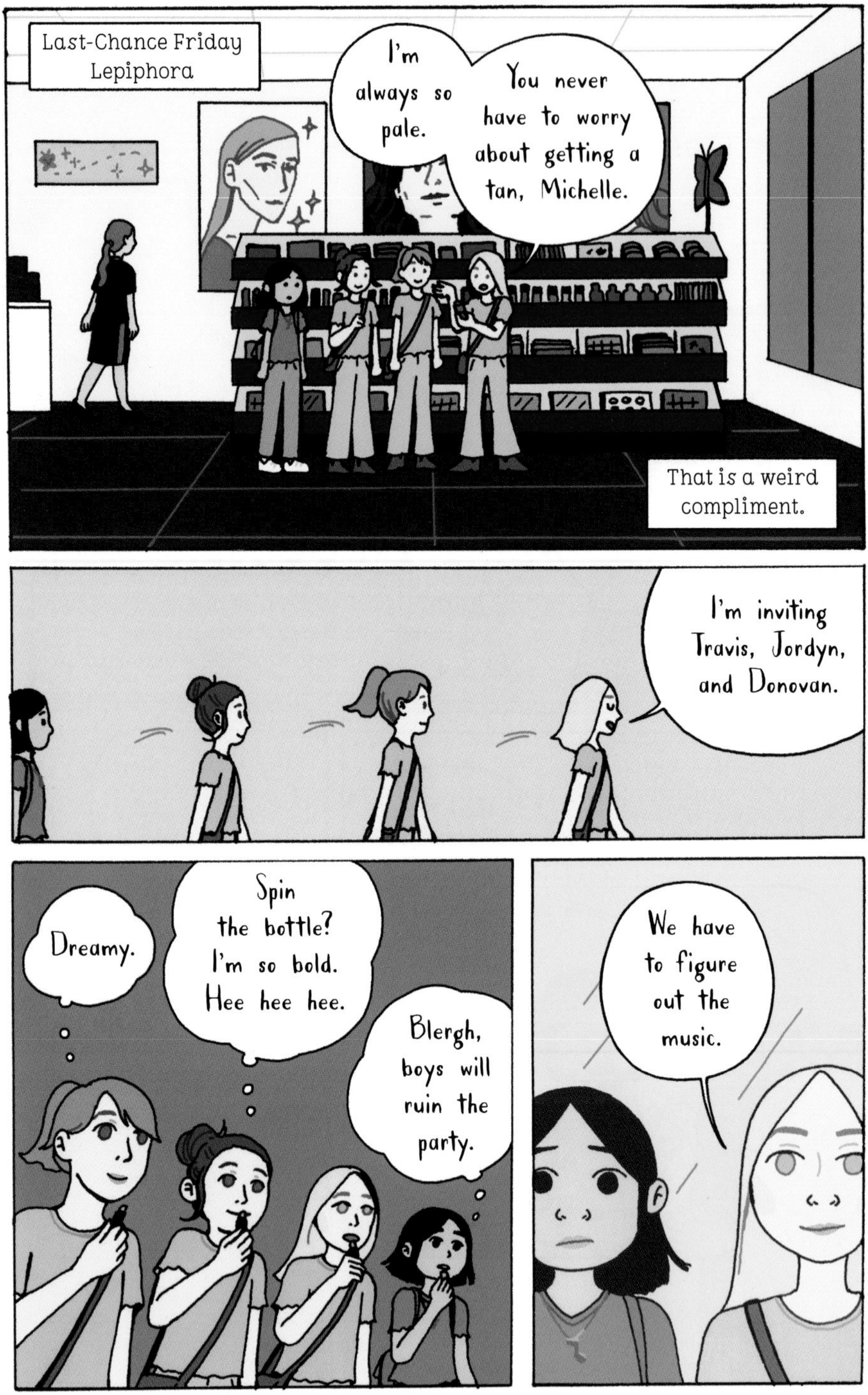
Last-Chance Friday
Lepiphora
I'm always so pale.
You never have to worry about getting a tan, Michelle.
That is a weird compliment.
I'm inviting Travis, Jordyn, and Donovan.
Dreamy.
Spin the bottle? I'm so bold. Hee hee hee.
Blergh, boys will ruin the party.
We have to figure out the music.

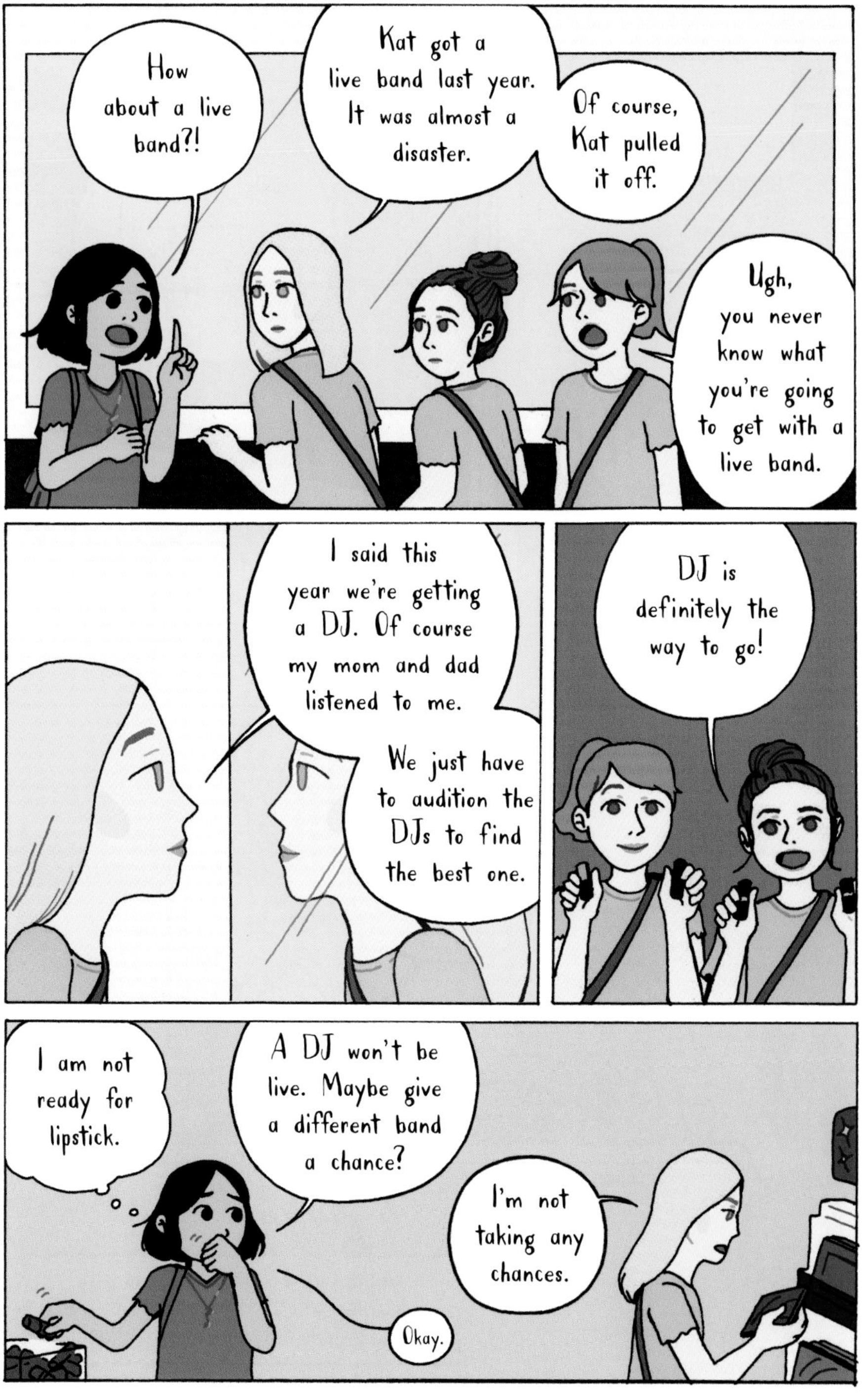
How about a live band?!
Kat got a live band last year. It was almost a disaster.
Of course, Kat pulled it off.
Ugh, you never know what you're going to get with a live band.
I said this year we're getting a DJ. Of course my mom and dad listened to me.
We just have to audition the DJs to find the best one.
DJ is definitely the way to go!
I am not ready for lipstick.
A DJ won't be live. Maybe give a different band a chance?
I'm not taking any chances.
Okay.

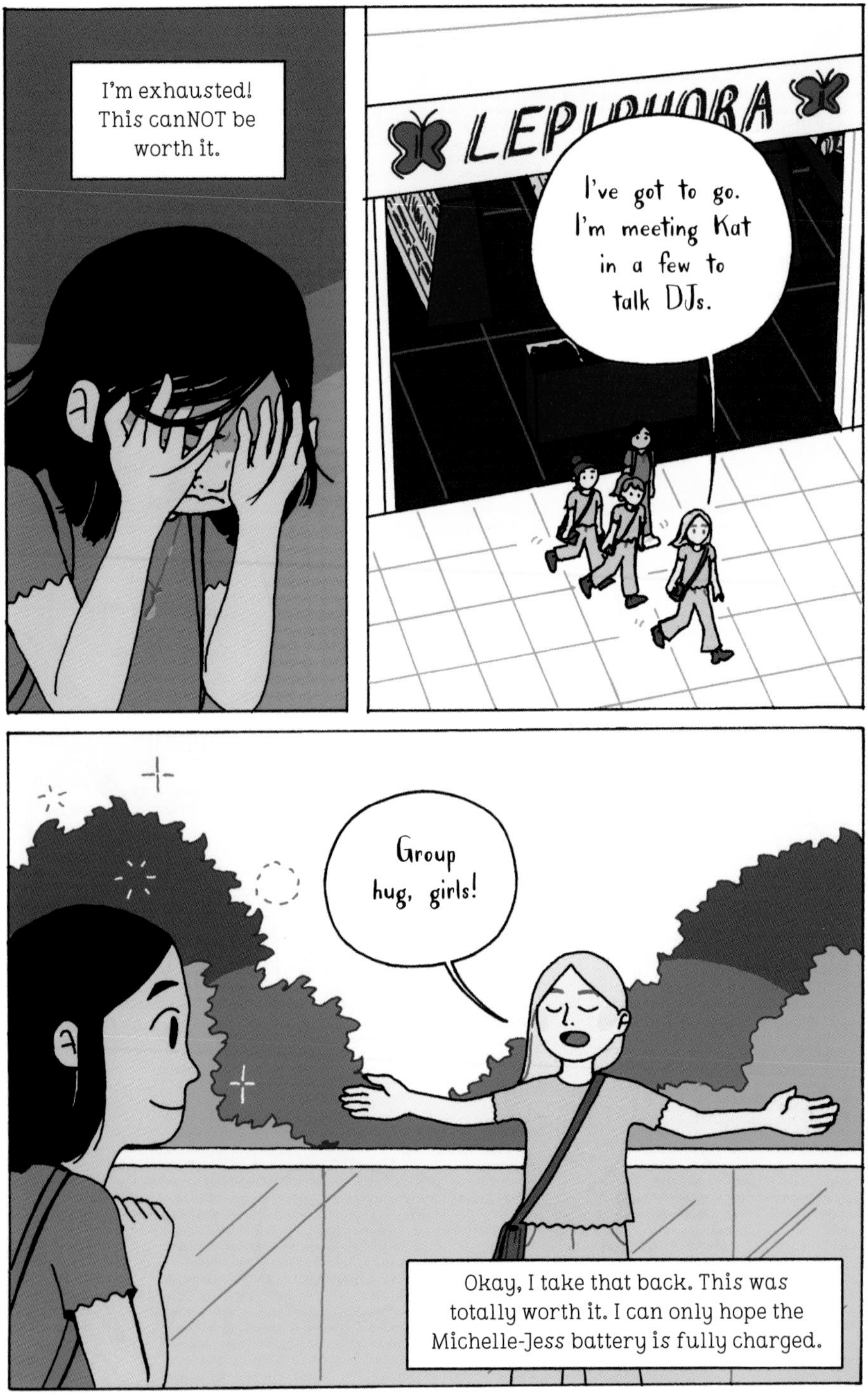
I'm exhausted! This canNOT be worth it.
LEPIDOPTERA
I've got to go. I'm meeting Kat in a few to talk DJs.
Group hug, girls!
Okay, I take that back. This was totally worth it. I can only hope the Michelle-Jess battery is fully charged.

chapter FIVE

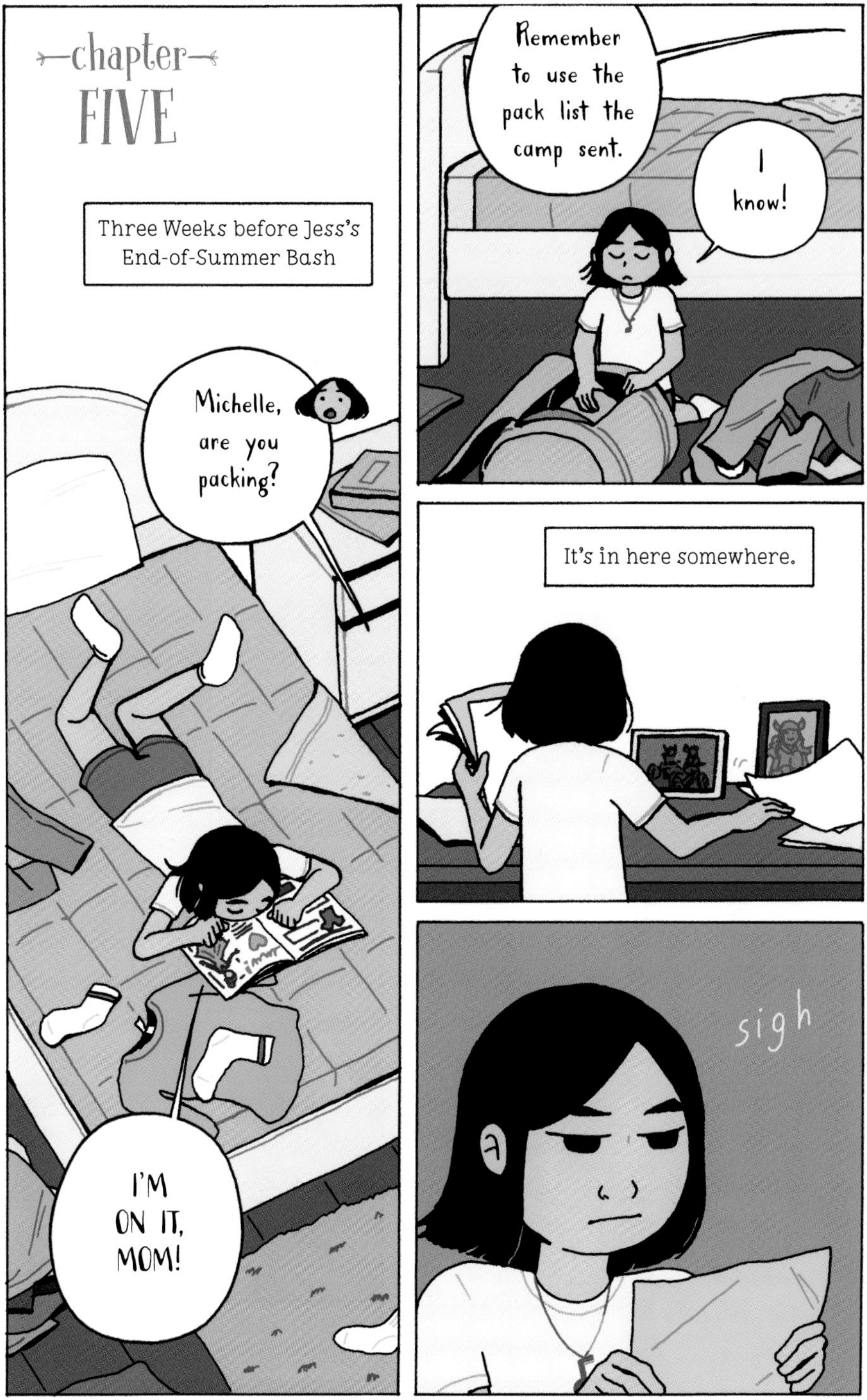
Three Weeks before Jess's End-of-Summer Bash
Michelle, are you packing?
I'M ON IT, MOM!
Remember to use the pack list the camp sent.
I know!
It's in here somewhere.
sigh

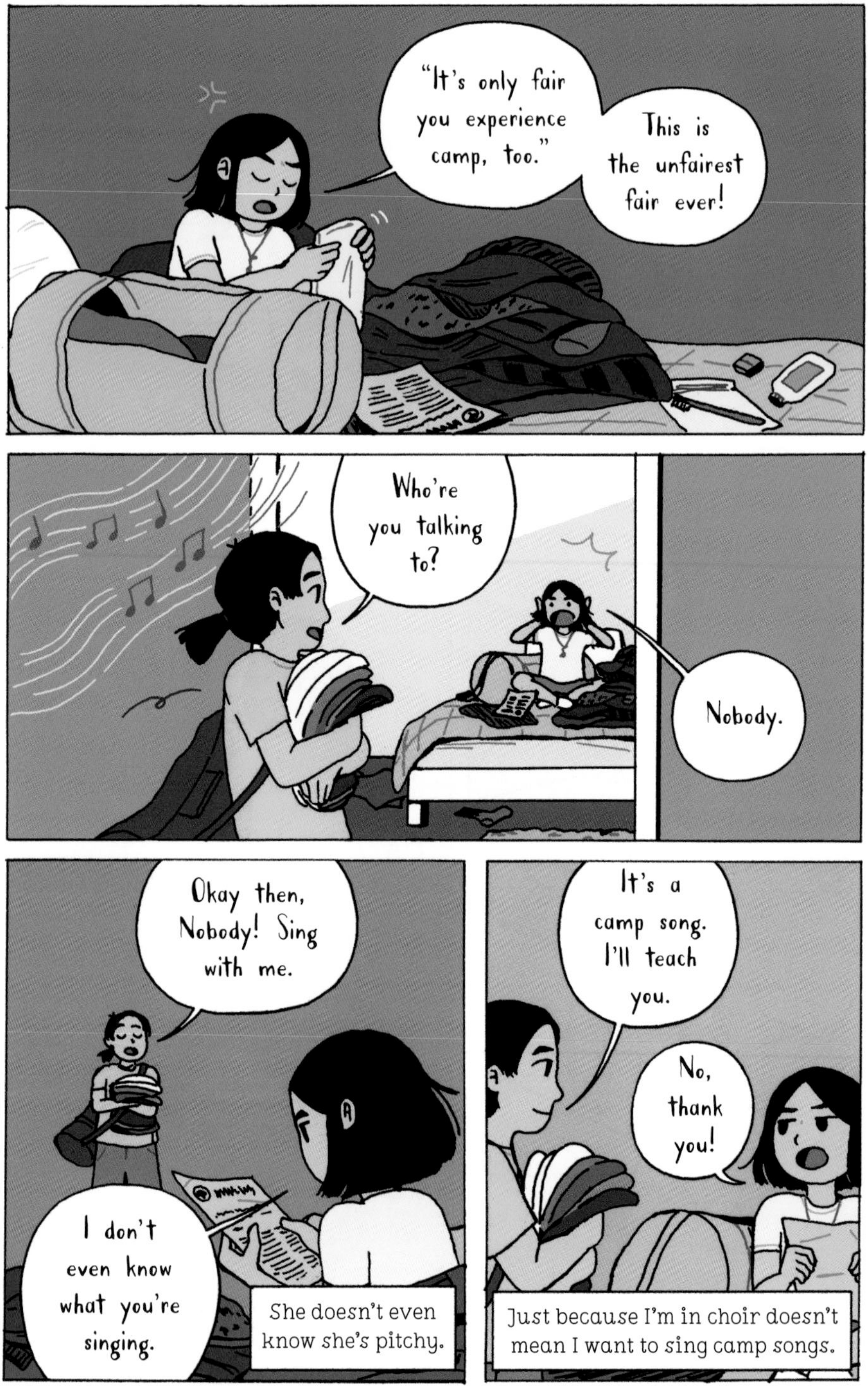
"It's only fair you experience camp, too."
This is the unfairest fair ever!
Who're you talking to?
Nobody.
Okay then, Nobody! Sing with me.
I don't even know what you're singing.
She doesn't even know she's pitchy.
It's a camp song. I'll teach you.
No, thank you!
Just because I'm in choir doesn't mean I want to sing camp songs.

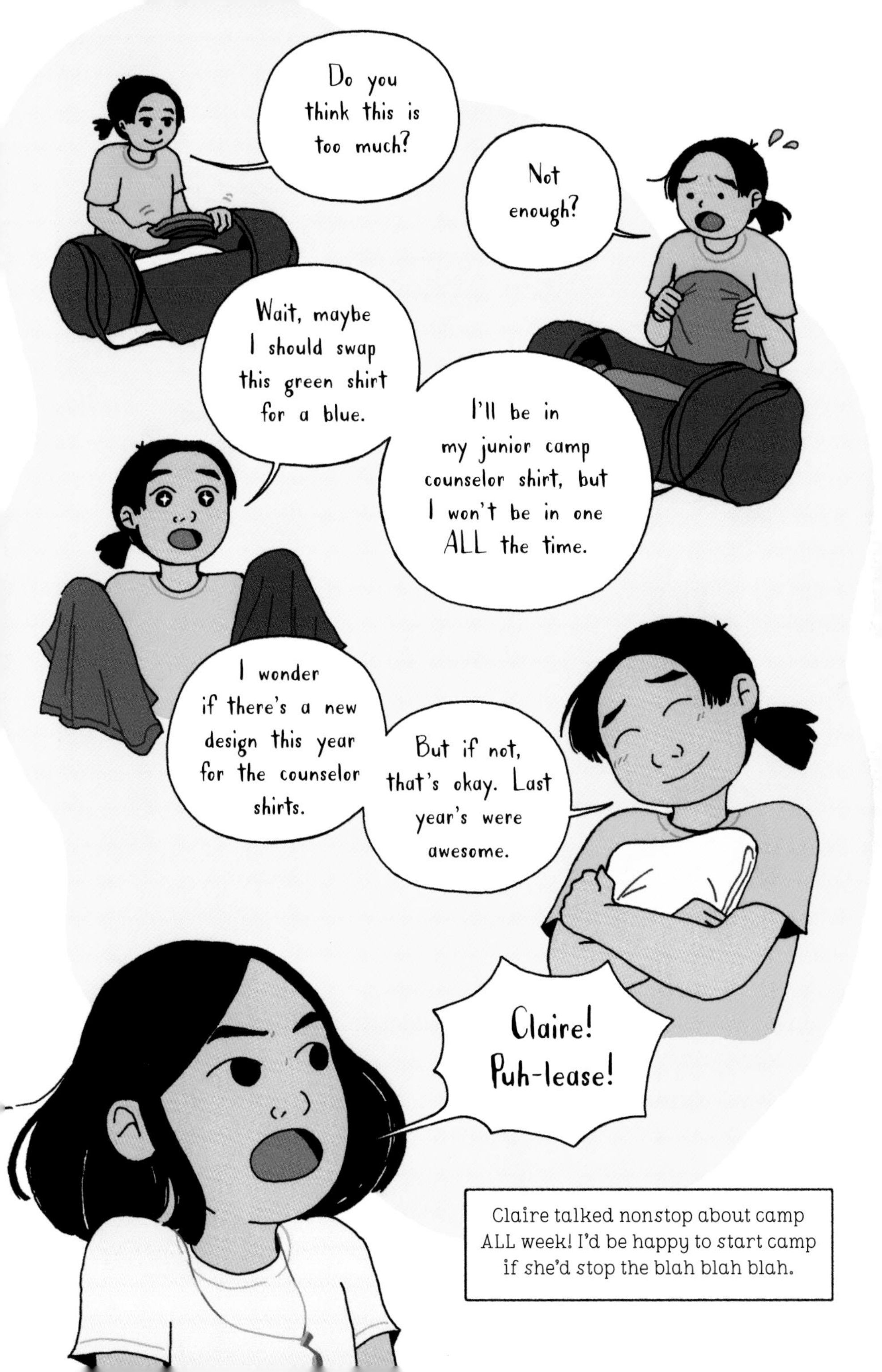
Do you think this is too much?
Not enough?
Wait, maybe I should swap this green shirt for a blue.
I'll be in my junior camp counselor shirt, but I won't be in one ALL the time.
I wonder if there's a new design this year for the counselor shirts.
But if not, that's okay. Last year's were awesome.
Claire! Puh-lease!
Claire talked nonstop about camp ALL week! I'd be happy to start camp if she'd stop the blah blah blah.

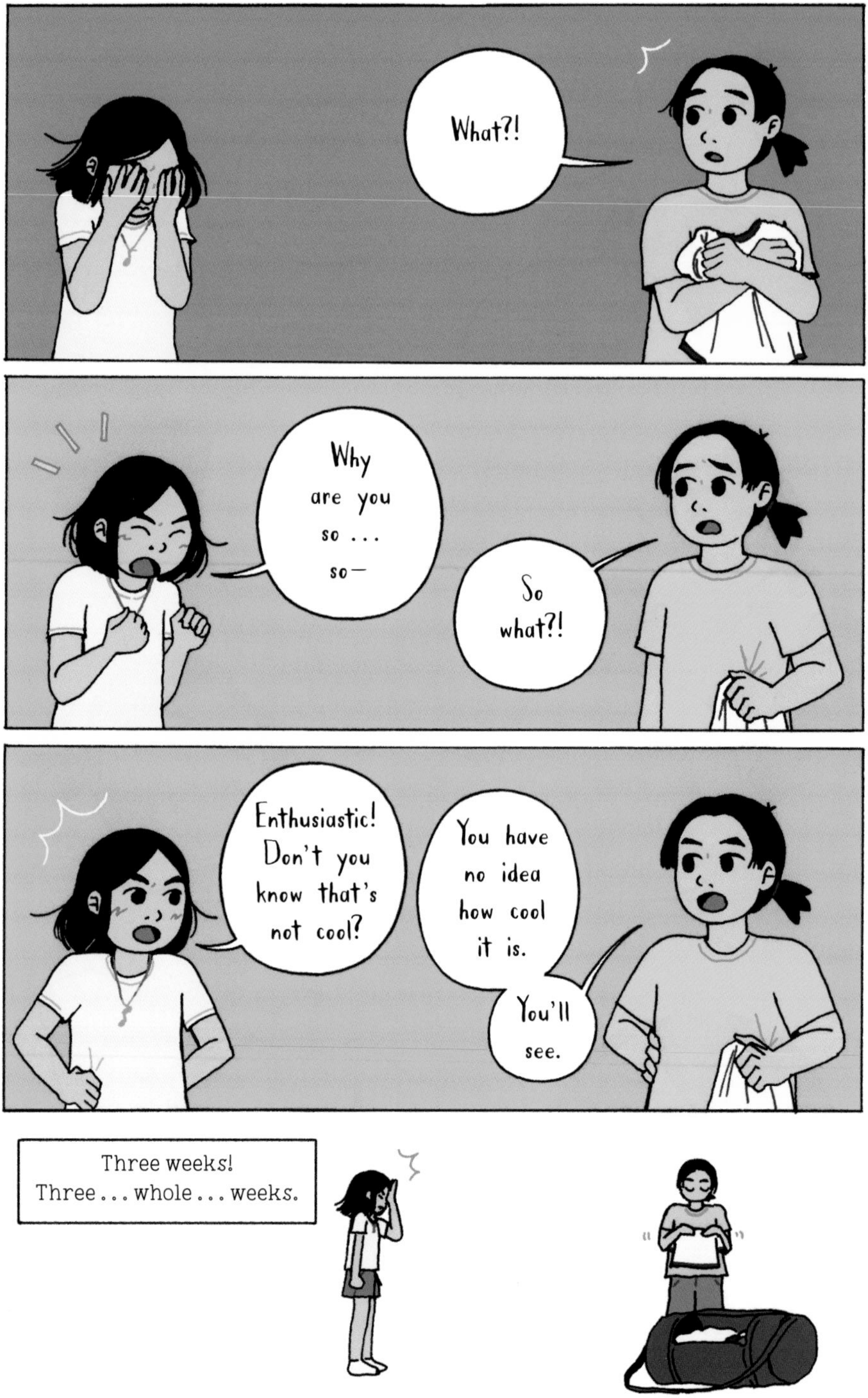
What?!
Why are you so . . . so—
So what?!
Enthusiastic! Don't you know that's not cool?
You have no idea how cool it is.
You'll see.
Three weeks!
Three . . . whole . . . weeks.

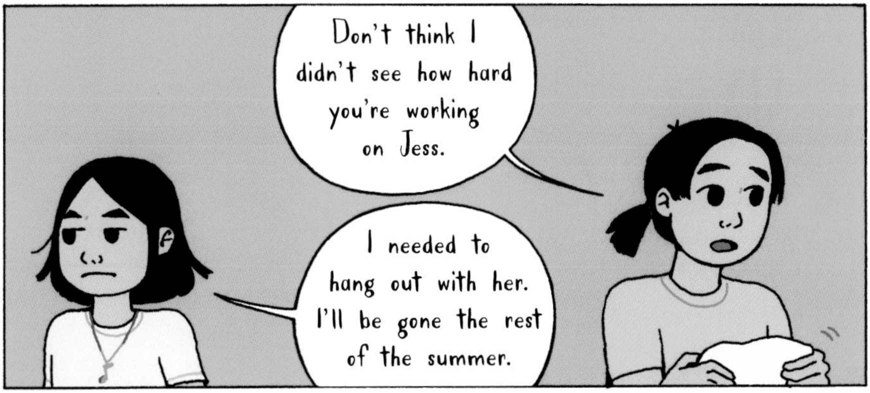
Don't think I didn't see how hard you're working on Jess.
I needed to hang out with her. I'll be gone the rest of the summer.

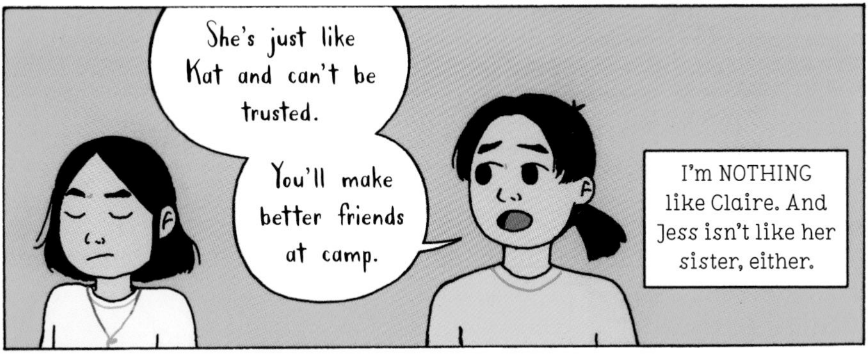
She's just like Kat and can't be trusted.
You'll make better friends at camp.
I'm NOTHING like Claire. And Jess isn't like her sister, either.

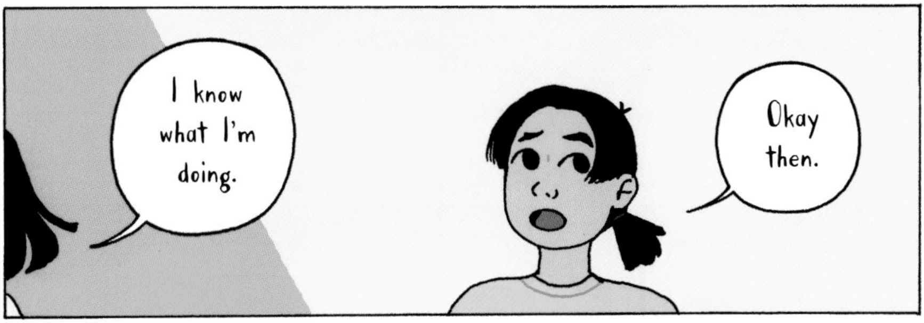
I know what I'm doing.
Okay then.

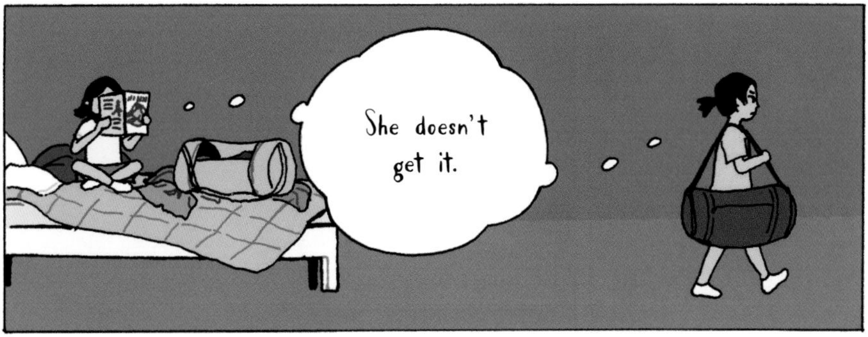
She doesn't get it.

chapter SIX

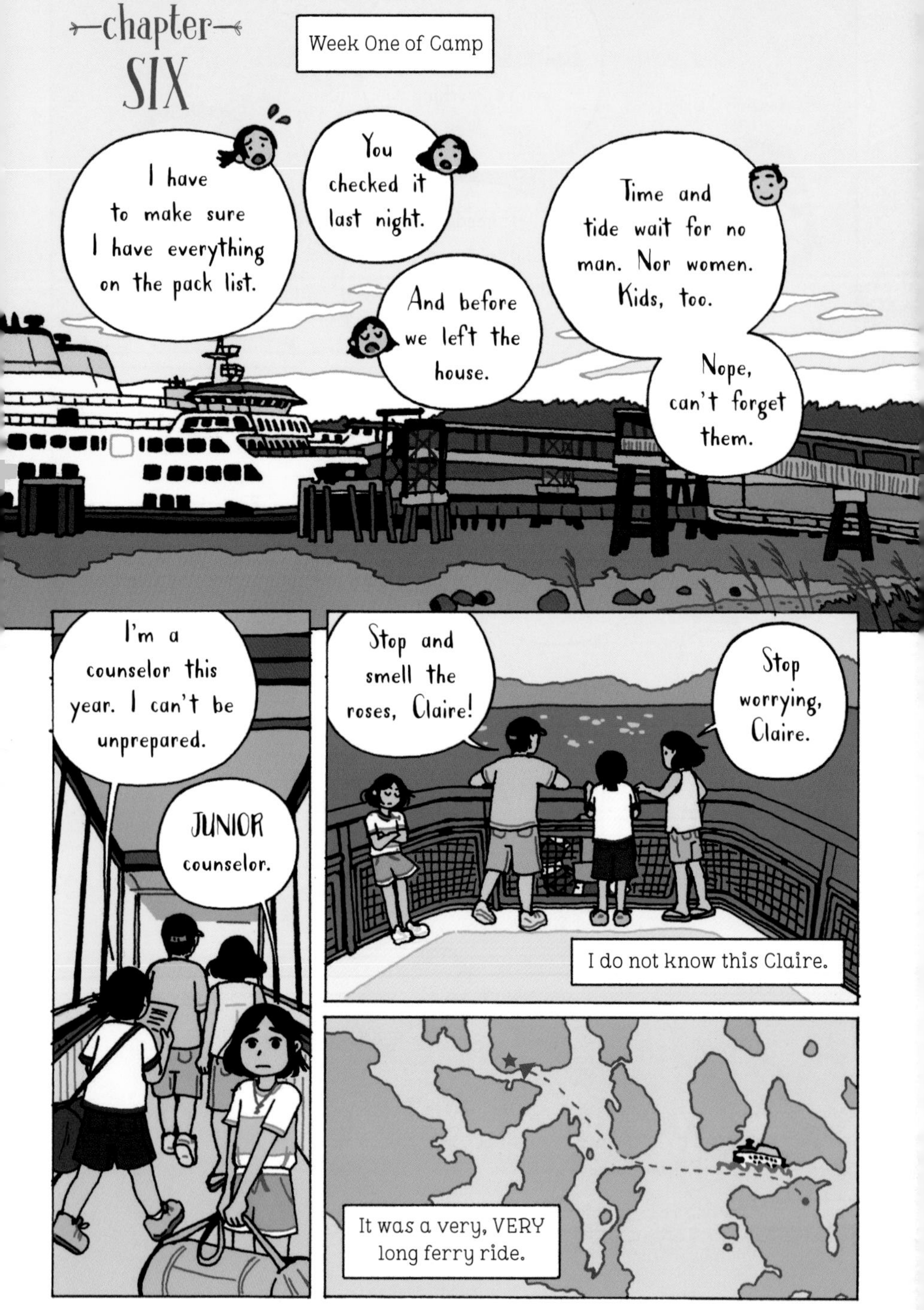
Week One of Camp
I have to make sure I have everything on the pack list.
You checked it last night.
And before we left the house.
Time and tide wait for no man. Nor women. Kids, too.
Nope, can't forget them.
I'm a counselor this year. I can't be unprepared.
JUNIOR counselor.
Stop and smell the roses, Claire!
Stop worrying, Claire.
I do not know this Claire.
It was a very, VERY long ferry ride.

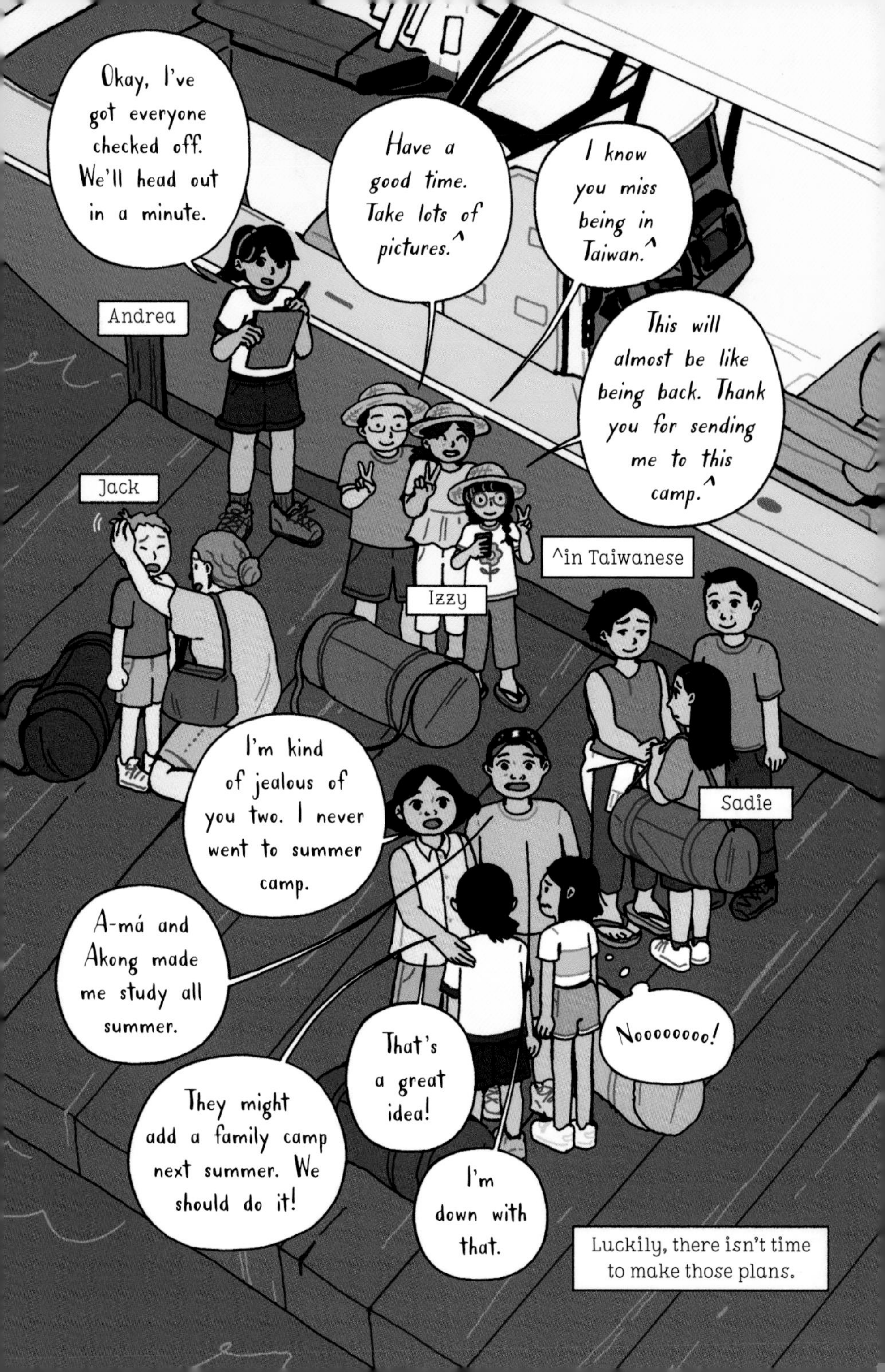
Okay, I've got everyone checked off. We'll head out in a minute.
Andrea
Have a good time. Take lots of pictures.^
I know you miss being in Taiwan.^
This will almost be like being back. Thank you for sending me to this camp.^
Jack
^in Taiwanese
Izzy
Sadie
I'm kind of jealous of you two. I never went to summer camp.
A-má and Akong made me study all summer.
Noooooooo!
That's a great idea!
They might add a family camp next summer. We should do it!
I'm down with that.
Luckily, there isn't time to make those plans.

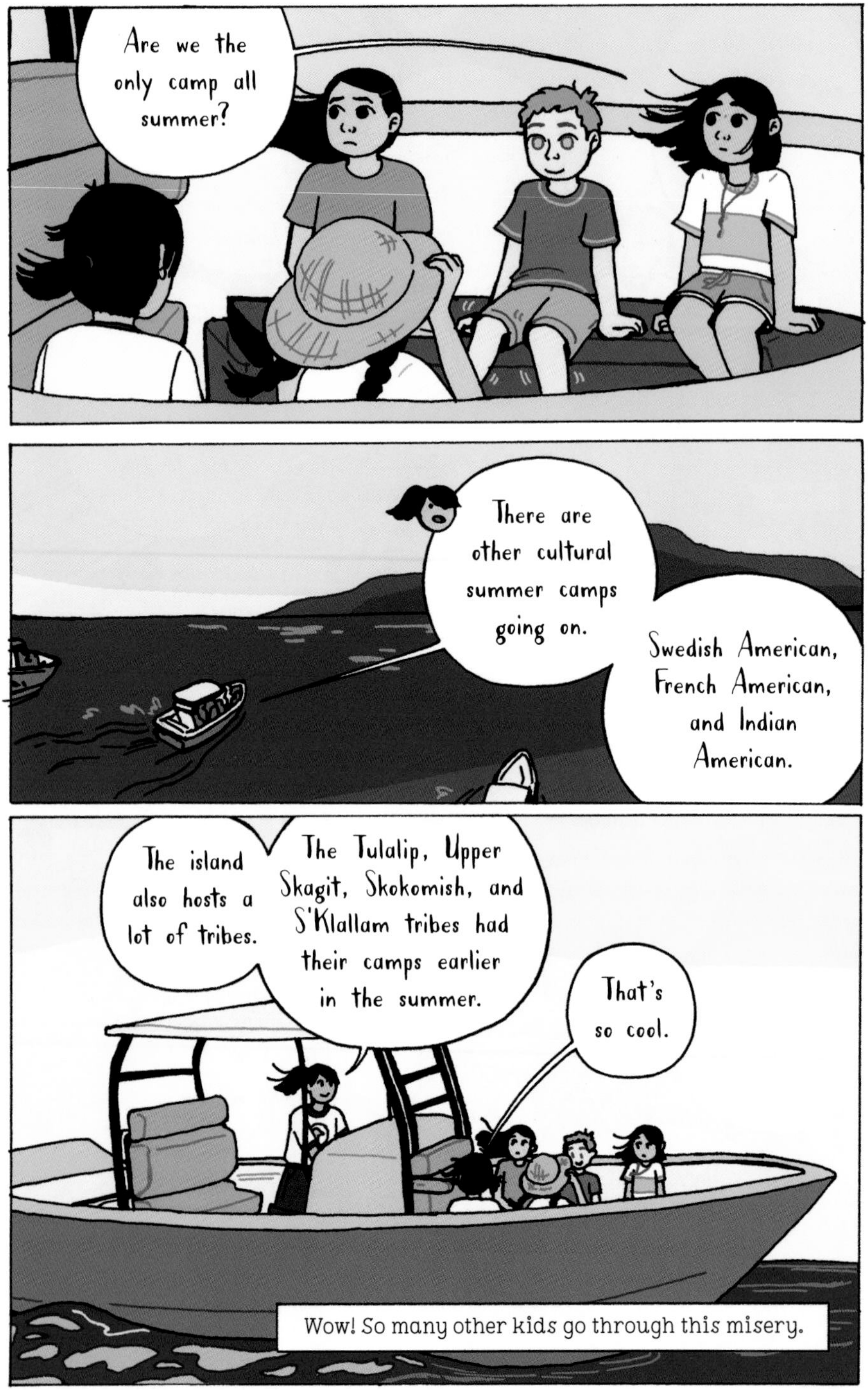

Are we the only camp all summer?
There are other cultural summer camps going on.
Swedish American, French American, and Indian American.
The island also hosts a lot of tribes.
The Tulalip, Upper Skagit, Skokomish, and S'Klallam tribes had their camps earlier in the summer.
That's so cool.
Wow! So many other kids go through this misery.

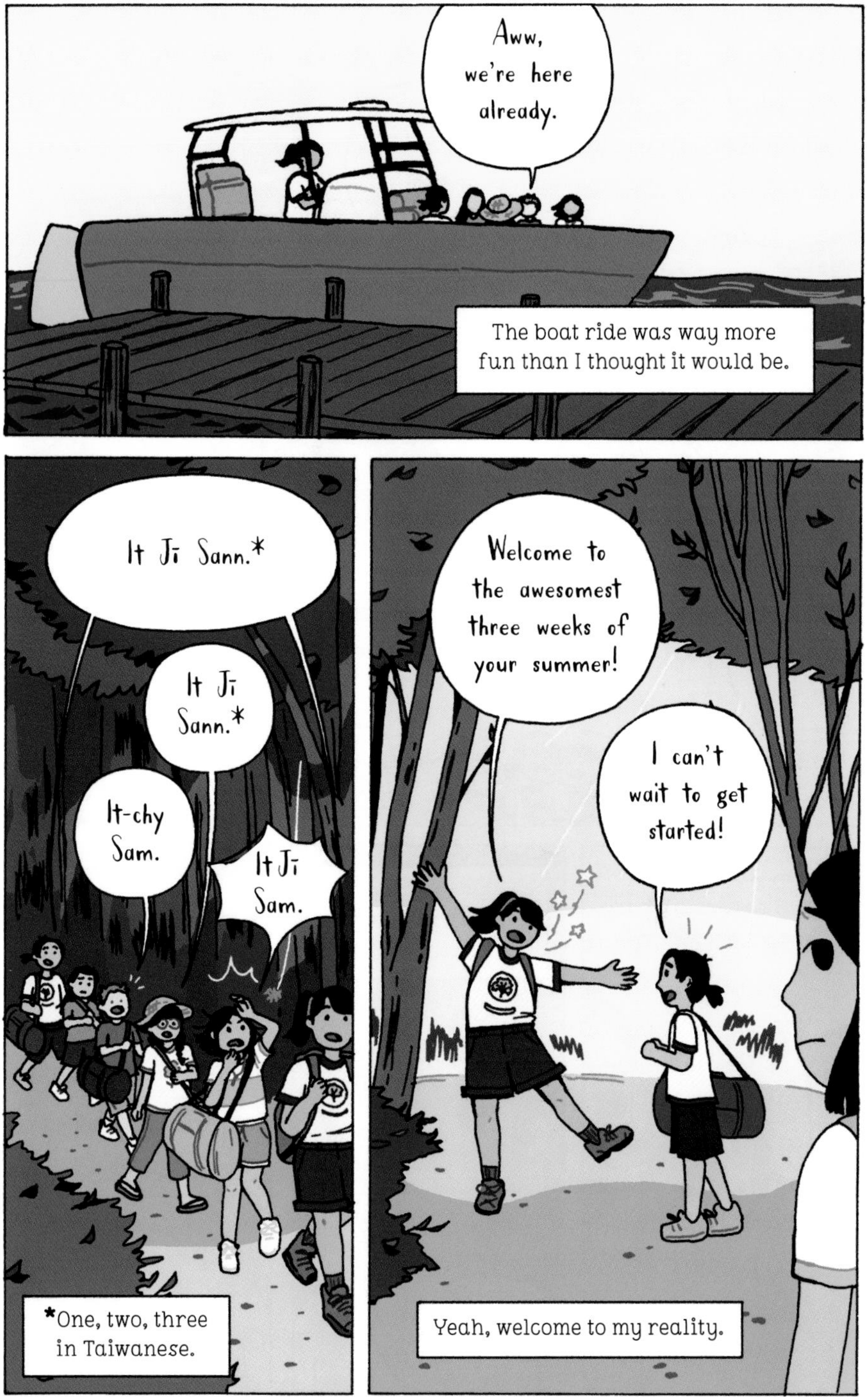

Aww, we're here already.
The boat ride was way more fun than I thought it would be.
It Jī Sann.*
It Jī Sann.*
It-chy Sam.
It Jī Sam.
*One, two, three in Taiwanese.
Welcome to the awesomest three weeks of your summer!
I can't wait to get started!
Yeah, welcome to my reality.

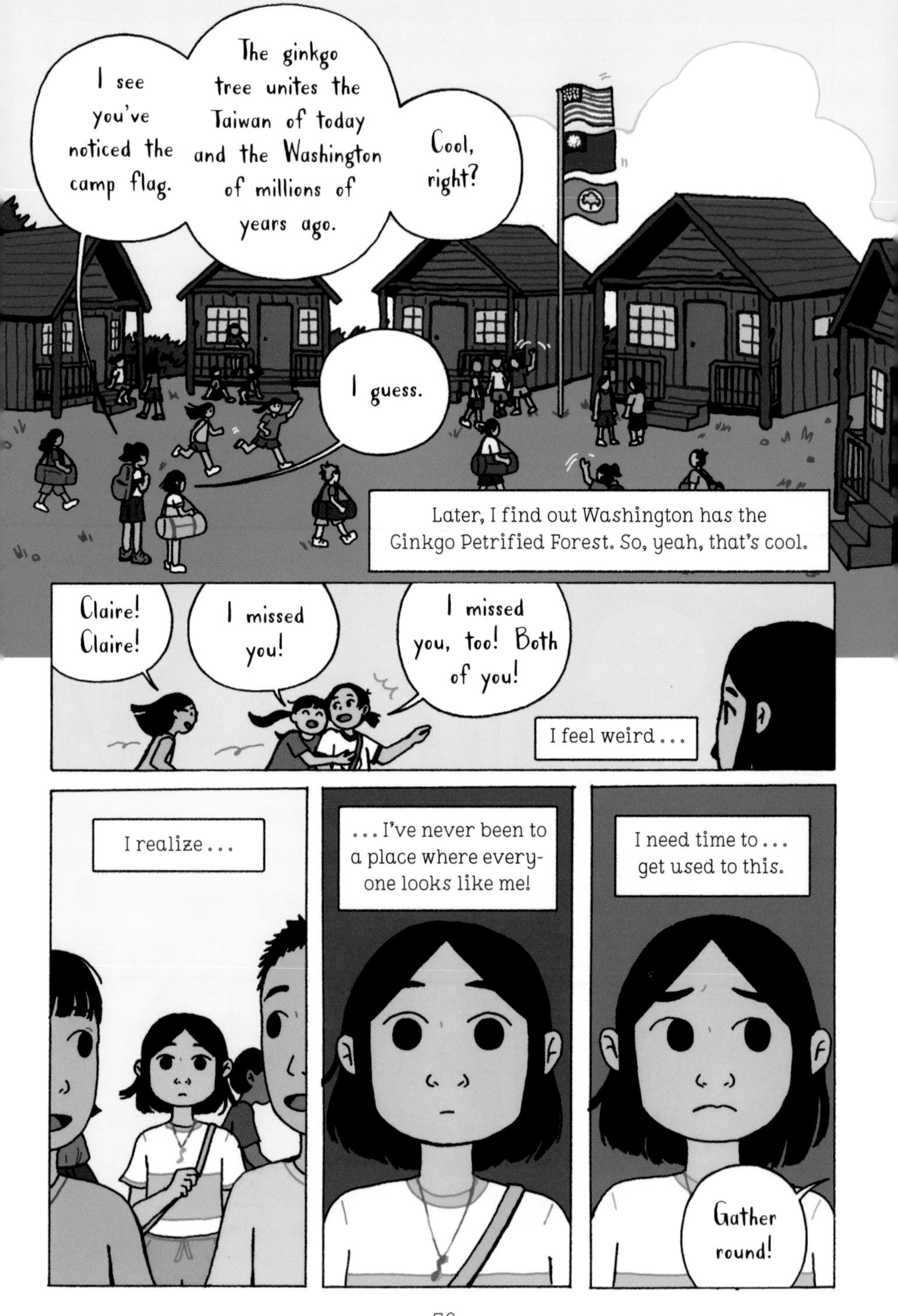

I see you've noticed the camp flag.
The ginkgo tree unites the Taiwan of today and the Washington of millions of years ago.
Cool, right?
I guess.
Later, I find out Washington has the Ginkgo Petrified Forest. So, yeah, that's cool.
Claire! Claire!
I missed you!
I missed you, too! Both of you!
I feel weird . . .
I realize . . .
. . . I've never been to a place where every-one looks like me!
I need time to . . . get used to this.
Gather round!

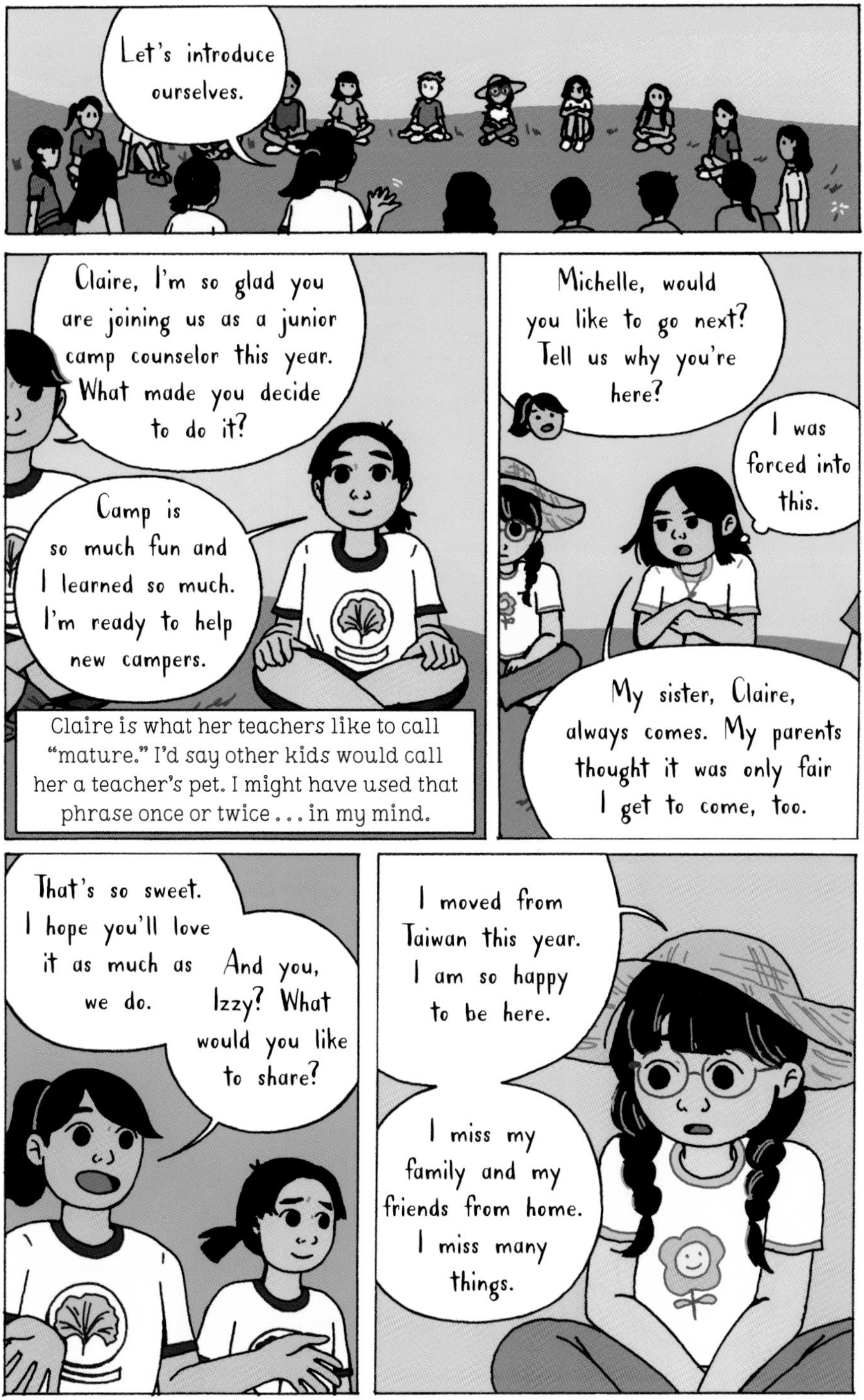
Let's introduce ourselves.
Claire, I'm so glad you are joining us as a junior camp counselor this year. What made you decide to do it?
Camp is so much fun and I learned so much. I'm ready to help new campers.
Claire is what her teachers like to call "mature." I'd say other kids would call her a teacher's pet. I might have used that phrase once or twice . . . in my mind.
Michelle, would you like to go next? Tell us why you're here?
I was forced into this.
My sister, Claire, always comes. My parents thought it was only fair I get to come, too.
That's so sweet. I hope you'll love it as much as we do.
And you, Izzy? What would you like to share?
I moved from Taiwan this year. I am so happy to be here.
I miss my family and my friends from home. I miss many things.

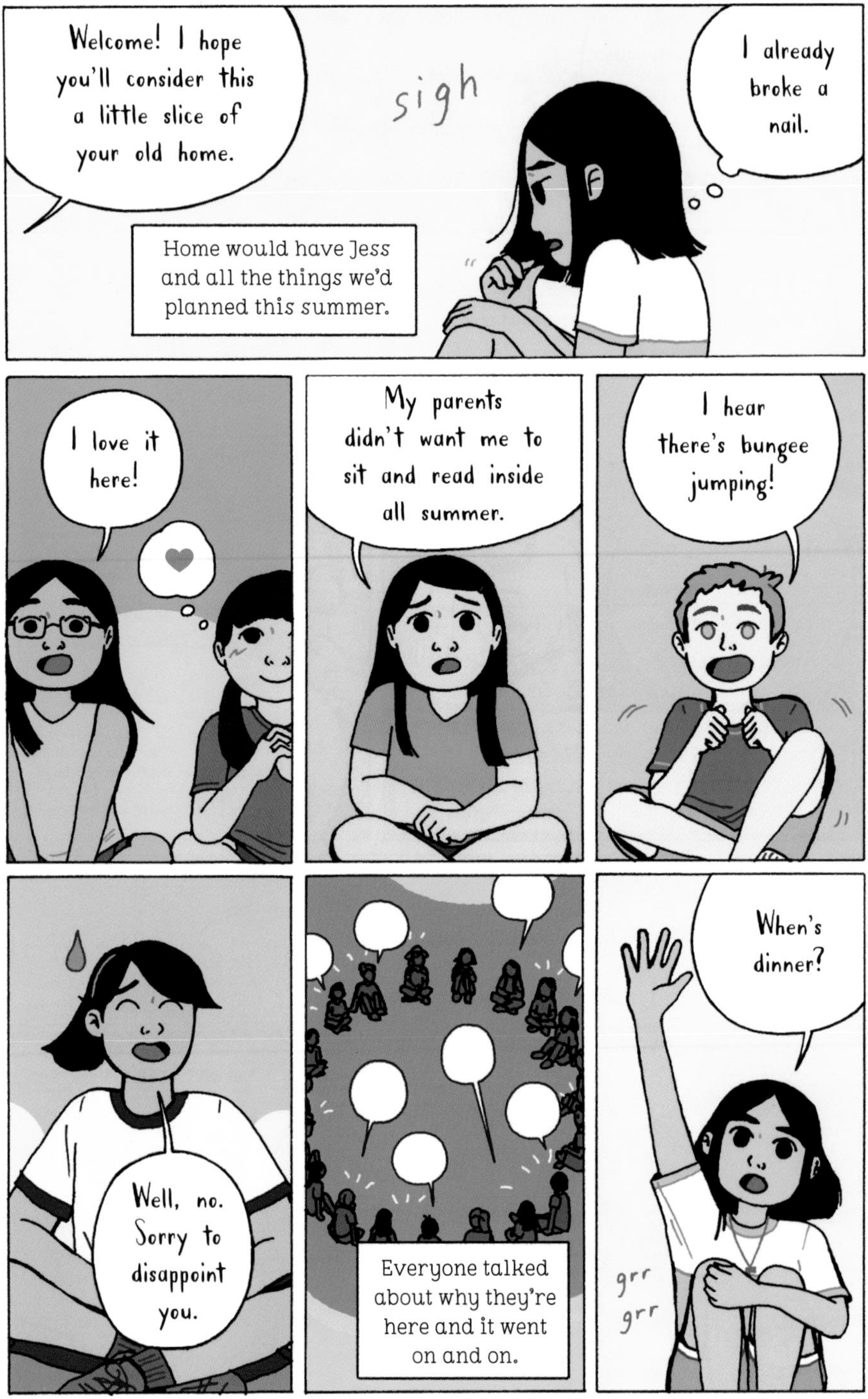
Welcome! I hope you'll consider this a little slice of your old home.
sigh
I already broke a nail.
Home would have Jess and all the things we'd planned this summer.
I love it here!
My parents didn't want me to sit and read inside all summer.
I hear there's bungee jumping!
Well, no. Sorry to disappoint you.
Everyone talked about why they're here and it went on and on.
When's dinner?
grr grr

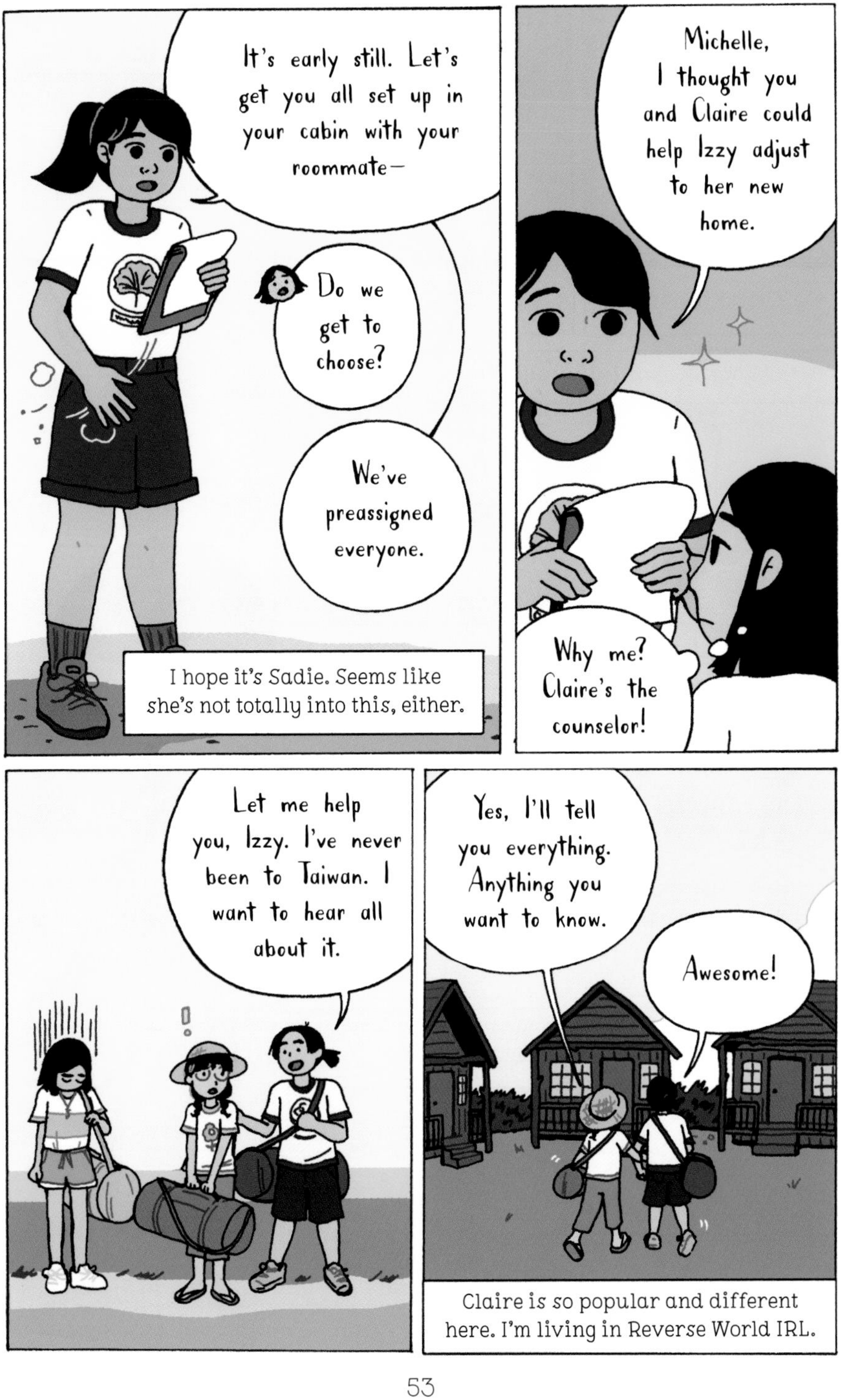
It's early still. Let's get you all set up in your cabin with your roommate—
Do we get to choose?
We've preassigned everyone.
I hope it's Sadie. Seems like she's not totally into this, either.
Michelle, I thought you and Claire could help Izzy adjust to her new home.
Why me? Claire's the counselor!
Let me help you, Izzy. I've never been to Taiwan. I want to hear all about it.
Yes, I'll tell you everything. Anything you want to know.
Awesome!
Claire is so popular and different here. I'm living in Reverse World IRL.

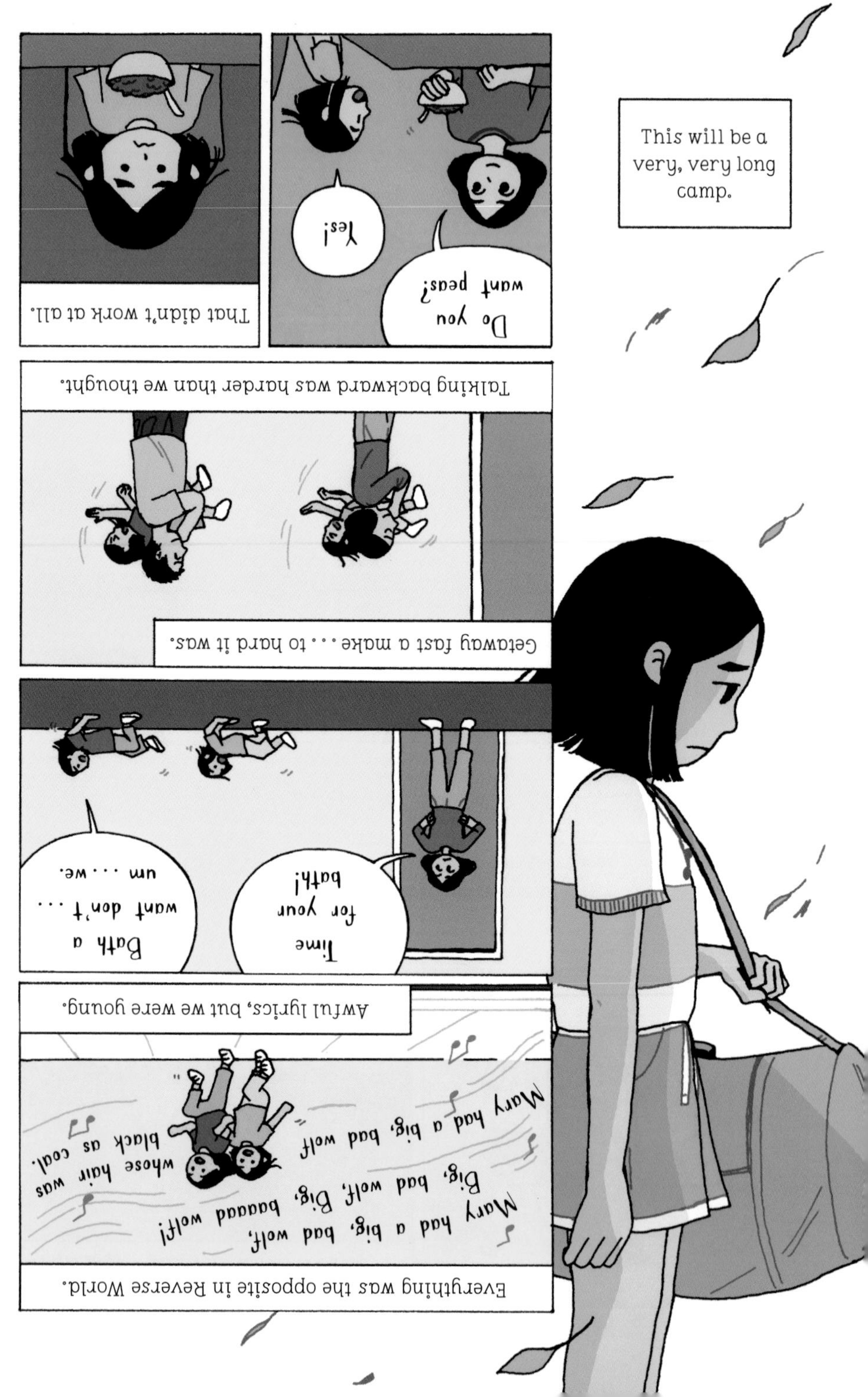
Everything was the opposite in Reverse World.
Mary had a big, bad wolf, Big, bad wolf, Big, baaaad wolf!
Mary had a big, bad wolf whose hair was black as coal.
Awful lyrics, but we were young.
Time for your bath!
Bath a want don't . . . um . . . we.
Getaway fast a make . . . to hard it was.
Talking backward was harder than we thought.
Do you want peas?
Yes!
That didn't work at all.
This will be a very, very long camp.

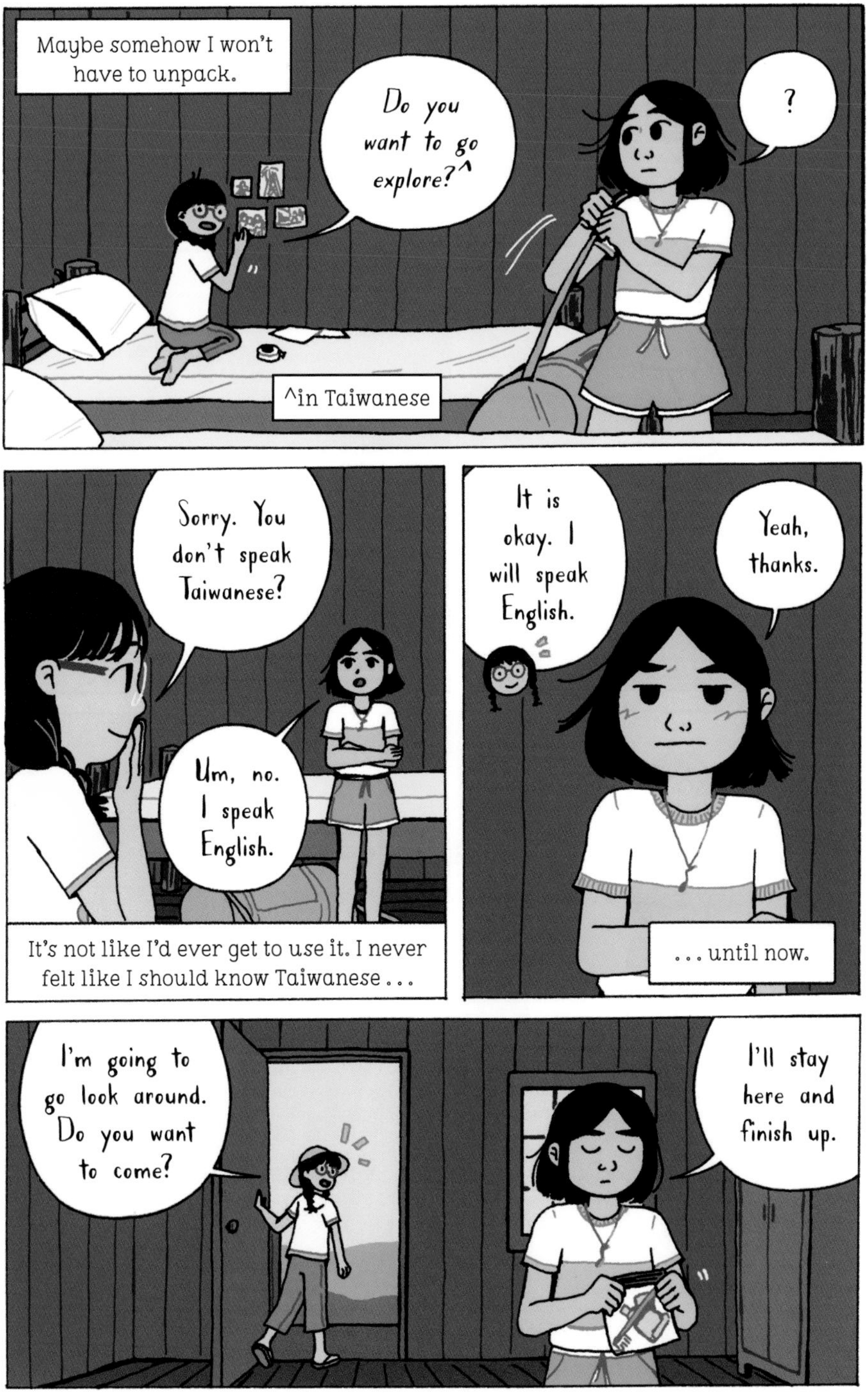
Maybe somehow I won't have to unpack.
Do you want to go explore?^
?
^in Taiwanese
Sorry. You don't speak Taiwanese?
Um, no. I speak English.
It's not like I'd ever get to use it. I never felt like I should know Taiwanese . . .
It is okay. I will speak English.
Yeah, thanks.
. . . until now.
I'm going to go look around. Do you want to come?
I'll stay here and finish up.

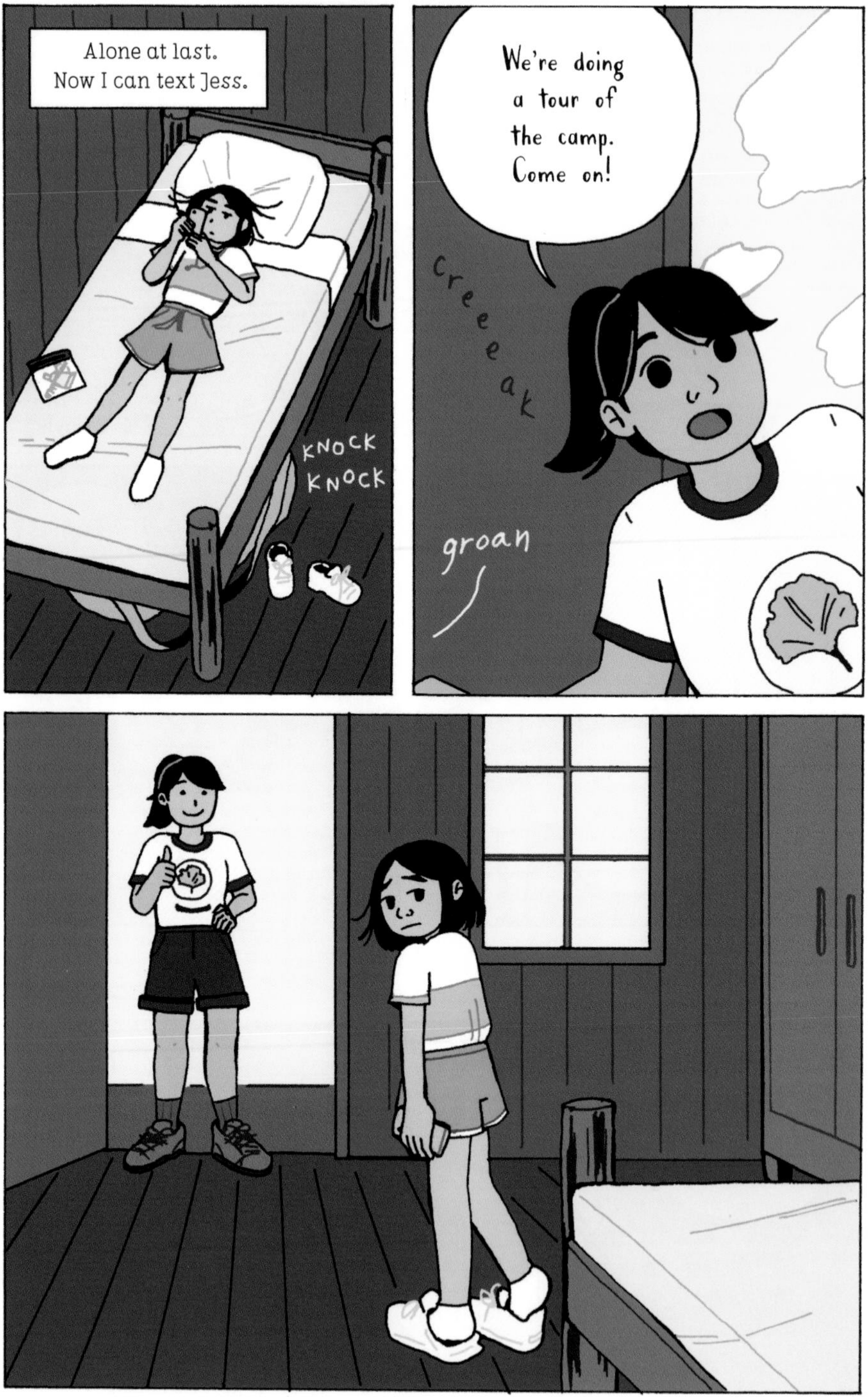

Alone at last.
Now I can text Jess.
KNOCK
KNOCK
We're doing a tour of the camp. Come on!
creeeeak
groan

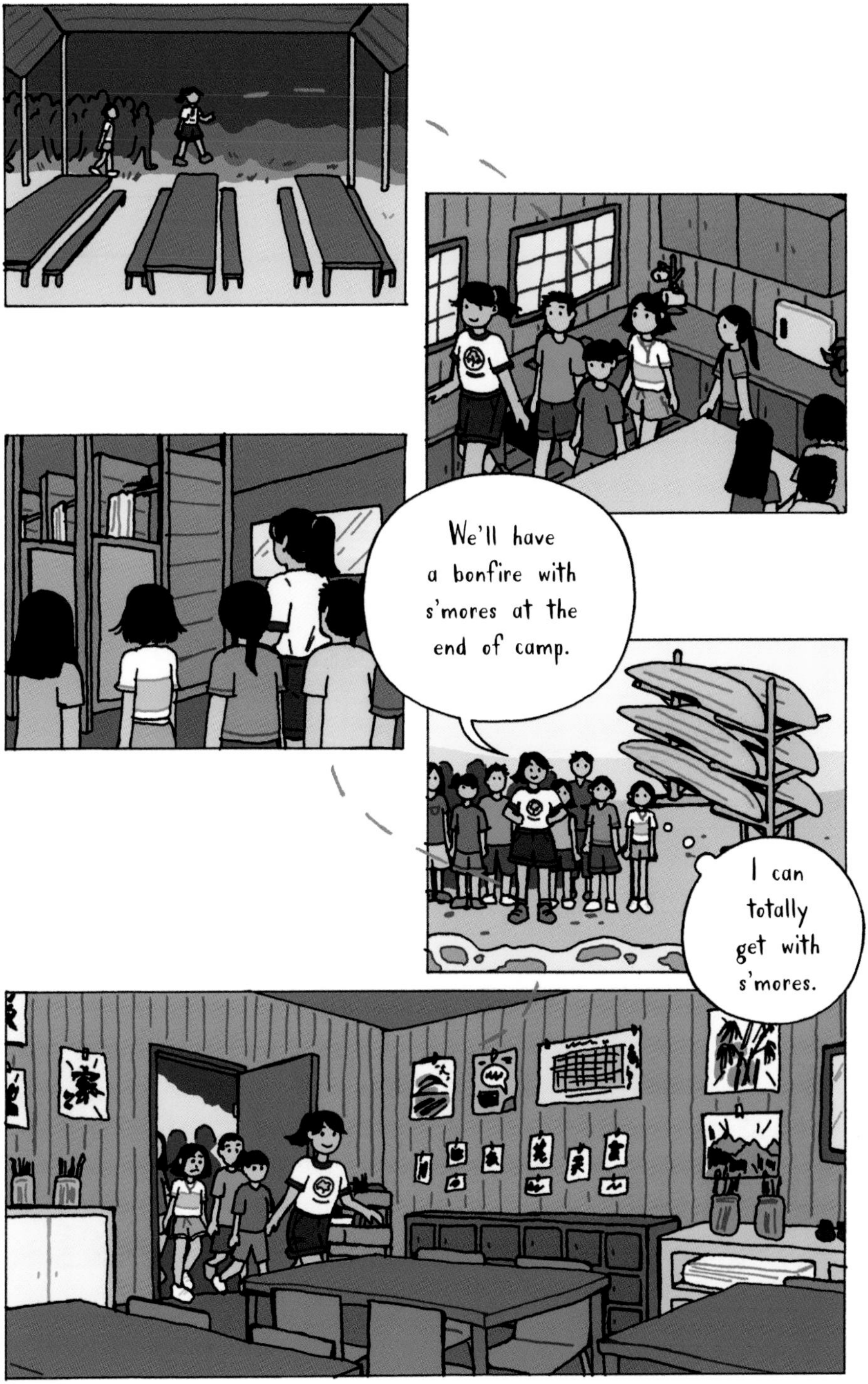
We'll have a bonfire with s'mores at the end of camp.
I can totally get with s'mores.

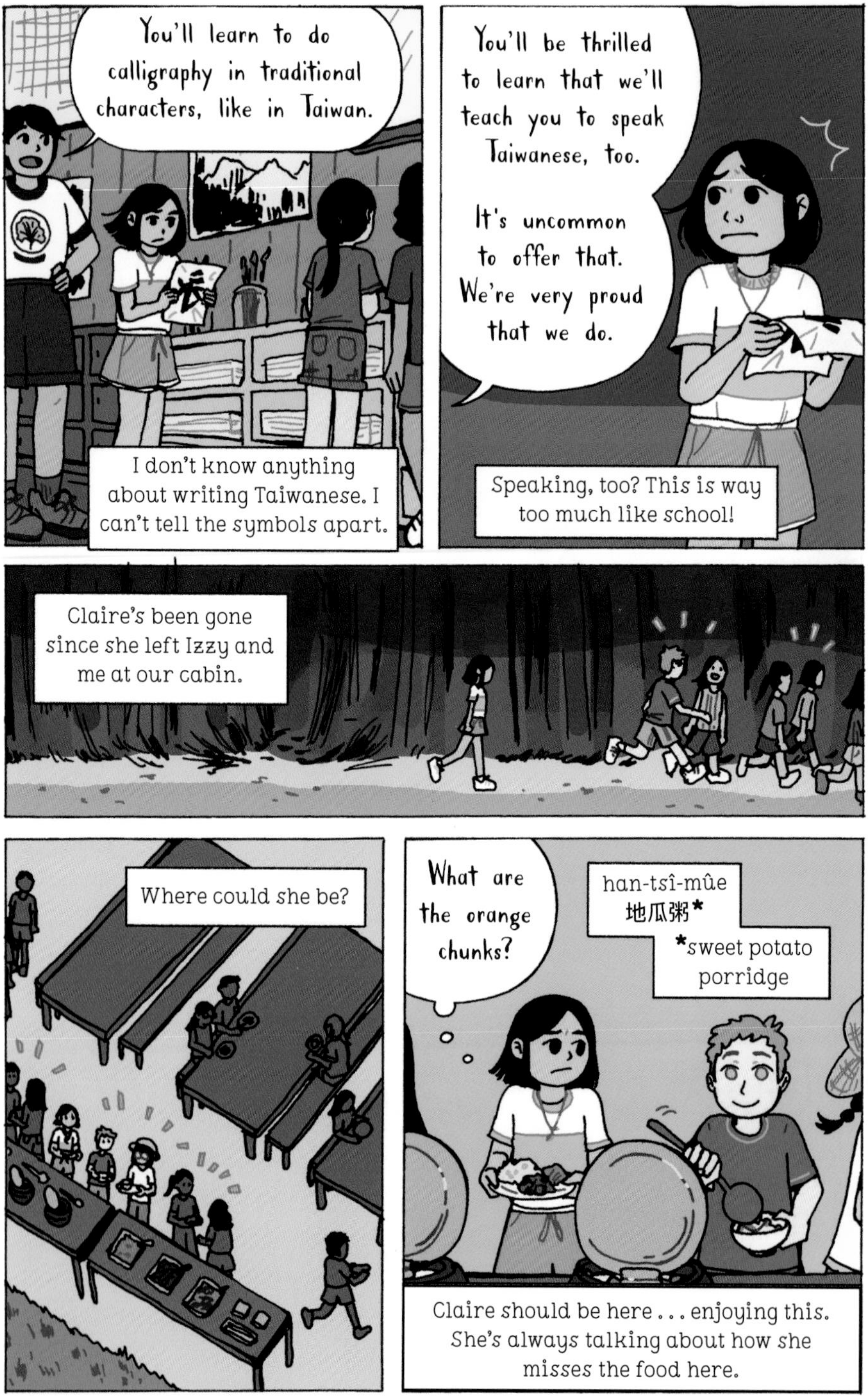

You'll learn to do calligraphy in traditional characters, like in Taiwan.
I don't know anything about writing Taiwanese. I can't tell the symbols apart.
You'll be thrilled to learn that we'll teach you to speak Taiwanese, too.
It's uncommon to offer that. We're very proud that we do.
Speaking, too? This is way too much like school!
Claire's been gone since she left Izzy and me at our cabin.
Where could she be?
What are the orange chunks?
han-tsî-mûe
地瓜粥*
*sweet potato porridge
Claire should be here . . . enjoying this. She's always talking about how she misses the food here.

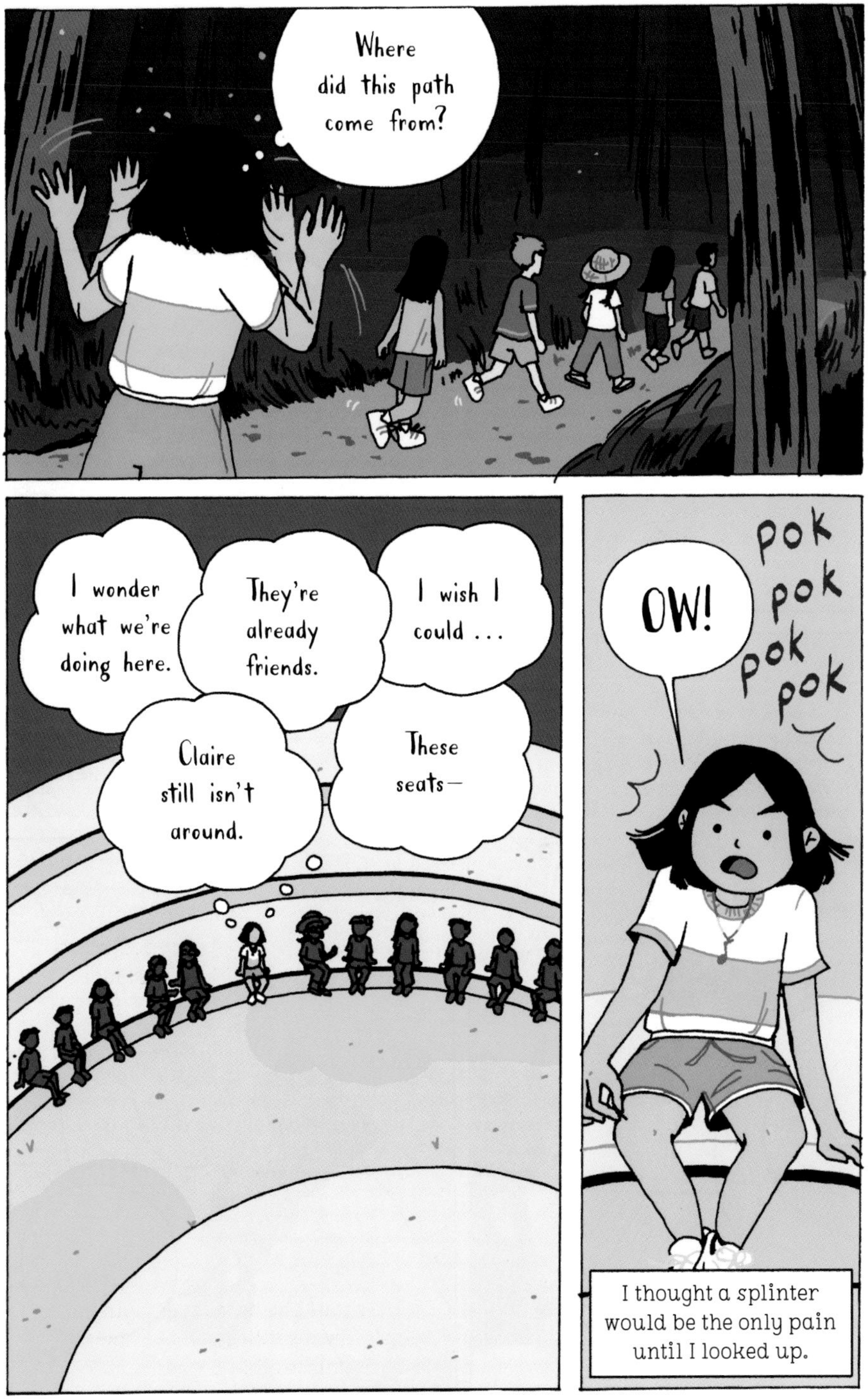
Where did this path come from?
I wonder what we're doing here.
They're already friends.
I wish I could . . .
Claire still isn't around.
These seats—
OW!
pok pok pok pok
I thought a splinter would be the only pain until I looked up.

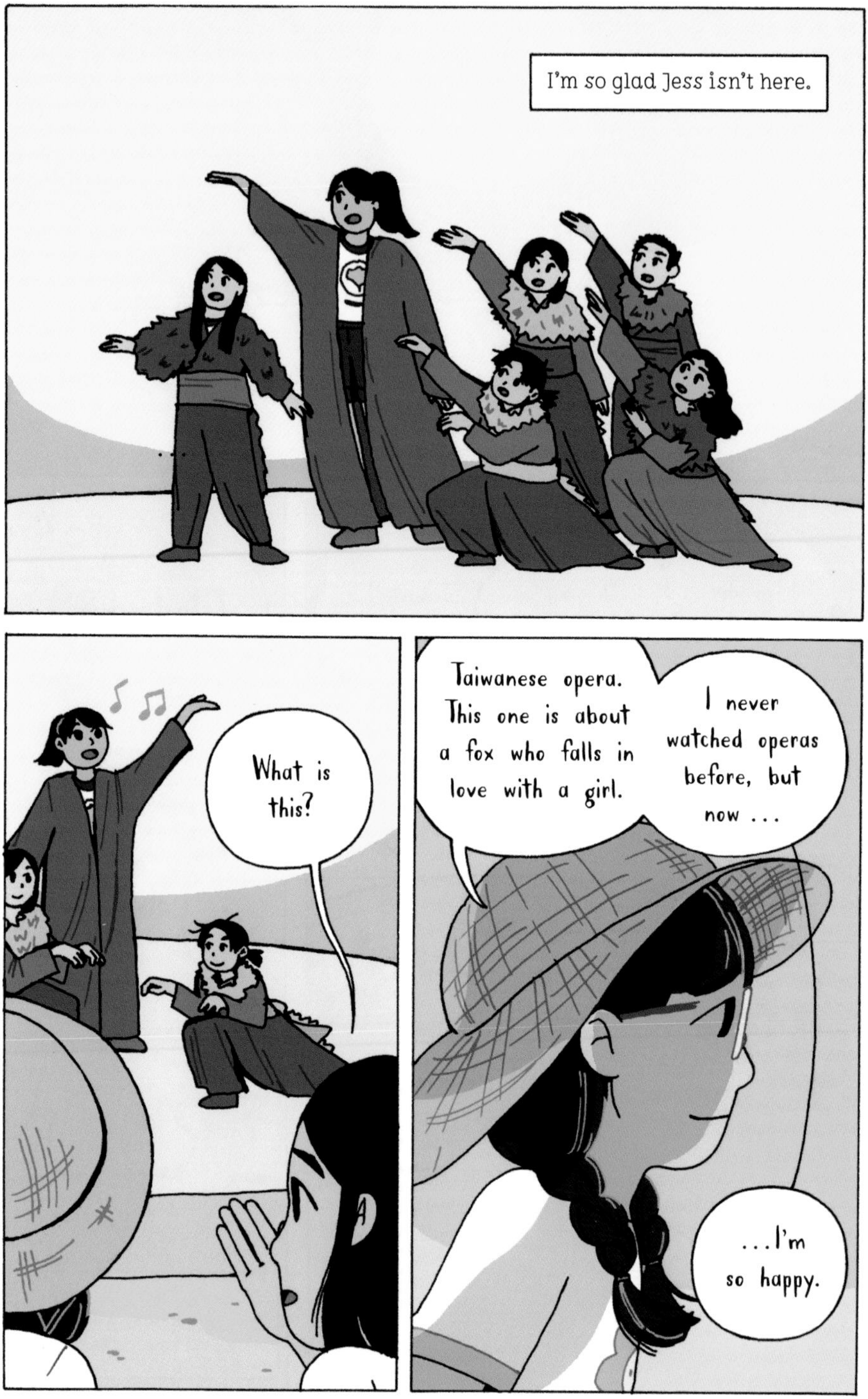
I'm so glad Jess isn't here.
What is this?
Taiwanese opera. This one is about a fox who falls in love with a girl.
I never watched operas before, but now . . .
. . . I'm so happy.

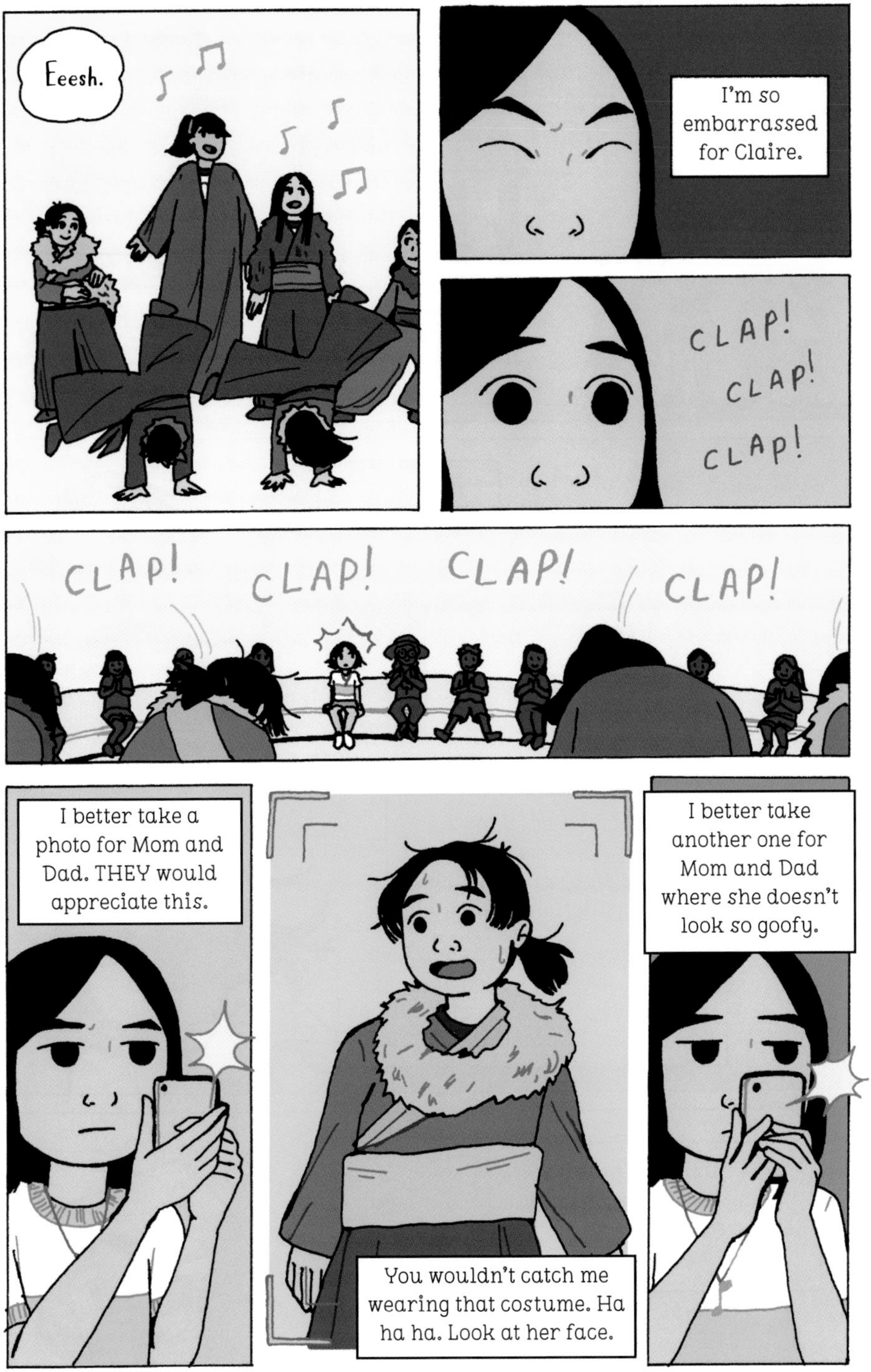

Eeesh.
I'm so embarrassed for Claire.
CLAP! CLAP! CLAP!
CLAP! CLAP! CLAP! CLAP!
I better take a photo for Mom and Dad. THEY would appreciate this.
You wouldn't catch me wearing that costume. Ha ha ha. Look at her face.
I better take another one for Mom and Dad where she doesn't look so goofy.

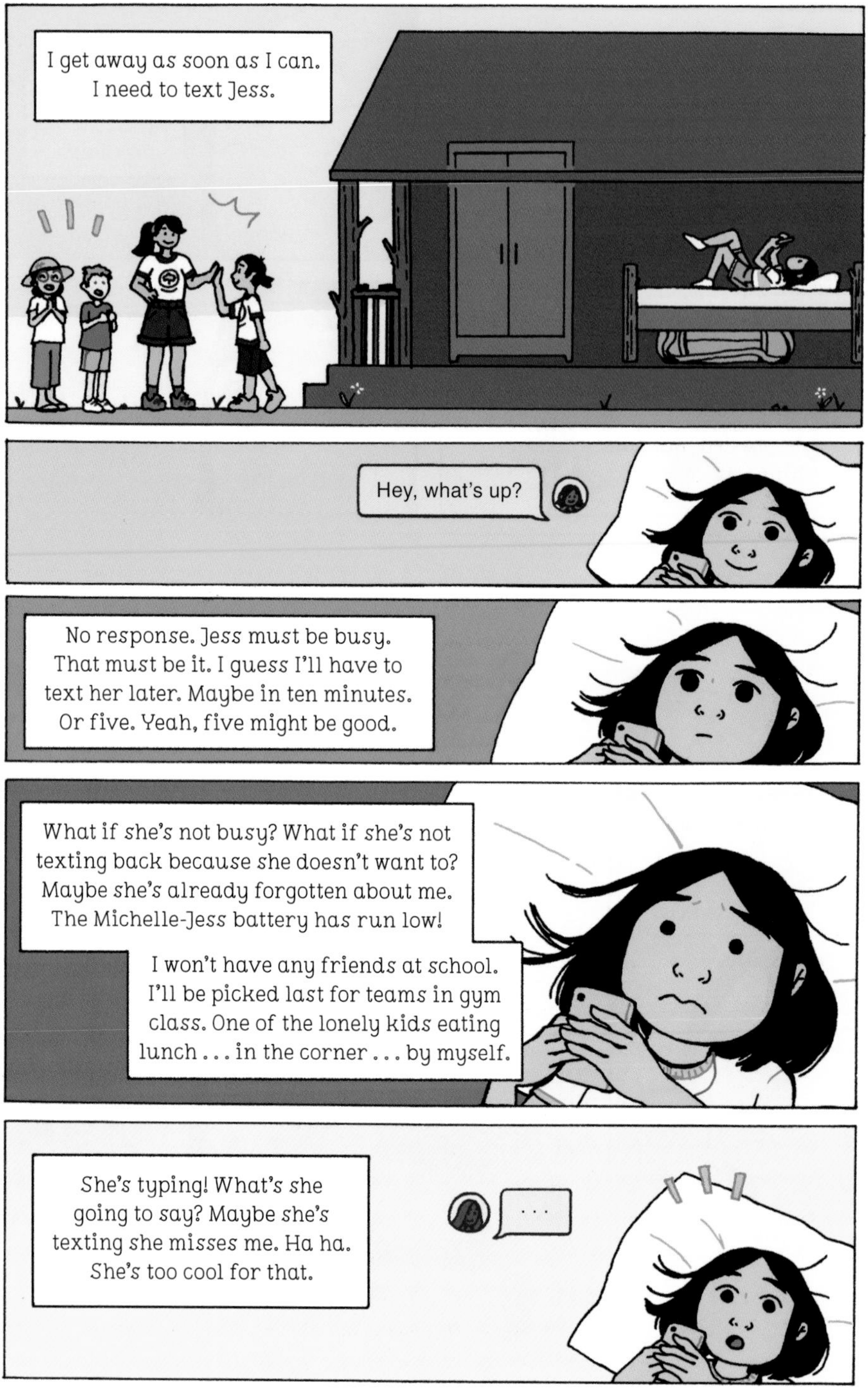

I get away as soon as I can. I need to text Jess.
Hey, what's up?
No response. Jess must be busy. That must be it. I guess I'll have to text her later. Maybe in ten minutes. Or five. Yeah, five might be good.
What if she's not busy? What if she's not texting back because she doesn't want to? Maybe she's already forgotten about me. The Michelle-Jess battery has run low!
I won't have any friends at school. I'll be picked last for teams in gym class. One of the lonely kids eating lunch . . . in the corner . . . by myself.
She's typing! What's she going to say? Maybe she's texting she misses me. Ha ha. She's too cool for that.
. . .

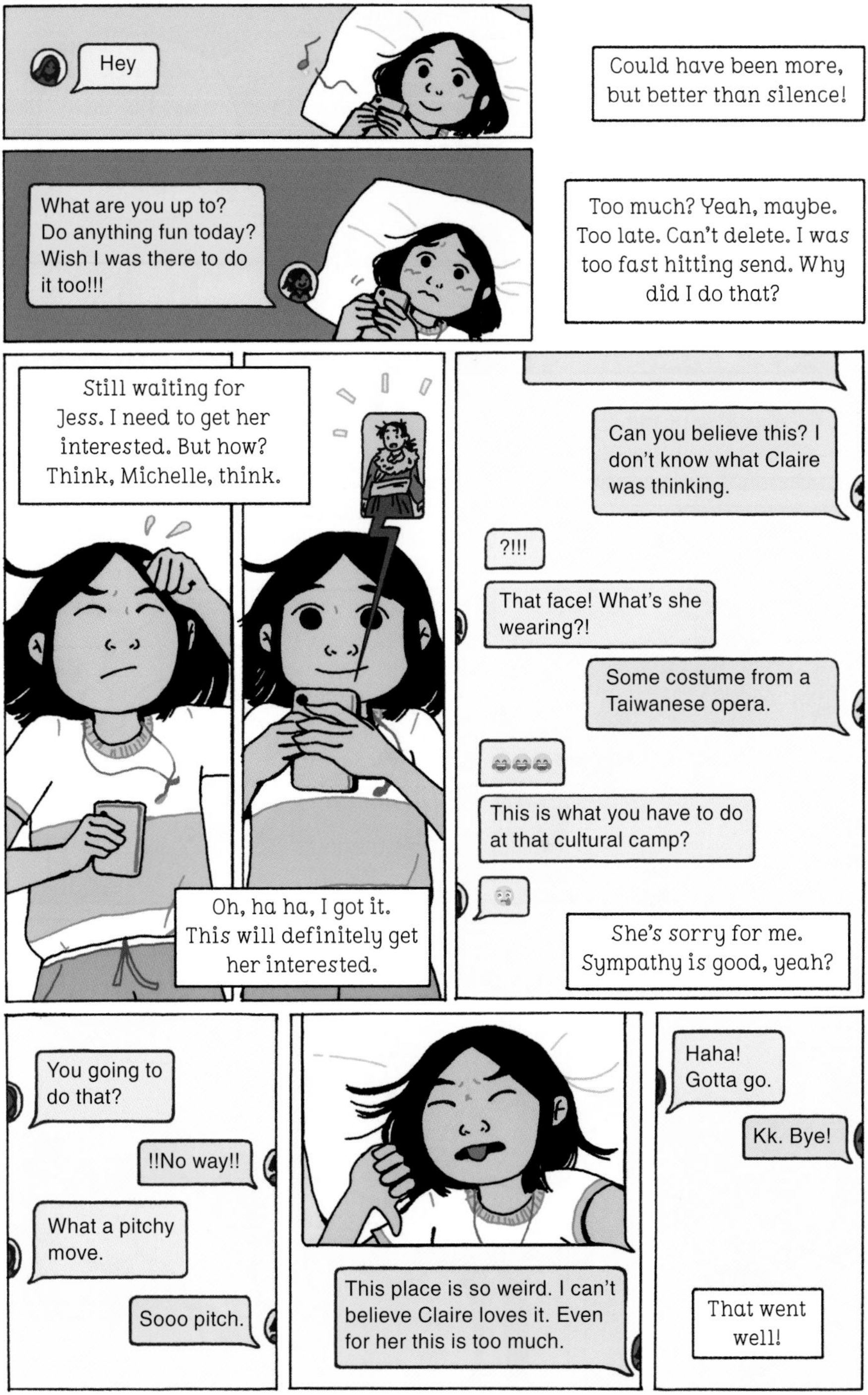
Hey
Could have been more, but better than silence!
What are you up to? Do anything fun today? Wish I was there to do it too!!!
Too much? Yeah, maybe. Too late. Can't delete. I was too fast hitting send. Why did I do that?
Still waiting for Jess. I need to get her interested. But how? Think, Michelle, think.
Oh, ha ha, I got it. This will definitely get her interested.
Can you believe this? I don't know what Claire was thinking.
?!!!
That face! What's she wearing?!
Some costume from a Taiwanese opera.
This is what you have to do at that cultural camp?
She's sorry for me. Sympathy is good, yeah?
You going to do that?
!!No way!!
What a pitchy move.
Sooo pitch.
This place is so weird. I can't believe Claire loves it. Even for her this is too much.
Haha! Gotta go.
Kk. Bye!
That went well!

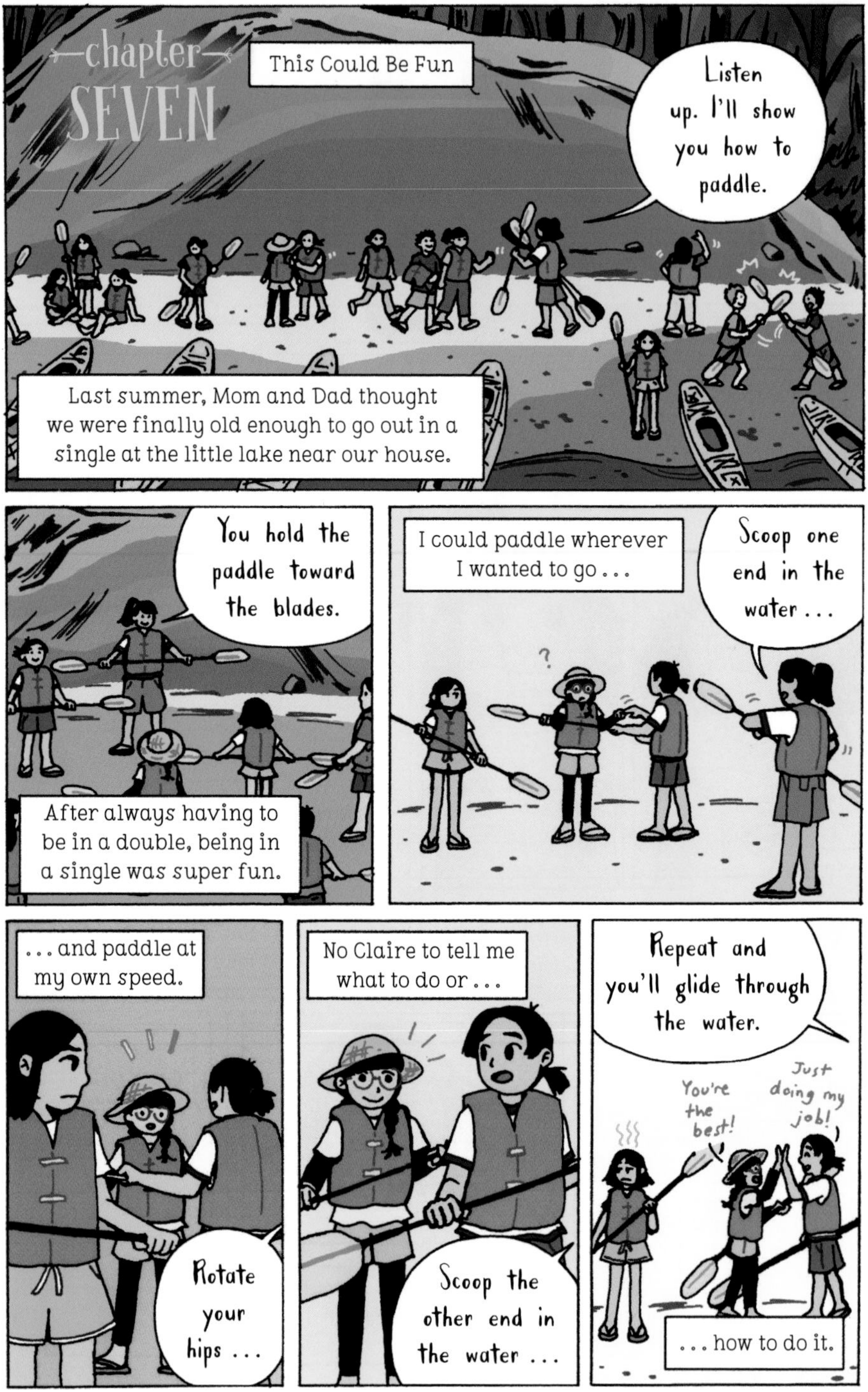
chapter SEVEN
This Could Be Fun
Listen up. I'll show you how to paddle.
Last summer, Mom and Dad thought we were finally old enough to go out in a single at the little lake near our house.
You hold the paddle toward the blades.
After always having to be in a double, being in a single was super fun.
I could paddle wherever I wanted to go . . .
Scoop one end in the water . . .
. . . and paddle at my own speed.
Rotate your hips . . .
No Claire to tell me what to do or . . .
Scoop the other end in the water . . .
Repeat and you'll glide through the water.
You're the best!
Just doing my job!
. . . how to do it.

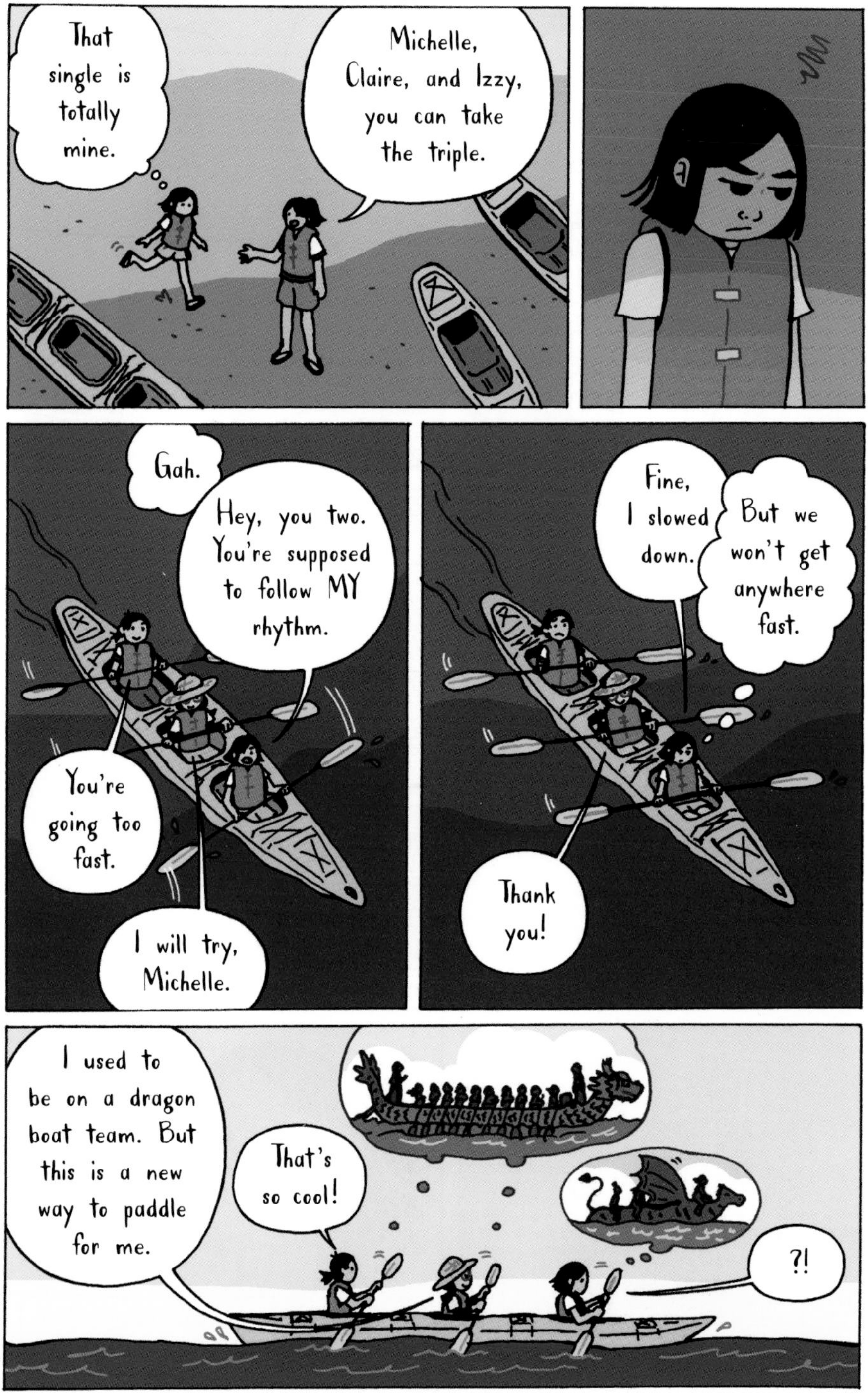
That single is totally mine.
Michelle, Claire, and Izzy, you can take the triple.
Gah.
Hey, you two. You're supposed to follow MY rhythm.
You're going too fast.
I will try, Michelle.
Fine, I slowed down.
But we won't get anywhere fast.
Thank you!
I used to be on a dragon boat team. But this is a new way to paddle for me.
That's so cool!
?!

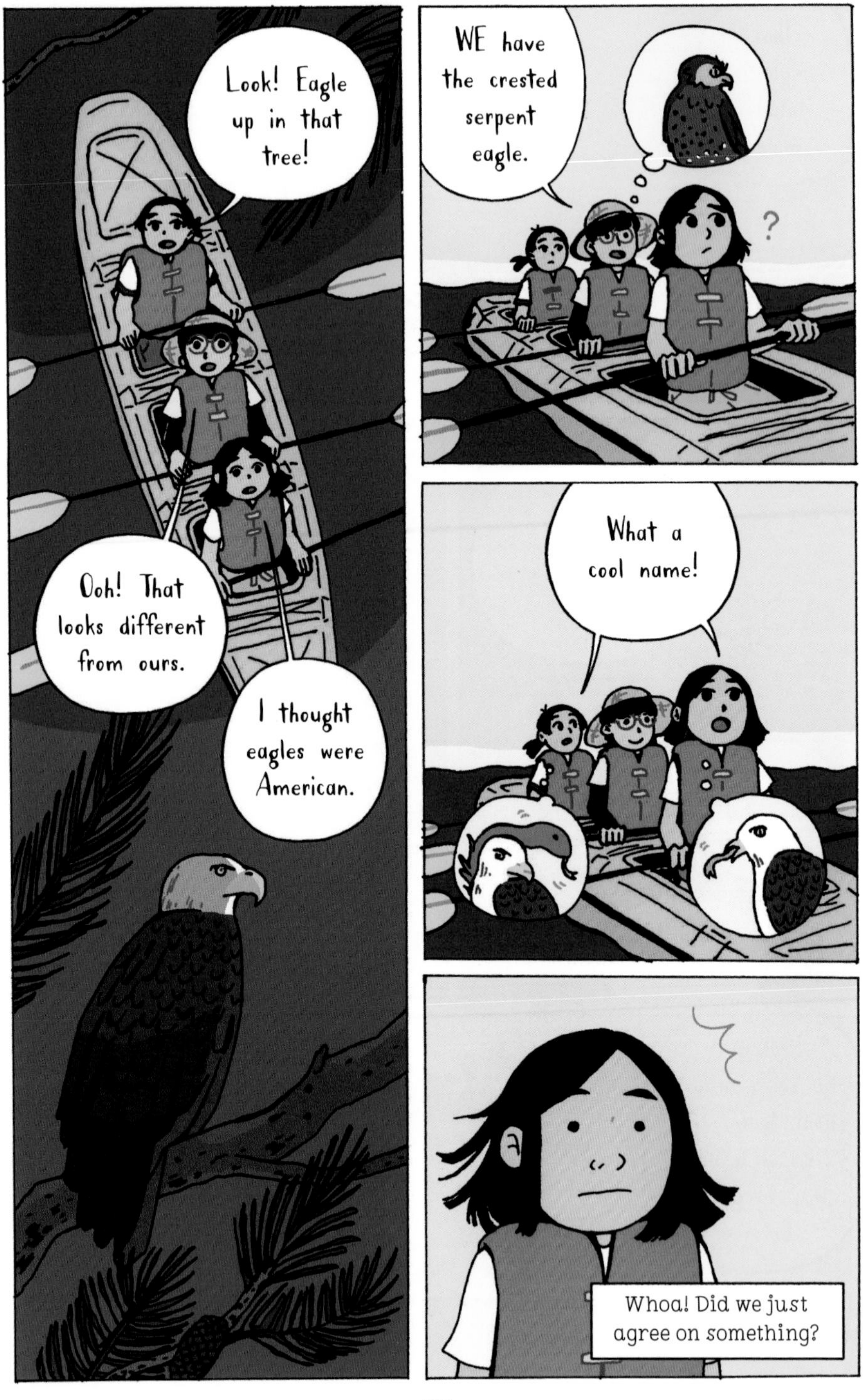
Look! Eagle up in that tree!
Ooh! That looks different from ours.
I thought eagles were American.
WE have the crested serpent eagle.
What a cool name!
Whoa! Did we just agree on something?

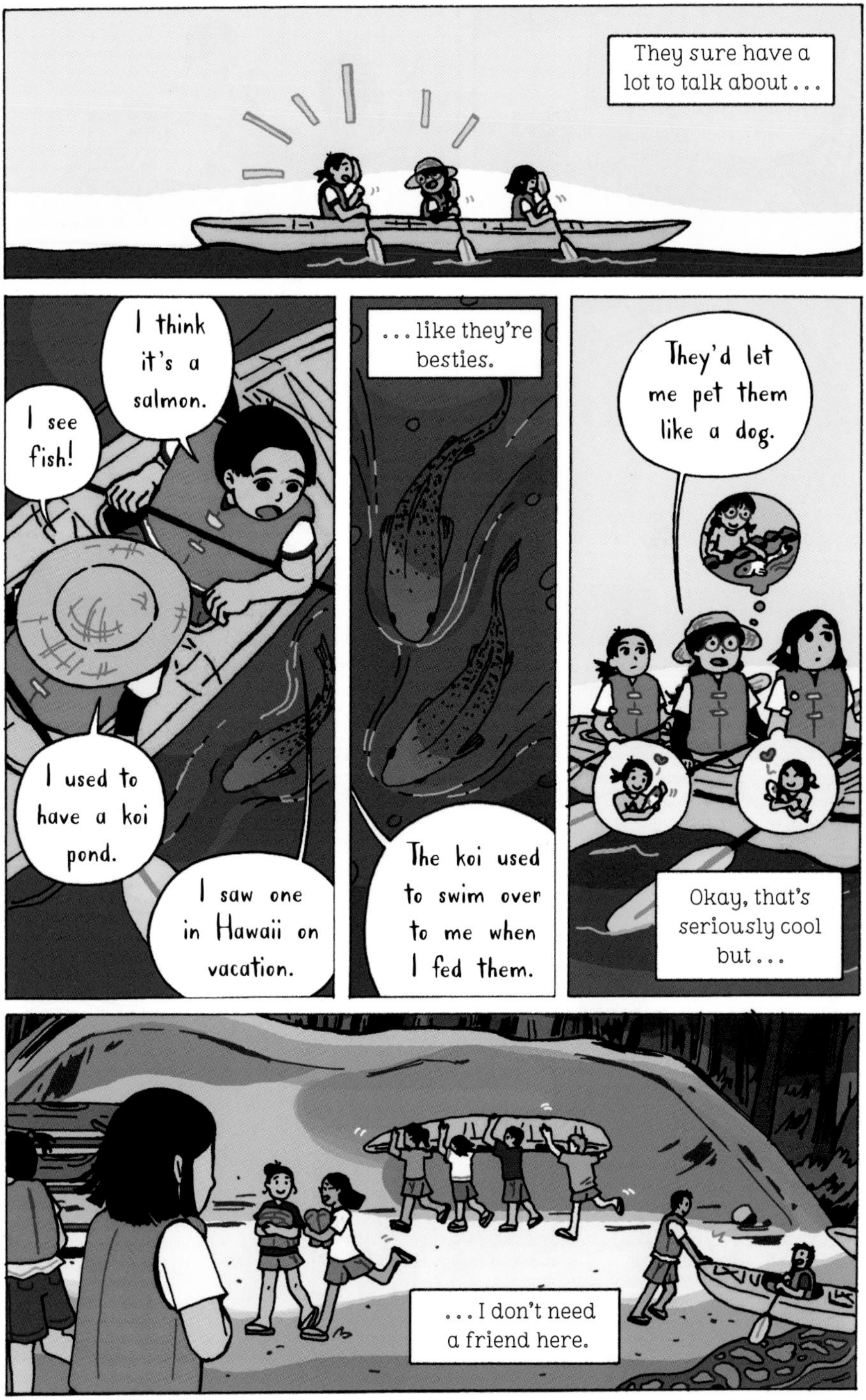
They sure have a lot to talk about . . .
I see fish!
I think it's a salmon.
I used to have a koi pond.
I saw one in Hawaii on vacation.
. . . like they're besties.
The koi used to swim over to me when I fed them.
They'd let me pet them like a dog.
Okay, that's seriously cool but . . .
. . . I don't need a friend here.

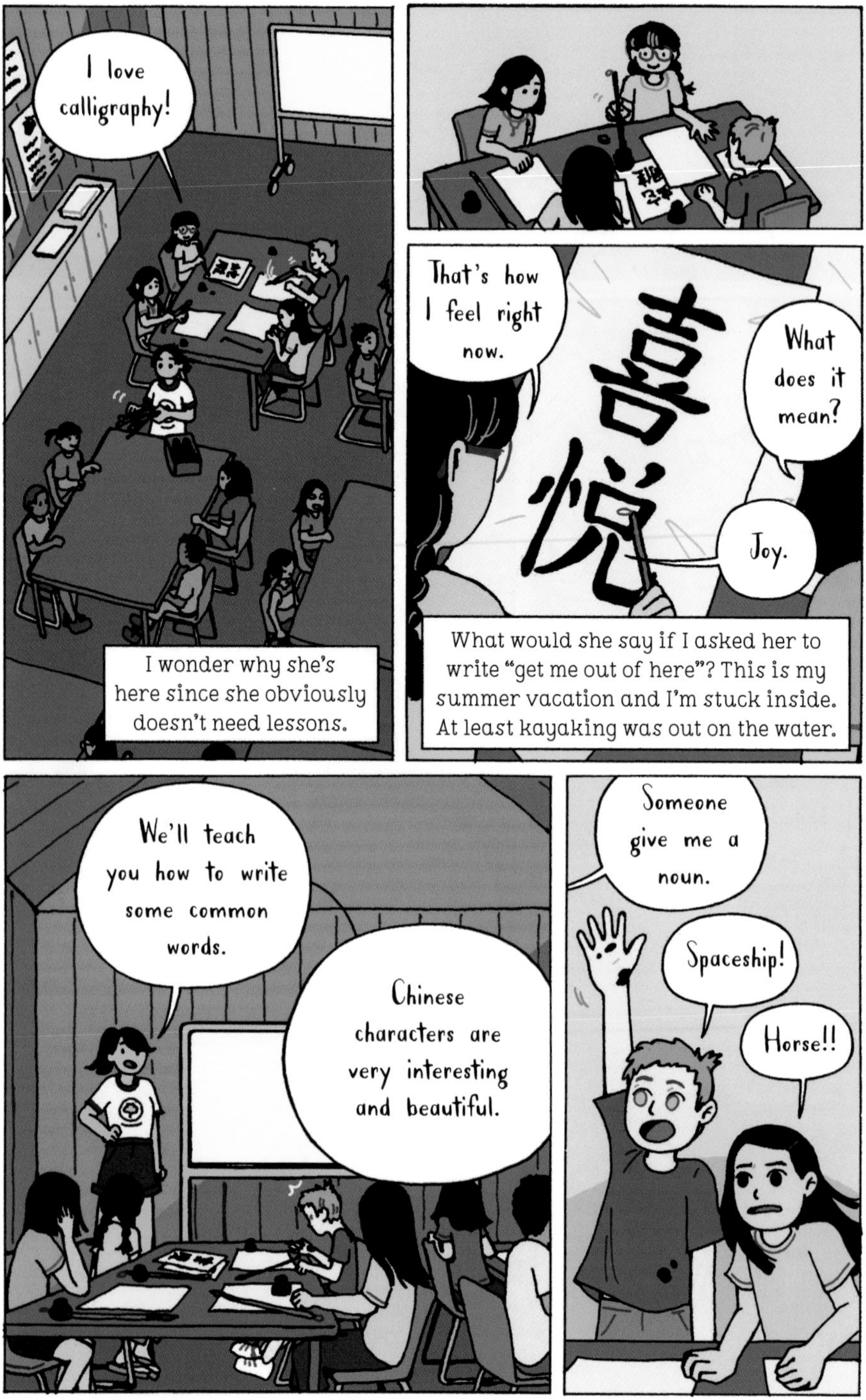
I love calligraphy!
I wonder why she's here since she obviously doesn't need lessons.
That's how I feel right now.
喜悦
What does it mean?
Joy.
What would she say if I asked her to write "get me out of here"? This is my summer vacation and I'm stuck inside. At least kayaking was out on the water.
We'll teach you how to write some common words.
Chinese characters are very interesting and beautiful.
Someone give me a noun.
Spaceship!
Horse!!

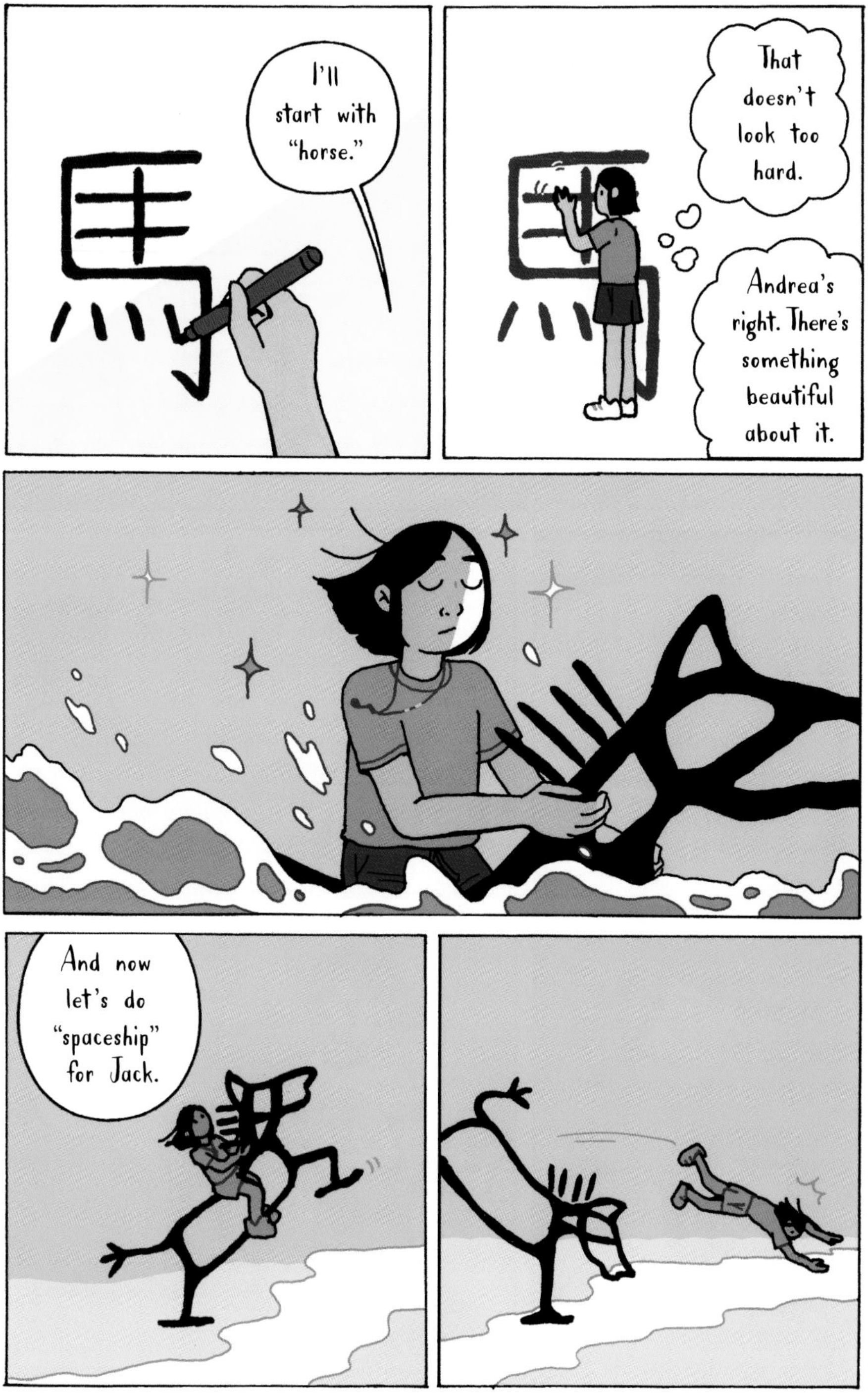
馬
I'll start with "horse."
馬
That doesn't look too hard.
Andrea's right. There's something beautiful about it.
And now let's do "spaceship" for Jack.

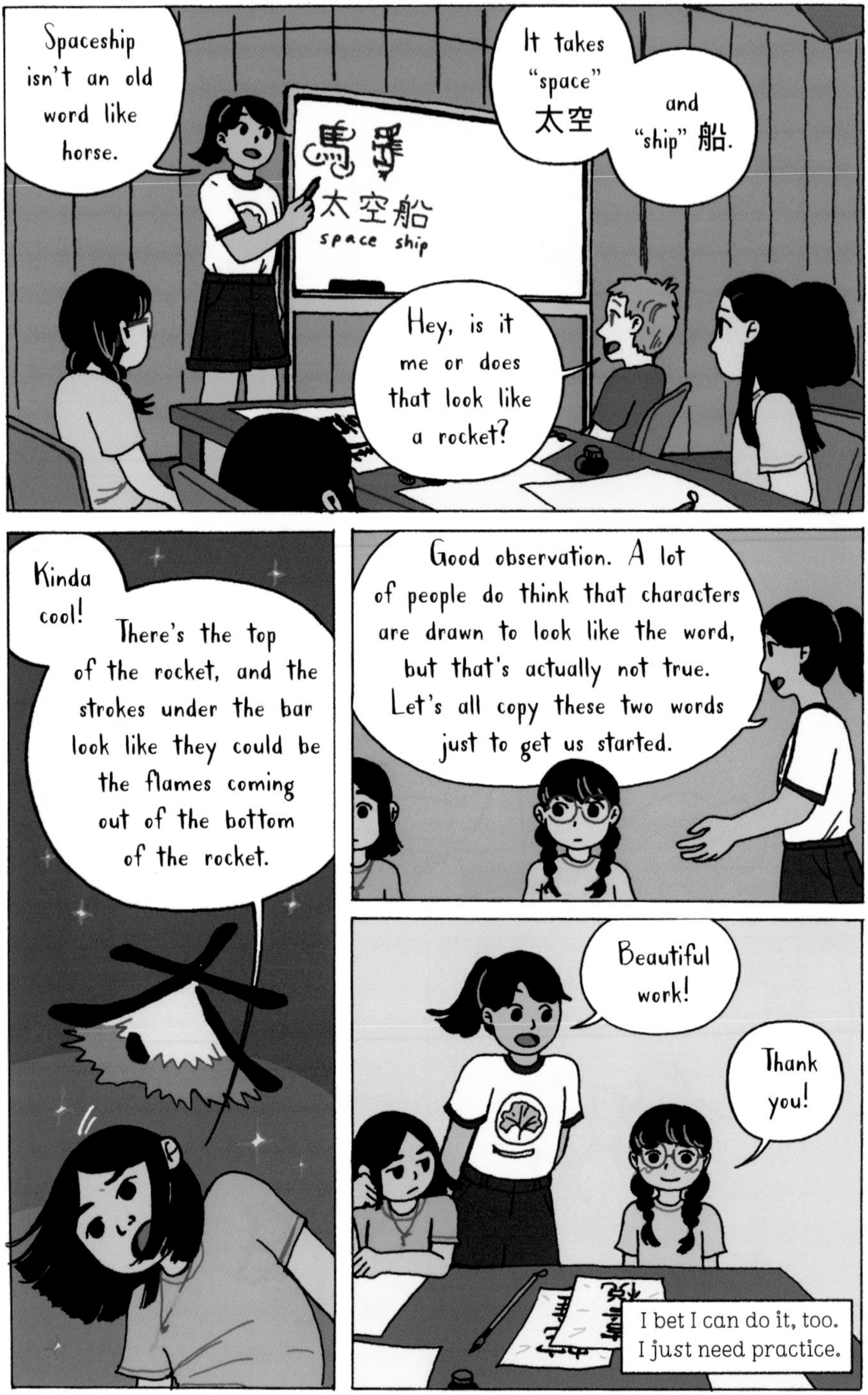
Spaceship isn't an old word like horse.
It takes "space" 太空
and "ship" 船.
馬
太空船
space ship
Hey, is it me or does that look like a rocket?
Kinda cool!
There's the top of the rocket, and the strokes under the bar look like they could be the flames coming out of the bottom of the rocket.
Good observation. A lot of people do think that characters are drawn to look like the word, but that's actually not true. Let's all copy these two words just to get us started.
Beautiful work!
Thank you!
I bet I can do it, too. I just need practice.

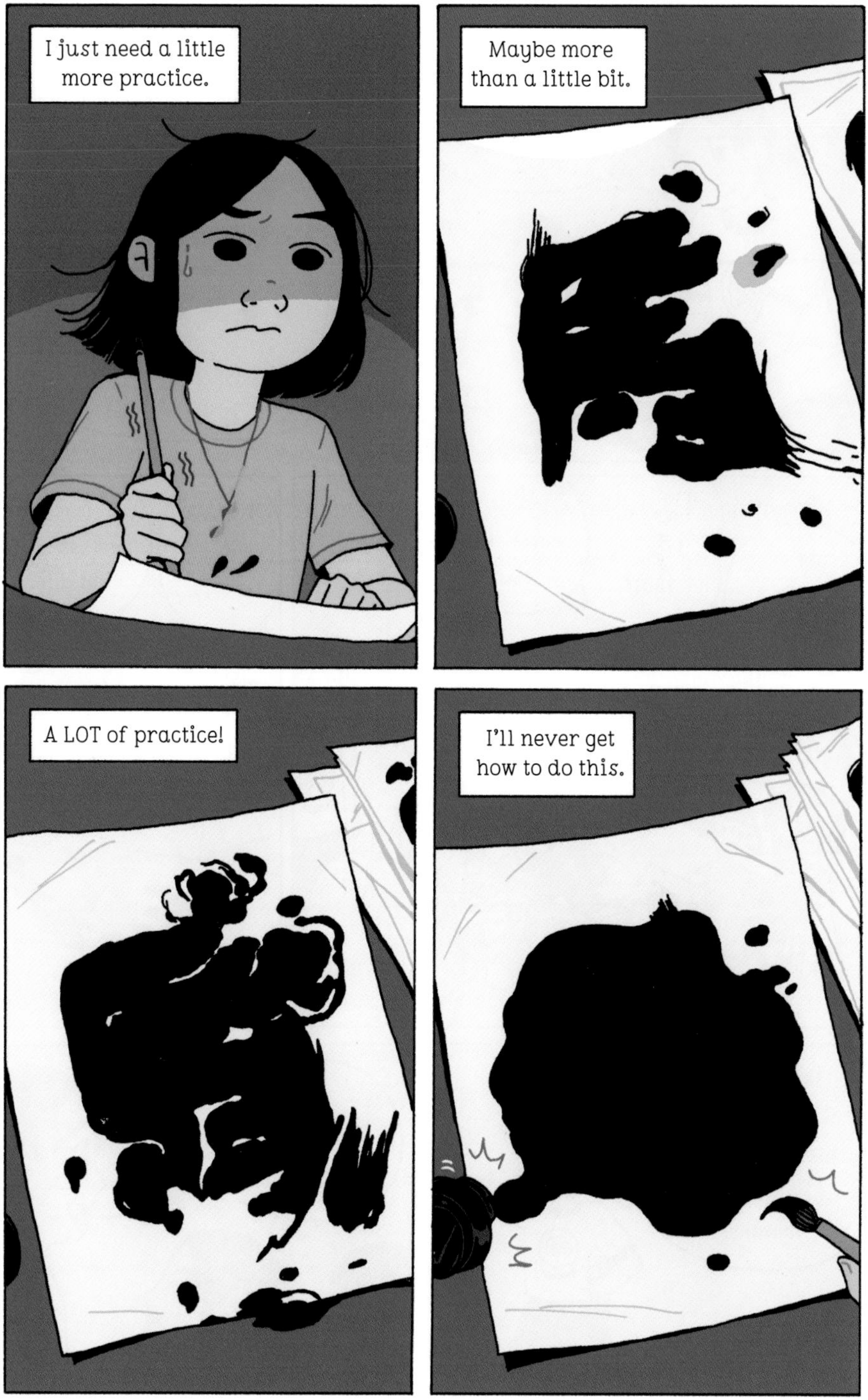
I just need a little more practice.
Maybe more than a little bit.
A LOT of practice!
I'll never get how to do this.

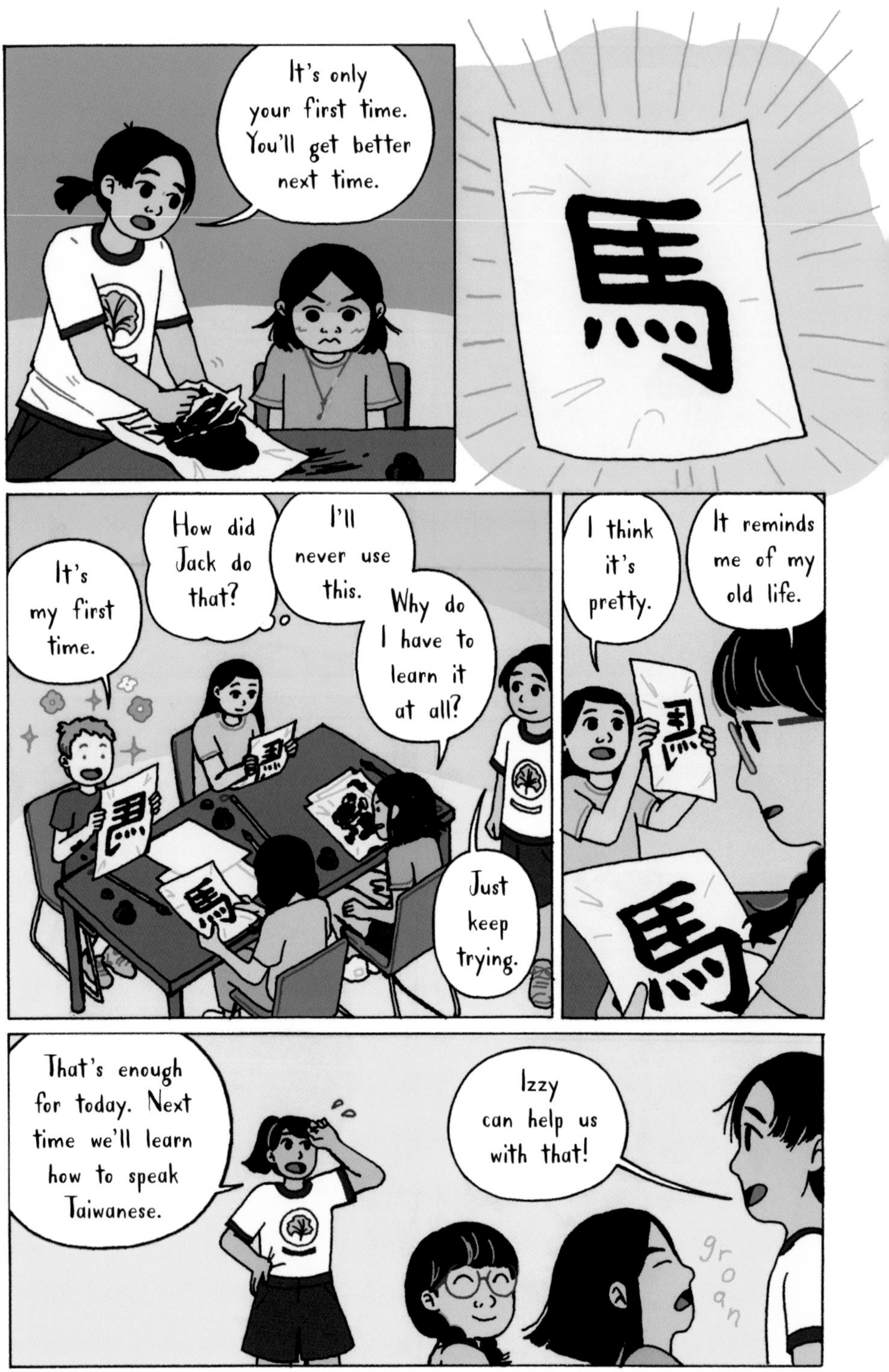
It's only your first time. You'll get better next time.
馬
It's my first time.
How did Jack do that?
I'll never use this.
Why do I have to learn it at all?
Just keep trying.
I think it's pretty.
It reminds me of my old life.
馬
That's enough for today. Next time we'll learn how to speak Taiwanese.
Izzy can help us with that!
groan

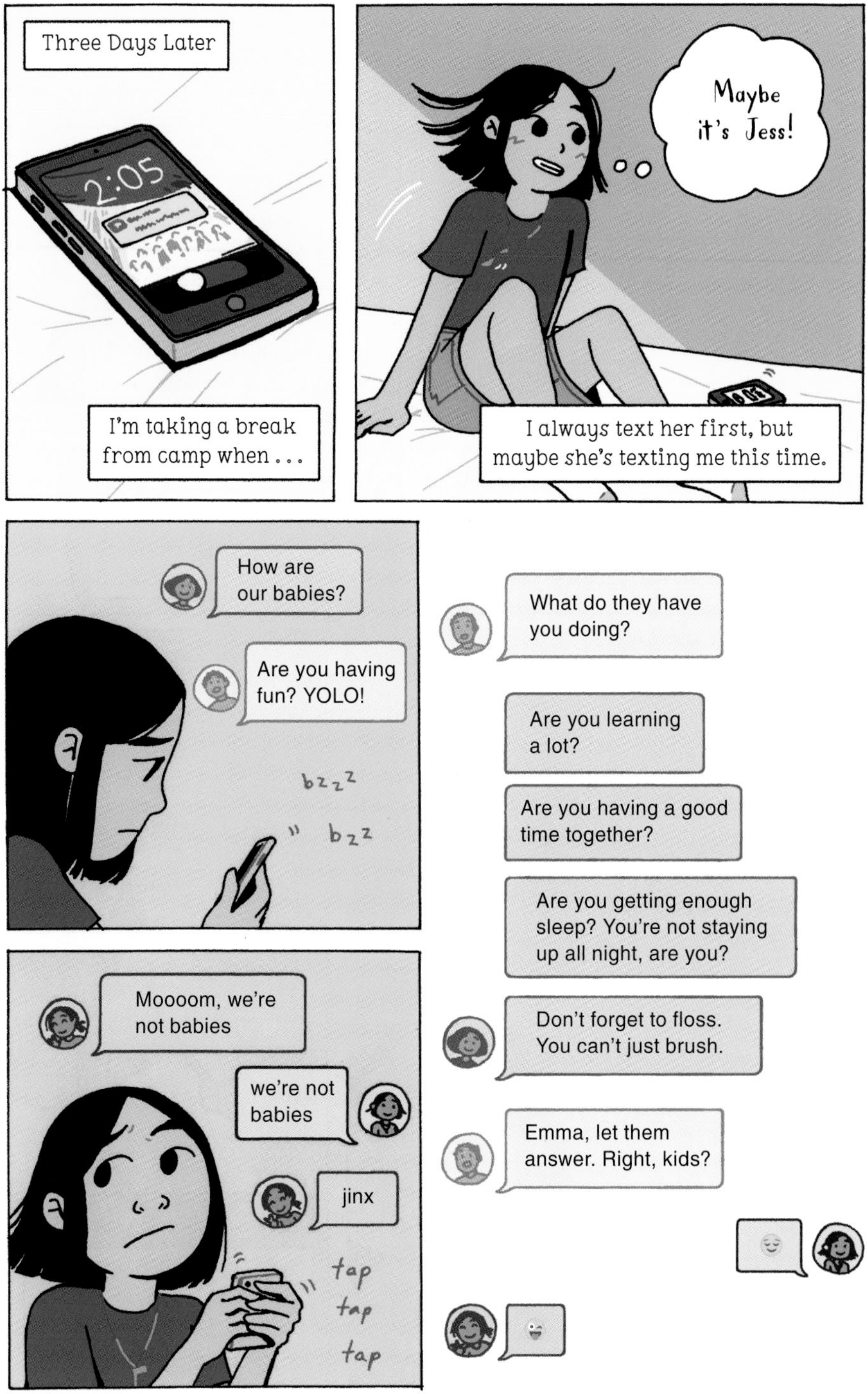
Three Days Later
2:05
I'm taking a break from camp when . . .
Maybe it's Jess!
I always text her first, but maybe she's texting me this time.
How are our babies?
Are you having fun? YOLO!
bzzz
bzz
What do they have you doing?
Are you learning a lot?
Are you having a good time together?
Are you getting enough sleep? You're not staying up all night, are you?
Don't forget to floss. You can't just brush.
Emma, let them answer. Right, kids?
Moooom, we're not babies
we're not babies
jinx
tap
tap
tap

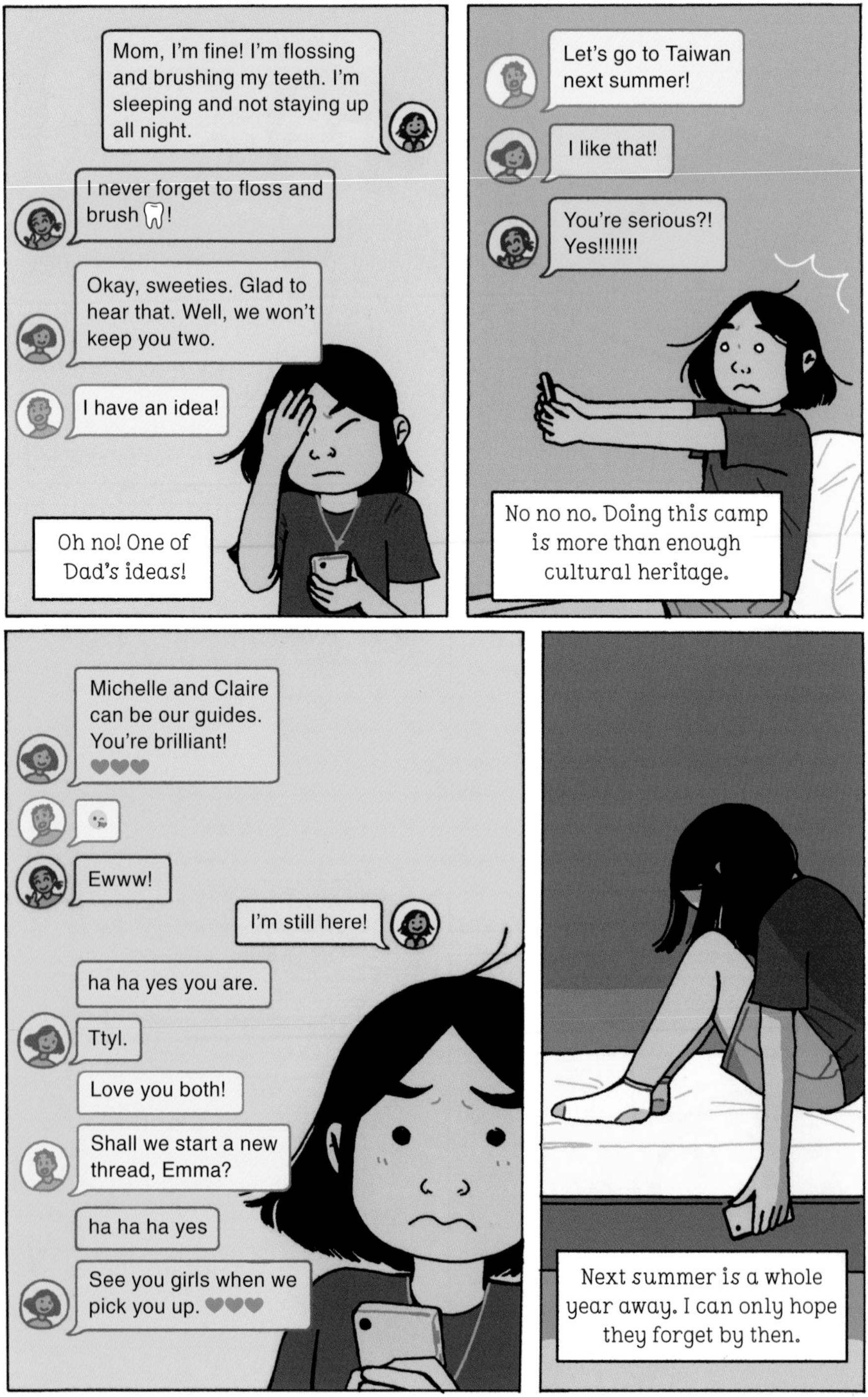

Mom, I'm fine! I'm flossing and brushing my teeth. I'm sleeping and not staying up all night.
I never forget to floss and brush 🦷!
Okay, sweeties. Glad to hear that. Well, we won't keep you two.
I have an idea!
Oh no! One of Dad's ideas!
Let's go to Taiwan next summer!
I like that!
You're serious?! Yes!!!!!!!
No no no. Doing this camp is more than enough cultural heritage.
Michelle and Claire can be our guides. You're brilliant! ❤❤❤
Ewww!
I'm still here!
ha ha yes you are.
Ttyl.
Love you both!
Shall we start a new thread, Emma?
ha ha ha yes
See you girls when we pick you up. ❤❤❤
Next summer is a whole year away. I can only hope they forget by then.

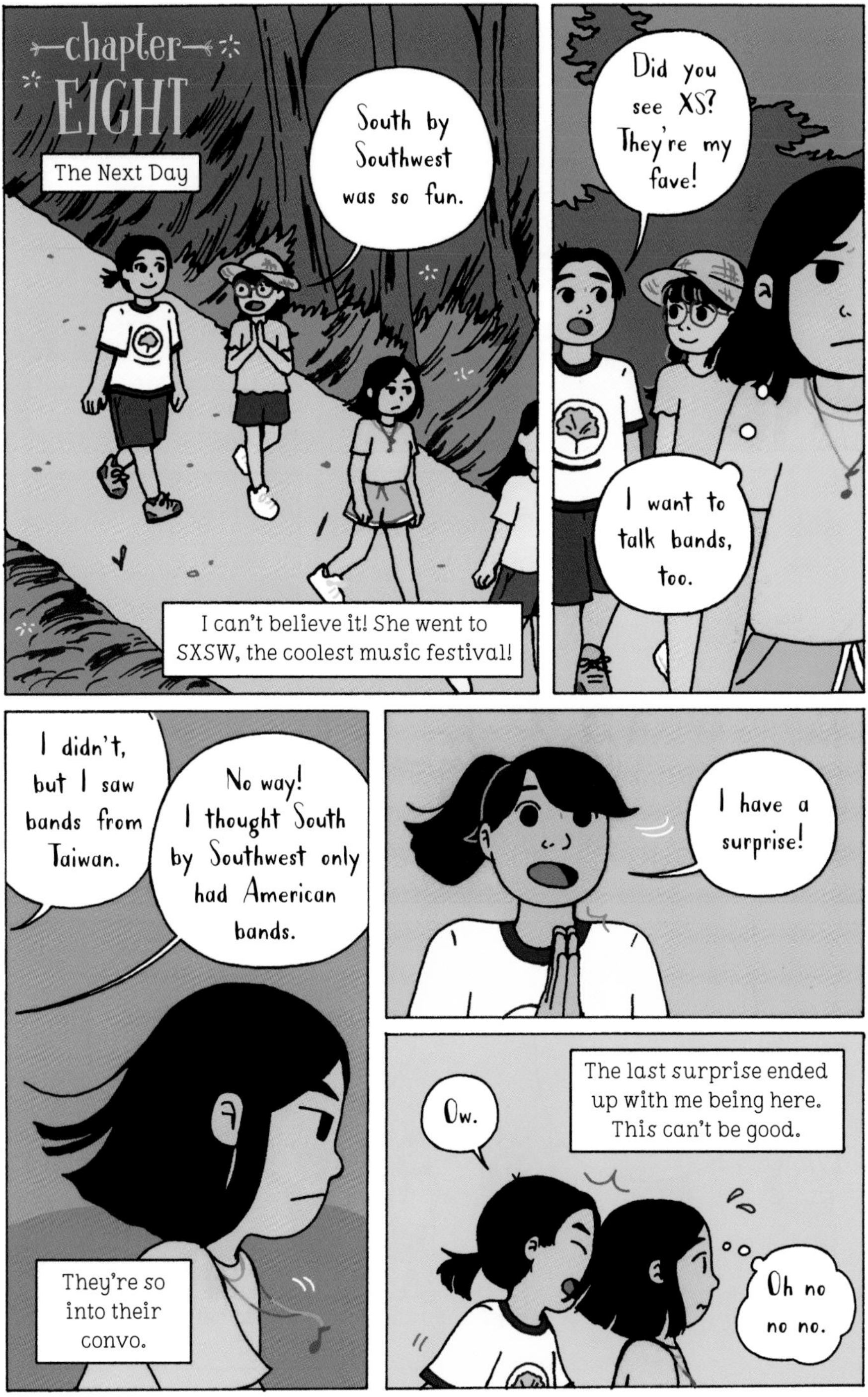
chapter EIGHT
The Next Day
South by Southwest was so fun.
I can't believe it! She went to SXSW, the coolest music festival!
Did you see XS? They're my fave!
I want to talk bands, too.
I didn't, but I saw bands from Taiwan.
No way! I thought South by Southwest only had American bands.
They're so into their convo.
I have a surprise!
Ow.
The last surprise ended up with me being here. This can't be good.
Oh no no no.

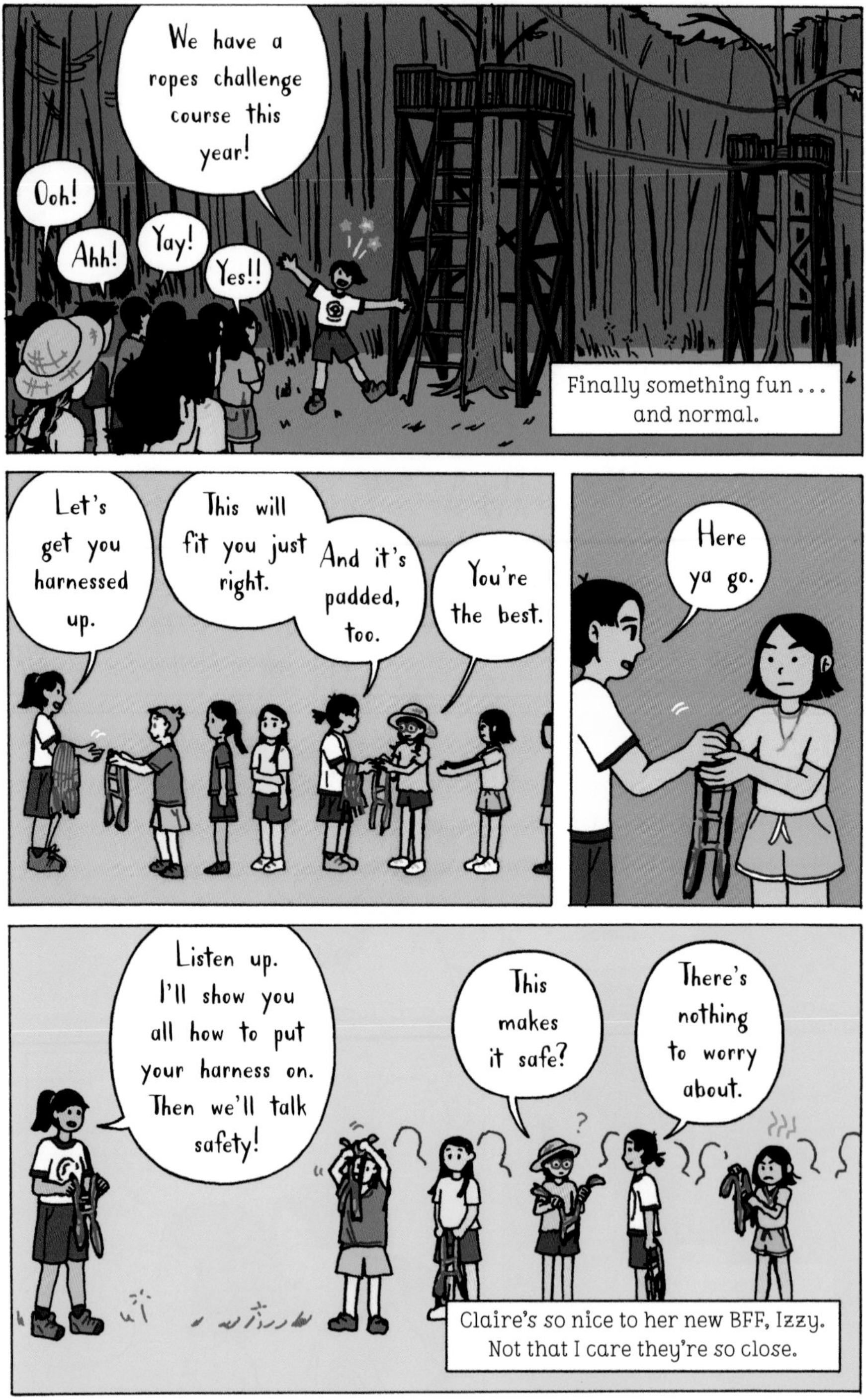
We have a ropes challenge course this year!
Ooh!
Ahh!
Yay!
Yes!!
Finally something fun . . . and normal.
Let's get you harnessed up.
This will fit you just right.
And it's padded, too.
You're the best.
Here ya go.
Listen up. I'll show you all how to put your harness on. Then we'll talk safety!
This makes it safe?
There's nothing to worry about.
Claire's so nice to her new BFF, Izzy. Not that I care they're so close.

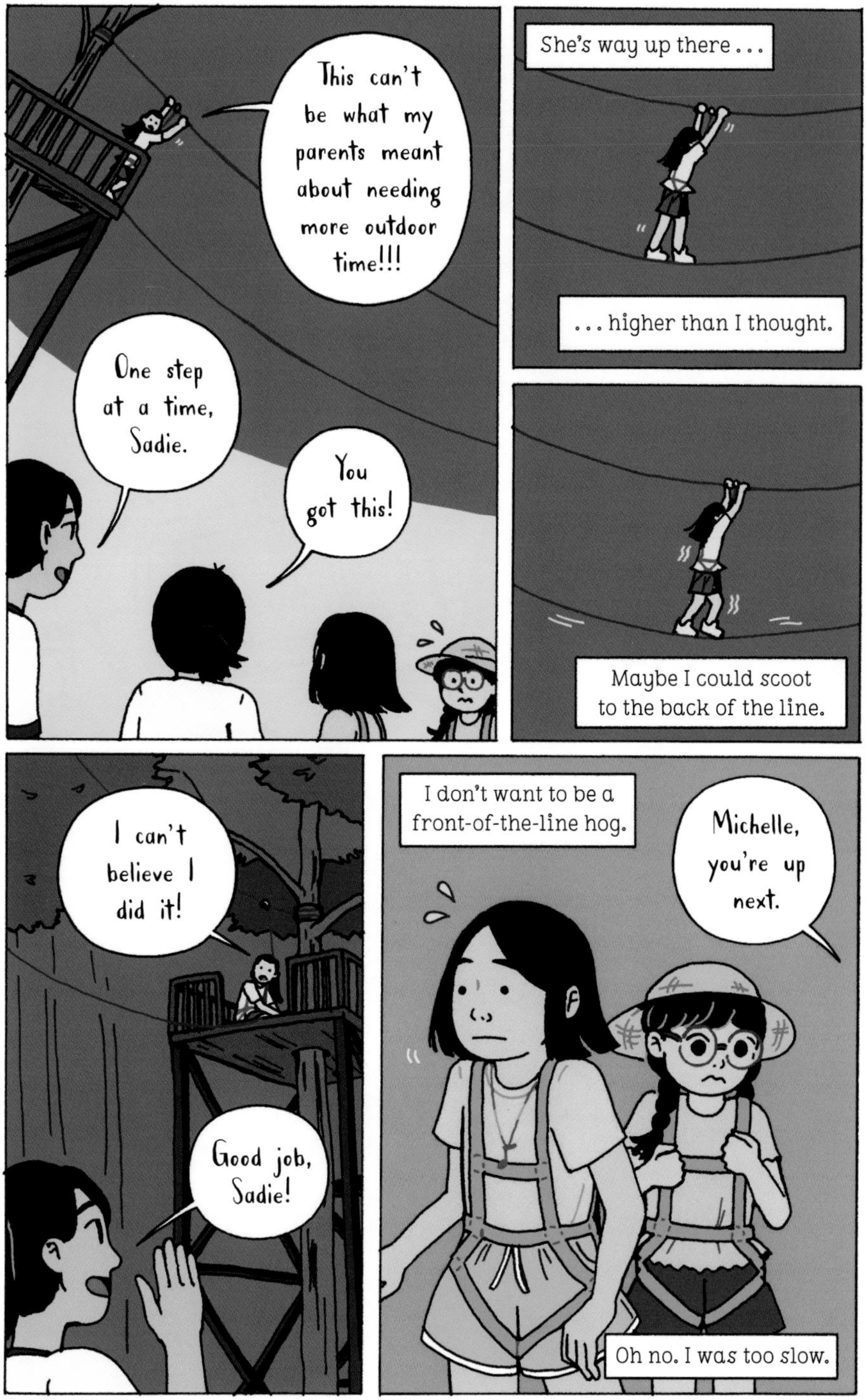

This can't be what my parents meant about needing more outdoor time!!!
One step at a time, Sadie.
You got this!
She's way up there . . .
. . . higher than I thought.
Maybe I could scoot to the back of the line.
I can't believe I did it!
Good job, Sadie!
I don't want to be a front-of-the-line hog.
Michelle, you're up next.
Oh no. I was too slow.

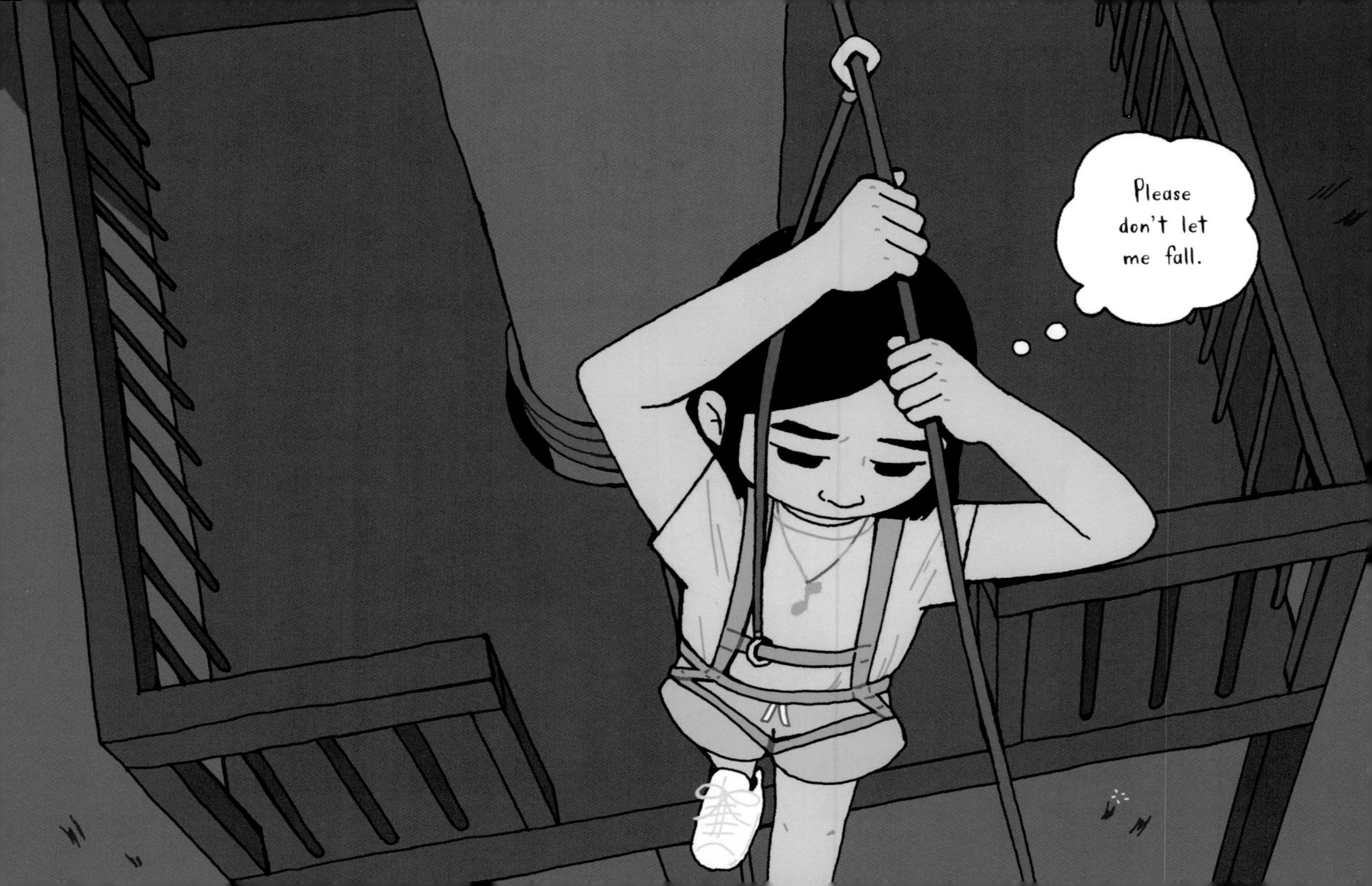
Please don't let me fall.

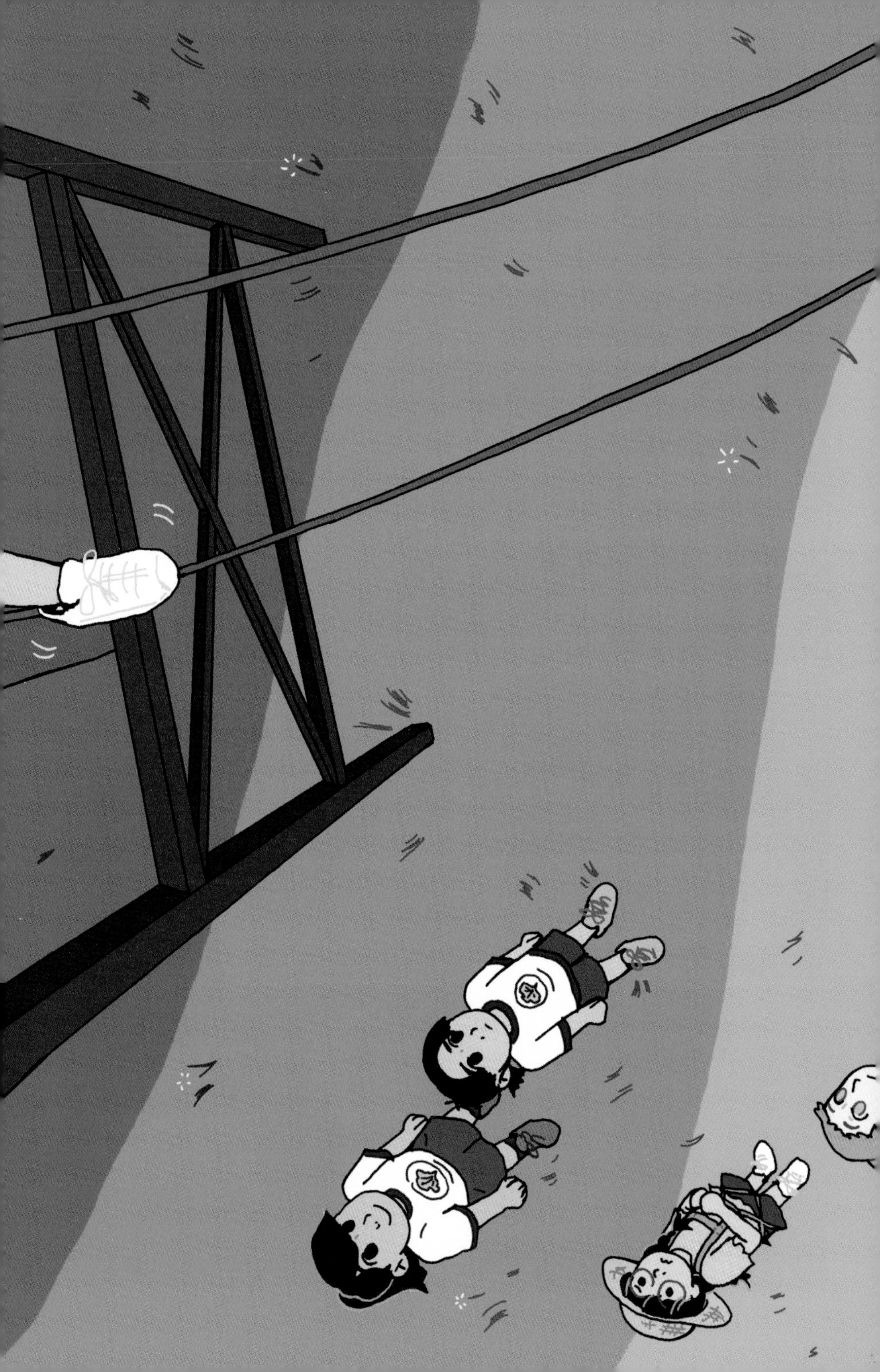

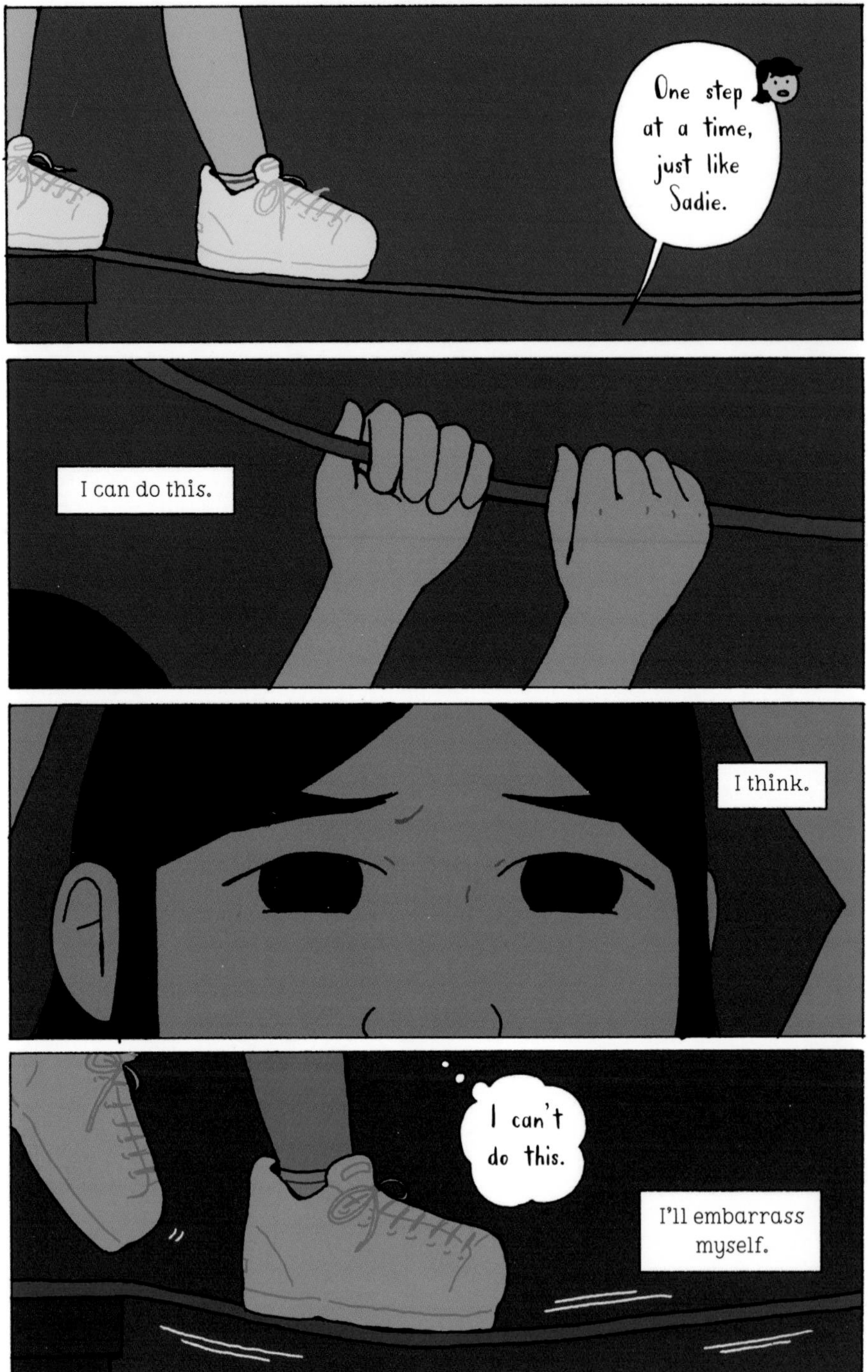
One step at a time, just like Sadie.
I can do this.
I think.
I can't do this.
I'll embarrass myself.

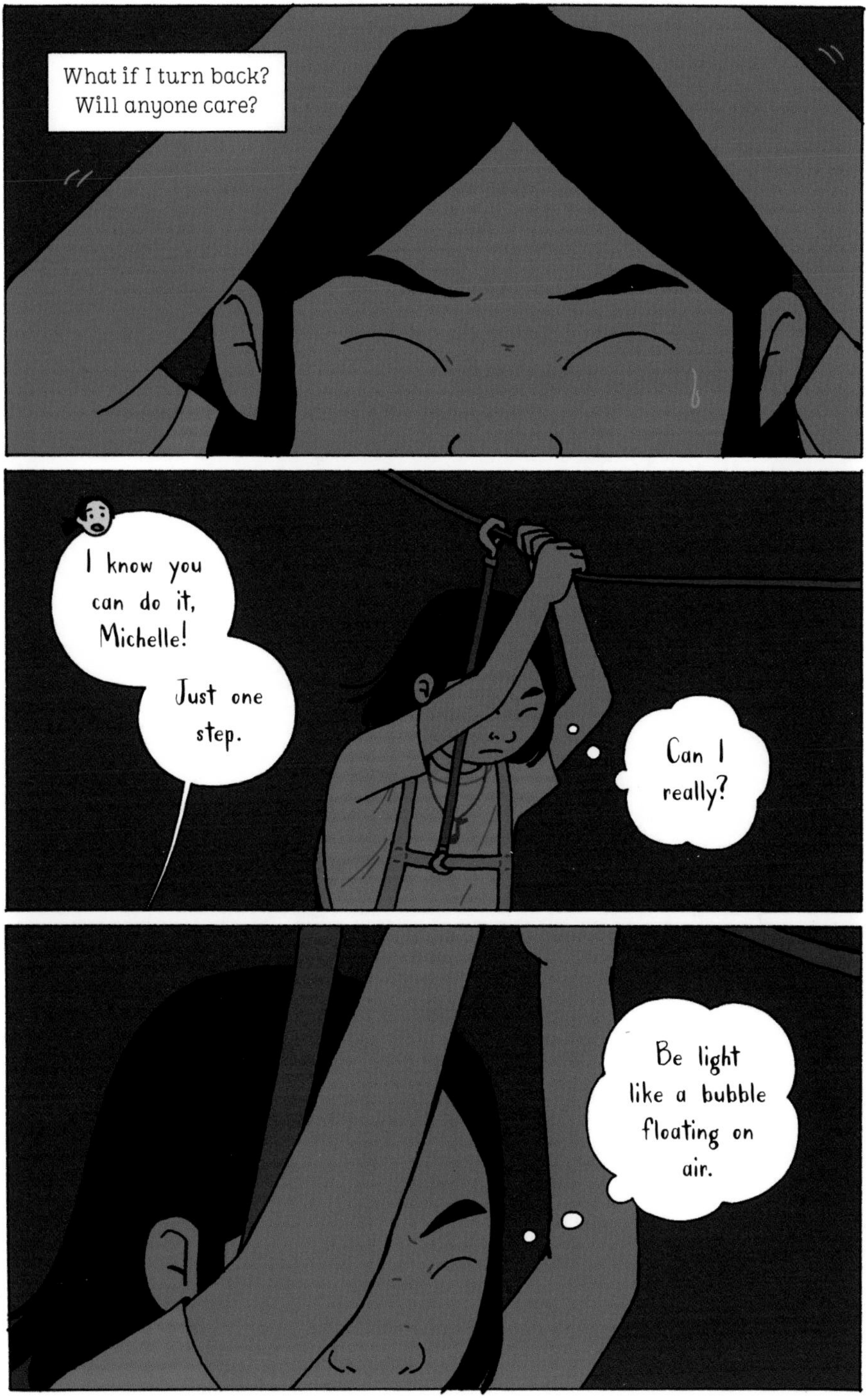
What if I turn back? Will anyone care?
I know you can do it, Michelle!
Just one step.
Can I really?
Be light like a bubble floating on air.

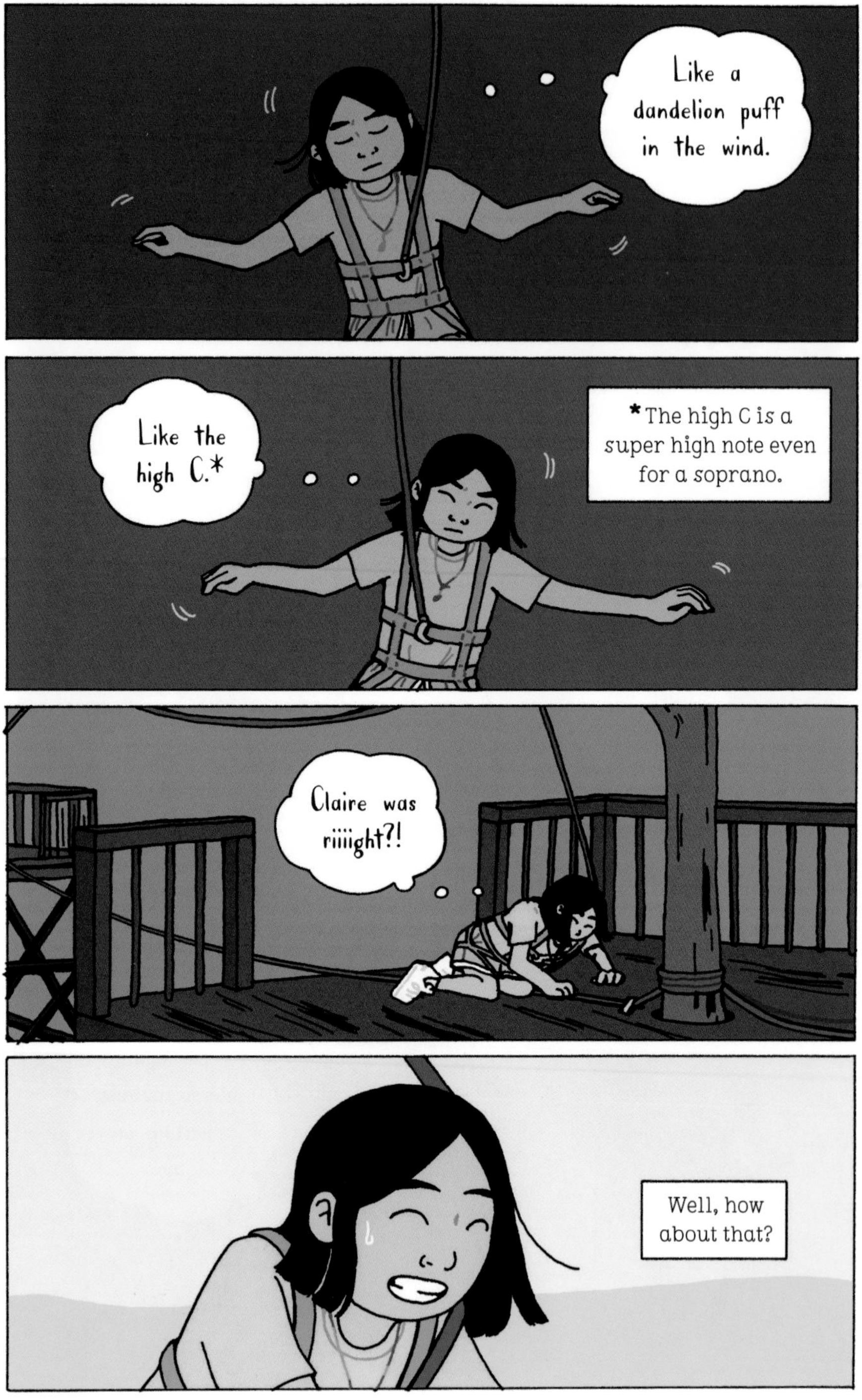

Like a dandelion puff in the wind.
Like the high C.*
*The high C is a super high note even for a soprano.
Claire was riiiight?!
Well, how about that?

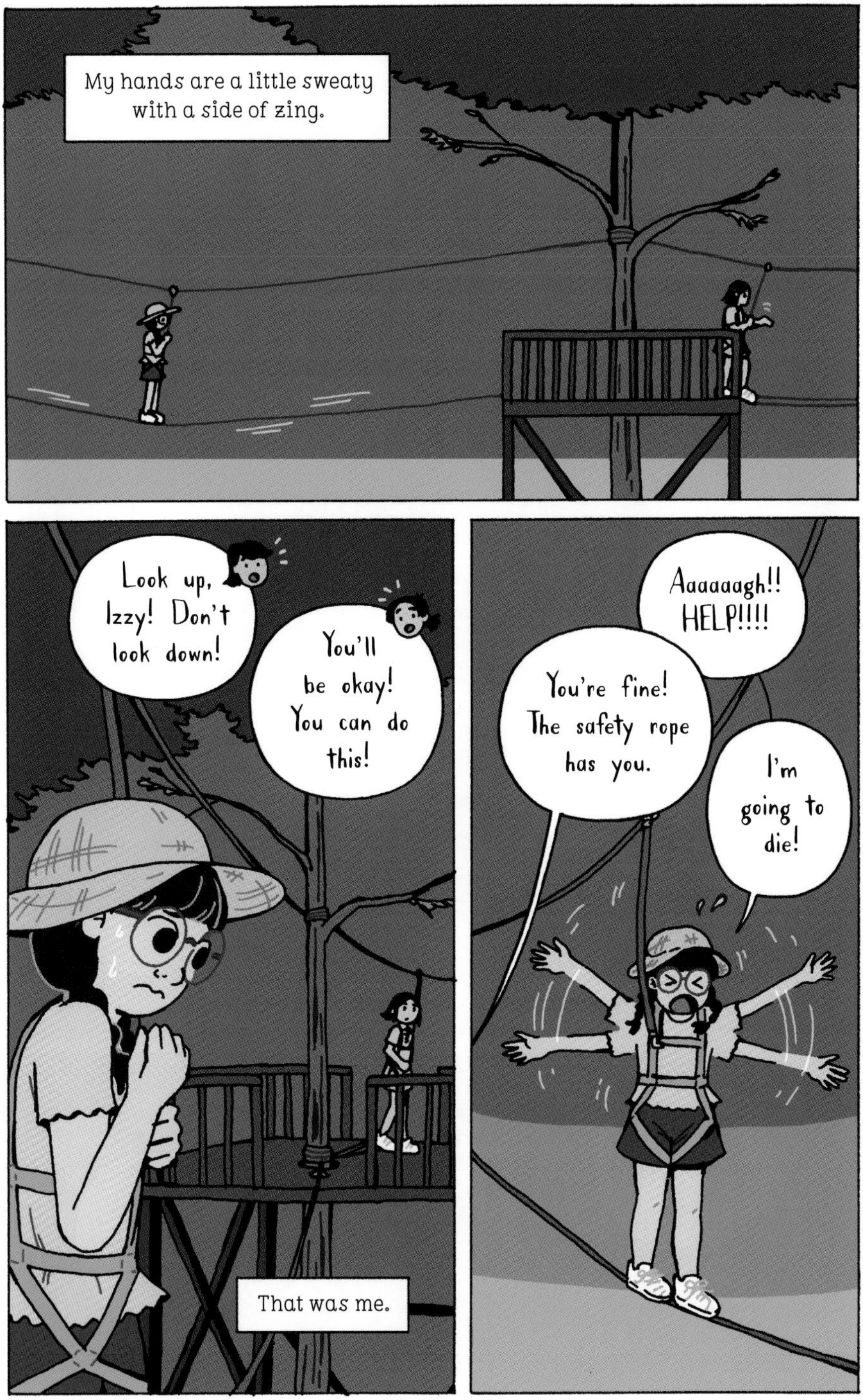
My hands are a little sweaty with a side of zing.
Look up, Izzy! Don't look down!
You'll be okay! You can do this!
That was me.
Aaaaaagh!! HELP!!!!
You're fine! The safety rope has you.
I'm going to die!

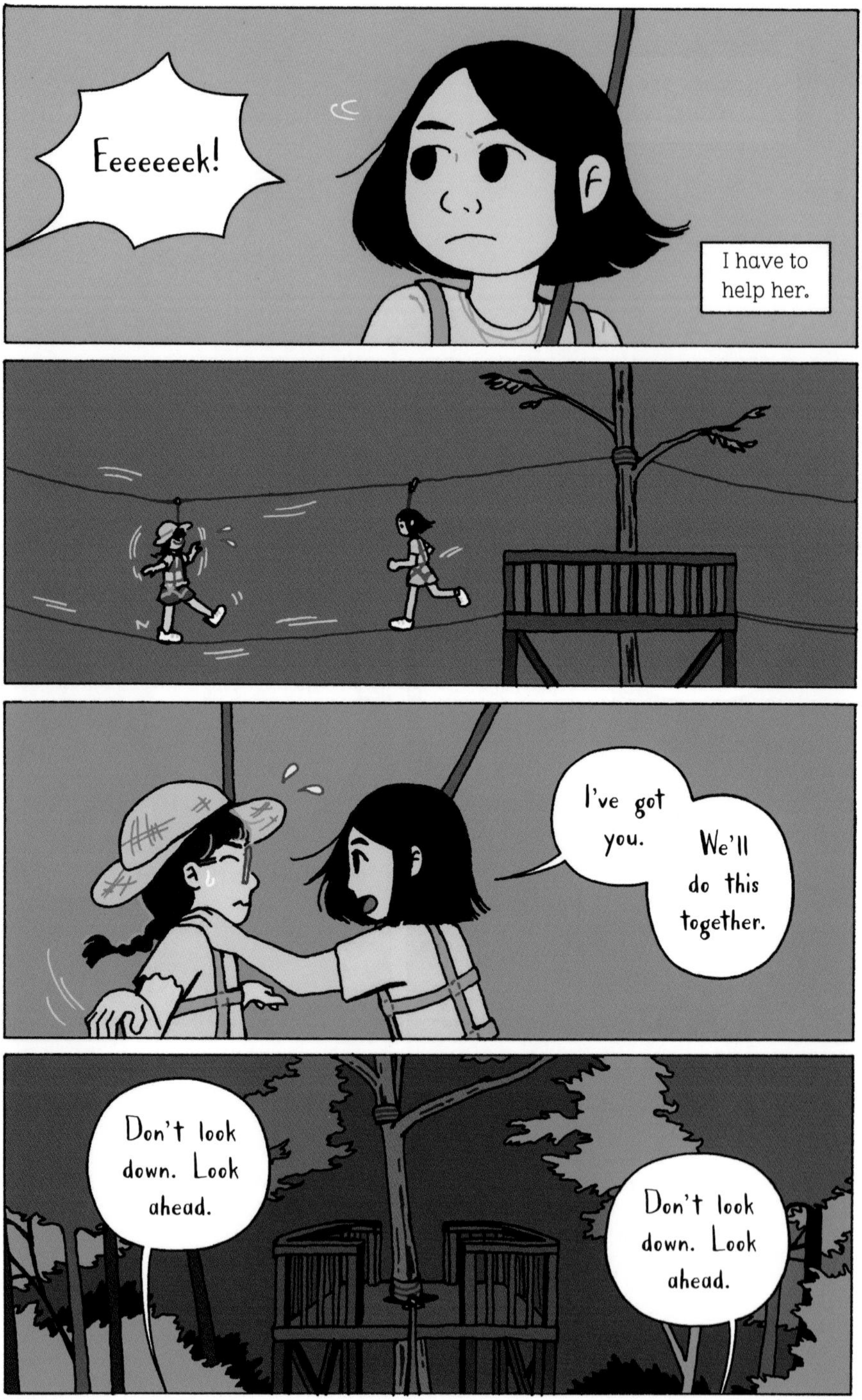
Eeeeeeek!
I have to help her.
I've got you.
We'll do this together.
Don't look down. Look ahead.
Don't look down. Look ahead.

Left hand over right. Right over left.
Left hand over right. Right over left.
Right foot step. Left foot step.
Right foot step. Left foot step.
You're safe.
Thank you. You're the best.
I feel pretty good then . . .

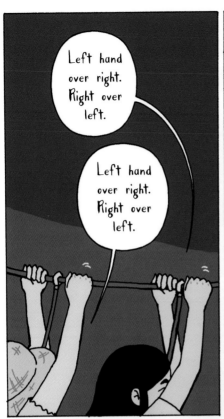

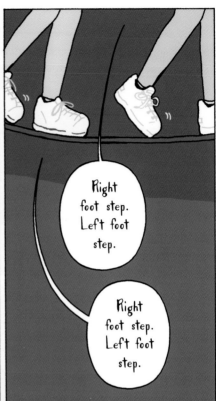

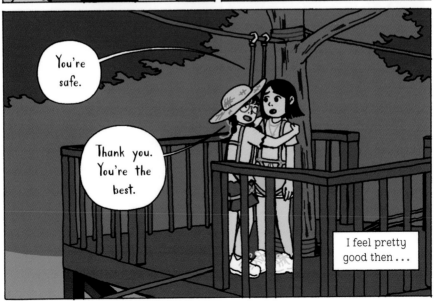

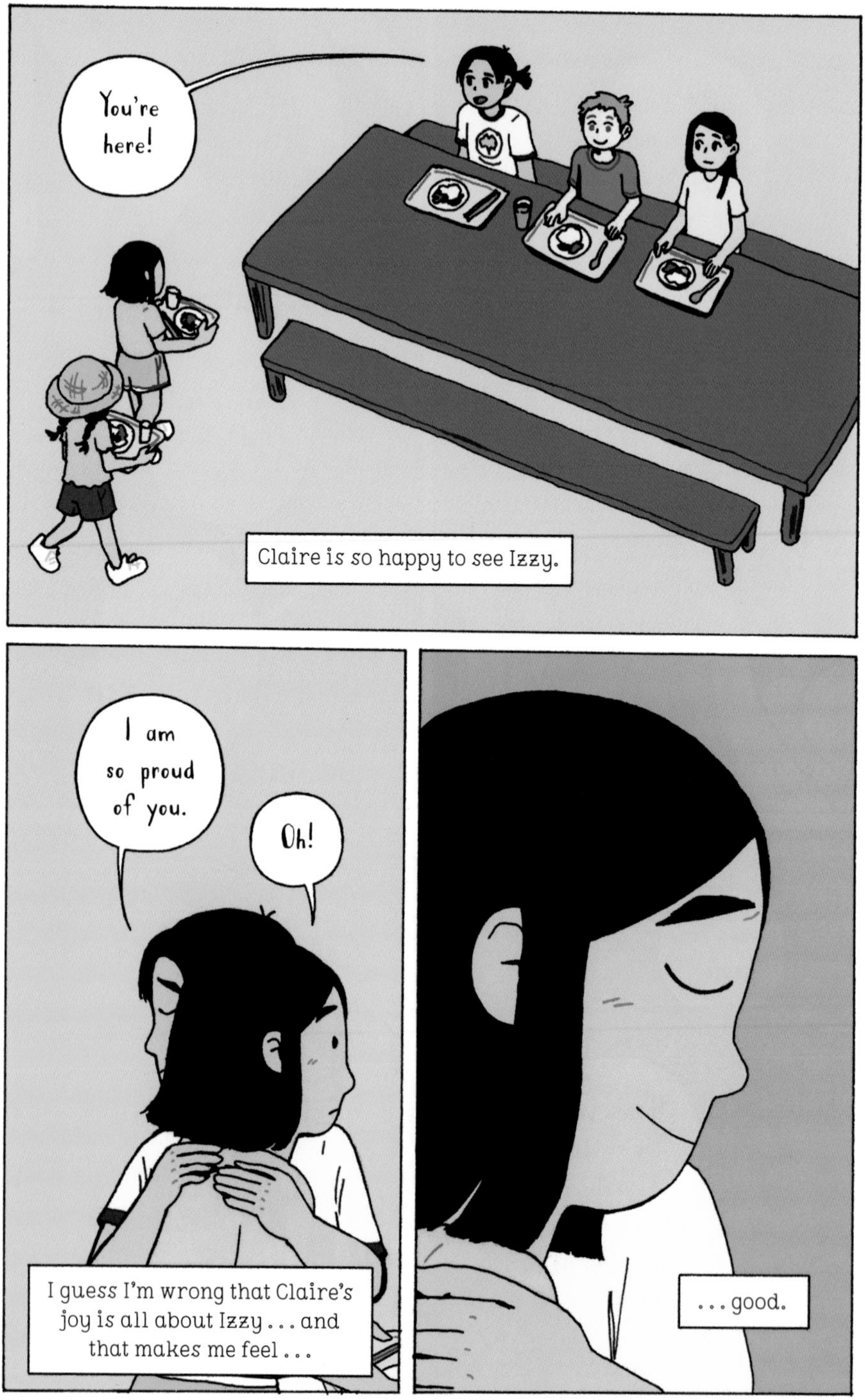
You're here!
Claire is so happy to see Izzy.
I am so proud of you.
Oh!
I guess I'm wrong that Claire's joy is all about Izzy . . . and that makes me feel . . .
. . . good.

On a surprisingly hot day a couple of days later, Andrea explained how to make Taiwanese shaved ice.

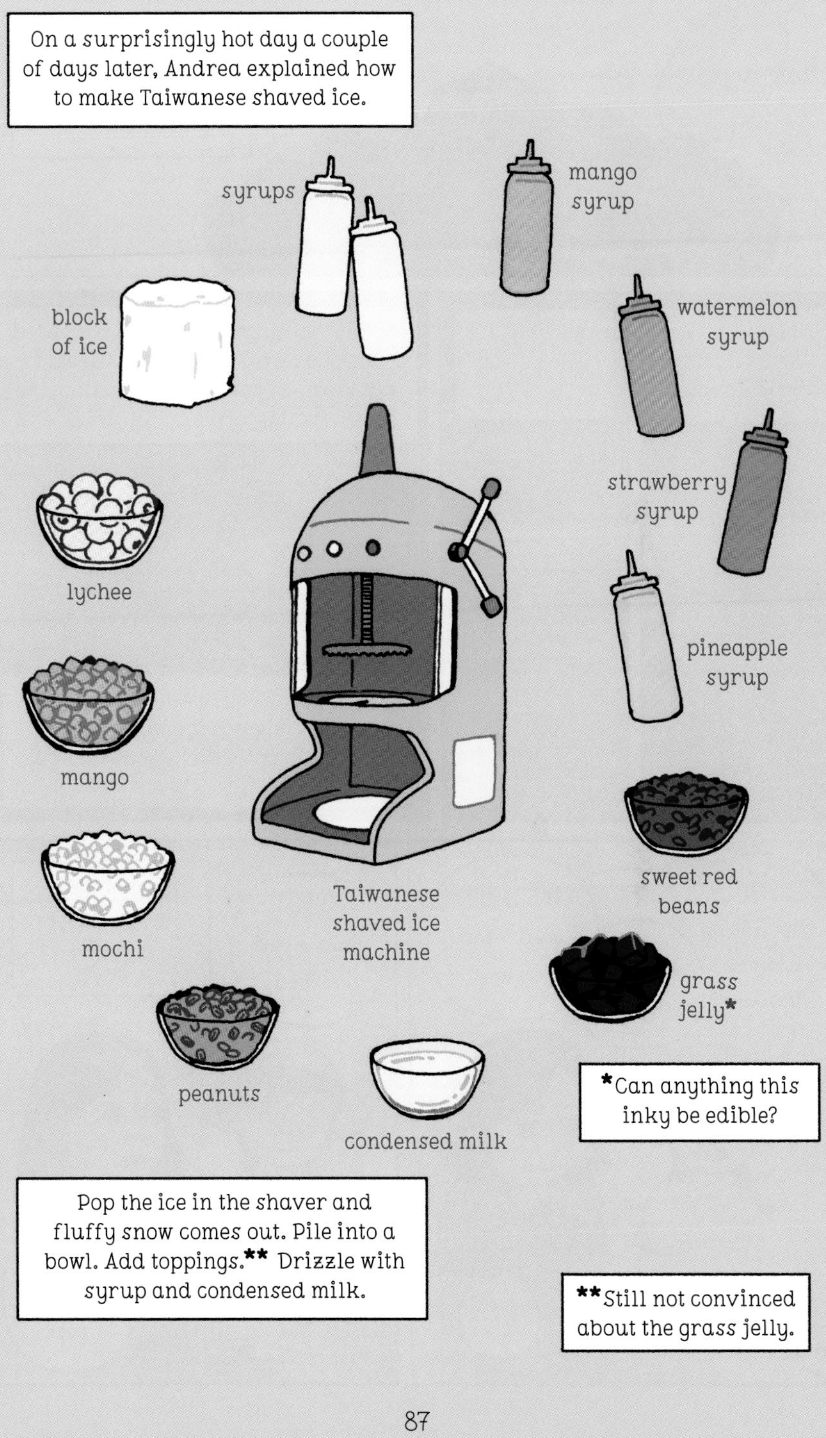
syrups
mango syrup
block of ice
watermelon syrup
strawberry syrup
lychee
pineapple syrup
mango
sweet red beans
mochi
Taiwanese shaved ice machine
grass jelly*
peanuts
condensed milk

*Can anything this inky be edible?

Pop the ice in the shaver and fluffy snow comes out. Pile into a bowl. Add toppings.** Drizzle with syrup and condensed milk.

**Still not convinced about the grass jelly.

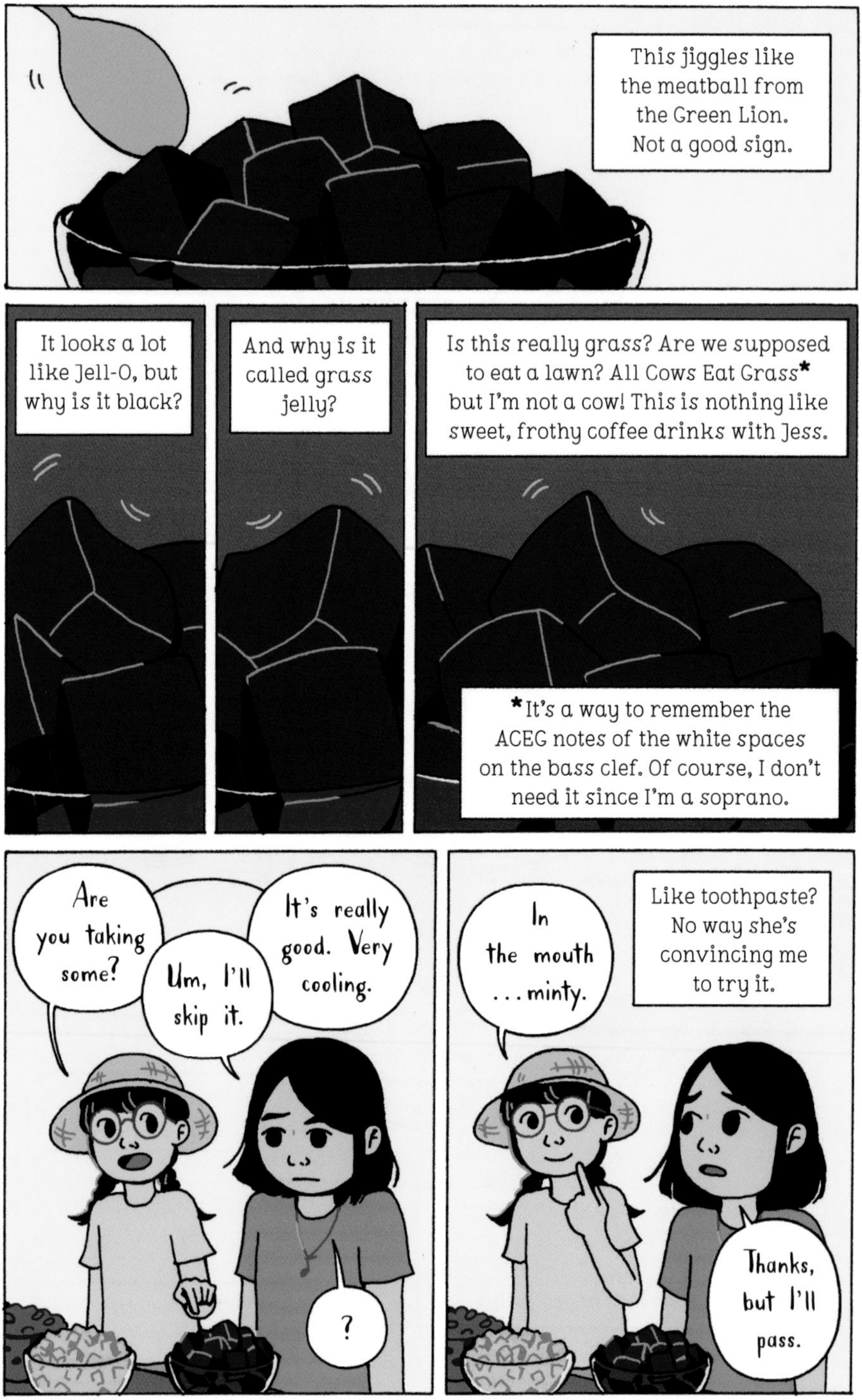
This jiggles like the meatball from the Green Lion. Not a good sign.
It looks a lot like Jell-O, but why is it black?
And why is it called grass jelly?
Is this really grass? Are we supposed to eat a lawn? All Cows Eat Grass* but I'm not a cow! This is nothing like sweet, frothy coffee drinks with Jess.
*It's a way to remember the ACEG notes of the white spaces on the bass clef. Of course, I don't need it since I'm a soprano.
Are you taking some?
Um, I'll skip it.
It's really good. Very cooling.
?
In the mouth ...minty.
Like toothpaste? No way she's convincing me to try it.
Thanks, but I'll pass.

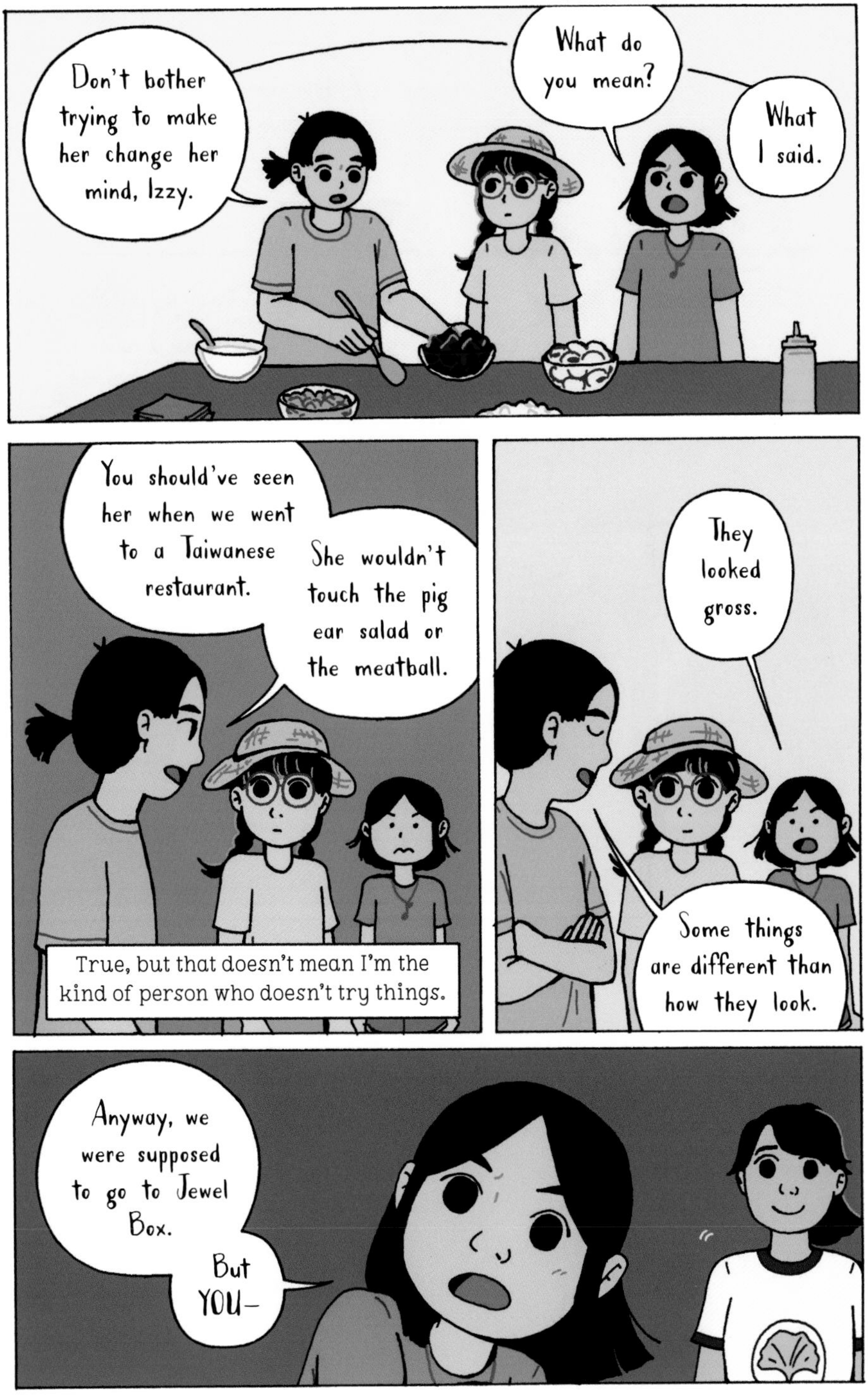

Don't bother trying to make her change her mind, Izzy.
What do you mean?
What I said.
You should've seen her when we went to a Taiwanese restaurant.
She wouldn't touch the pig ear salad or the meatball.
True, but that doesn't mean I'm the kind of person who doesn't try things.
They looked gross.
Some things are different than how they look.
Anyway, we were supposed to go to Jewel Box.
But YOU–

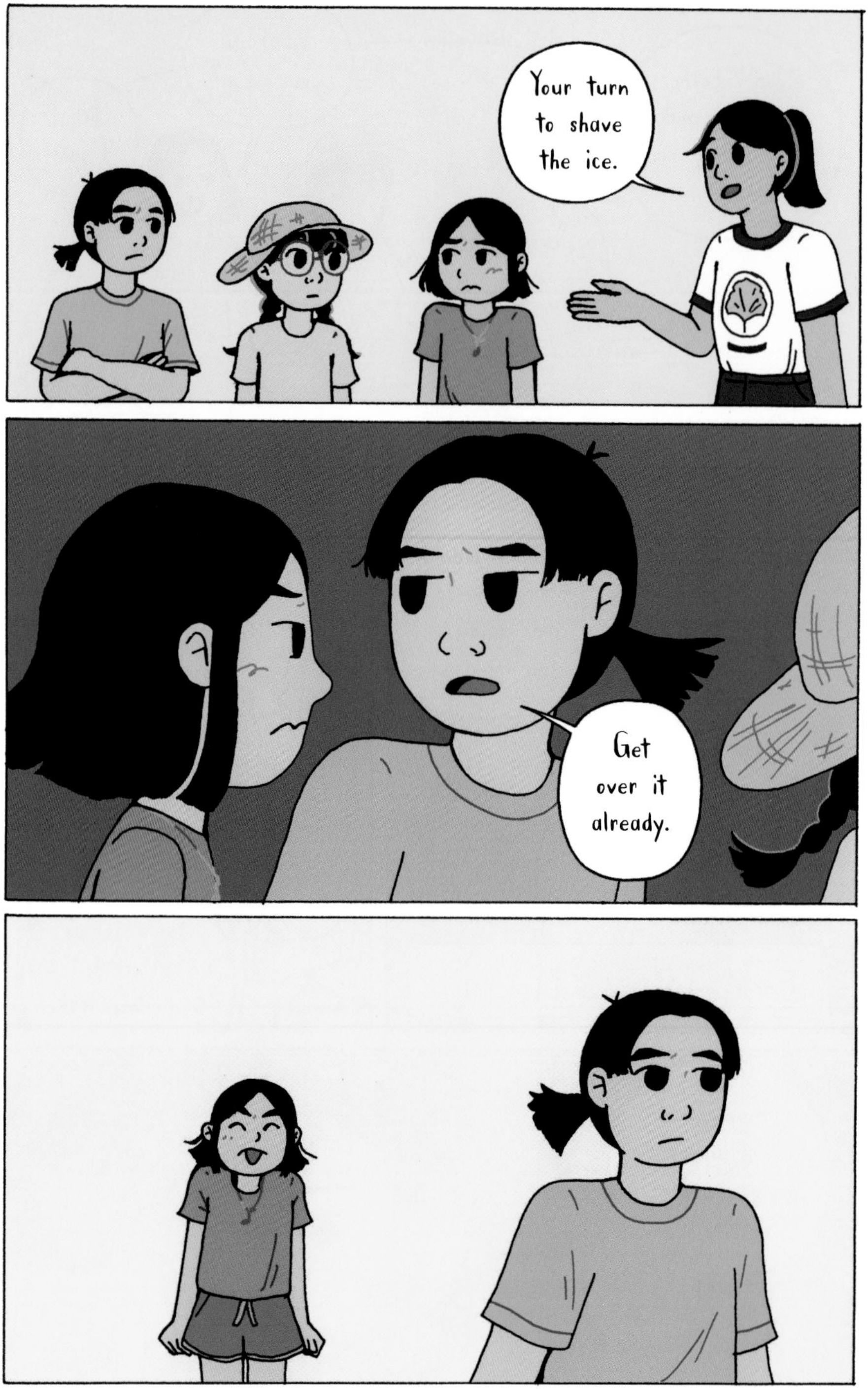
Your turn to shave the ice.
Get over it already.

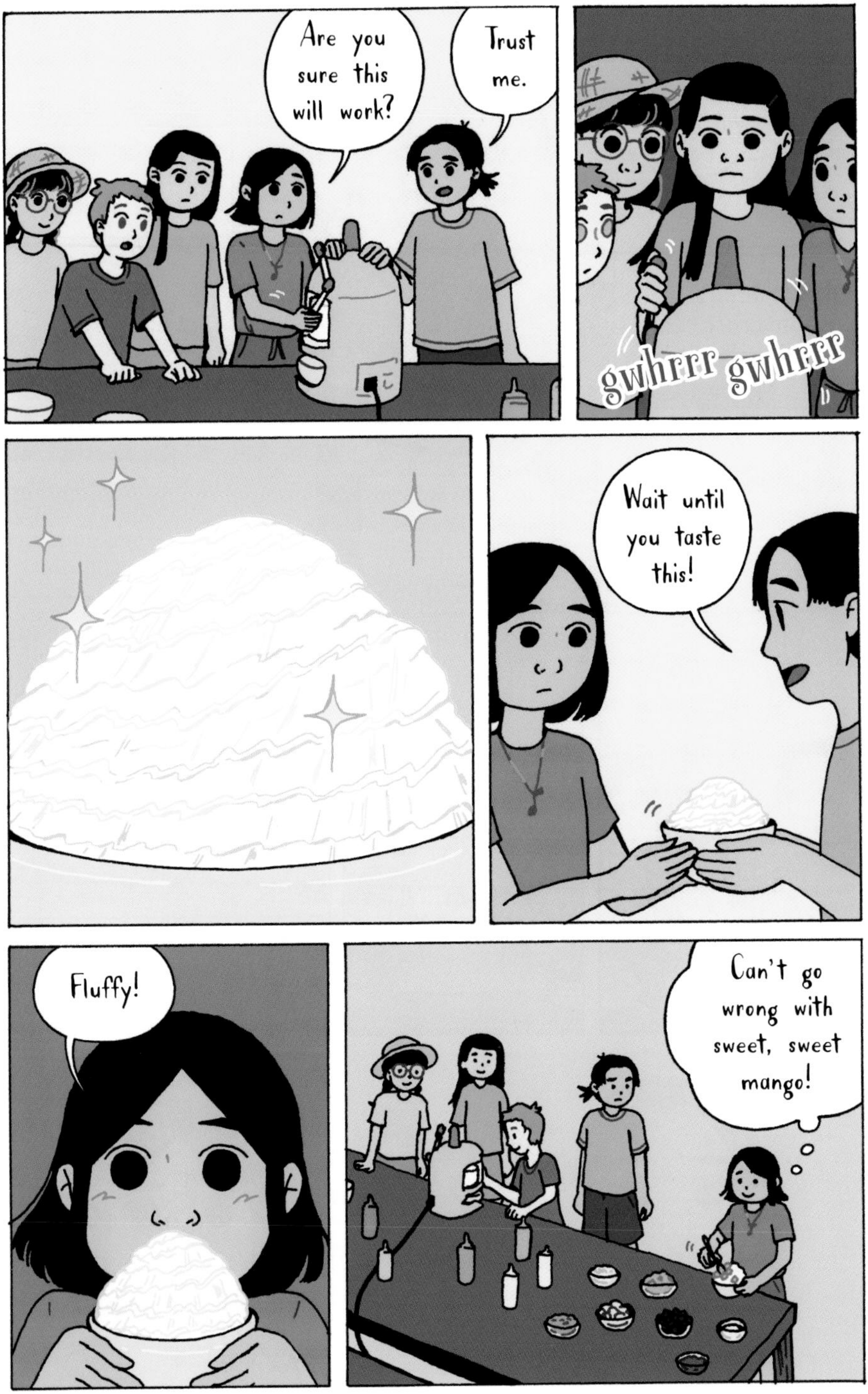
Are you sure this will work?
Trust me.
gwhrrr gwhrrr
Wait until you taste this!
Fluffy!
Can't go wrong with sweet, sweet mango!

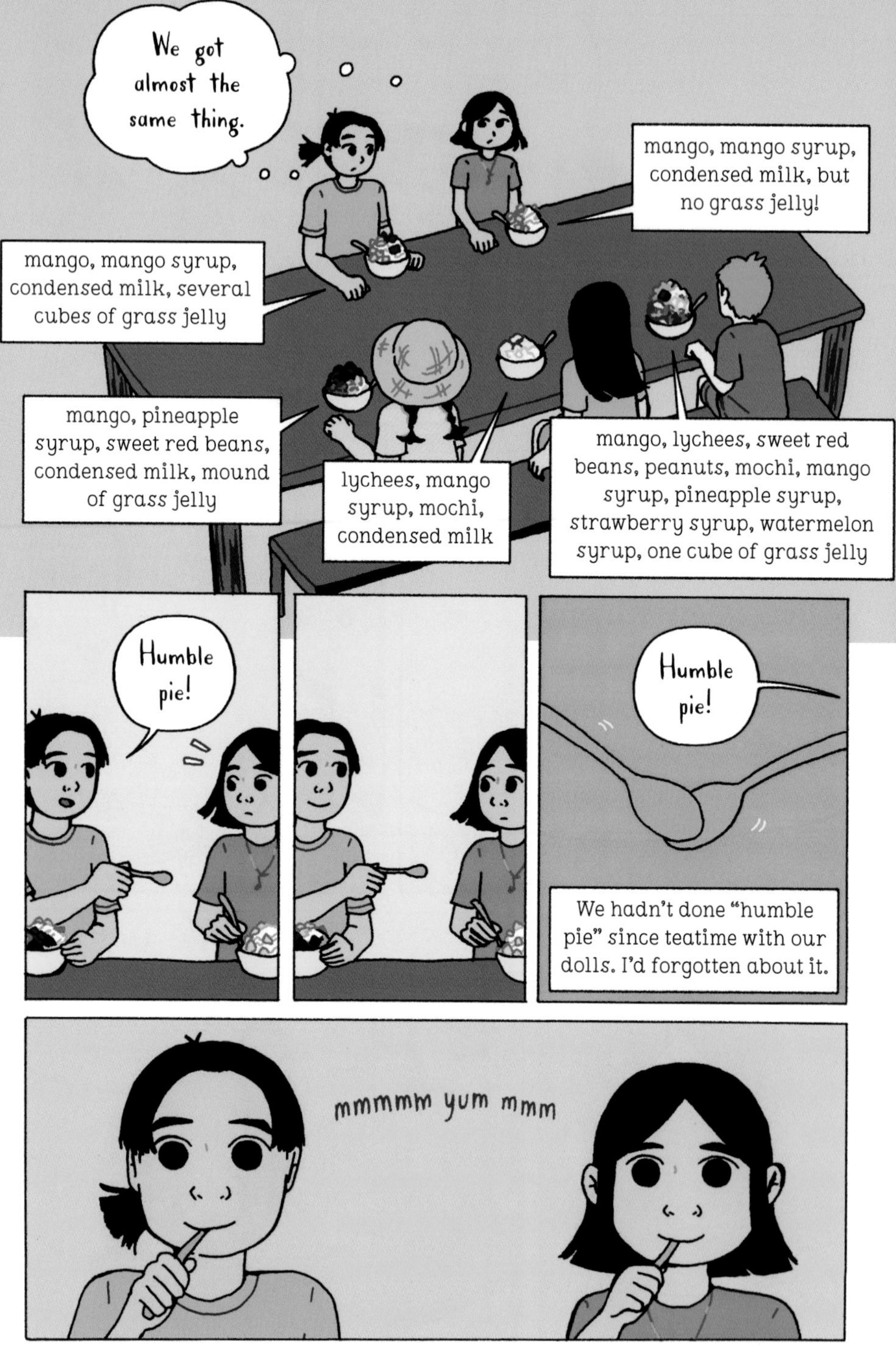
We got almost the same thing.
mango, mango syrup, condensed milk, but no grass jelly!
mango, mango syrup, condensed milk, several cubes of grass jelly
mango, pineapple syrup, sweet red beans, condensed milk, mound of grass jelly
lychees, mango syrup, mochi, condensed milk
mango, lychees, sweet red beans, peanuts, mochi, mango syrup, pineapple syrup, strawberry syrup, watermelon syrup, one cube of grass jelly
Humble pie!
Humble pie!
We hadn't done "humble pie" since teatime with our dolls. I'd forgotten about it.
mmmmm yum mmm

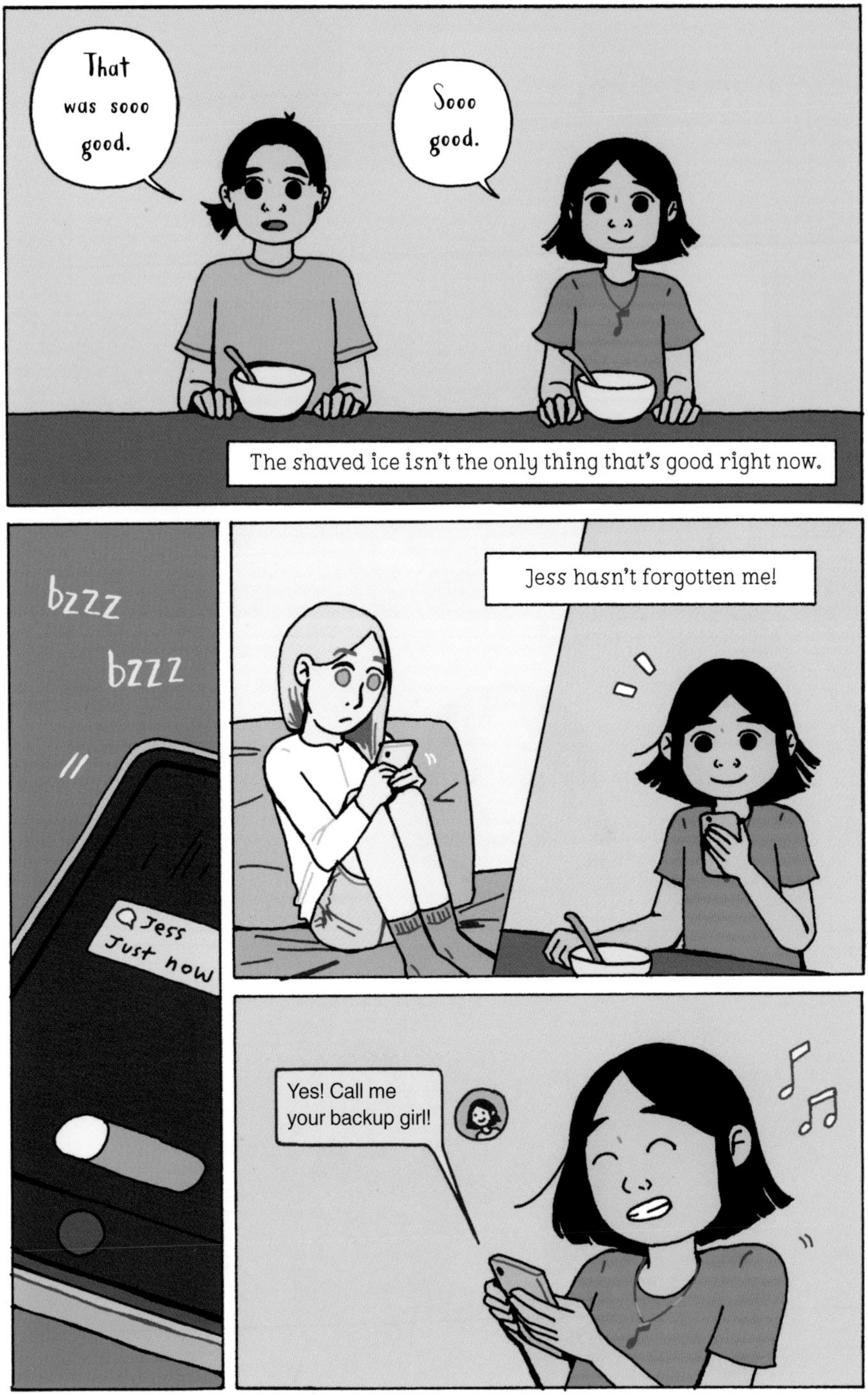
That was sooo good.
Sooo good.
The shaved ice isn't the only thing that's good right now.
bzzz
bzzz
Jess
Just now
Jess hasn't forgotten me!
Yes! Call me your backup girl!

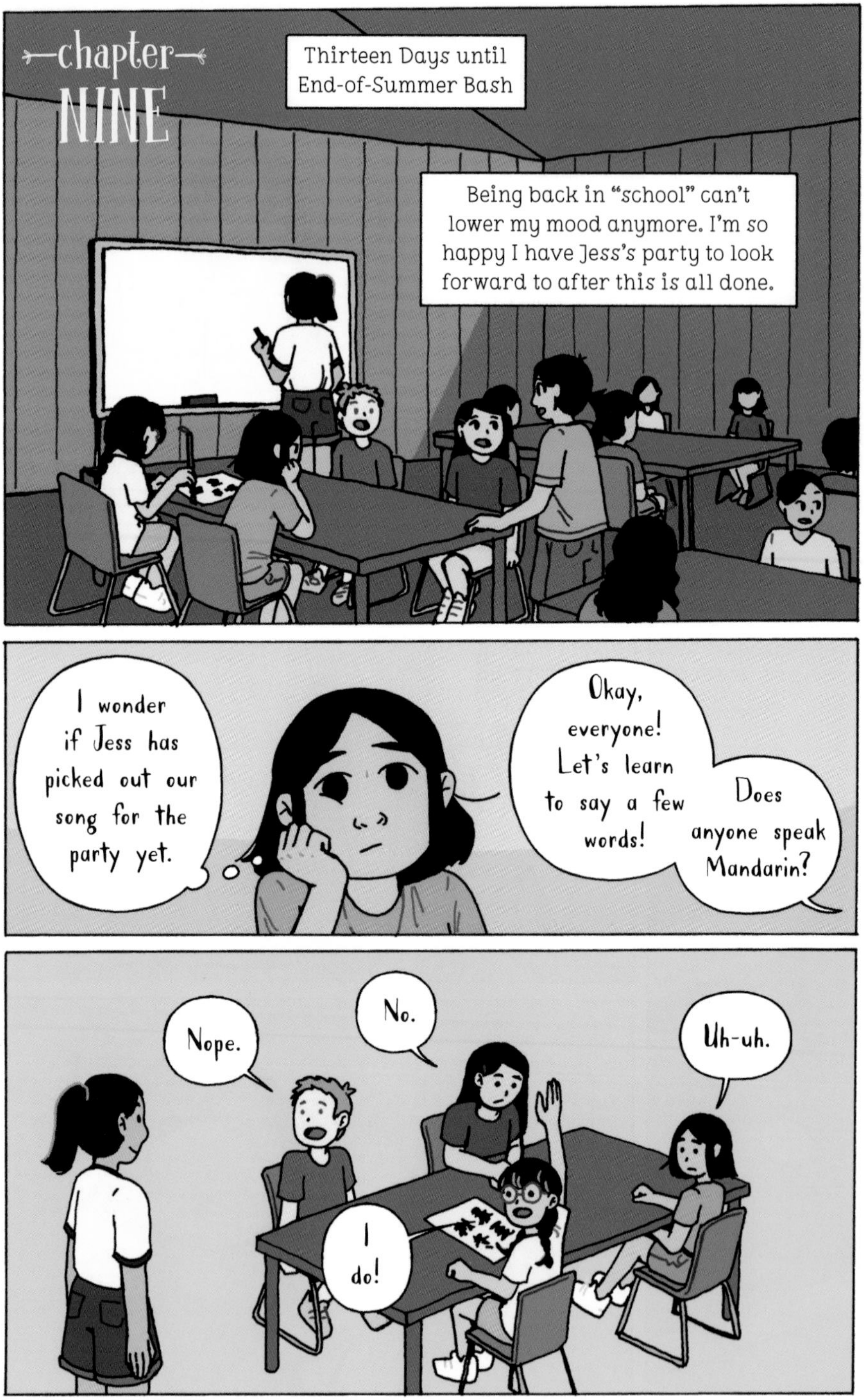
chapter NINE
Thirteen Days until End-of-Summer Bash
Being back in "school" can't lower my mood anymore. I'm *so* happy I have Jess's party to look forward to after this is all done.
I wonder if Jess has picked out our song for the party yet.
Okay, everyone! Let's learn to say a few words!
Does anyone speak Mandarin?
Nope.
No.
Uh-uh.
I do!

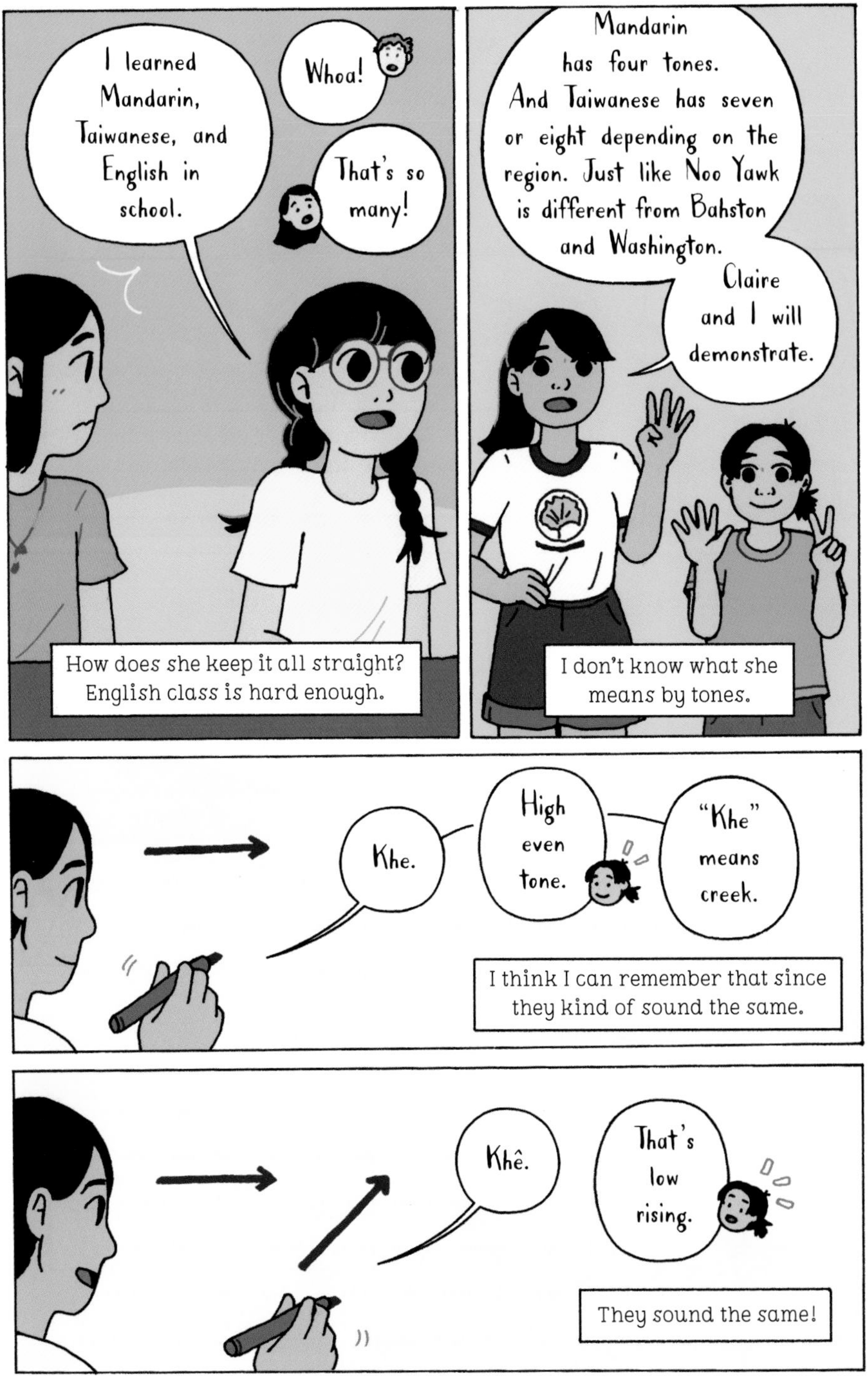
I learned Mandarin, Taiwanese, and English in school.
Whoa!
That's so many!
How does she keep it all straight? English class is hard enough.
Mandarin has four tones. And Taiwanese has seven or eight depending on the region. Just like Noo Yawk is different from Bahston and Washington.
Claire and I will demonstrate.
I don't know what she means by tones.
Khe.
High even tone.
"Khe" means creek.
I think I can remember that since they kind of sound the same.
Khê.
That's low rising.
They sound the same!

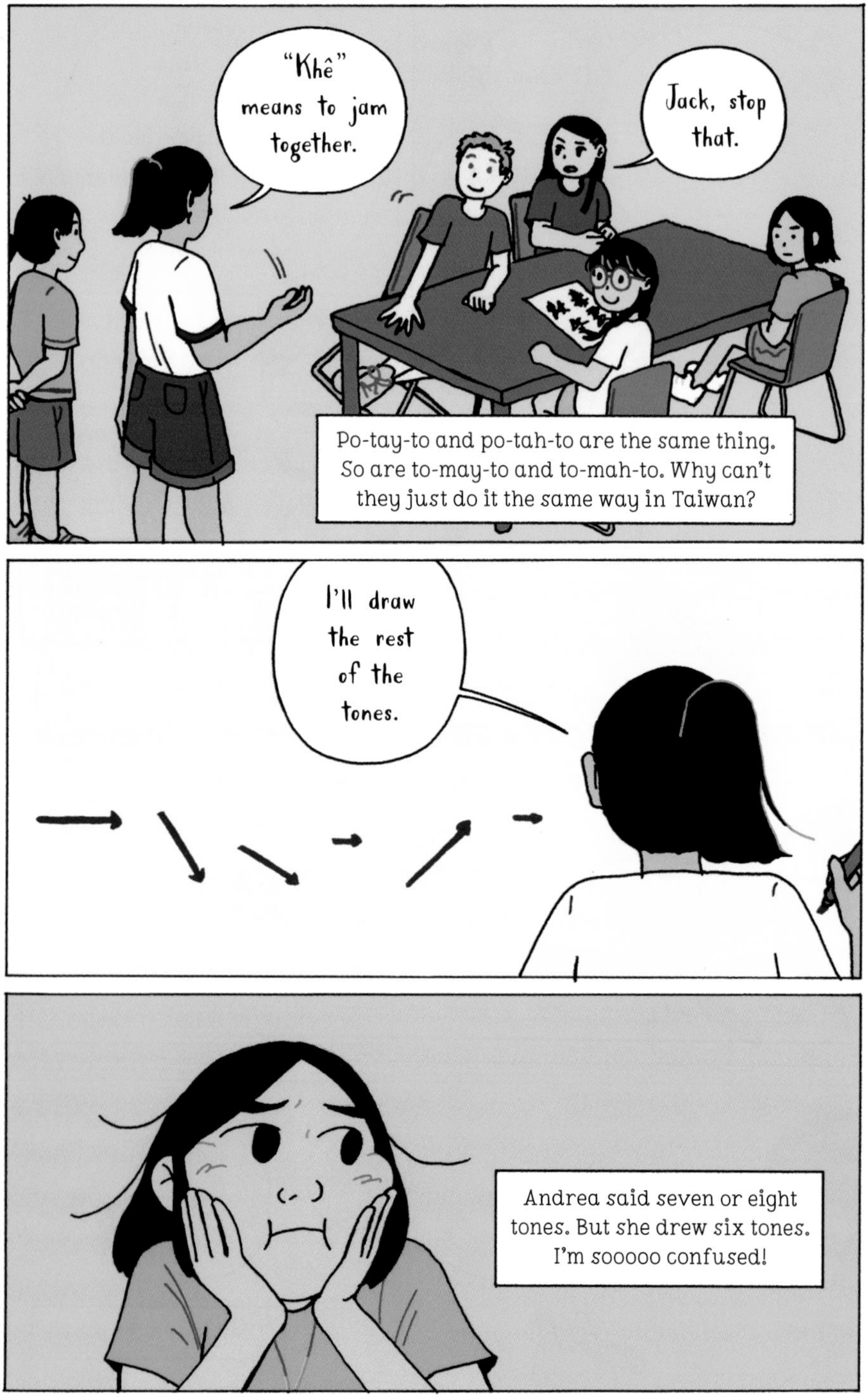
"Khê" means to jam together.
Jack, stop that.
Po-tay-to and po-tah-to are the same thing. So are to-may-to and to-mah-to. Why can't they just do it the same way in Taiwan?
I'll draw the rest of the tones.
Andrea said seven or eight tones. But she drew six tones. I'm sooooo confused!

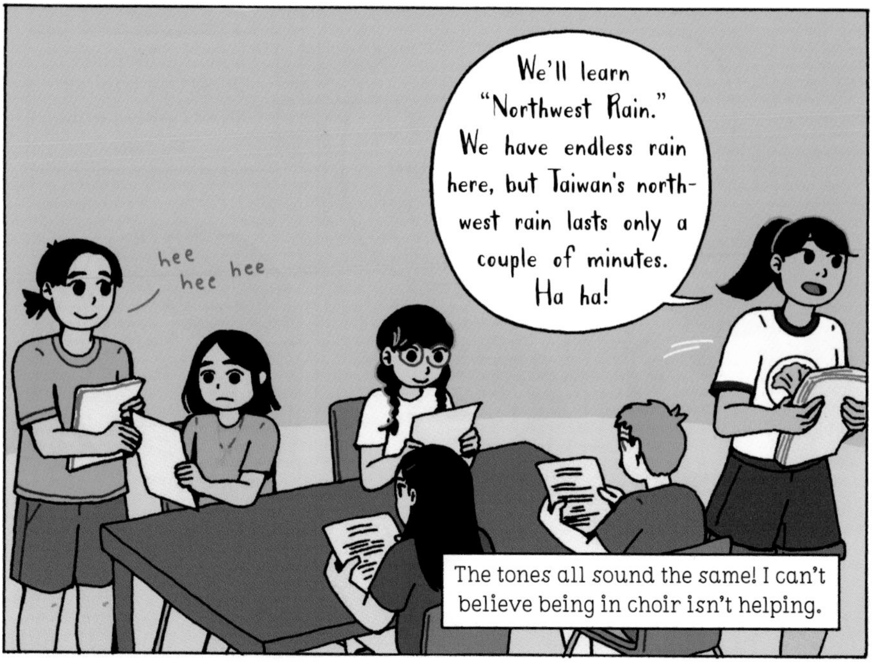
hee
hee hee
We'll learn "Northwest Rain." We have endless rain here, but Taiwan's northwest rain lasts only a couple of minutes. Ha ha!
The tones all sound the same! I can't believe being in choir isn't helping.

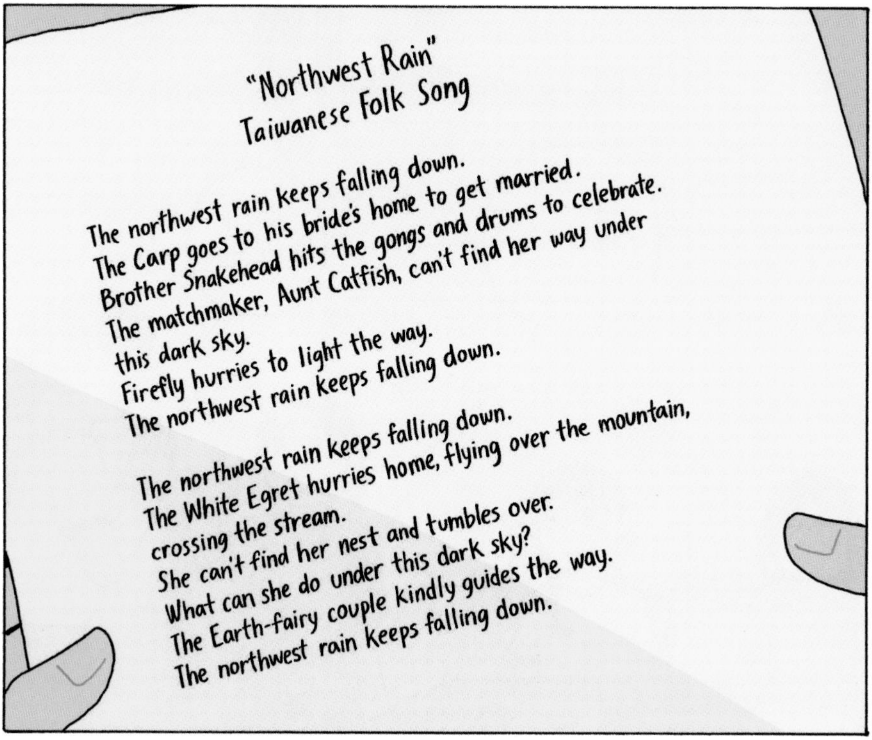
"Northwest Rain"
Taiwanese Folk Song
The northwest rain keeps falling down.
The Carp goes to his bride's home to get married.
Brother Snakehead hits the gongs and drums to celebrate.
The matchmaker, Aunt Catfish, can't find her way under
this dark sky.
Firefly hurries to light the way.
The northwest rain keeps falling down.
The northwest rain keeps falling down.
The White Egret hurries home, flying over the mountain,
crossing the stream.
She can't find her nest and tumbles over.
What can she do under this dark sky?
The Earth-fairy couple kindly guides the way.
The northwest rain keeps falling down.

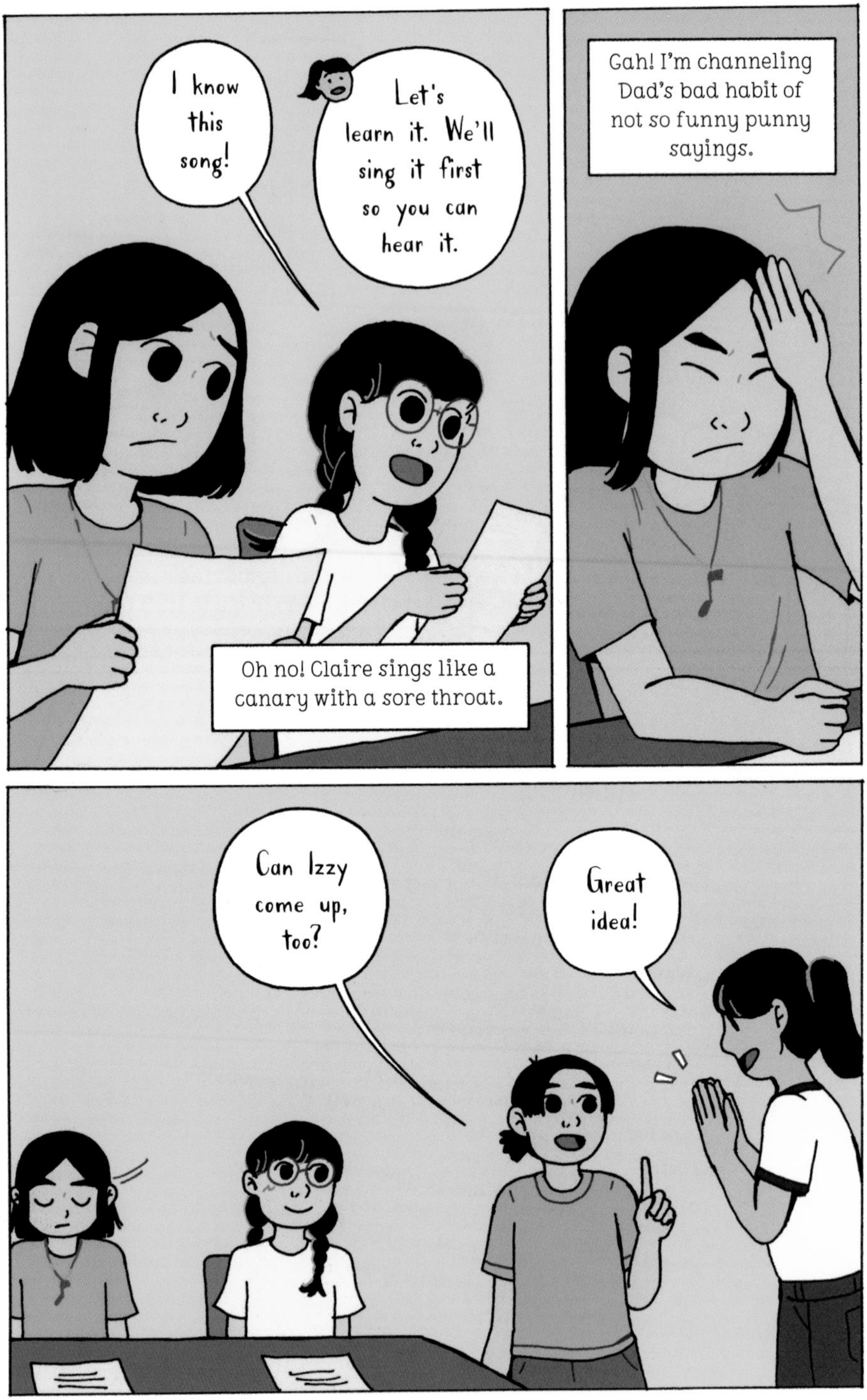

I know this song!
Let's learn it. We'll sing it first so you can hear it.
Oh no! Claire sings like a canary with a sore throat.
Gah! I'm channeling Dad's bad habit of not so funny punny sayings.
Can Izzy come up, too?
Great idea!

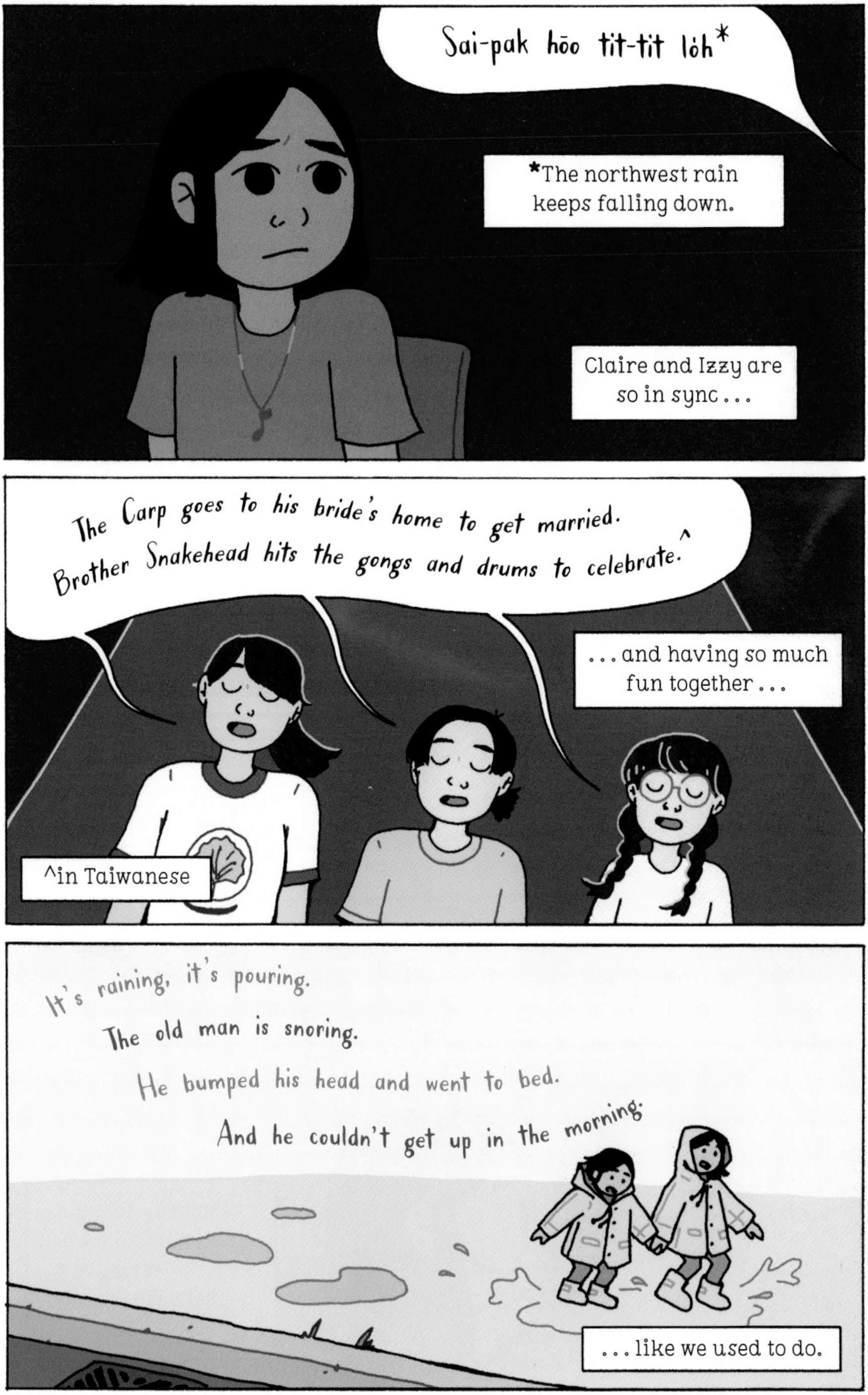

Sai-pak hōo tit-tit lòh*
*The northwest rain keeps falling down.
Claire and Izzy are so in sync . . .
The Carp goes to his bride's home to get married. Brother Snakehead hits the gongs and drums to celebrate.^
. . . and having so much fun together . . .
^in Taiwanese
It's raining, it's pouring.
The old man is snoring.
He bumped his head and went to bed.
And he couldn't get up in the morning.
. . . like we used to do.

The Earth-fairy couple kindly guides the way. The northwest rain keeps falling down.^

Now it's as if Izzy is her sister instead of me.

^in Taiwanese

I should be singing with Claire...

...but she didn't ask me.

I know, I know... I don't know the words.

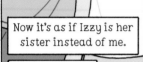
Let's all sing now. Don't worry. We'll go slow.

I'm in elite choir, so I know I can carry a tune. But can I figure out the words?

Let's try the first line together. Remember, it's "Sai-pak hōo tit-tit lòh."

I'm game to try. Besides, it's like when we first learn a song in choir. We don't get it all right.

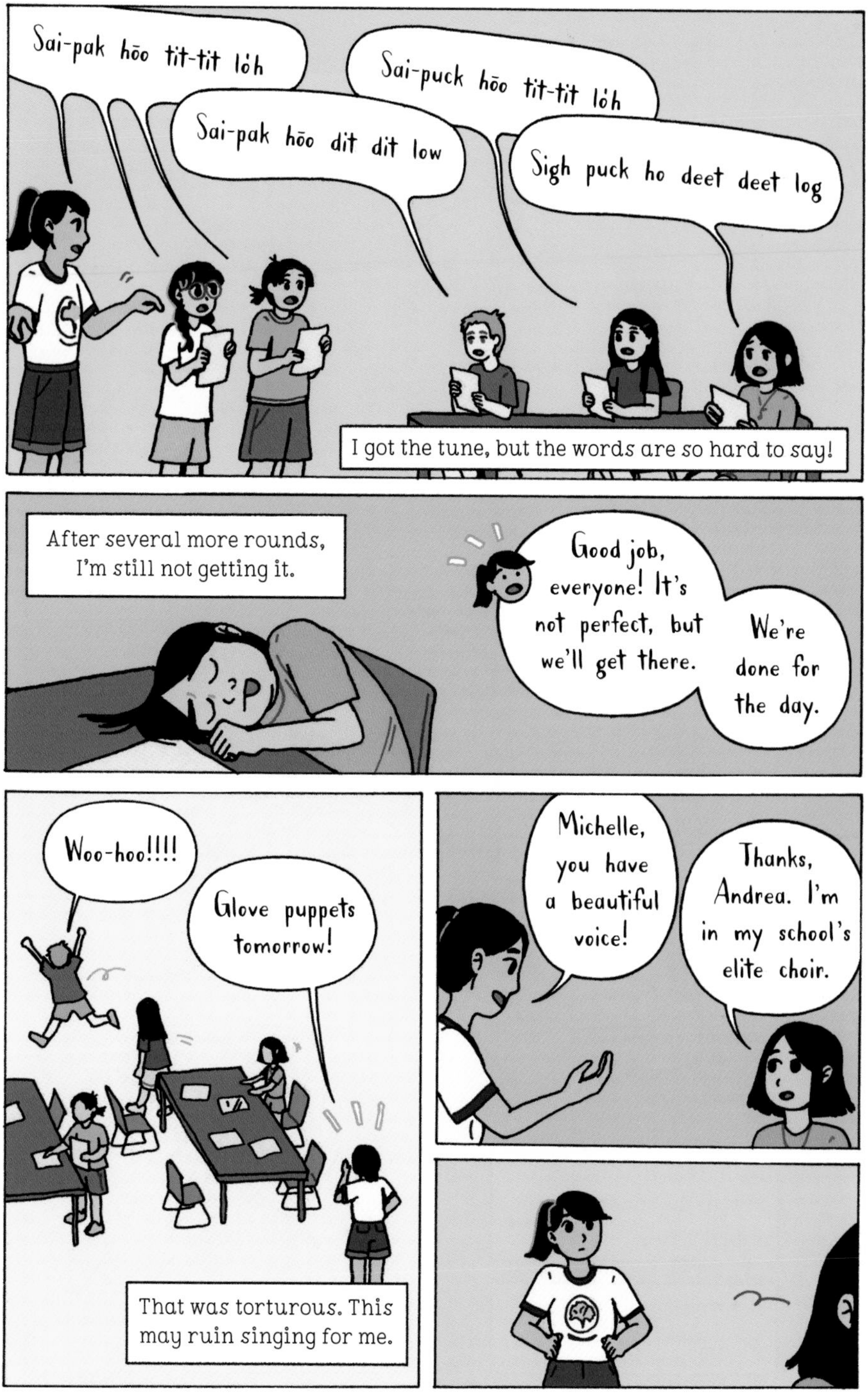
Sai-pak hōo tit-tit lòh
Sai-puck hōo tit-tit lòh
Sai-pak hōo dit dit low
Sigh puck ho deet deet log
I got the tune, but the words are so hard to say!
After several more rounds, I'm still not getting it.
Good job, everyone! It's not perfect, but we'll get there.
We're done for the day.
Woo-hoo!!!!
Glove puppets tomorrow!
That was torturous. This may ruin singing for me.
Michelle, you have a beautiful voice!
Thanks, Andrea. I'm in my school's elite choir.

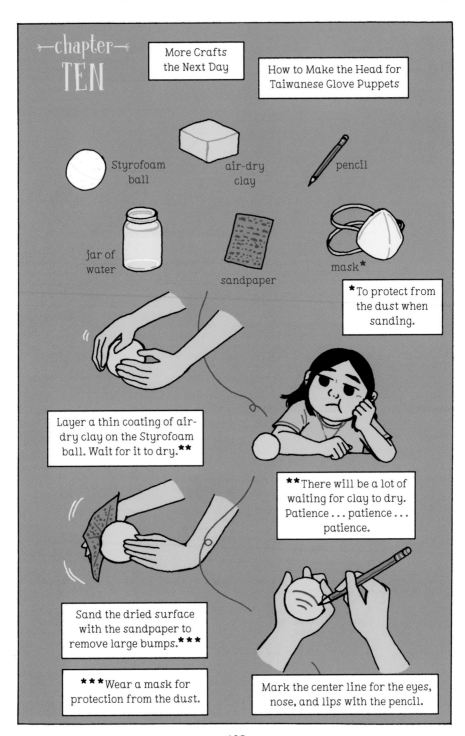

More Crafts the Next Day

How to Make the Head for Taiwanese Glove Puppets

Styrofoam ball

air-dry clay

pencil

jar of water

sandpaper

mask*

*To protect from the dust when sanding.

Layer a thin coating of air-dry clay on the Styrofoam ball. Wait for it to dry.**

**There will be a lot of waiting for clay to dry. Patience ... patience ... patience.

Sand the dried surface with the sandpaper to remove large bumps.***

***Wear a mask for protection from the dust.

Mark the center line for the eyes, nose, and lips with the pencil.

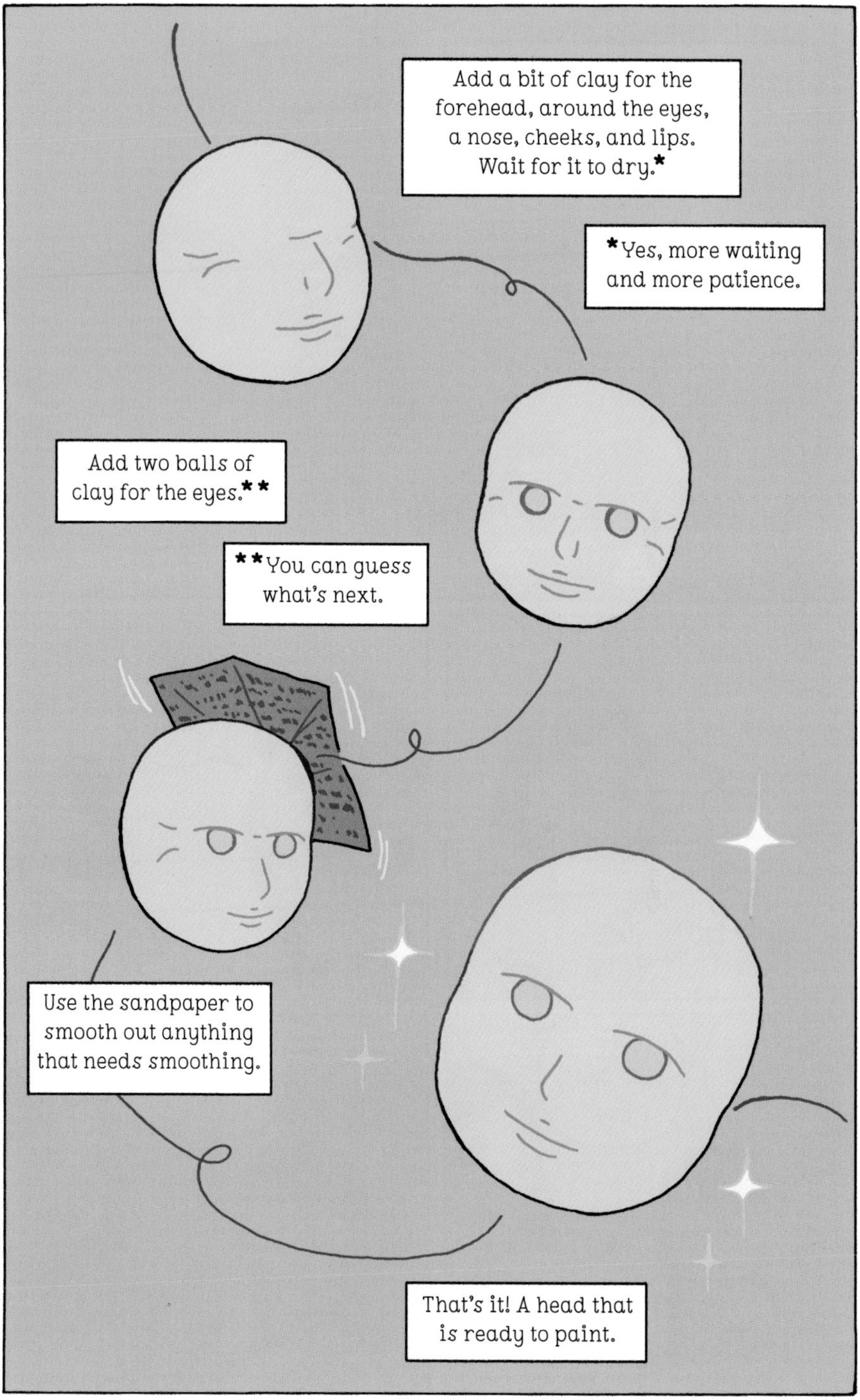
Add a bit of clay for the forehead, around the eyes, a nose, cheeks, and lips. Wait for it to dry.*
*Yes, more waiting and more patience.
Add two balls of clay for the eyes.**
**You can guess what's next.
Use the sandpaper to smooth out anything that needs smoothing.
That's it! A head that is ready to paint.

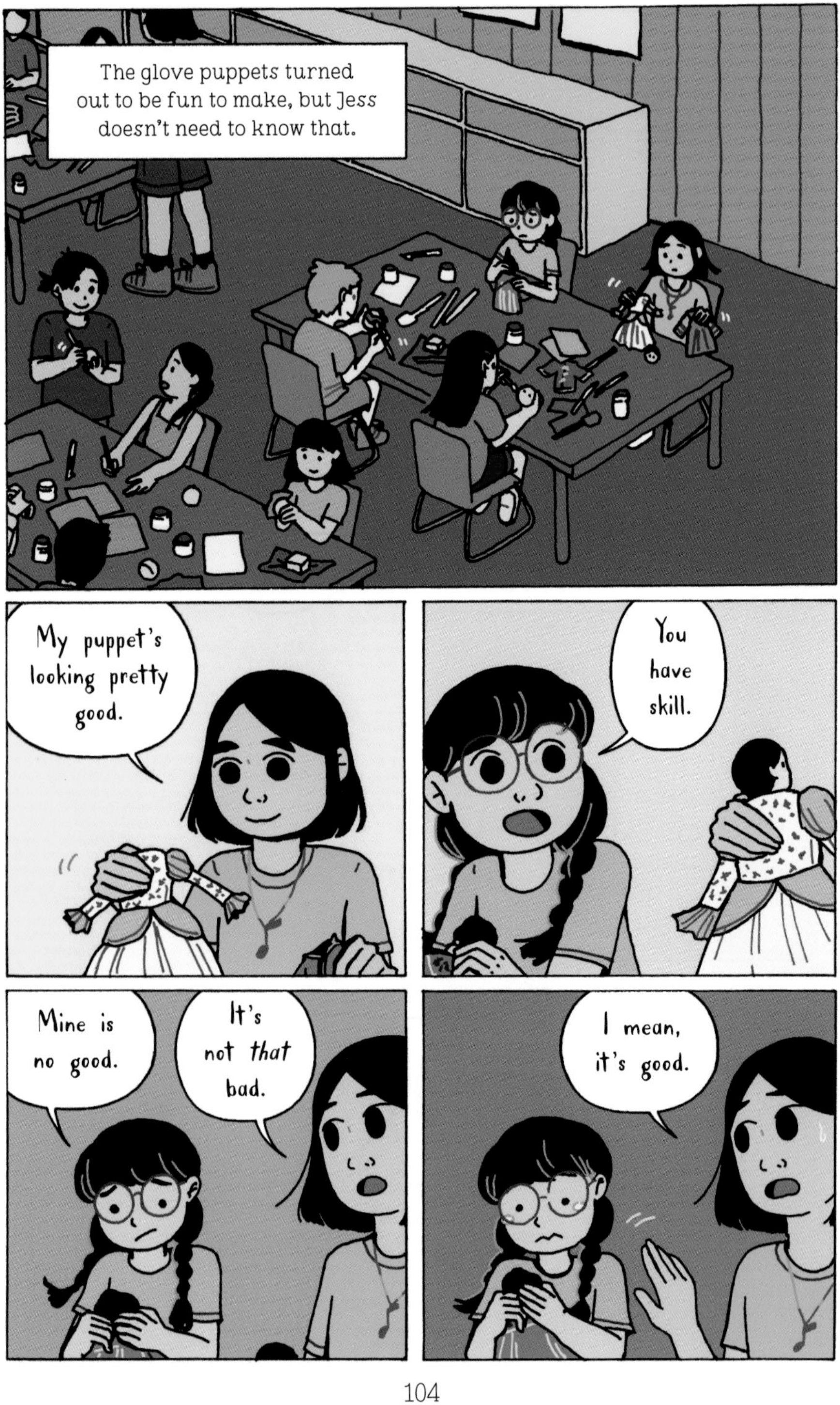
The glove puppets turned out to be fun to make, but Jess doesn't need to know that.
My puppet's looking pretty good.
You have skill.
Mine is no good.
It's not *that* bad.
I mean, it's good.

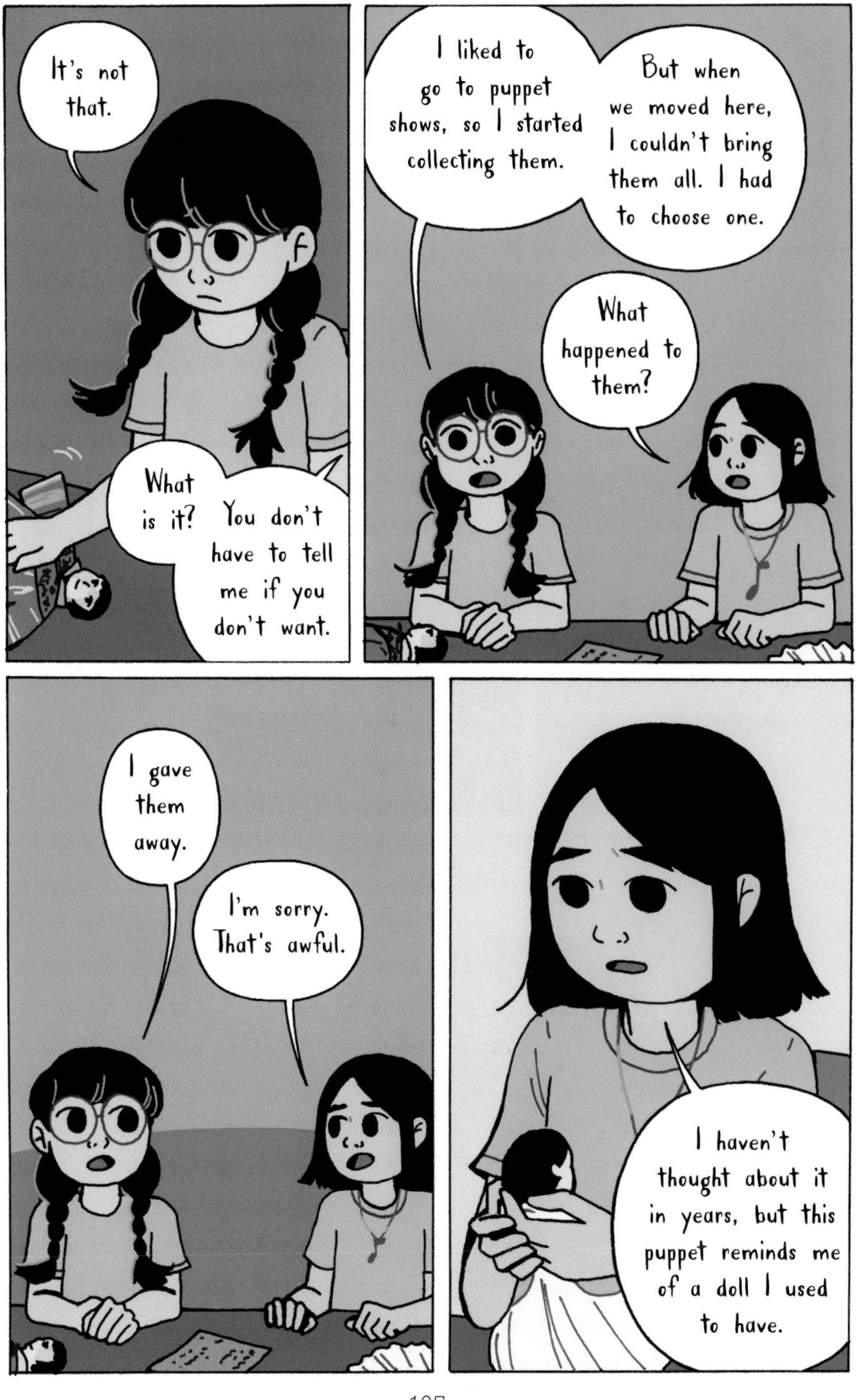
It's not that.
What is it? You don't have to tell me if you don't want.
I liked to go to puppet shows, so I started collecting them.
But when we moved here, I couldn't bring them all. I had to choose one.
What happened to them?
I gave them away.
I'm sorry. That's awful.
I haven't thought about it in years, but this puppet reminds me of a doll I used to have.

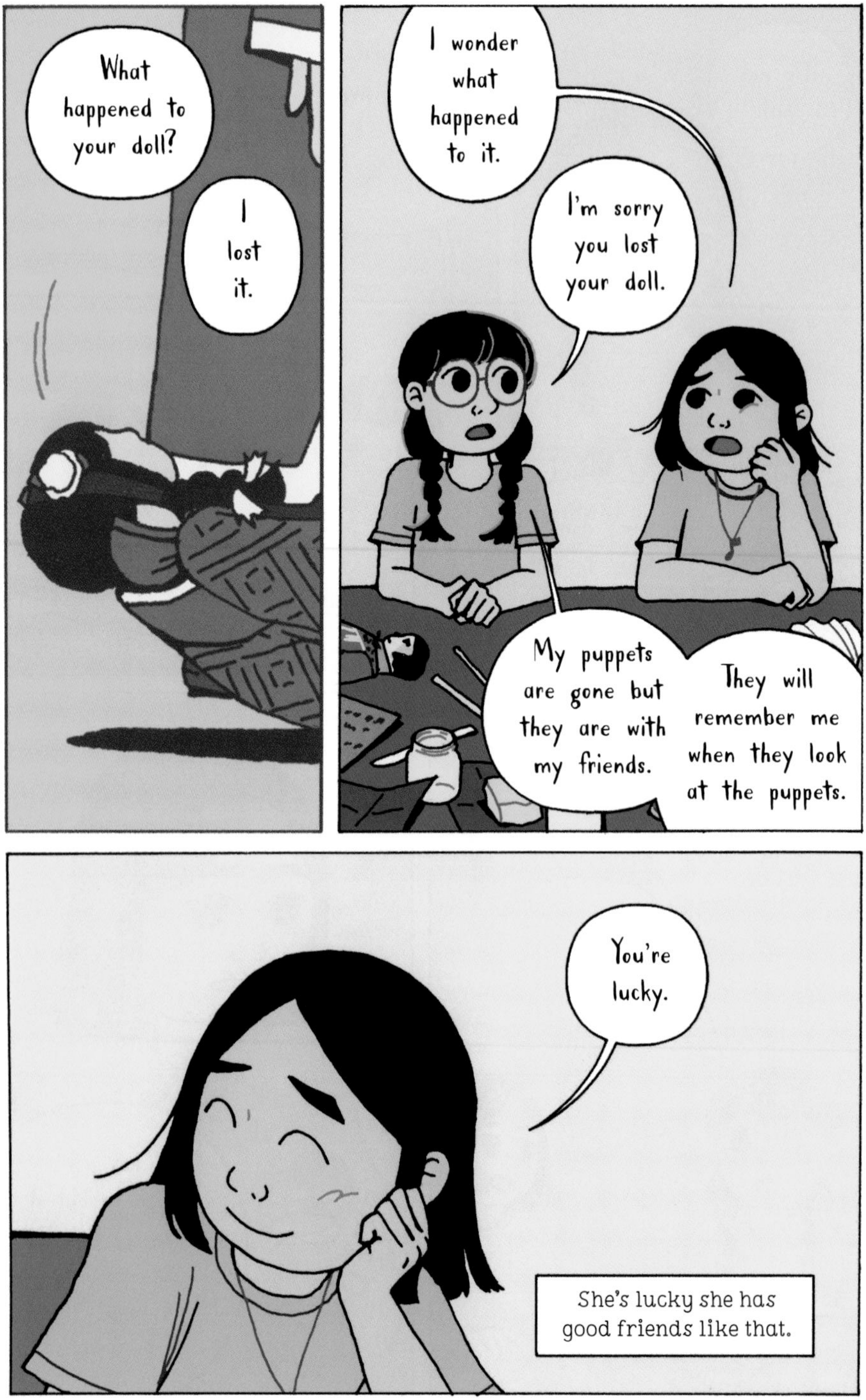
What happened to your doll?
I lost it.
I wonder what happened to it.
I'm sorry you lost your doll.
My puppets are gone but they are with my friends.
They will remember me when they look at the puppets.
You're lucky.
She's lucky she has good friends like that.

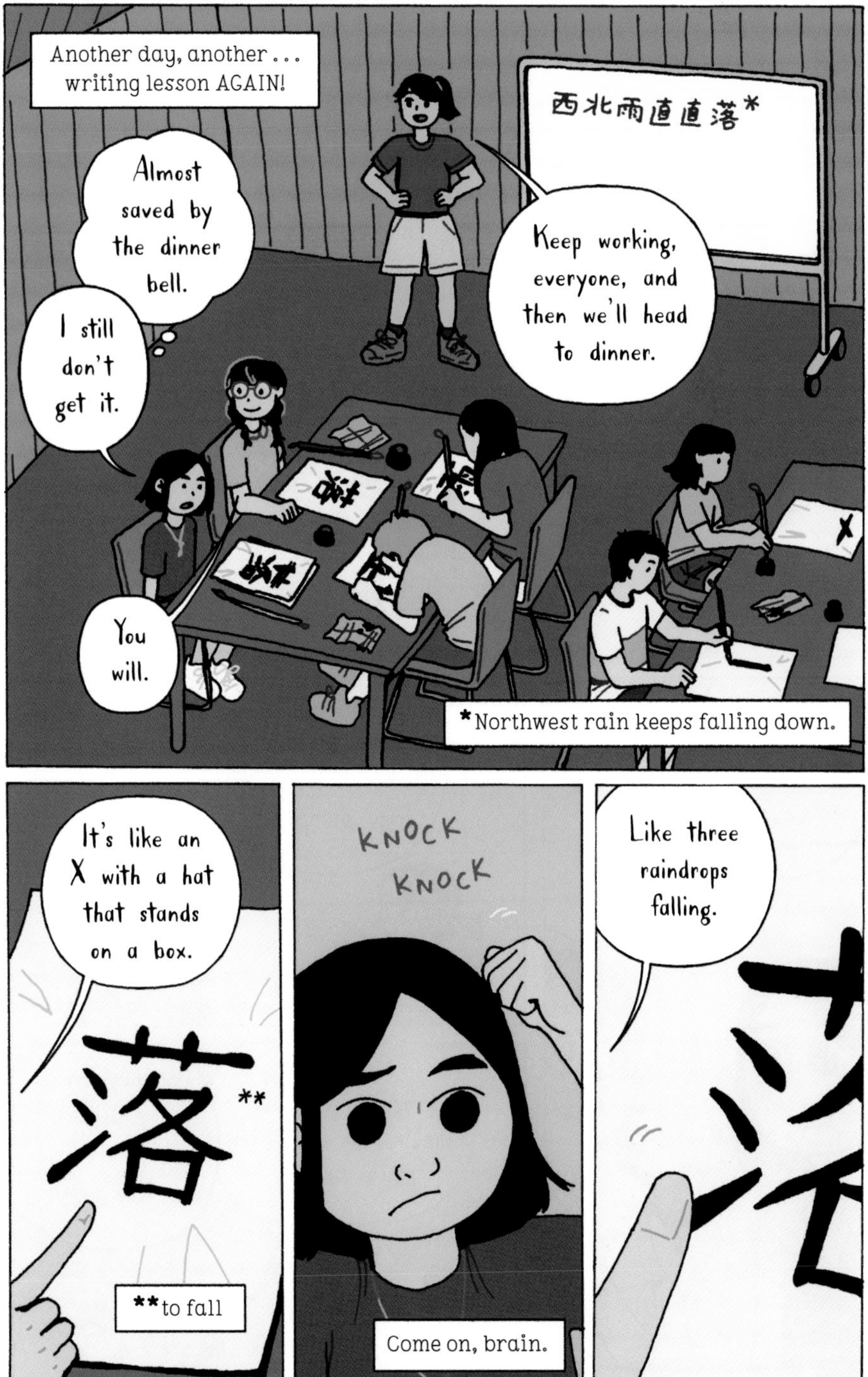
Another day, another . . . writing lesson AGAIN!
西北雨直直落*
Almost saved by the dinner bell.
Keep working, everyone, and then we'll head to dinner.
I still don't get it.
You will.
*Northwest rain keeps falling down.
It's like an X with a hat that stands on a box.
落**
**to fall
KNOCK
KNOCK
Come on, brain.
Like three raindrops falling.

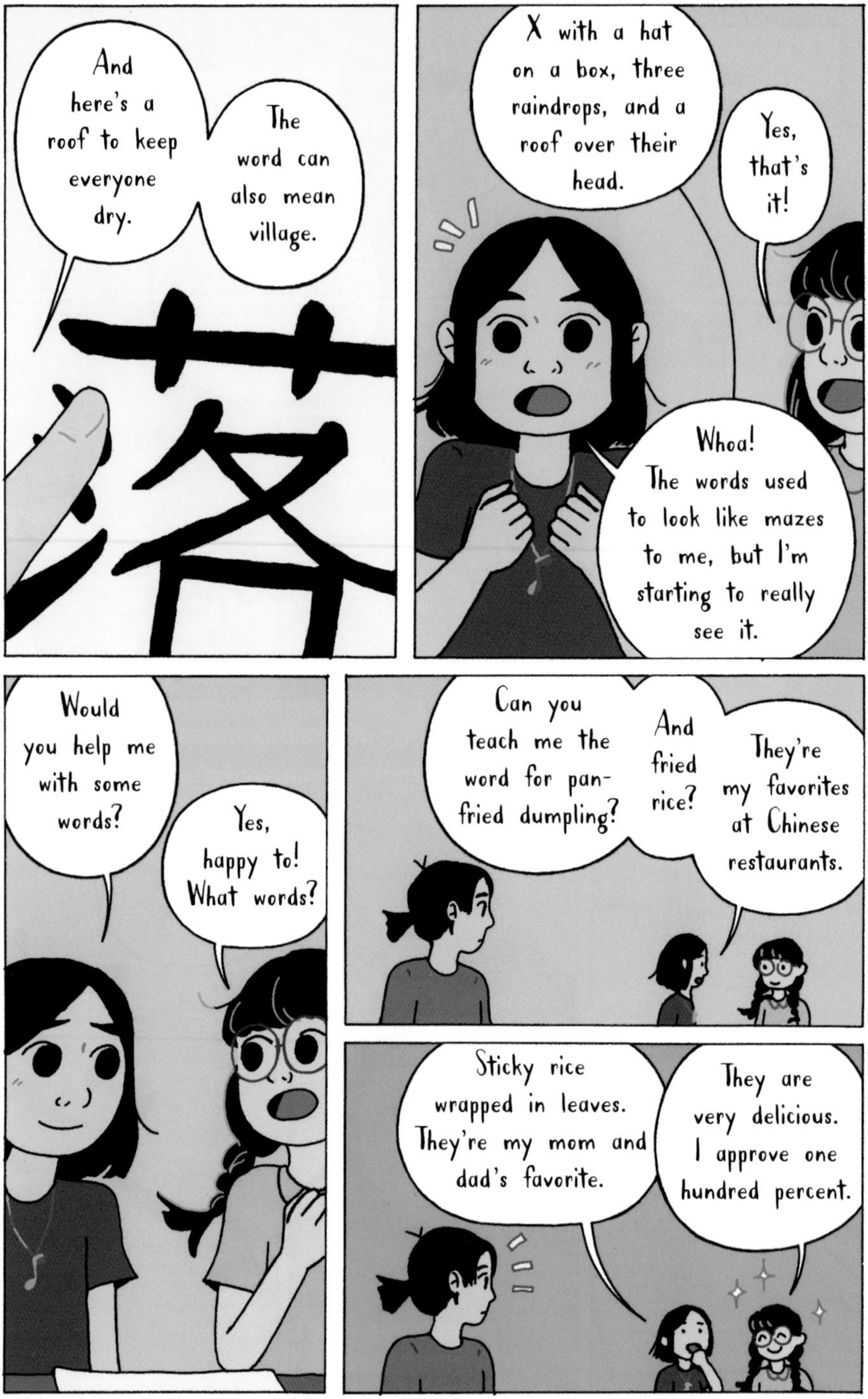
And here's a roof to keep everyone dry.
The word can also mean village.
落
X with a hat on a box, three raindrops, and a roof over their head.
Yes, that's it!
Whoa! The words used to look like mazes to me, but I'm starting to really see it.
Would you help me with some words?
Yes, happy to! What words?
Can you teach me the word for pan-fried dumpling?
And fried rice?
They're my favorites at Chinese restaurants.
Sticky rice wrapped in leaves. They're my mom and dad's favorite.
They are very delicious. I approve one hundred percent.

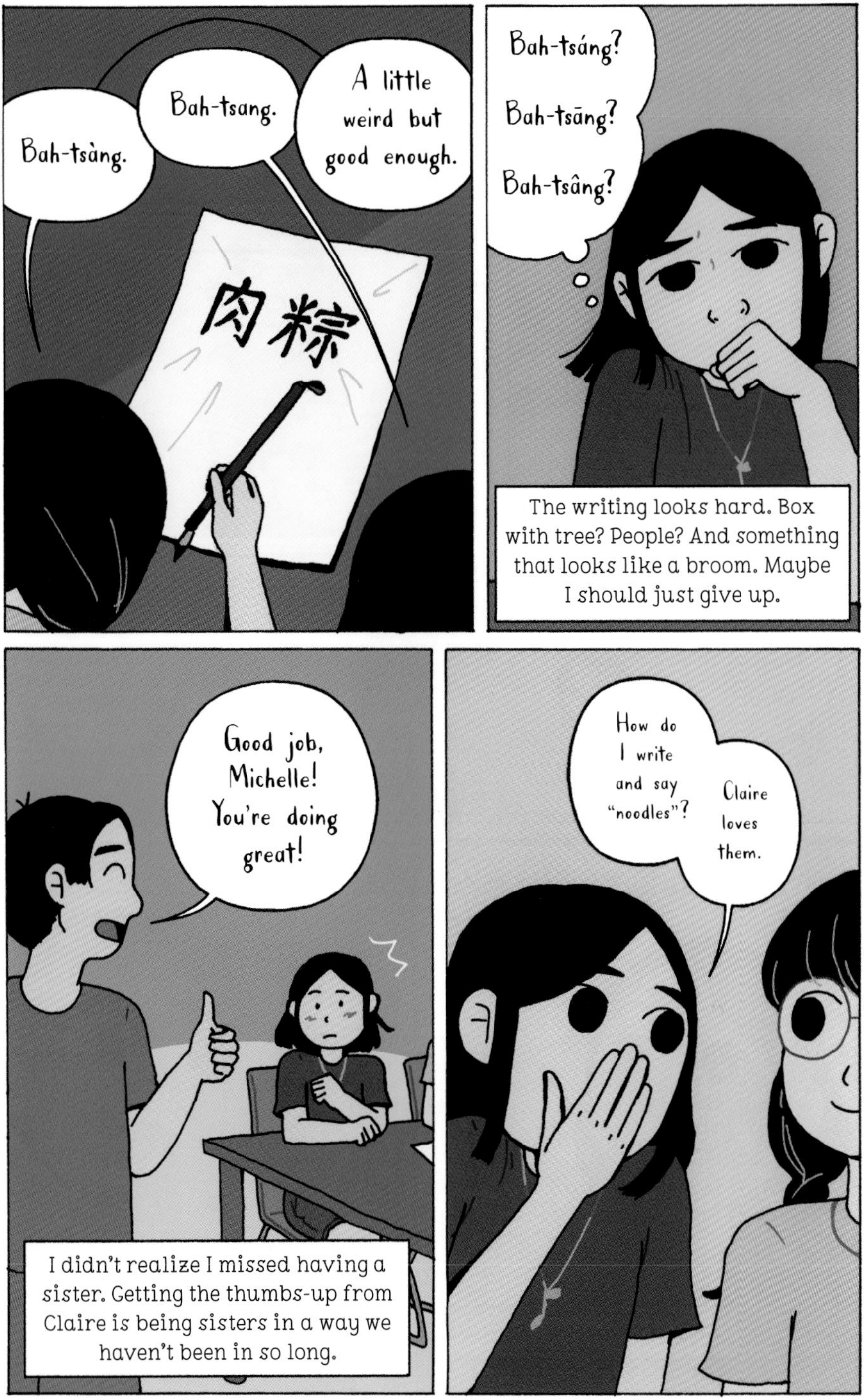
Bah-tsàng.
Bah-tsang.
A little weird but good enough.
肉粽
Bah-tsáng?
Bah-tsāng?
Bah-tsâng?
The writing looks hard. Box with tree? People? And something that looks like a broom. Maybe I should just give up.
Good job, Michelle! You're doing great!
I didn't realize I missed having a sister. Getting the thumbs-up from Claire is being sisters in a way we haven't been in so long.
How do I write and say "noodles"?
Claire loves them.

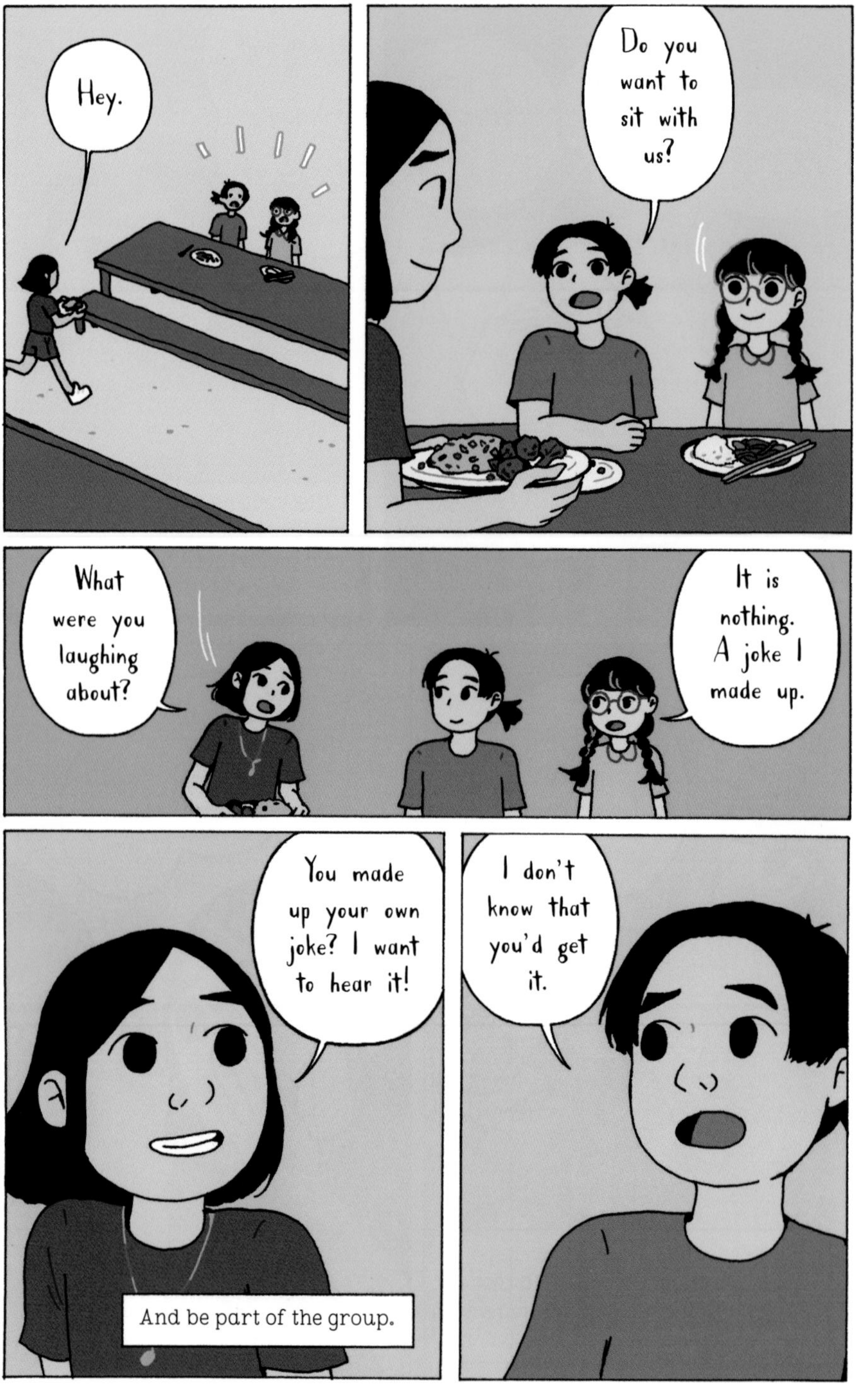
Hey.
Do you want to sit with us?
What were you laughing about?
It is nothing. A joke I made up.
You made up your own joke? I want to hear it!
And be part of the group.
I don't know that you'd get it.

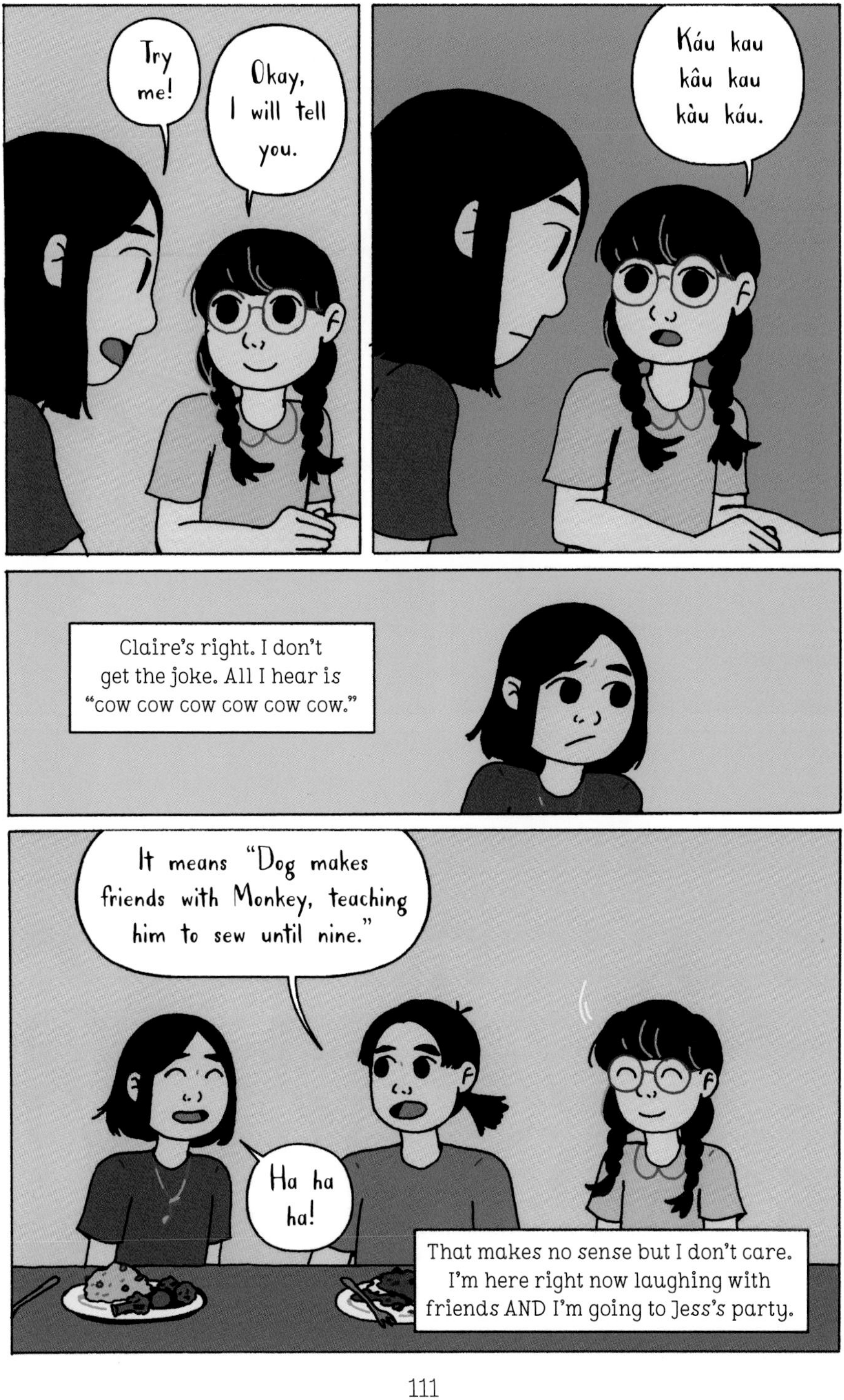
Try me!
Okay, I will tell you.
Káu kau kâu kau kàu káu.
Claire's right. I don't get the joke. All I hear is "COW COW COW COW COW COW."
It means "Dog makes friends with Monkey, teaching him to sew until nine."
Ha ha ha!
That makes no sense but I don't care. I'm here right now laughing with friends AND I'm going to Jess's party.

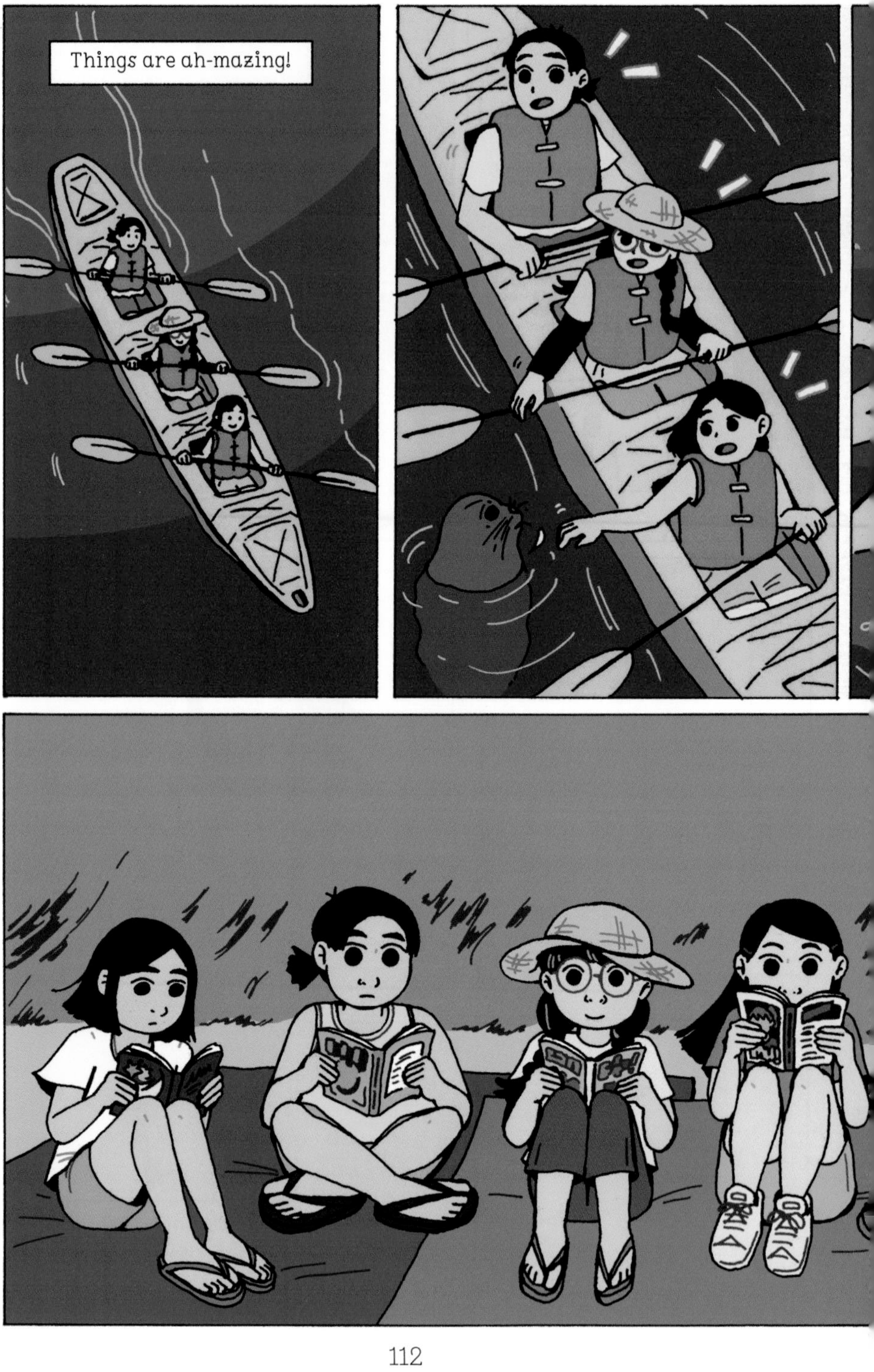
Things are ah-mazing!

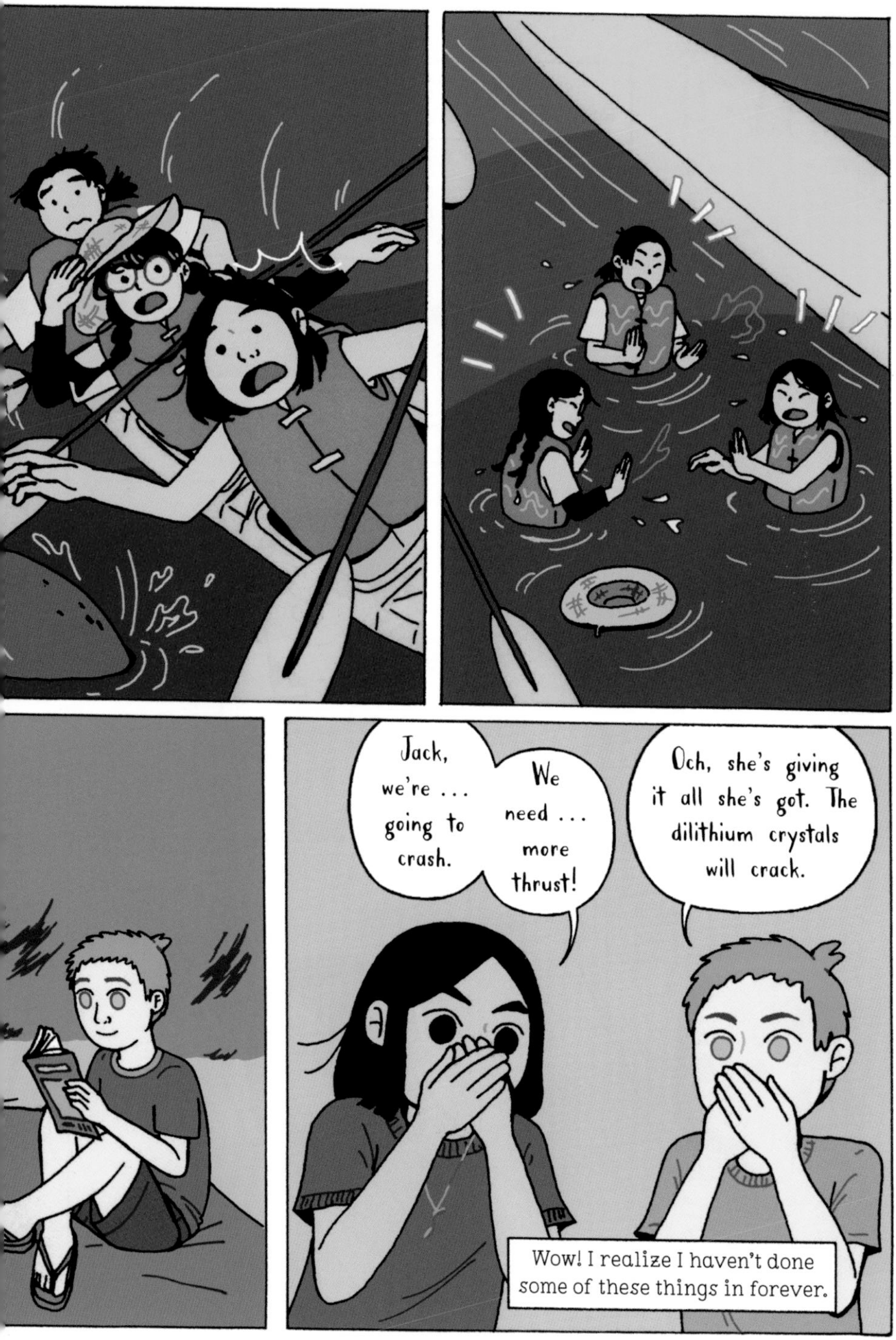

Jack, we're ... going to crash.
We need ... more thrust!
Och, she's giving it all she's got. The dilithium crystals will crack.
Wow! I realize I haven't done some of these things in forever.

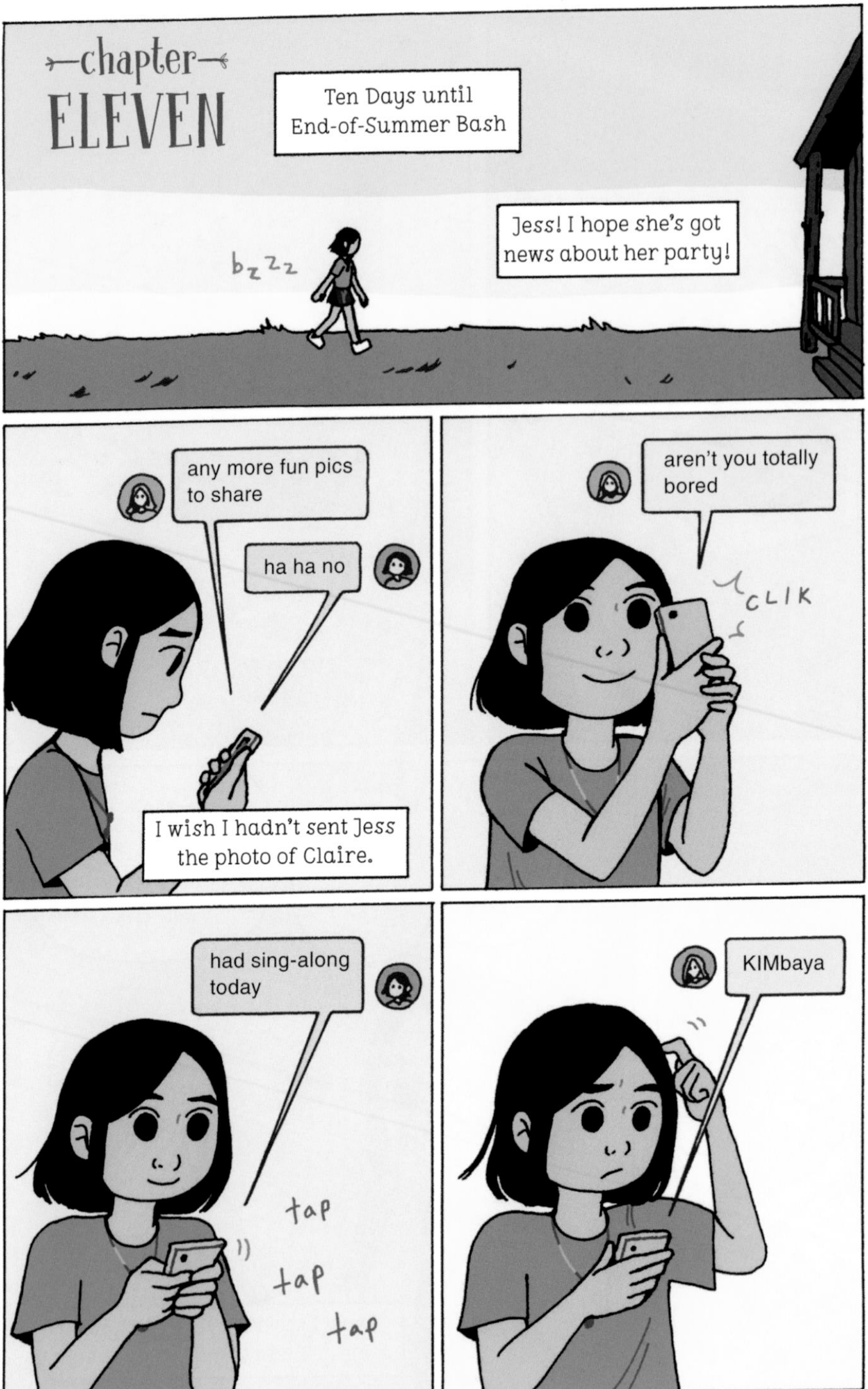
chapter
ELEVEN
Ten Days until End-of-Summer Bash
bzzz
Jess! I hope she's got news about her party!
any more fun pics to share
ha ha no
I wish I hadn't sent Jess the photo of Claire.
aren't you totally bored
CLIK
had sing-along today
tap
tap
tap
KIMbaya

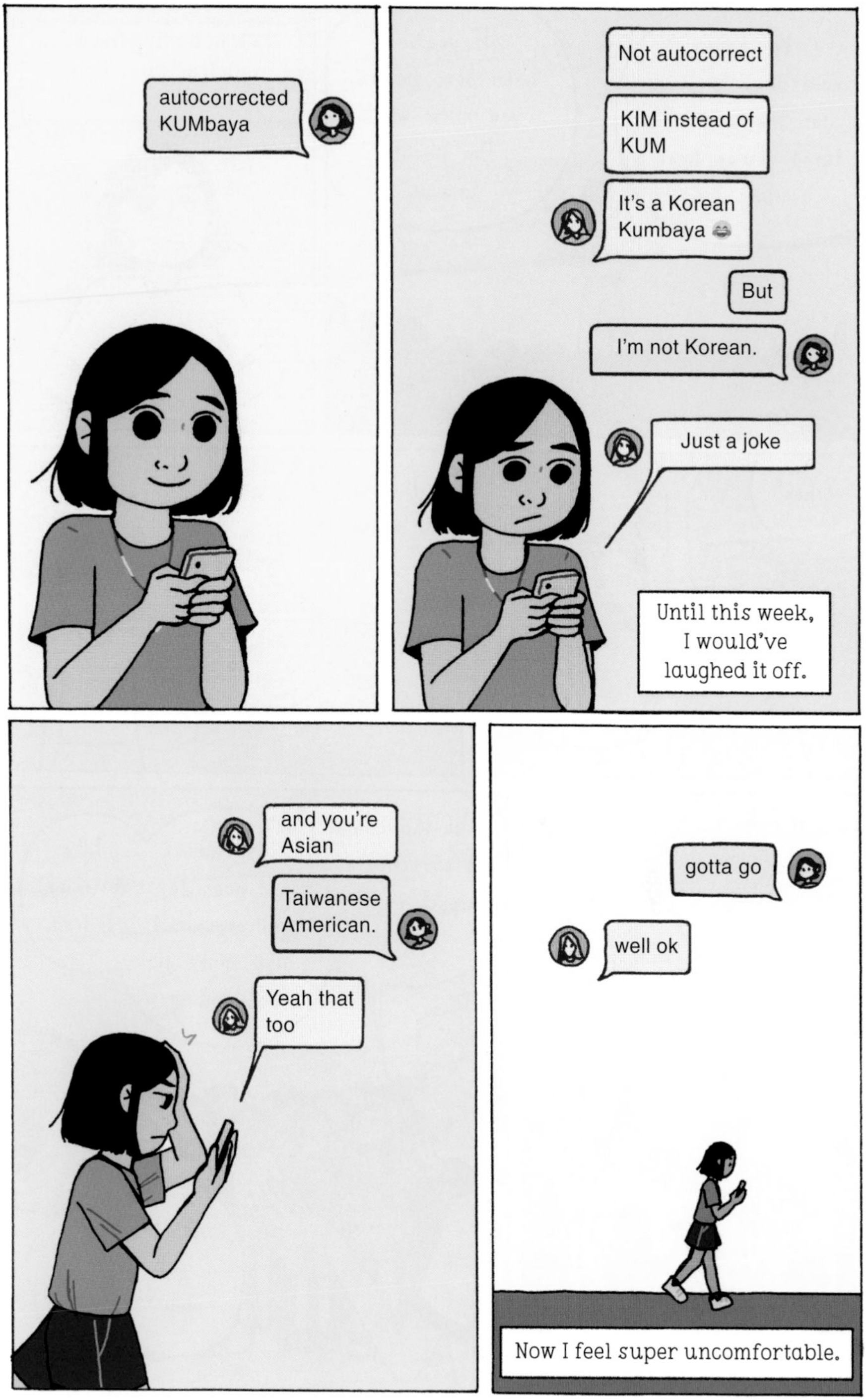
autocorrected KUMbaya
Not autocorrect
KIM instead of KUM
It's a Korean Kumbaya
But
I'm not Korean.
Just a joke
Until this week, I would've laughed it off.
and you're Asian
Taiwanese American.
Yeah that too
gotta go
well ok
Now I feel *super* uncomfortable.

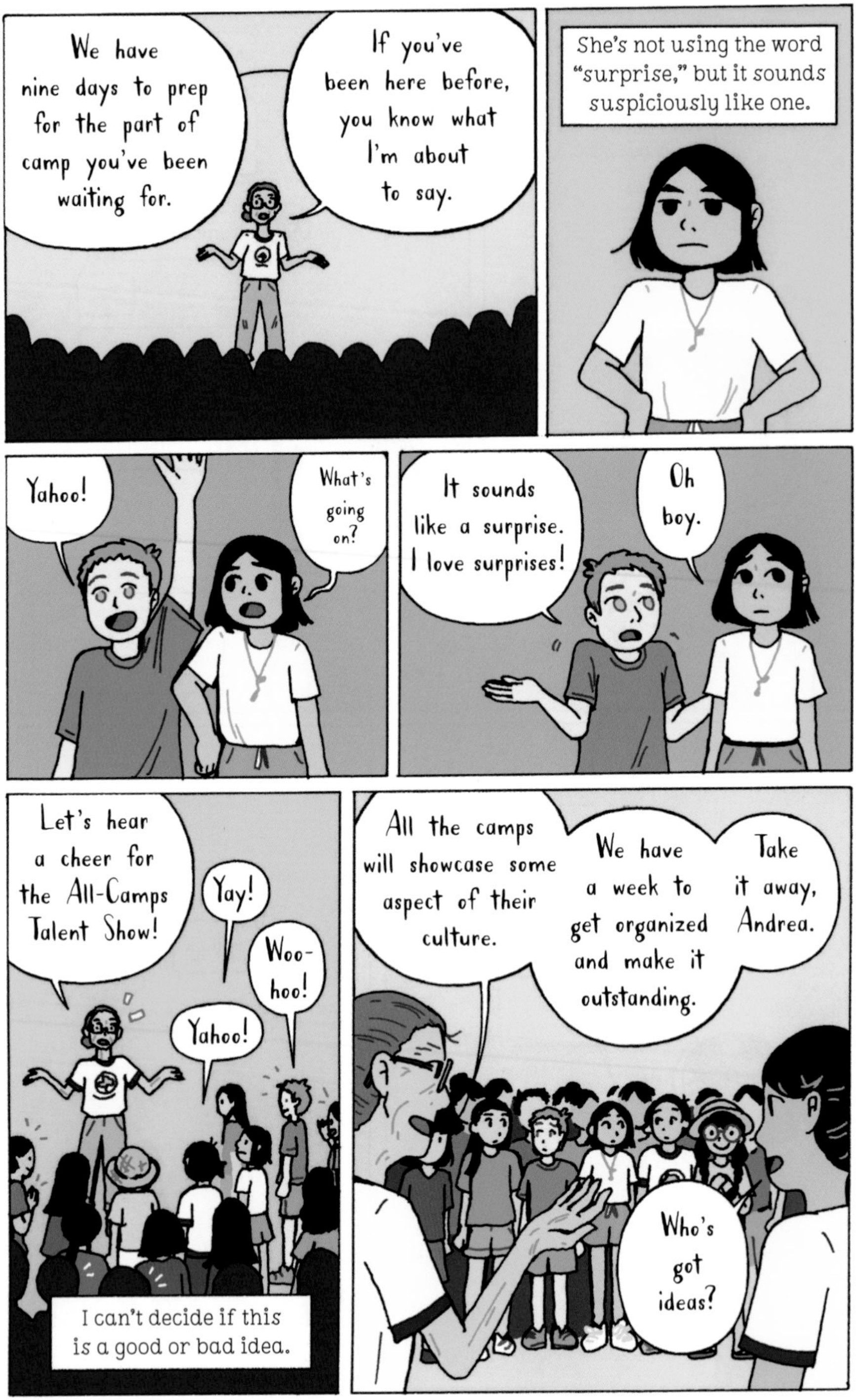
We have nine days to prep for the part of camp you've been waiting for.
If you've been here before, you know what I'm about to say.
She's not using the word "surprise," but it sounds suspiciously like one.
Yahoo!
What's going on?
It sounds like a surprise. I love surprises!
Oh boy.
Let's hear a cheer for the All-Camps Talent Show!
Yay!
Woo-hoo!
Yahoo!
I can't decide if this is a good or bad idea.
All the camps will showcase some aspect of their culture.
We have a week to get organized and make it outstanding.
Take it away, Andrea.
Who's got ideas?

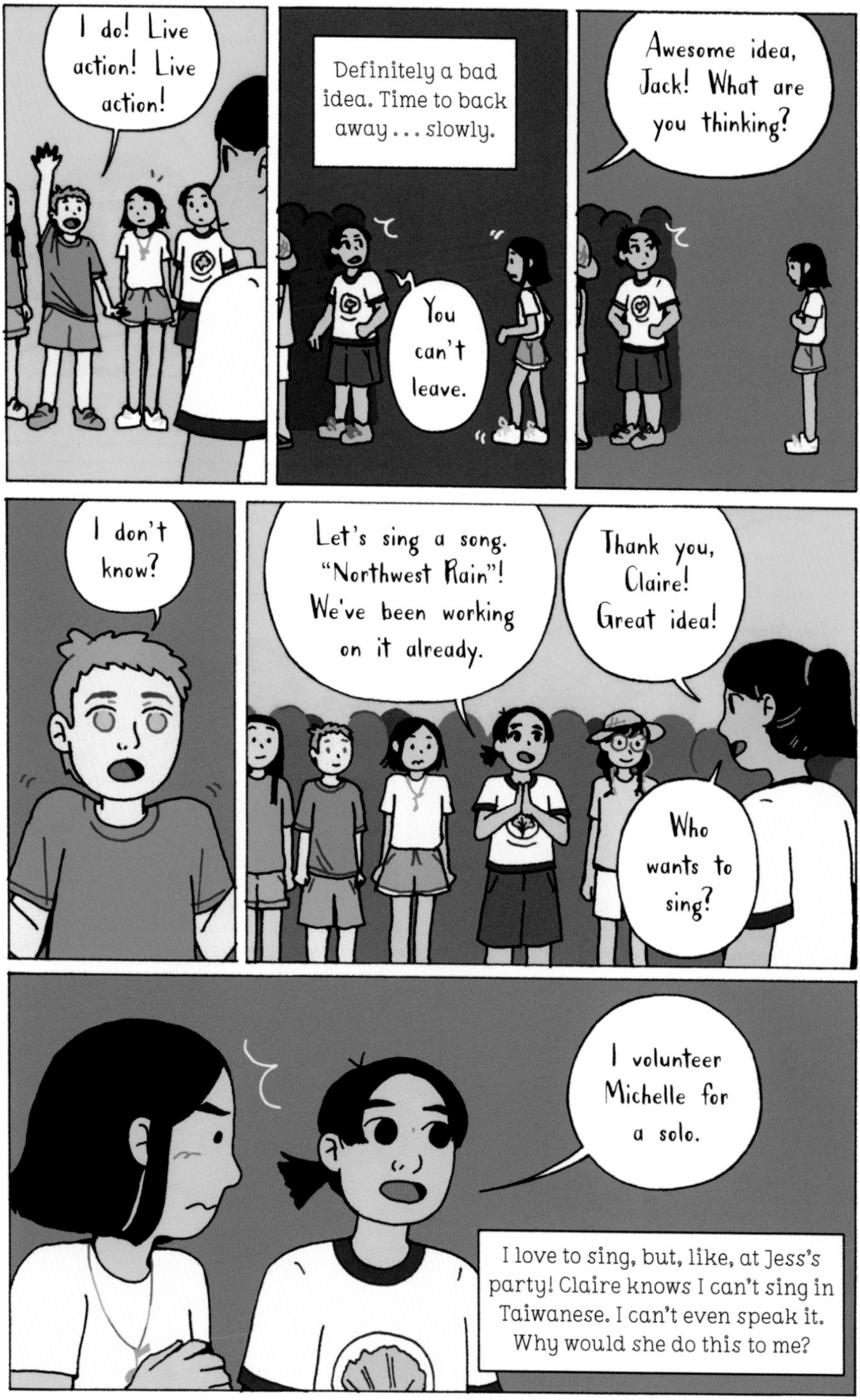
I do! Live action! Live action!
Definitely a bad idea. Time to back away . . . slowly.
You can't leave.
Awesome idea, Jack! What are you thinking?
I don't know?
Let's sing a song. "Northwest Rain"! We've been working on it already.
Thank you, Claire! Great idea!
Who wants to sing?
I volunteer Michelle for a solo.
I love to sing, but, like, at Jess's party! Claire knows I can't sing in Taiwanese. I can't even speak it. Why would she do this to me?

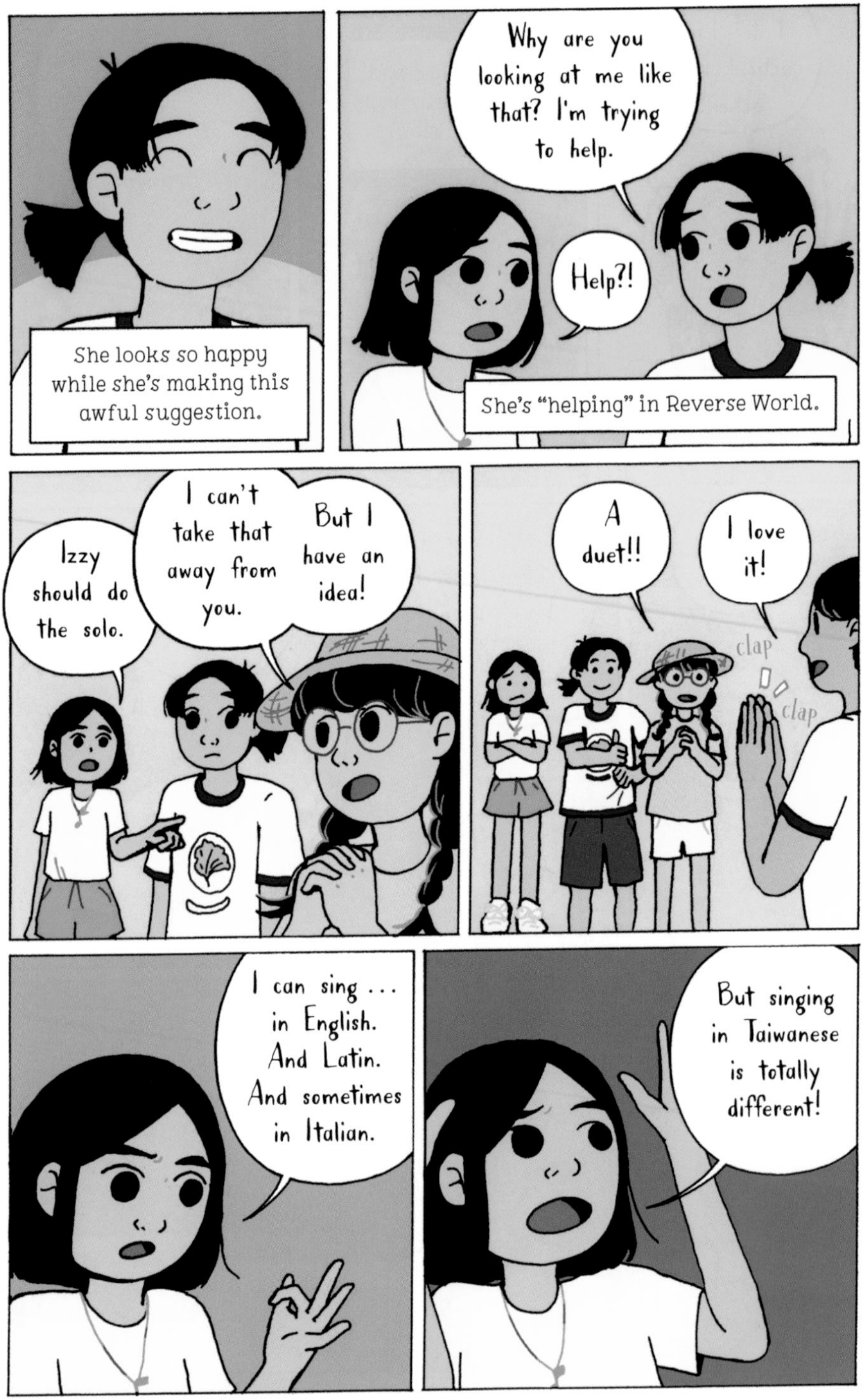
She looks so happy while she's making this awful suggestion.
Why are you looking at me like that? I'm trying to help.
Help?!
She's "helping" in Reverse World.
Izzy should do the solo.
I can't take that away from you.
But I have an idea!
A duet!!
I love it!
clap
clap
I can sing . . . in English. And Latin. And sometimes in Italian.
But singing in Taiwanese is totally different!

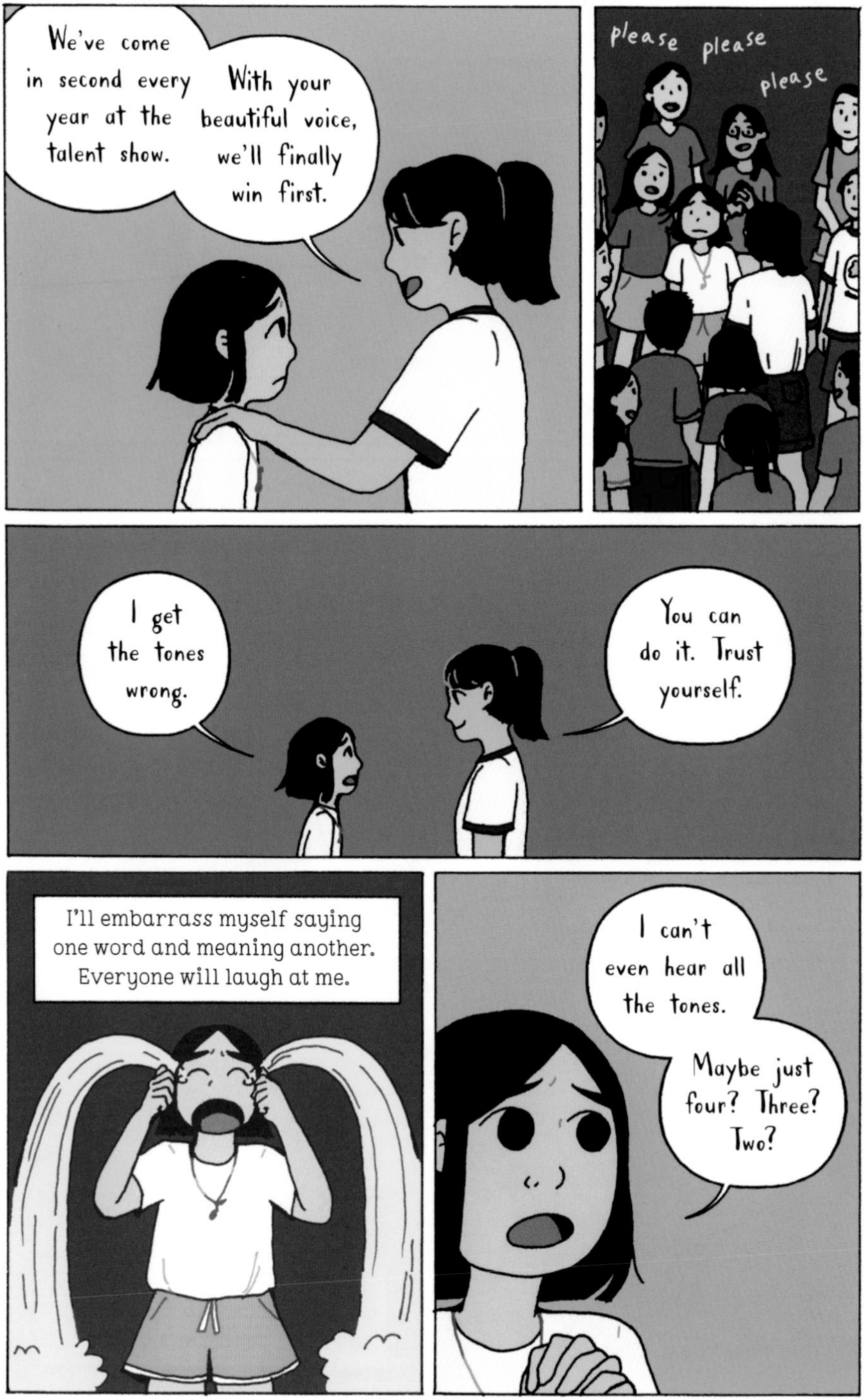
We've come in second every year at the talent show.
With your beautiful voice, we'll finally win first.
please please please
I get the tones wrong.
You can do it. Trust yourself.
I'll embarrass myself saying one word and meaning another. Everyone will laugh at me.
I can't even hear all the tones.
Maybe just four? Three? Two?

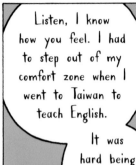

Listen, I know how you feel. I had to step out of my comfort zone when I went to Taiwan to teach English.

It was hard being in a foreign country.

But... but—

This camp must feel like a foreign country to you.

She knows how I feel!

By stepping out of my comfort zone, I learned so much about Taiwanese culture and about myself.

I was scared, but I'm so happy I did it. You will be, too.

I don't want to force you, but maybe you could just try, and we can see how it goes?

They're all looking at me to give us a chance to win. If I don't do it, I'll be the outsider here.

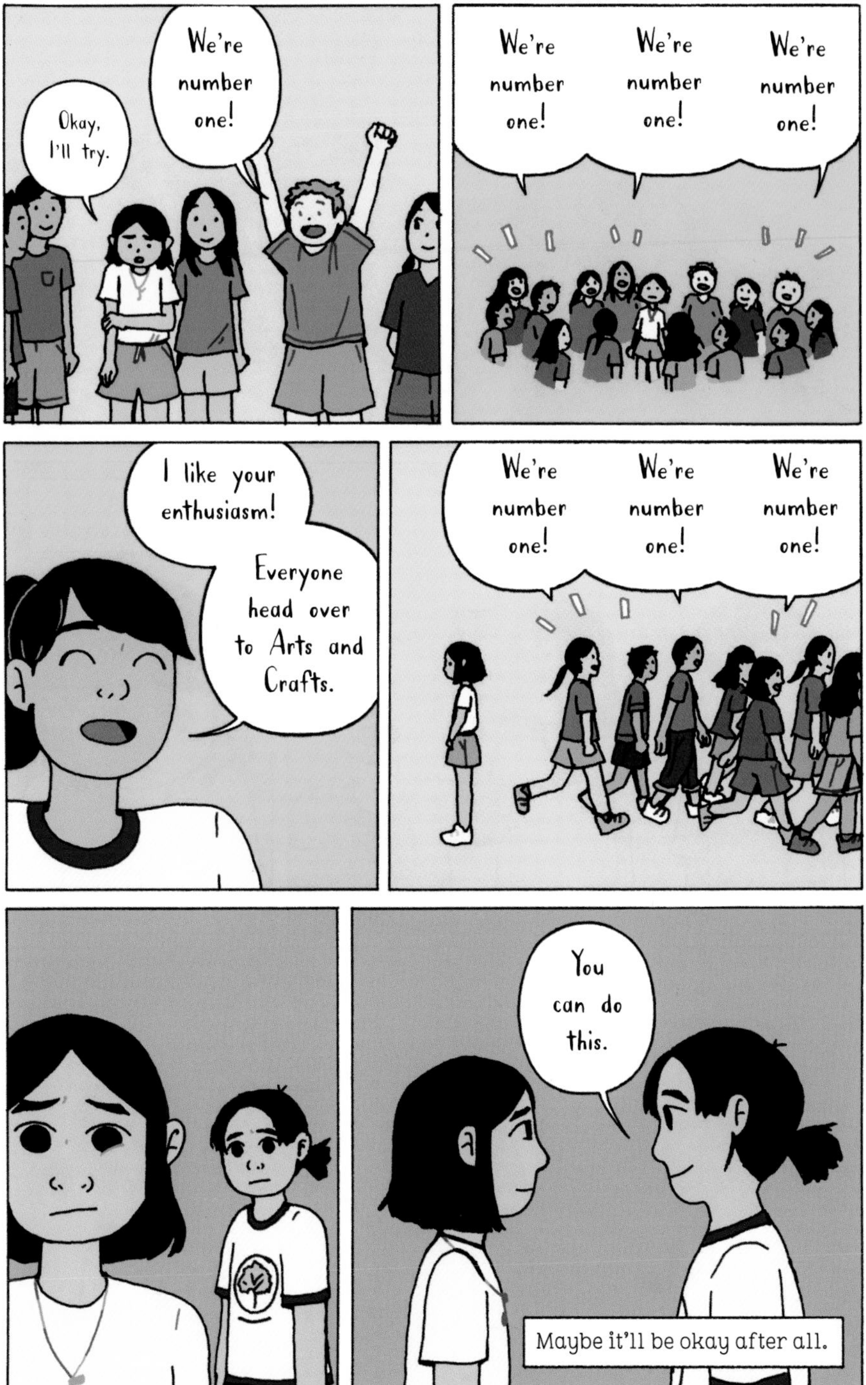
Okay, I'll try.
We're number one!
We're number one!
We're number one!
We're number one!
I like your enthusiasm!
Everyone head over to Arts and Crafts.
We're number one!
We're number one!
We're number one!
You can do this.
Maybe it'll be okay after all.

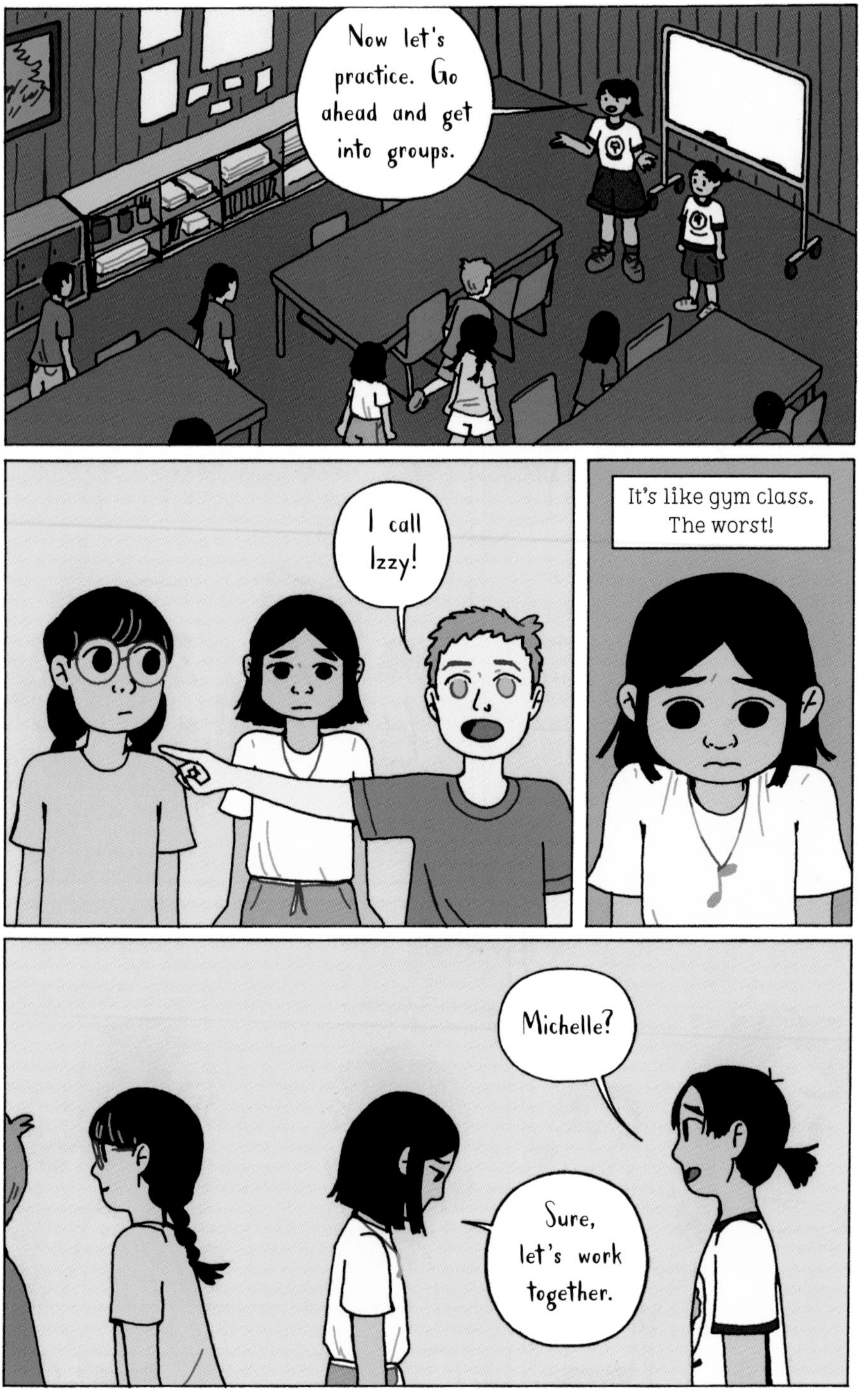
Now let's practice. Go ahead and get into groups.
I call Izzy!
It's like gym class. The worst!
Michelle?
Sure, let's work together.

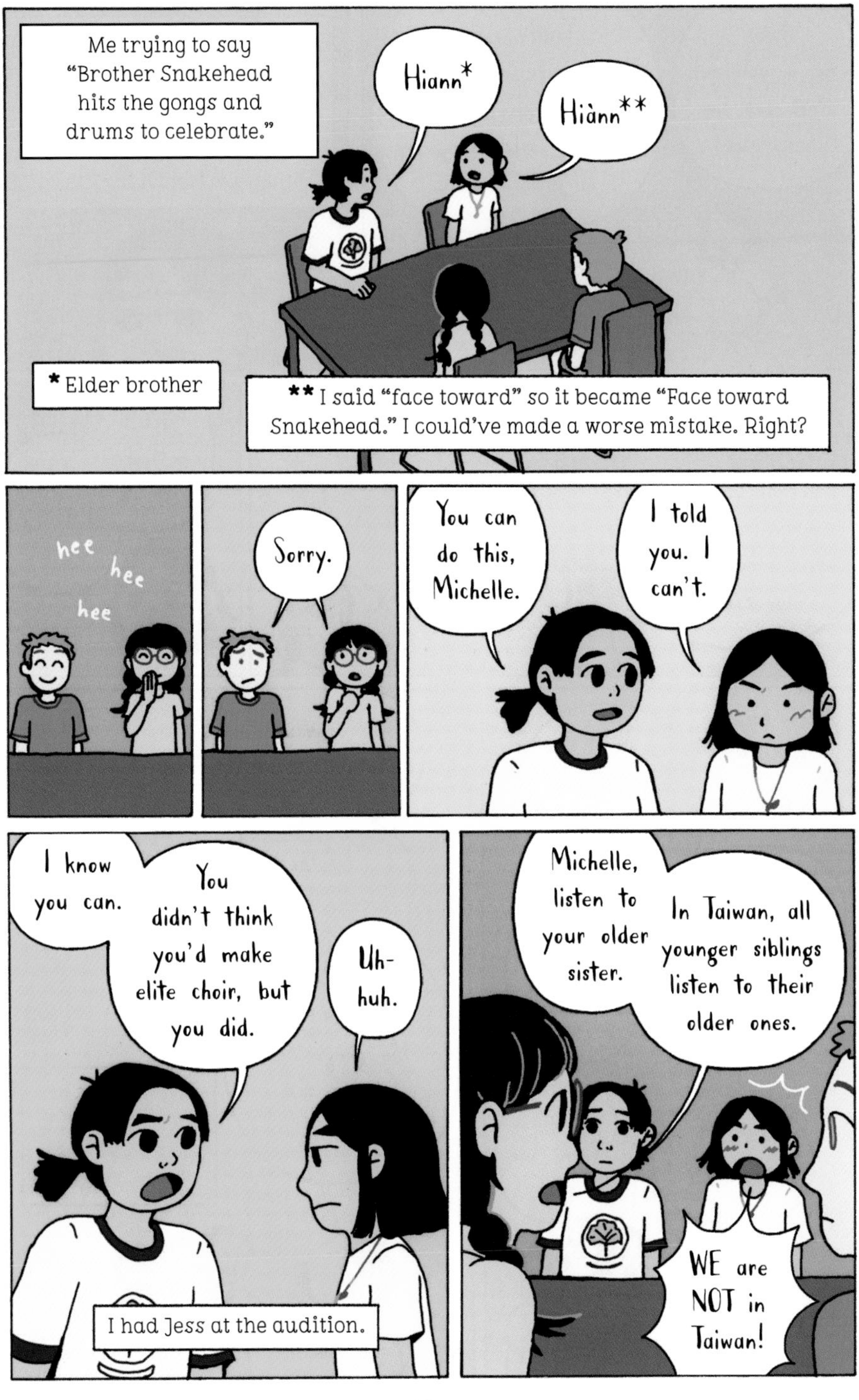
Me trying to say "Brother Snakehead hits the gongs and drums to celebrate."
Hiann*
Hiànn**
* Elder brother
** I said "face toward" so it became "Face toward Snakehead." I could've made a worse mistake. Right?
hee hee hee
Sorry.
You can do this, Michelle.
I told you. I can't.
I know you can.
You didn't think you'd make elite choir, but you did.
Uh-huh.
I had Jess at the audition.
Michelle, listen to your older sister.
In Taiwan, all younger siblings listen to their older ones.
WE are NOT in Taiwan!

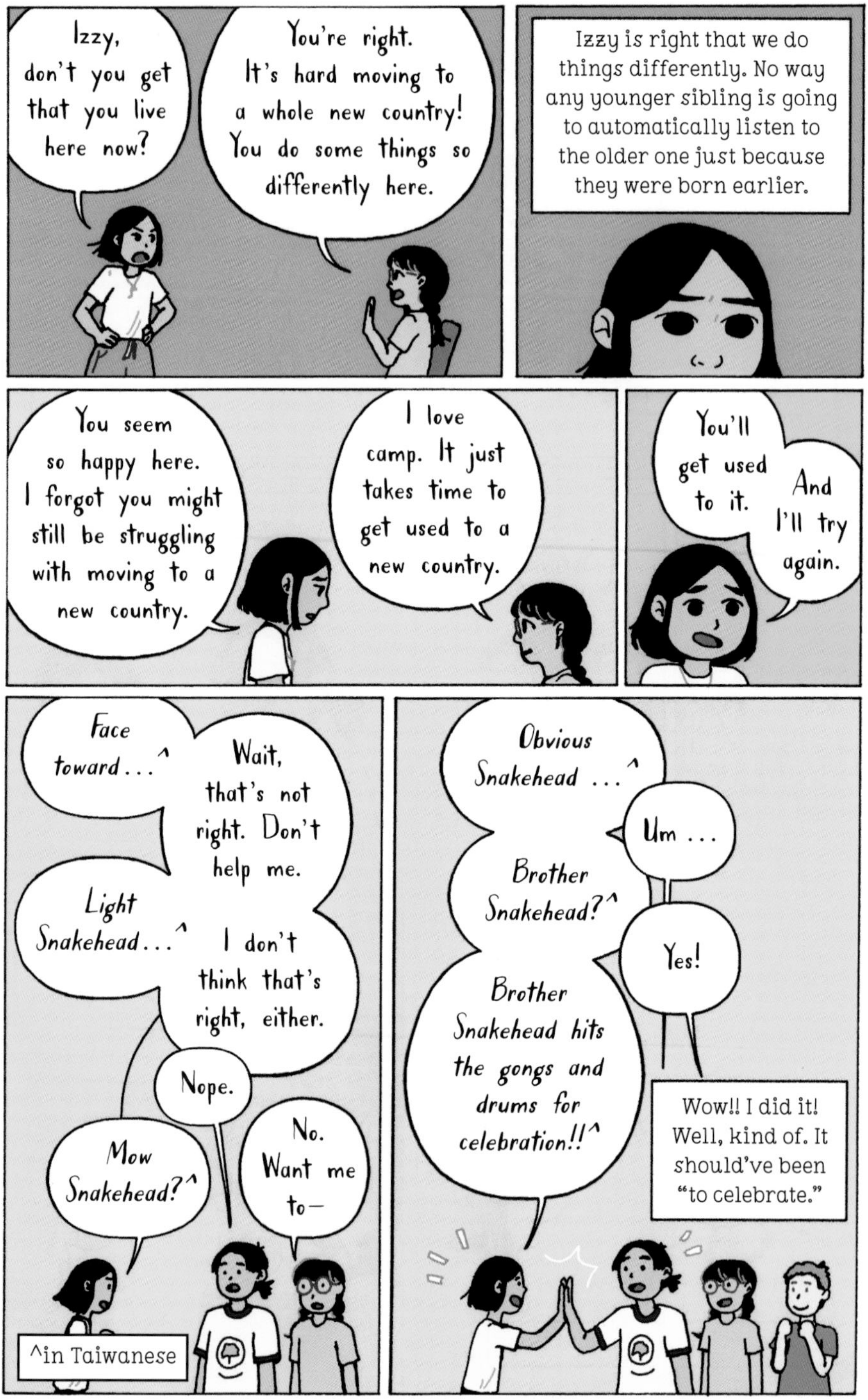
Izzy, don't you get that you live here now?
You're right. It's hard moving to a whole new country! You do some things so differently here.
Izzy is right that we do things differently. No way any younger sibling is going to automatically listen to the older one just because they were born earlier.
You seem so happy here. I forgot you might still be struggling with moving to a new country.
I love camp. It just takes time to get used to a new country.
You'll get used to it.
And I'll try again.
Face toward . . .^
Wait, that's not right. Don't help me.
Light Snakehead . . .^
I don't think that's right, either.
Nope.
Mow Snakehead?^
No. Want me to—
^in Taiwanese
Obvious Snakehead . . .^
Um . . .
Brother Snakehead?^
Yes!
Brother Snakehead hits the gongs and drums for celebration!!^
Wow!! I did it! Well, kind of. It should've been "to celebrate."

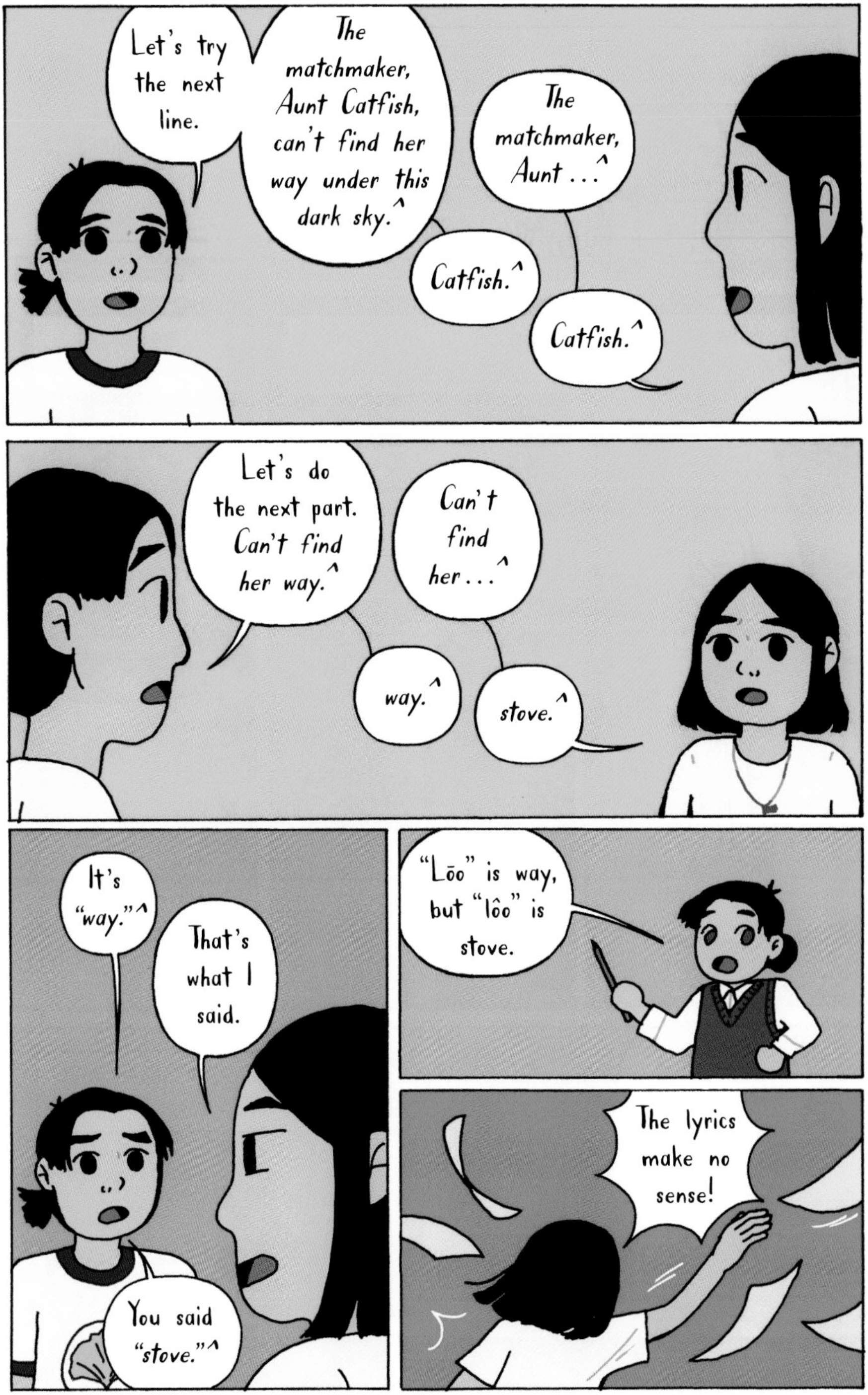
Let's try the next line.
The matchmaker, Aunt Catfish, can't find her way under this dark sky.^
The matchmaker, Aunt . . .^
Catfish.^
Catfish.^
Let's do the next part. Can't find her way.^
Can't find her . . .^
way.^
stove.^
It's "way."^
That's what I said.
You said "stove."^
"Lōo" is way, but "lôo" is stove.
The lyrics make no sense!

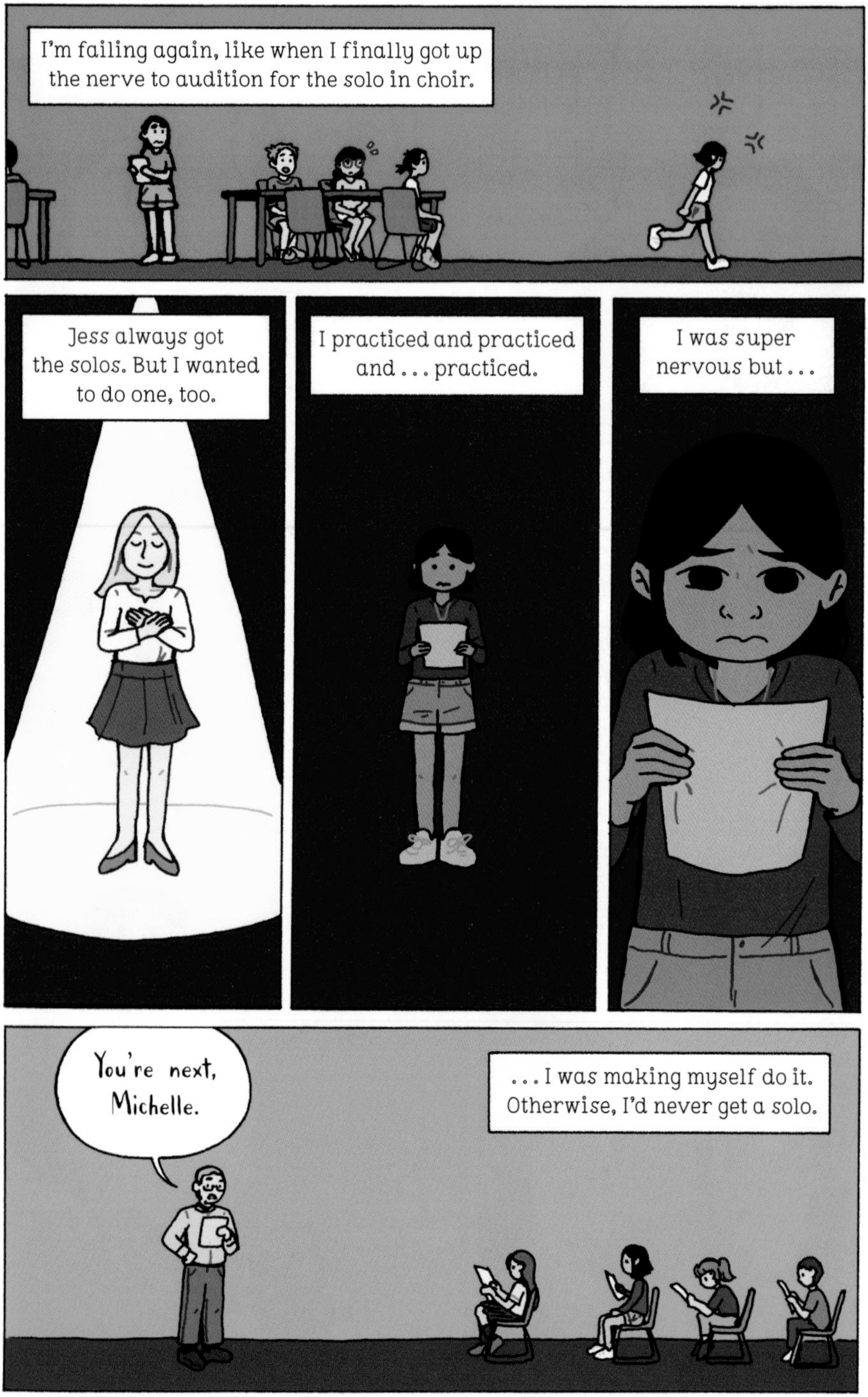
I'm failing again, like when I finally got up the nerve to audition for the solo in choir.
Jess always got the solos. But I wanted to do one, too.
I practiced and practiced and . . . practiced.
I was super nervous but . . .
You're next, Michelle.
. . . I was making myself do it. Otherwise, I'd never get a solo.

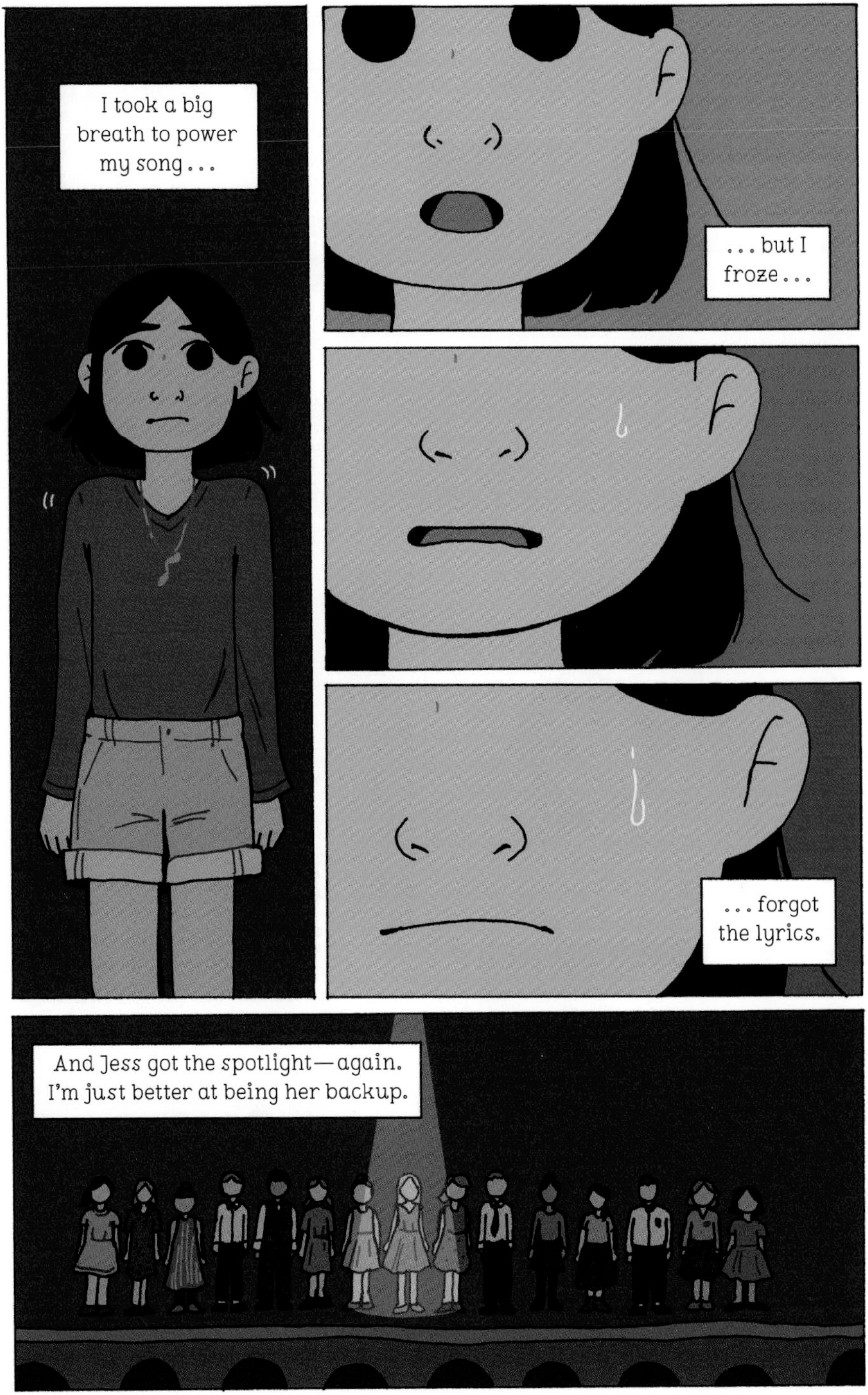
I took a big breath to power my *song* . . .
. . . but I froze . . .
. . . forgot the lyrics.
And Jess got the spotlight—again. I'm just better at being her backup.

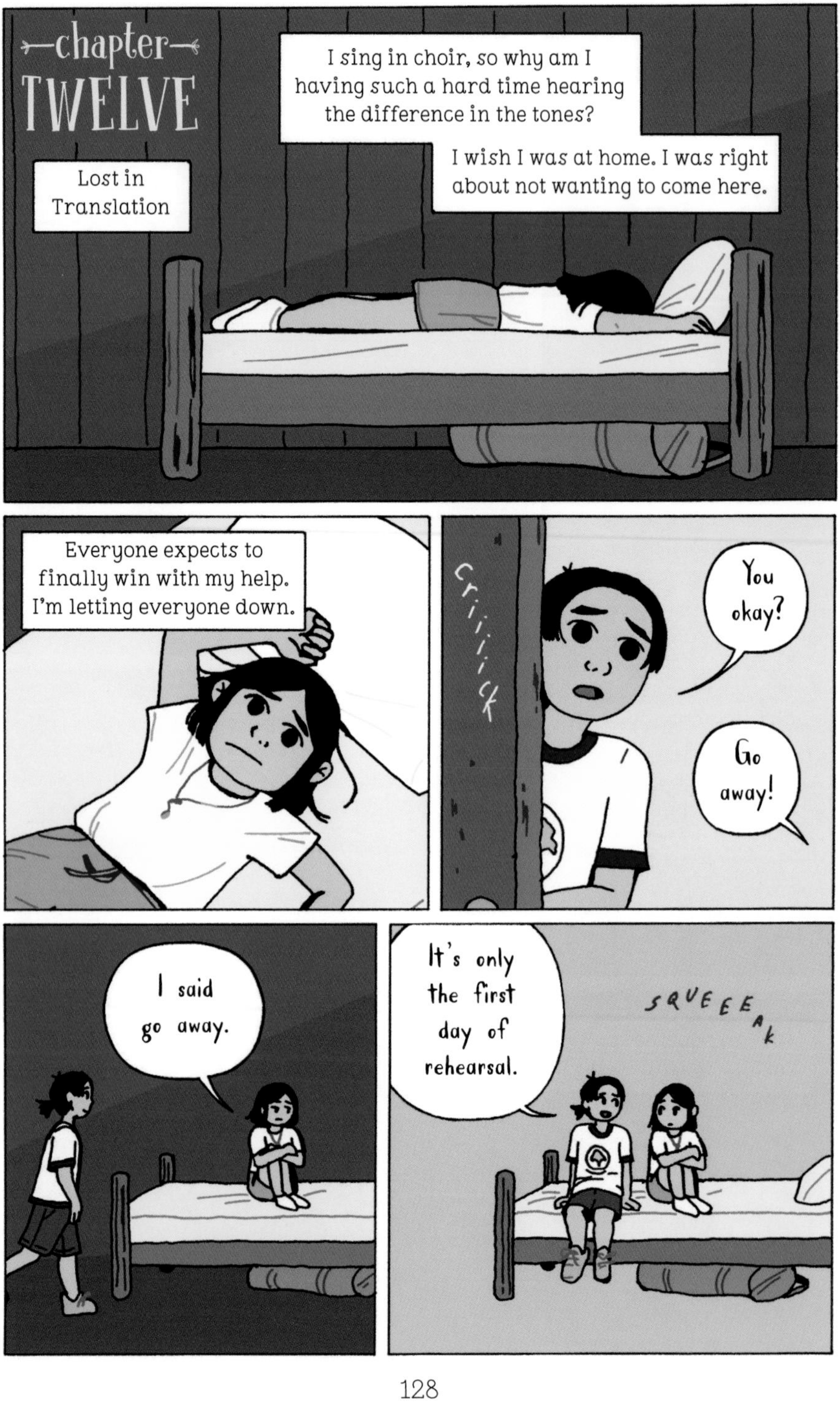
chapter
TWELVE
Lost in Translation
I sing in choir, so why am I having such a hard time hearing the difference in the tones?
I wish I was at home. I was right about not wanting to come here.
Everyone expects to finally win with my help. I'm letting everyone down.
Criiiick
You okay?
Go away!
I said go away.
It's only the first day of rehearsal.
SQUEEEAk

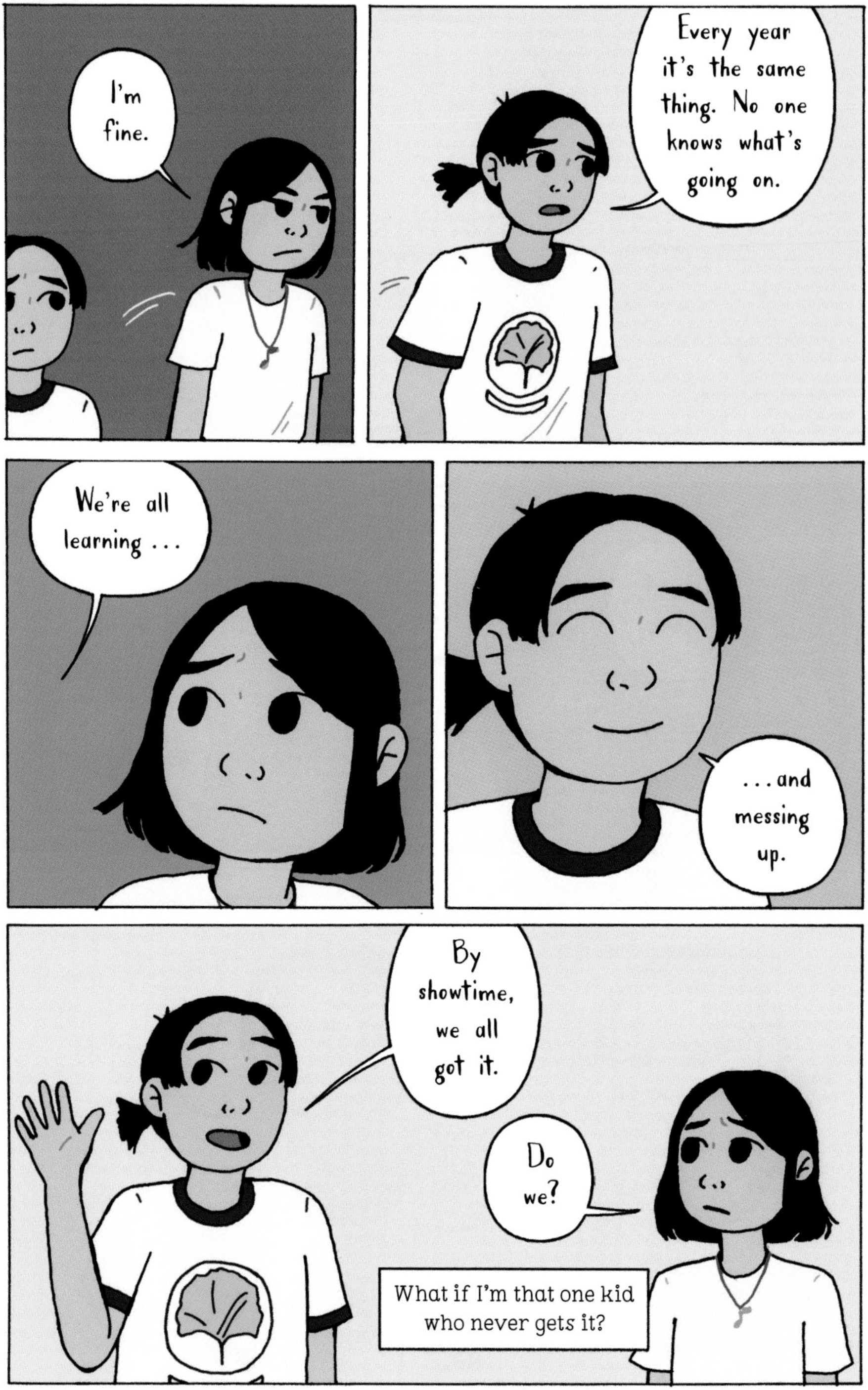
I'm fine.
Every year it's the same thing. No one knows what's going on.
We're all learning . . .
. . . and messing up.
By showtime, we all got it.
Do we?
What if I'm that one kid who never gets it?

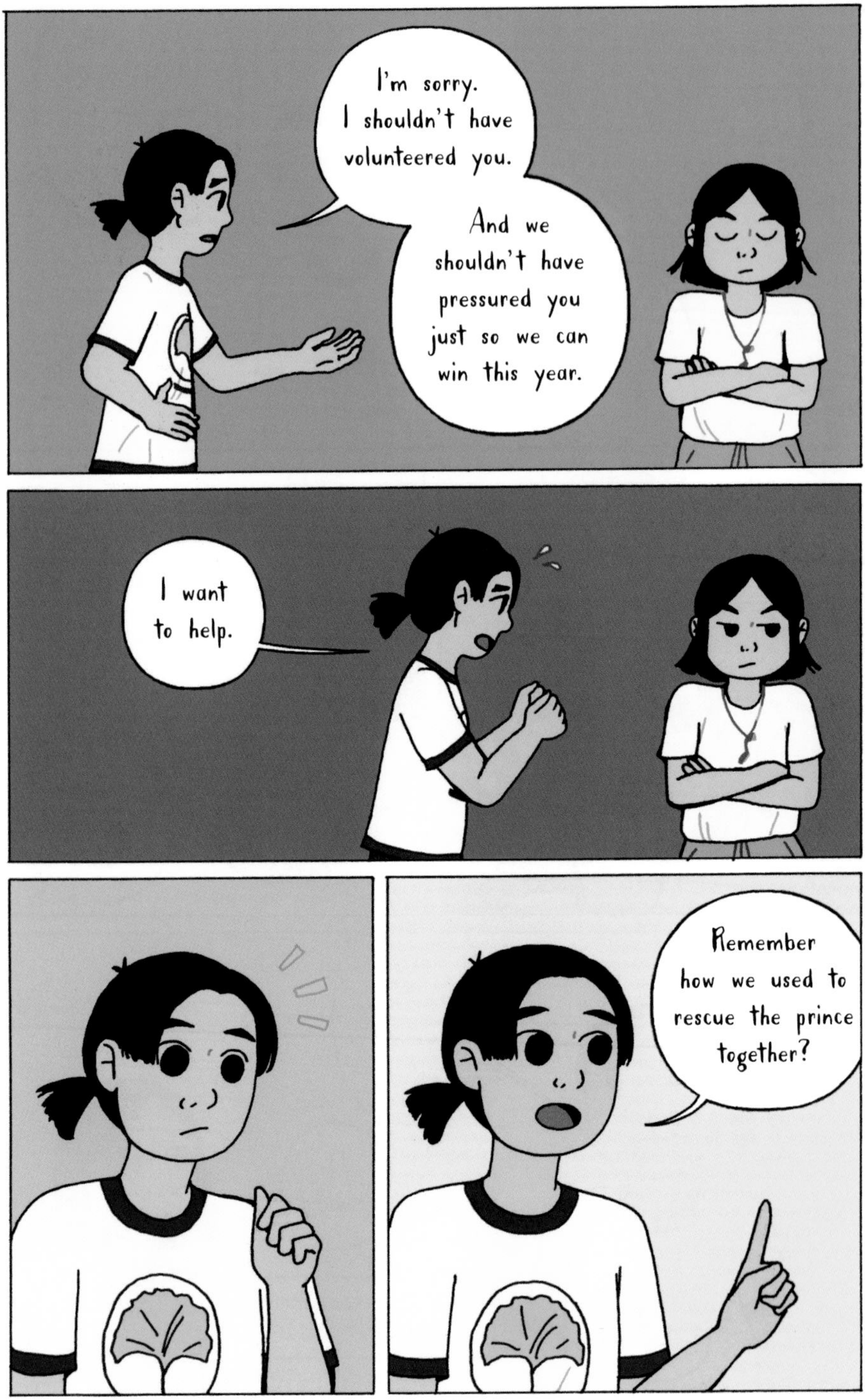
I'm sorry. I shouldn't have volunteered you.
And we shouldn't have pressured you just so we can win this year.
I want to help.
Remember how we used to rescue the prince together?

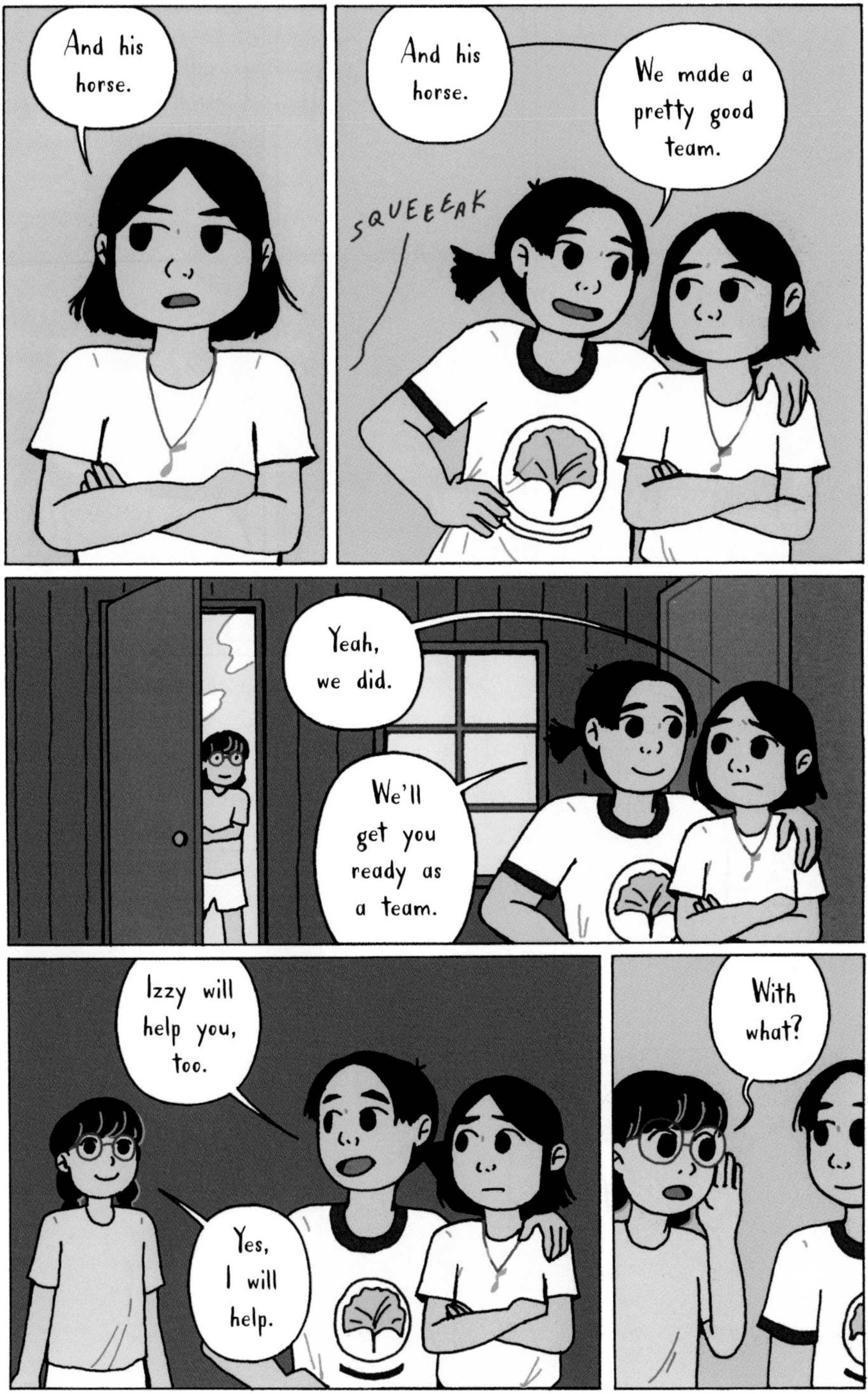
And his horse.
And his horse.
We made a pretty good team.
SQUEEEAK
Yeah, we did.
We'll get you ready as a team.
Izzy will help you, too.
Yes, I will help.
With what?

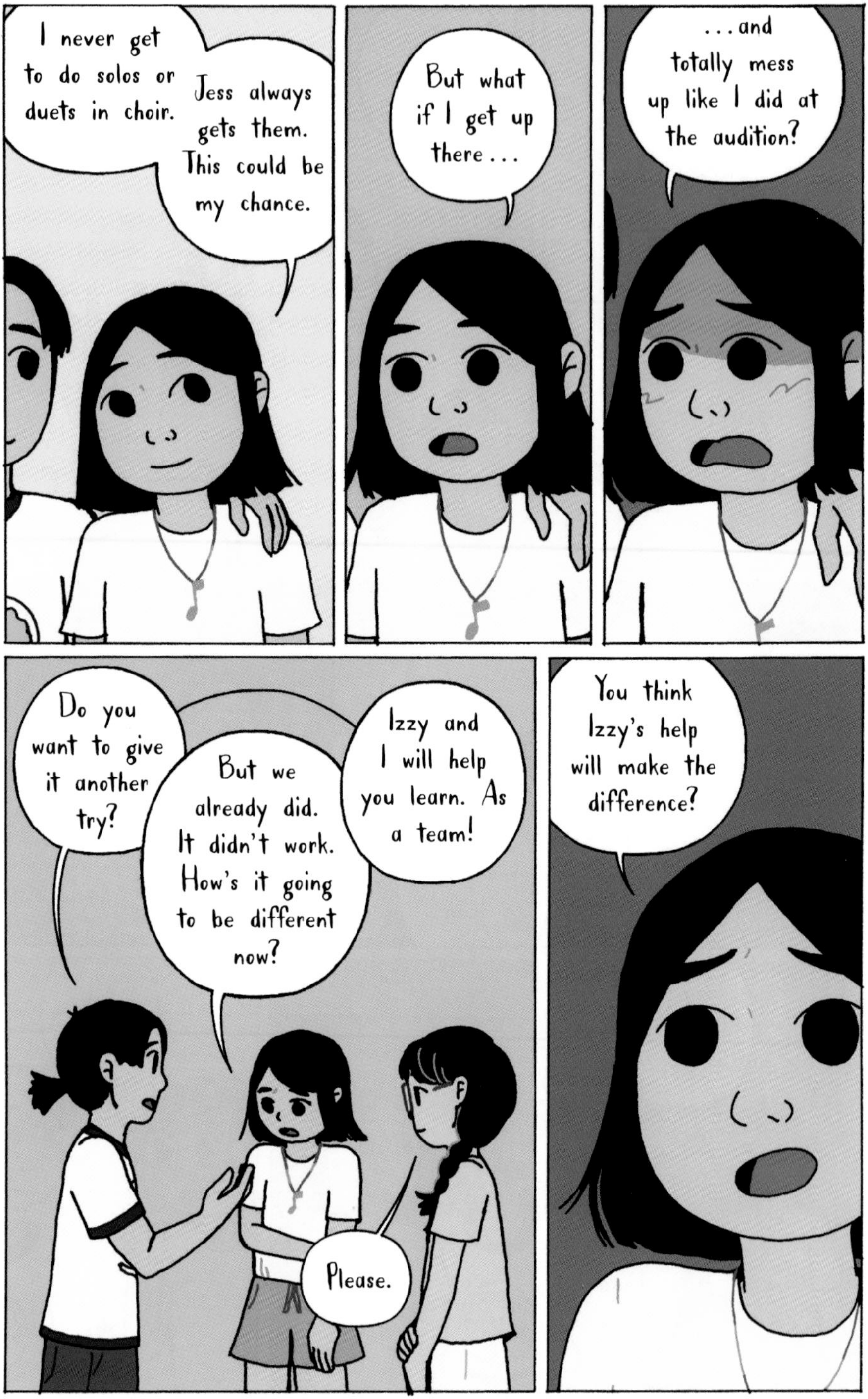
I never get to do solos or duets in choir.
Jess always gets them. This could be my chance.
But what if I get up there . . .
. . . and totally mess up like I did at the audition?
Do you want to give it another try?
But we already did. It didn't work. How's it going to be different now?
Izzy and I will help you learn. As a team!
Please.
You think Izzy's help will make the difference?

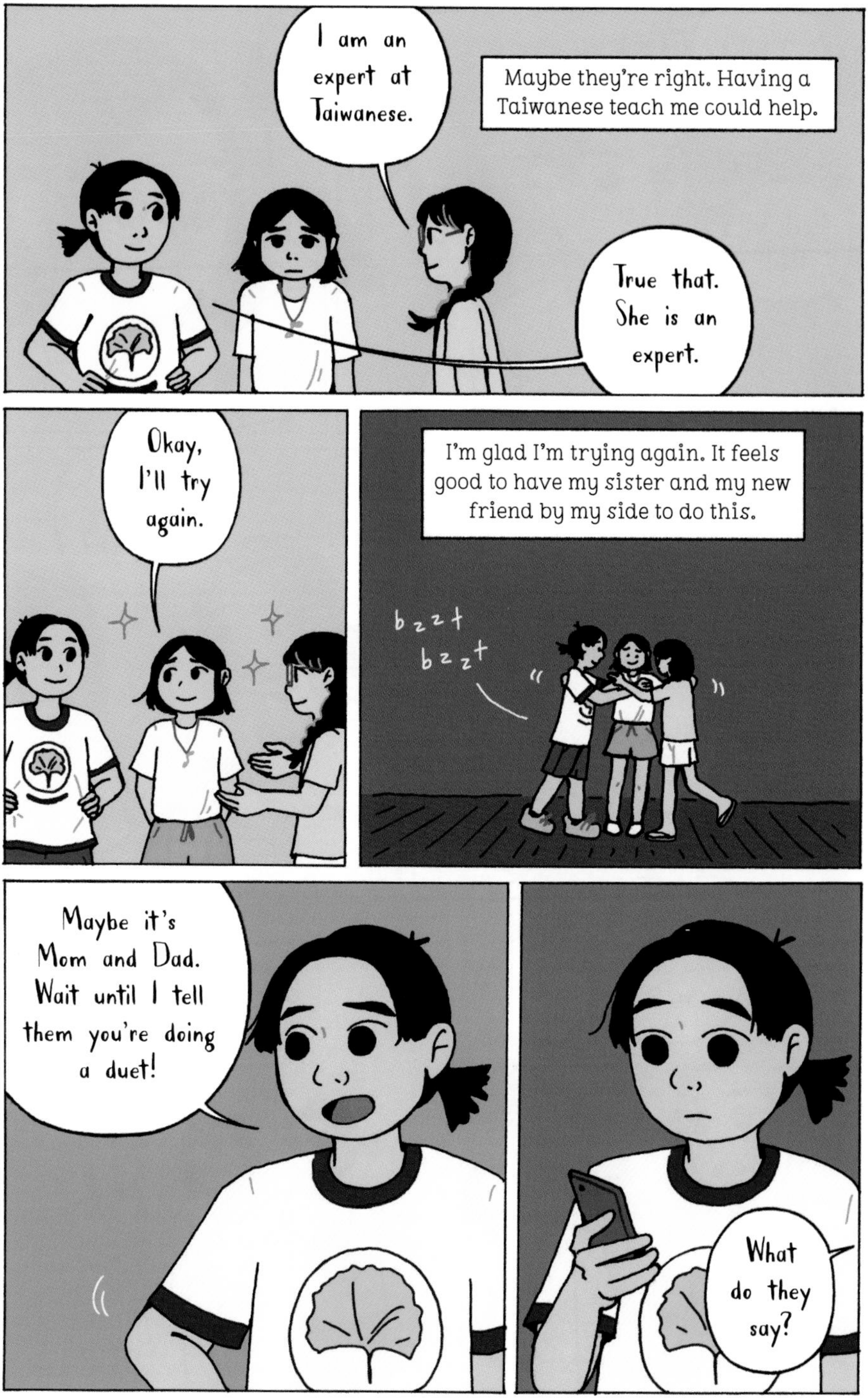
I am an expert at Taiwanese.
Maybe they're right. Having a Taiwanese teach me could help.
True that. She is an expert.
Okay, I'll try again.
I'm glad I'm trying again. It feels good to have my sister and my new friend by my side to do this.
bzzt
bzzt
Maybe it's Mom and Dad. Wait until I tell them you're doing a duet!
What do they say?

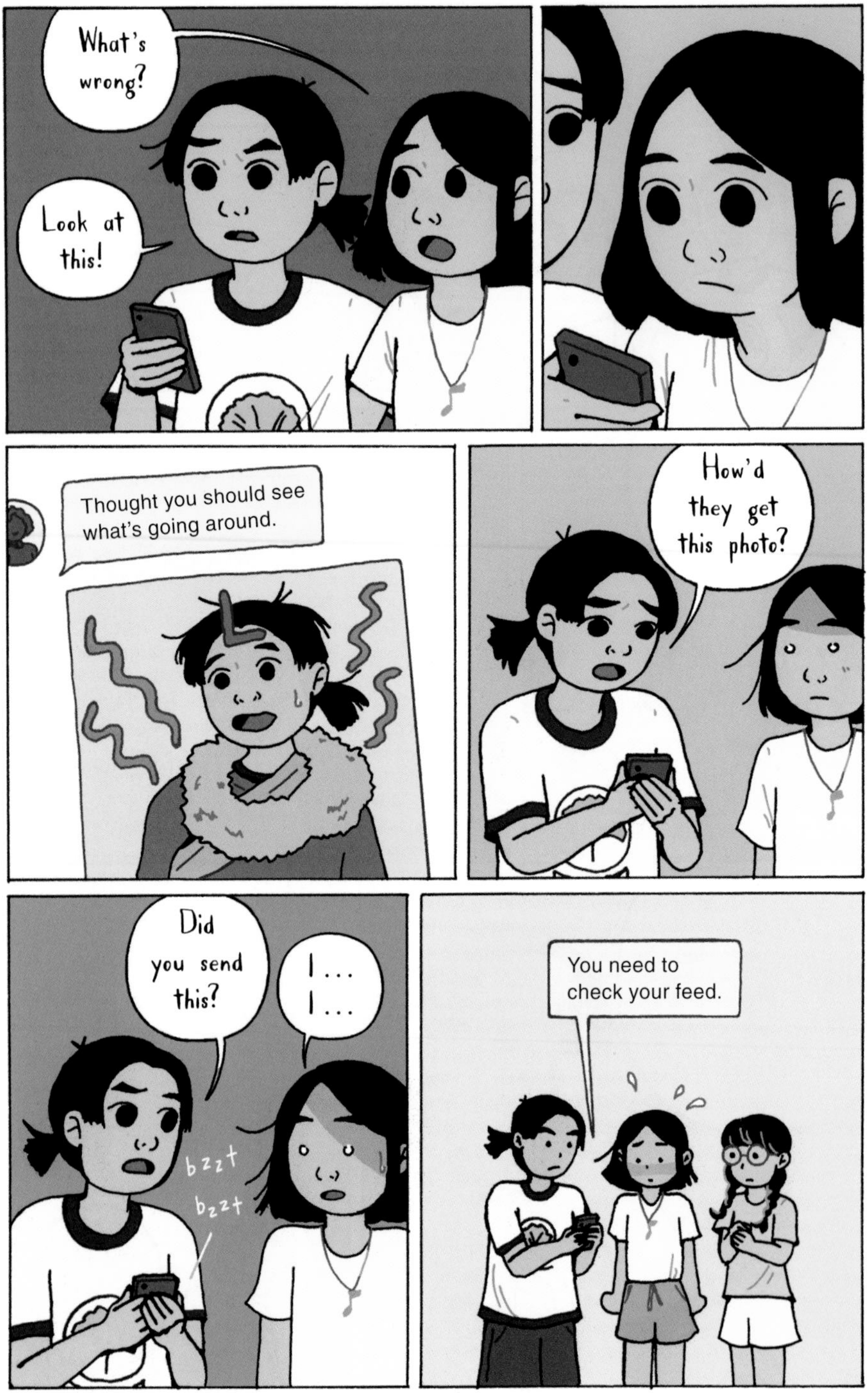
What's wrong?
Look at this!
Thought you should see what's going around.
How'd they get this photo?
Did you send this?
I... I...
bzzt bzzt
You need to check your feed.

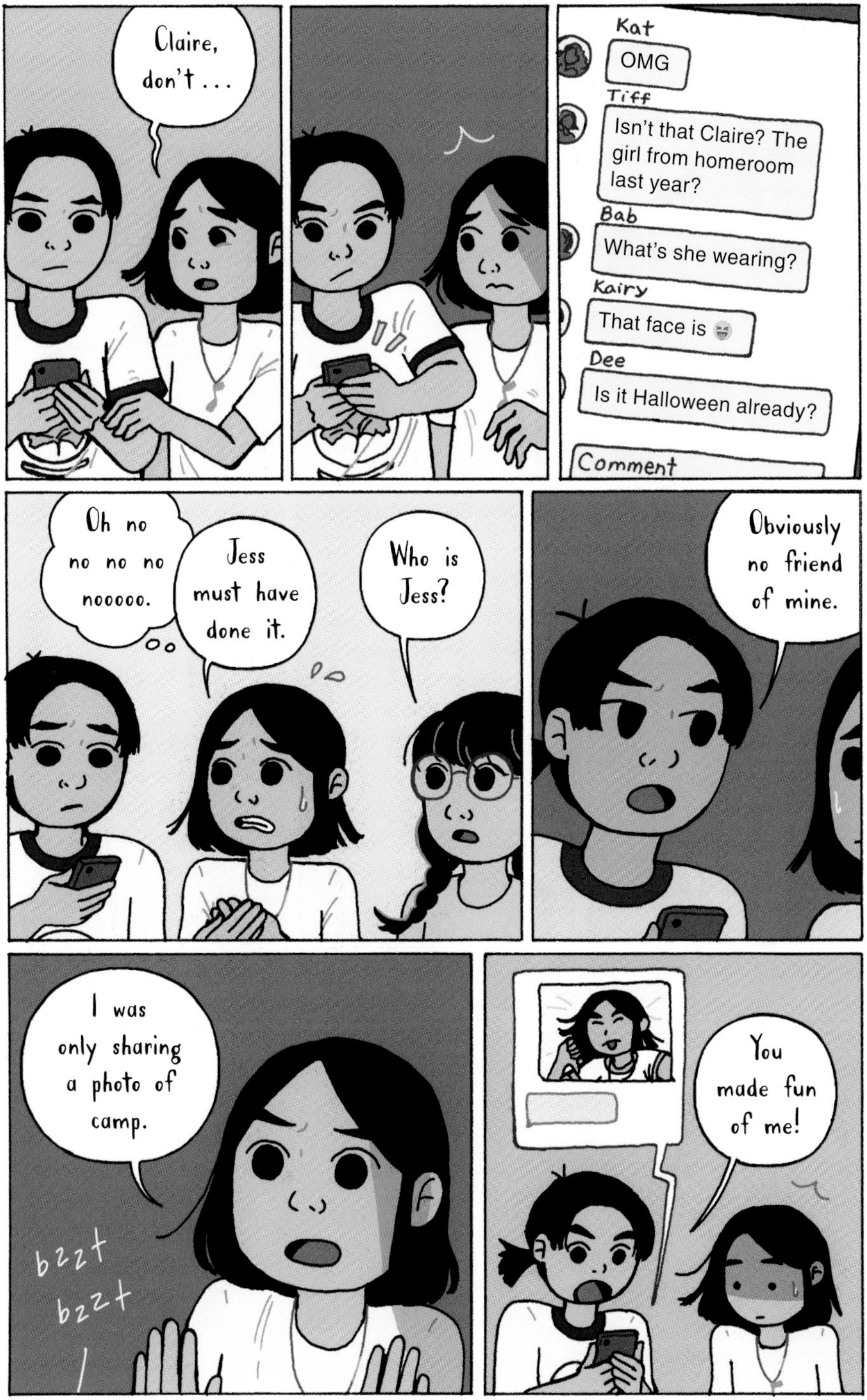
Claire, don't . . .
Kat
OMG
Tiff
Isn't that Claire? The girl from homeroom last year?
Bab
What's she wearing?
Kairy
That face is 😆
Dee
Is it Halloween already?
Comment
Oh no no no no nooooo.
Jess must have done it.
Who is Jess?
Obviously no friend of mine.
I was only sharing a photo of camp.
bzzt
bzzt
You made fun of me!

I'm your sister. Why would you do that?

Jess made more fun of you than I did. I only sent the photo. I didn't put the "L" for...

Gee, thanks for that.

bzzt
bzzt

What a loser!

No one wants to be friends with her

I always knew there was something wrong with that girl

You're not my sister!

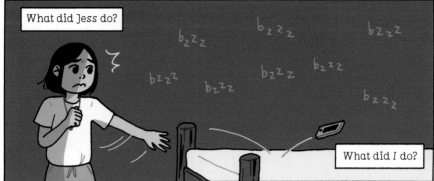

What did Jess do?

bzzz
bzzz
bzzz
bzzz
bzzz
bzzz
bzzz
bzzz

What did I do?

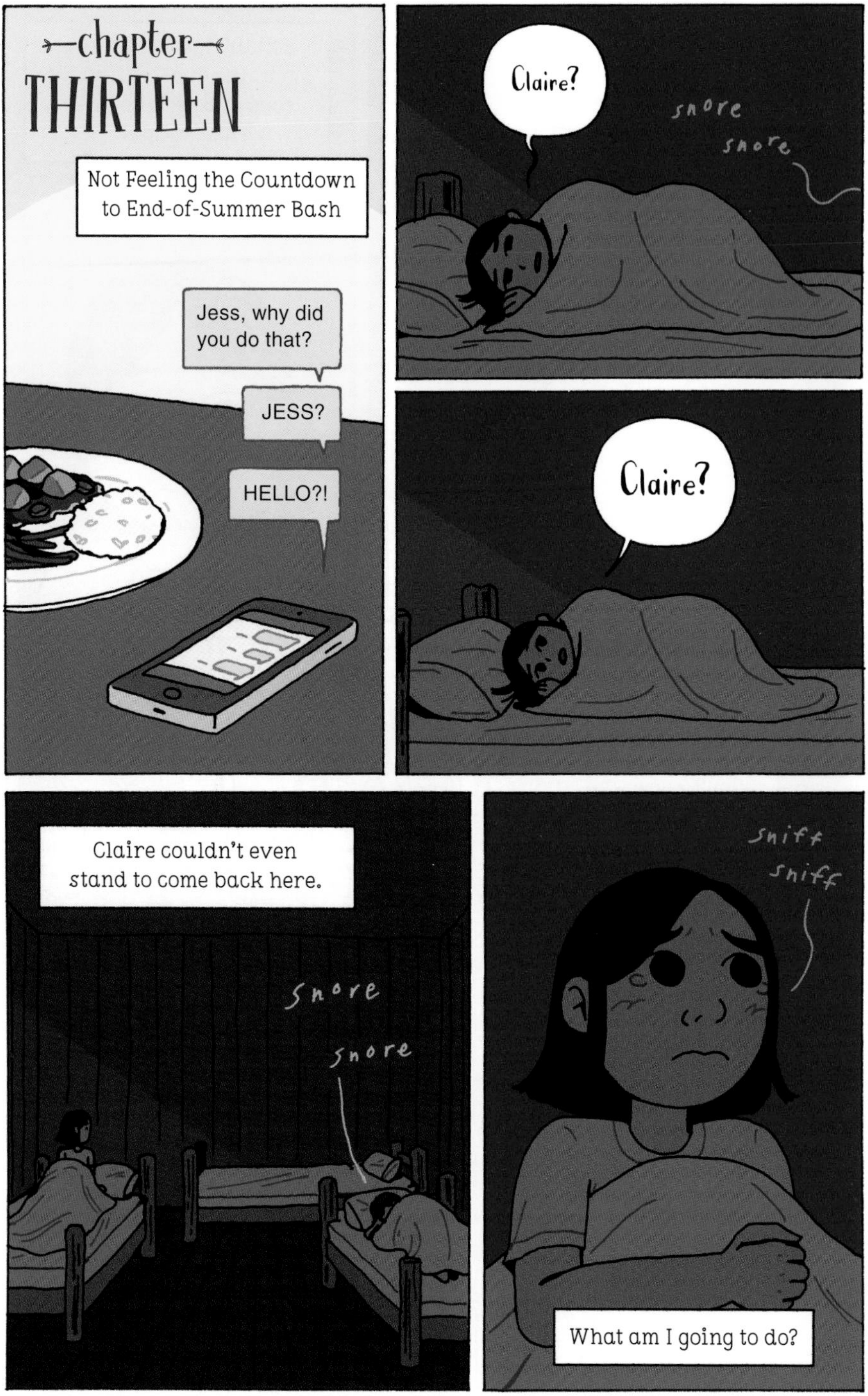

chapter
THIRTEEN
Not Feeling the Countdown to End-of-Summer Bash
Jess, why did you do that?
JESS?
HELLO?!
Claire?
snore
snore
Claire?
Claire couldn't even stand to come back here.
snore
snore
sniff
sniff
What am I going to do?

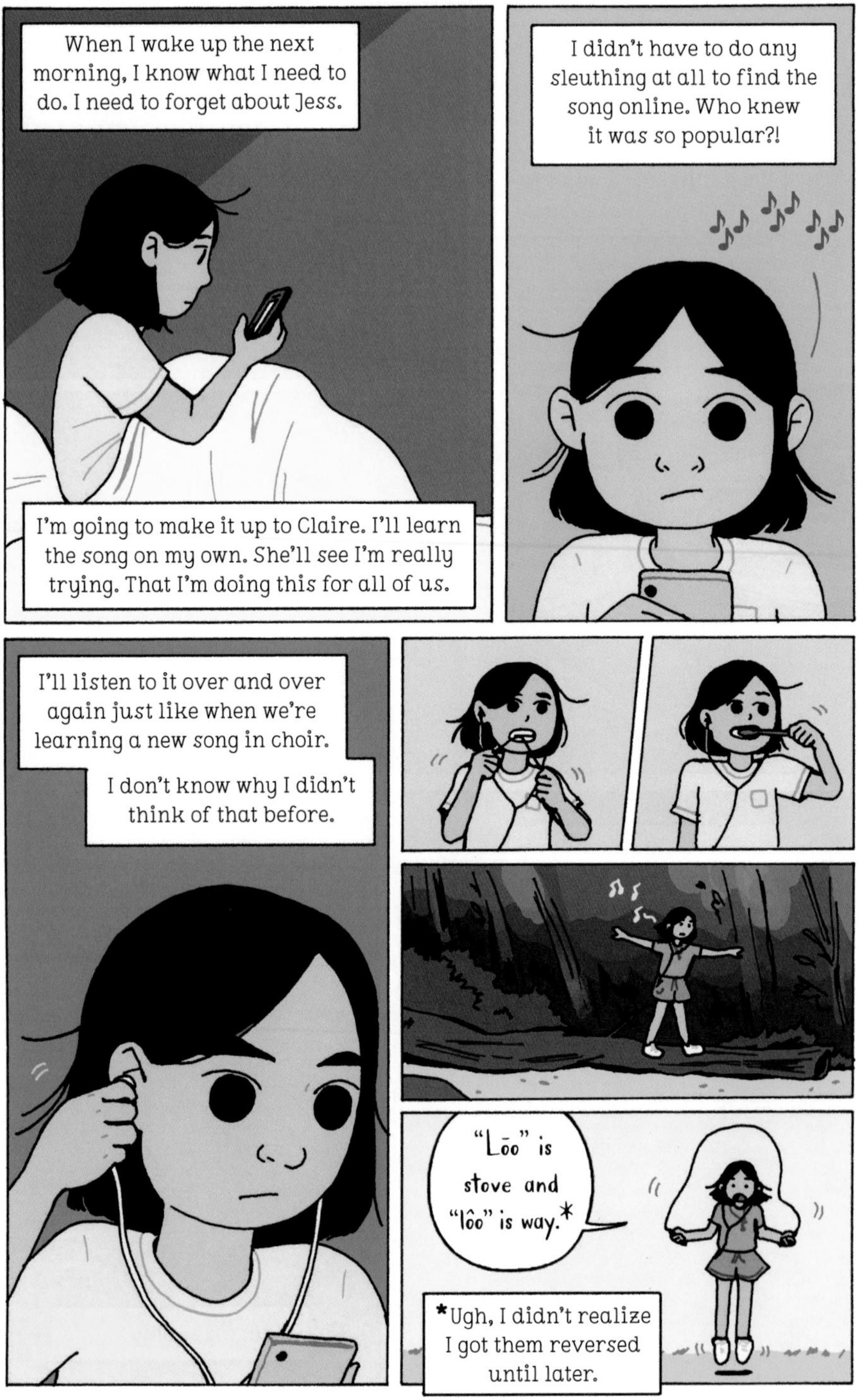
When I wake up the next morning, I know what I need to do. I need to forget about Jess.
I'm going to make it up to Claire. I'll learn the song on my own. She'll see I'm really trying. That I'm doing this for all of us.
I didn't have to do any sleuthing at all to find the song online. Who knew it was so popular?!
I'll listen to it over and over again just like when we're learning a new song in choir.
I don't know why I didn't think of that before.
"Lōo" is stove and "lôo" is way.*
*Ugh, I didn't realize I got them reversed until later.

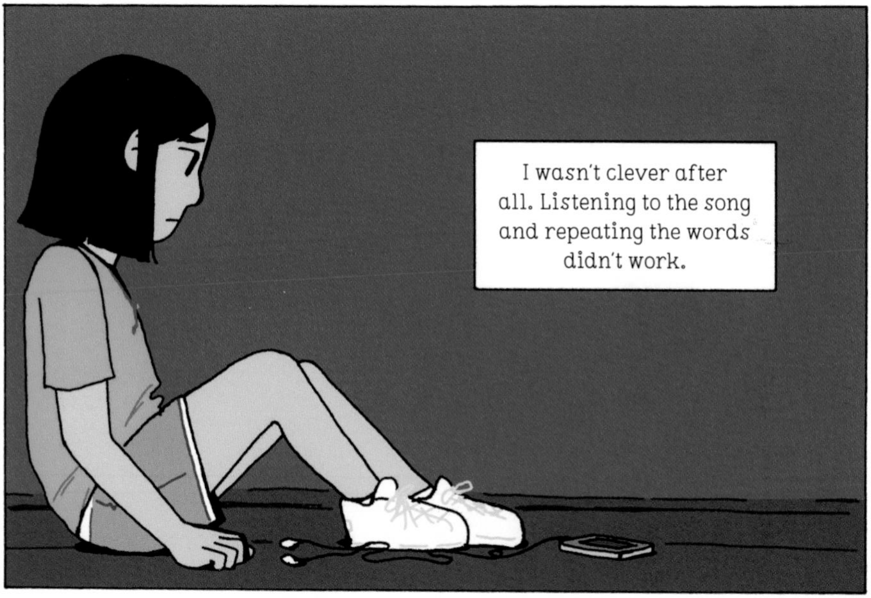
I wasn't clever after all. Listening to the song and repeating the words didn't work.

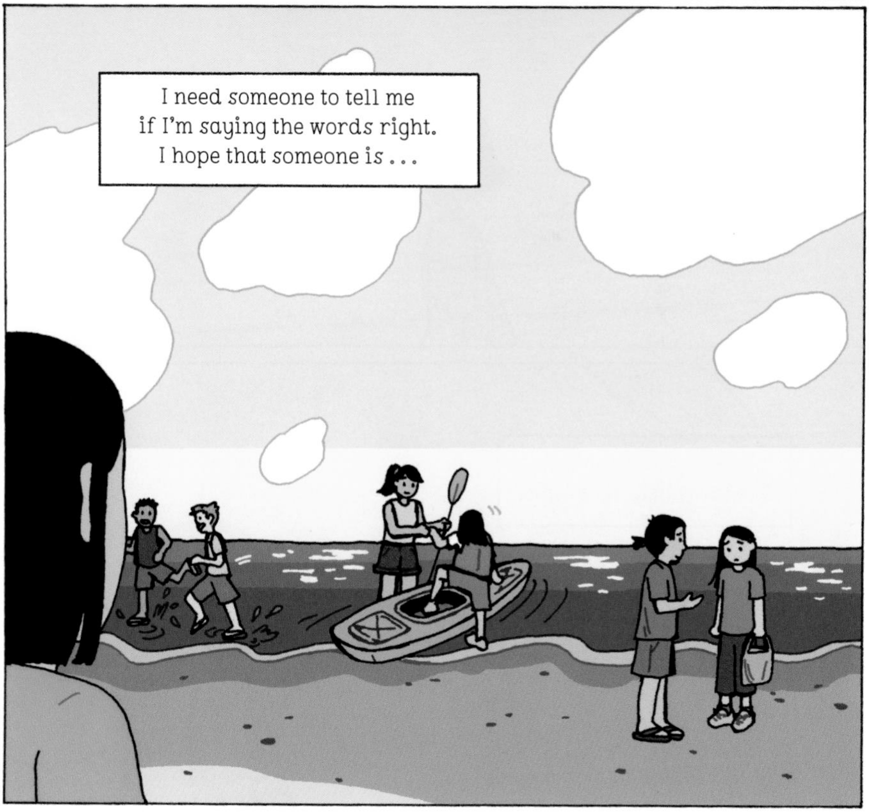
I need someone to tell me if I'm saying the words right. I hope that someone is . . .

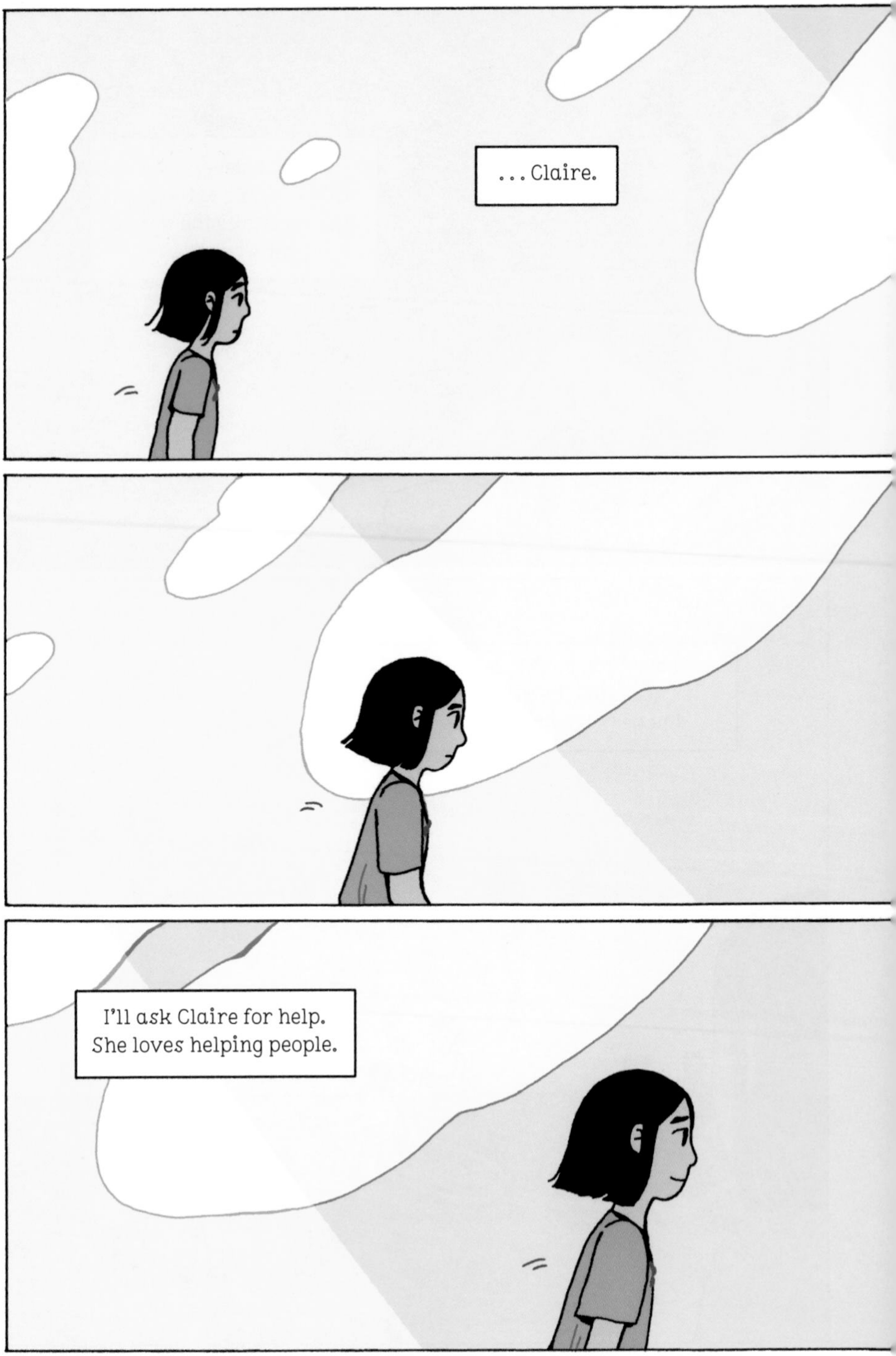
...Claire.
I'll ask Claire for help. She loves helping people.

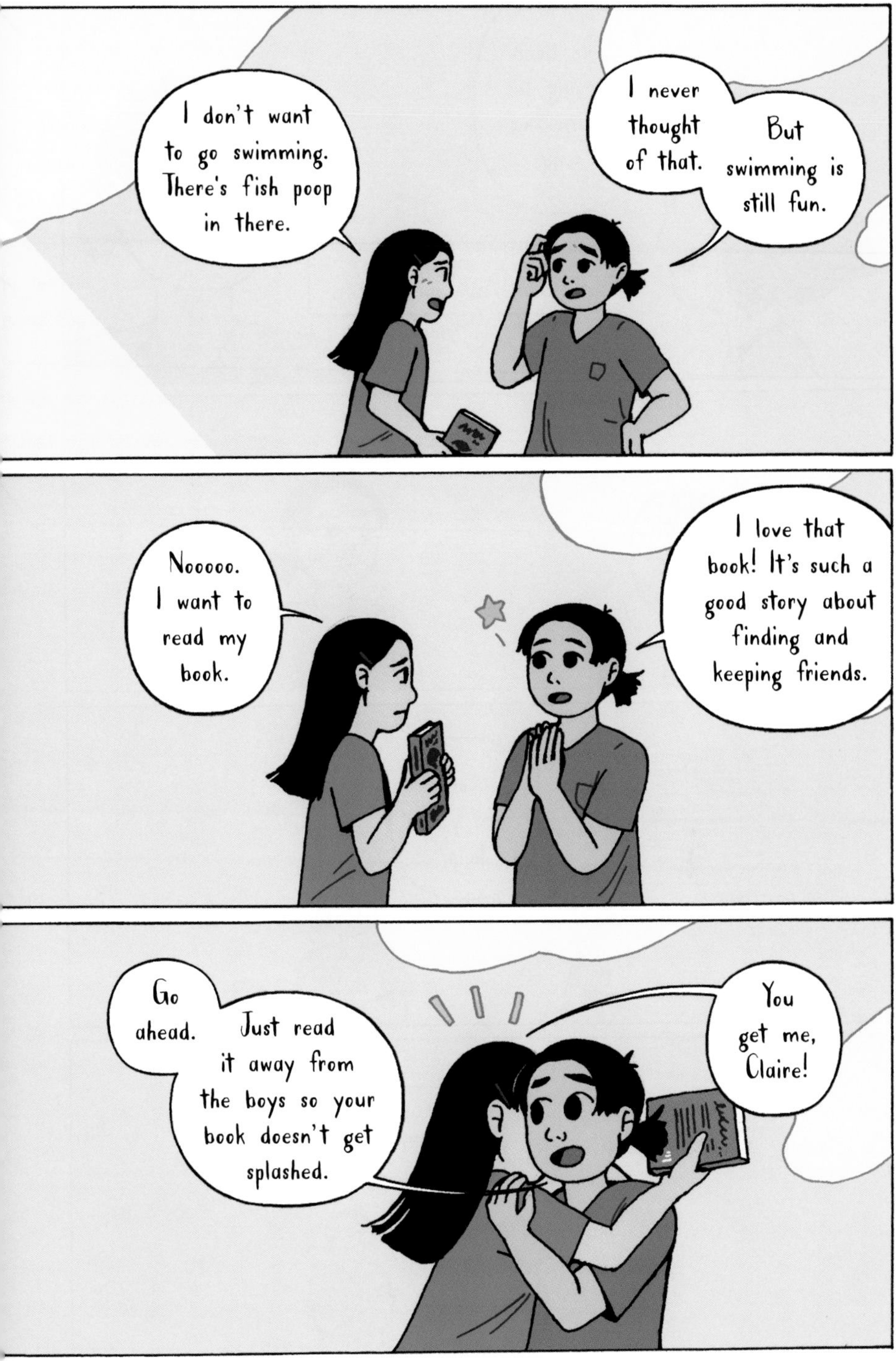
I don't want to go swimming. There's fish poop in there.
I never thought of that.
But swimming is still fun.
Nooooo. I want to read my book.
I love that book! It's such a good story about finding and keeping friends.
Go ahead.
Just read it away from the boys so your book doesn't get splashed.
You get me, Claire!

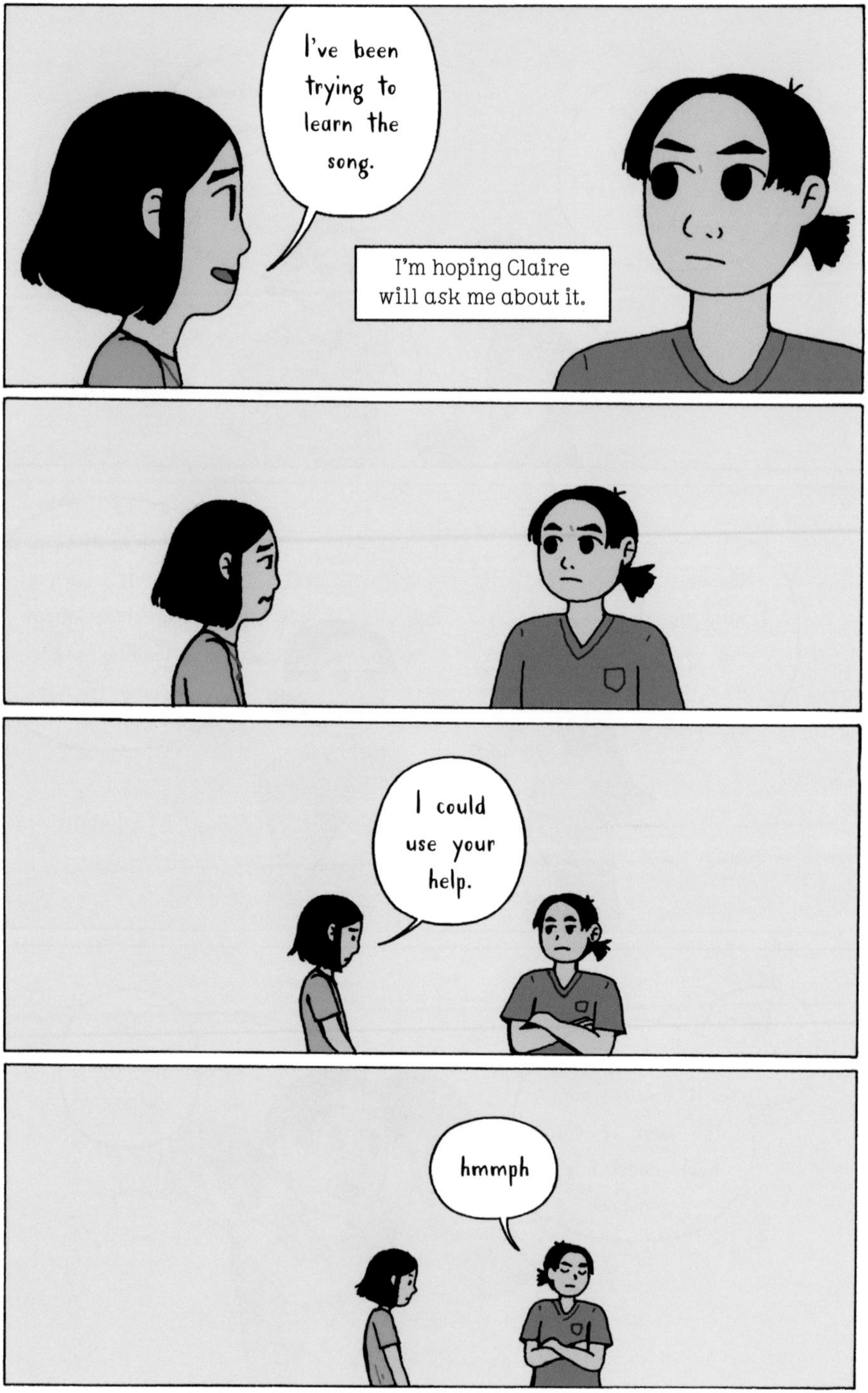
I've been trying to learn the song.
I'm hoping Claire will ask me about it.
I could use your help.
hmmph

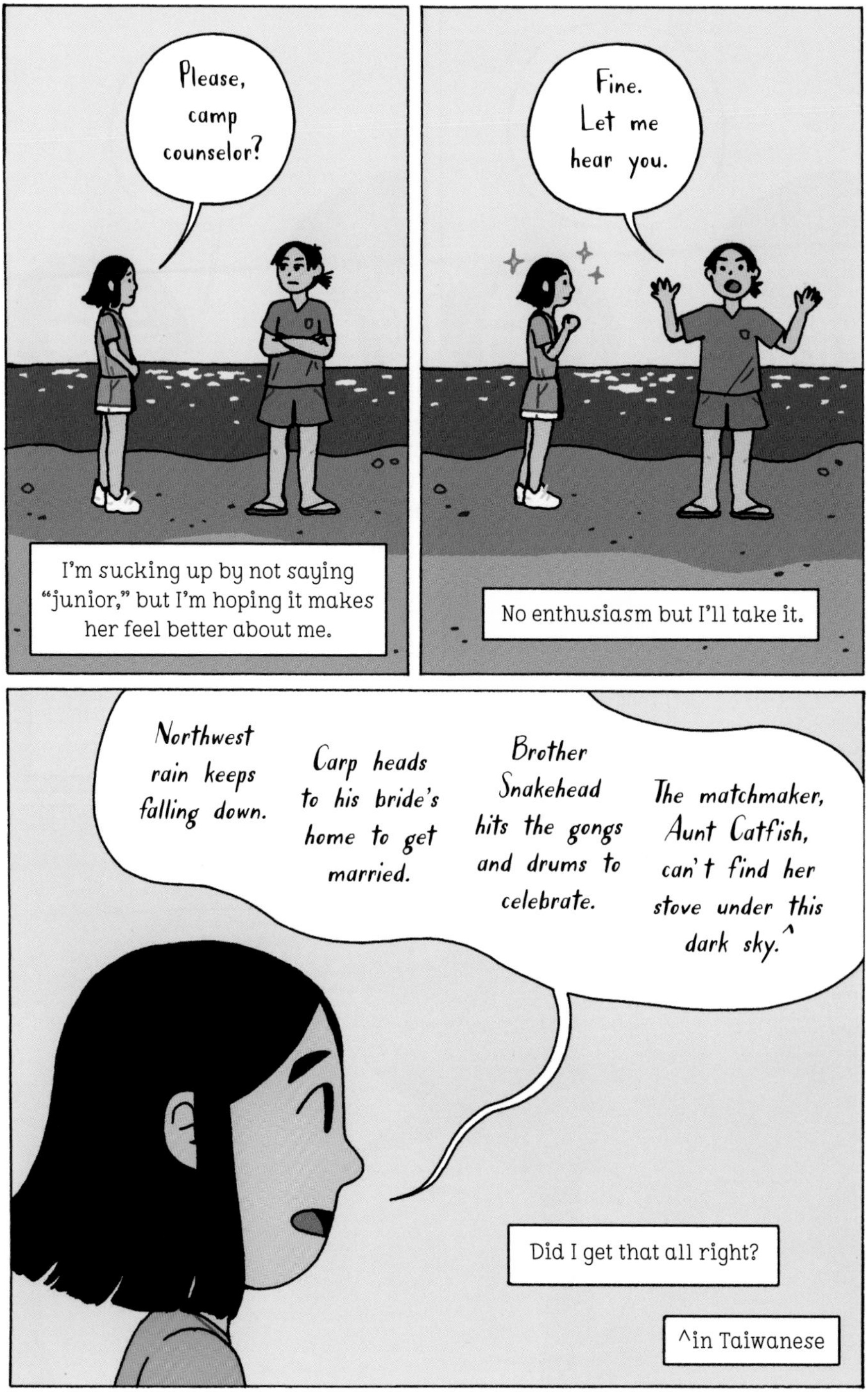
Please, camp counselor?
I'm sucking up by not saying "junior," but I'm hoping it makes her feel better about me.
Fine. Let me hear you.
No enthusiasm but I'll take it.
Northwest rain keeps falling down. Carp heads to his bride's home to get married. Brother Snakehead hits the gongs and drums to celebrate. The matchmaker, Aunt Catfish, can't find her stove under this dark sky.^
Did I get that all right?
^in Taiwanese

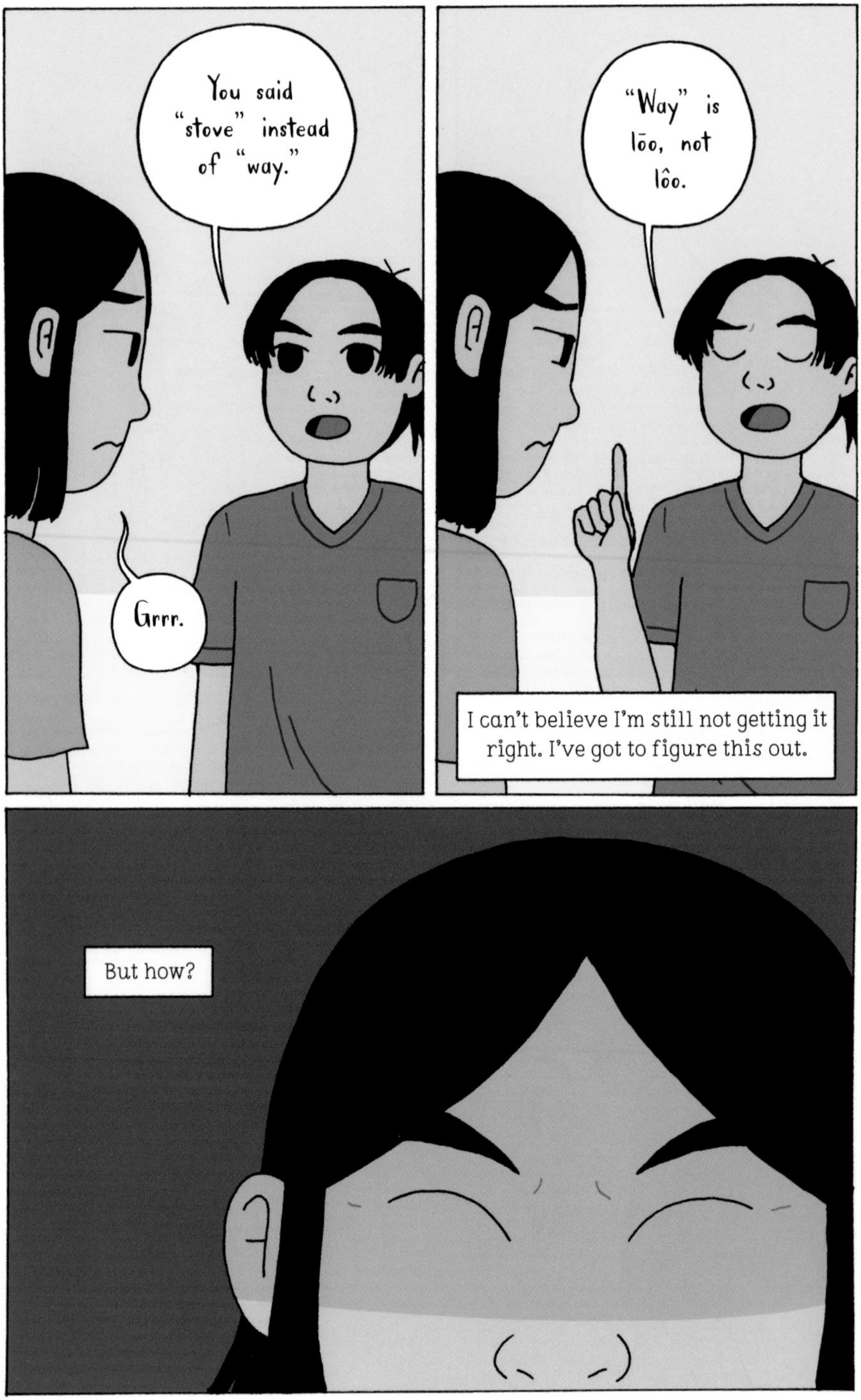
You said "stove" instead of "way."
Grrr.
"Way" is lōo, not lôo.
I can't believe I'm still not getting it right. I've got to figure this out.
But how?

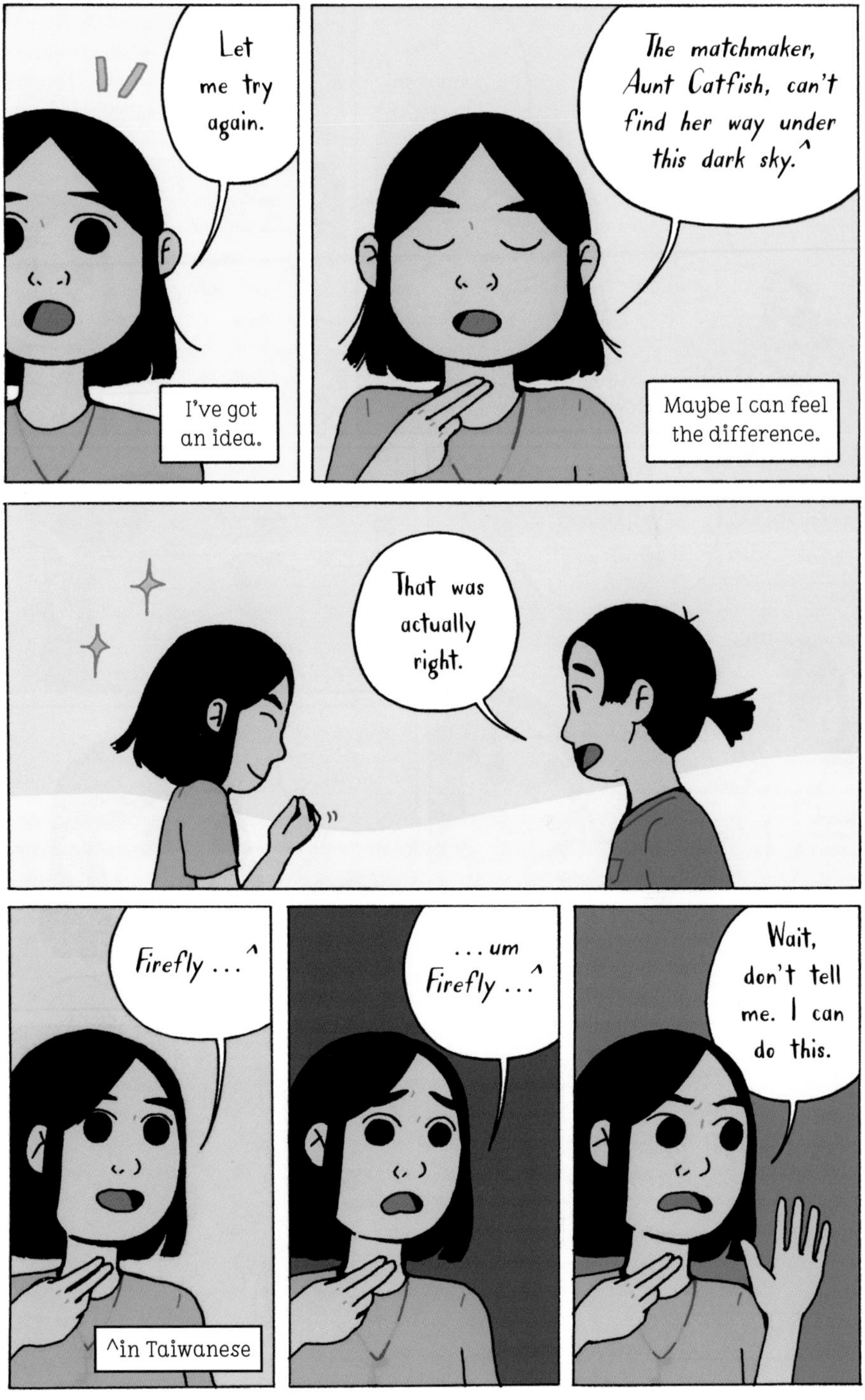
Let me try again.
I've got an idea.
The matchmaker, Aunt Catfish, can't find her way under this dark sky.^
Maybe I can feel the difference.
That was actually right.
Firefly . . .^
^in Taiwanese
. . . um Firefly . . .^
Wait, don't tell me. I can do this.

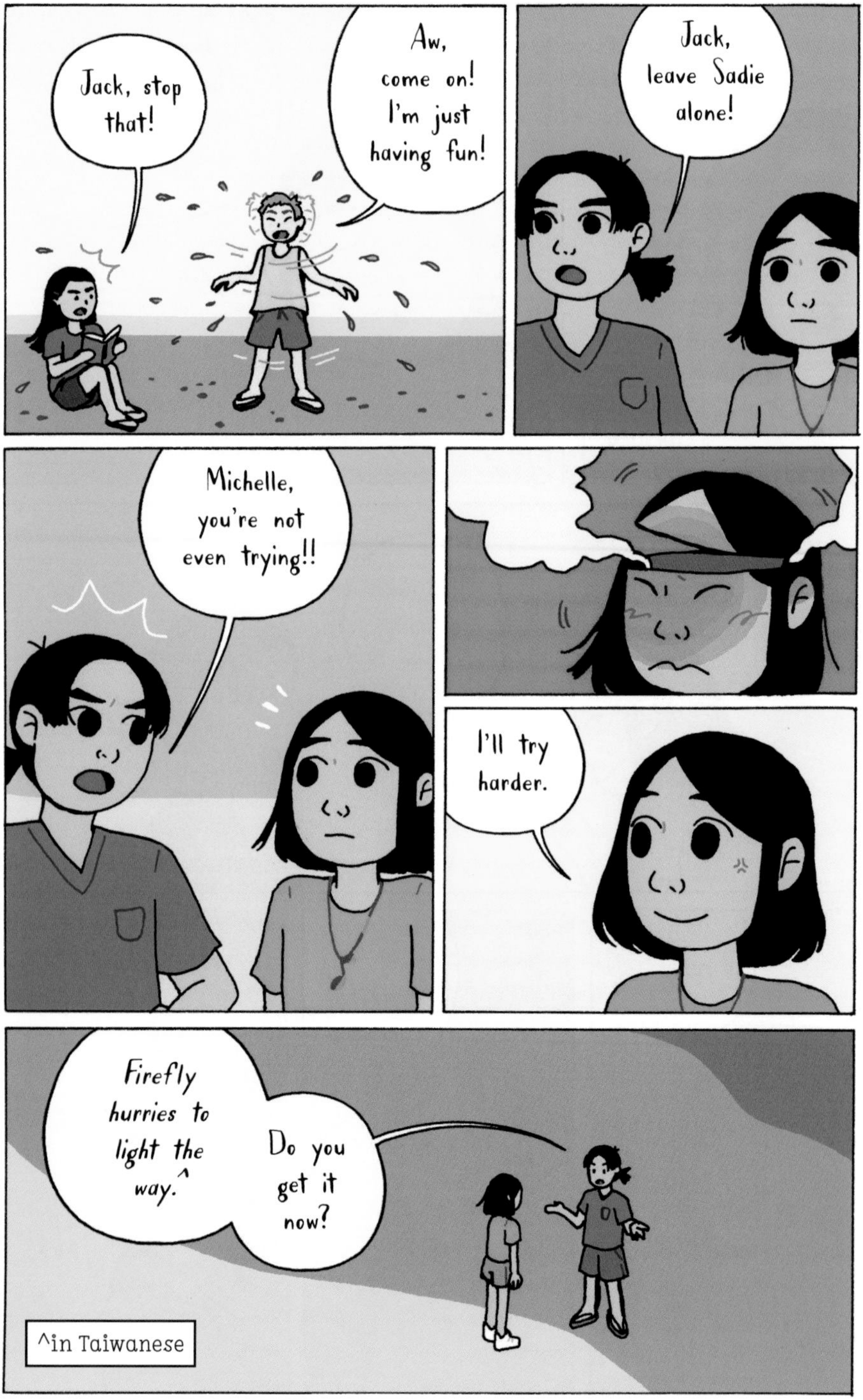
Jack, stop that!
Aw, come on! I'm just having fun!
Jack, leave Sadie alone!
Michelle, you're not even trying!!
I'll try harder.
Firefly hurries to light the way.^
Do you get it now?
^in Taiwanese

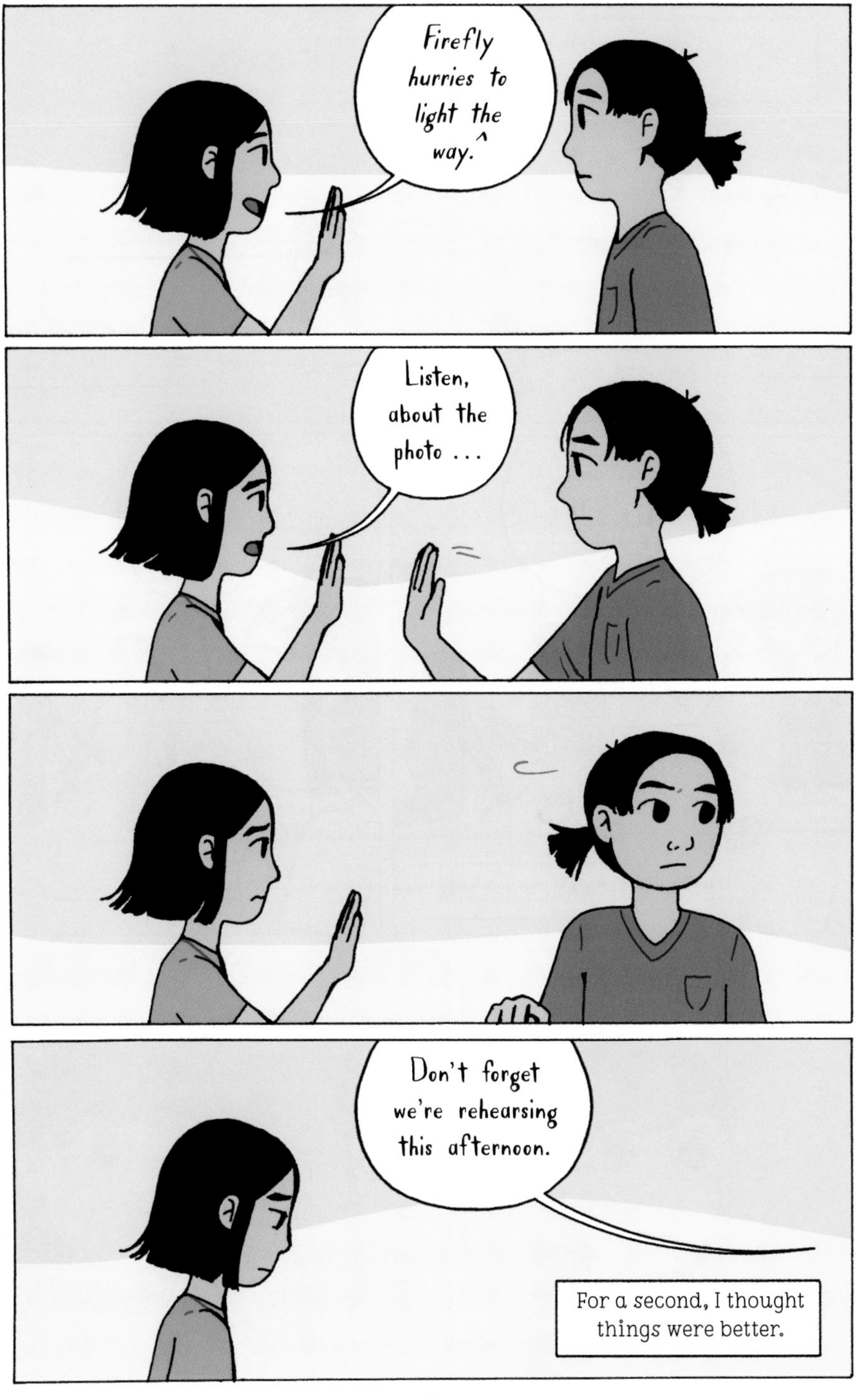
Firefly hurries to light the way.
Listen, about the photo . . .
Don't forget we're rehearsing this afternoon.
For a second, I thought things were better.

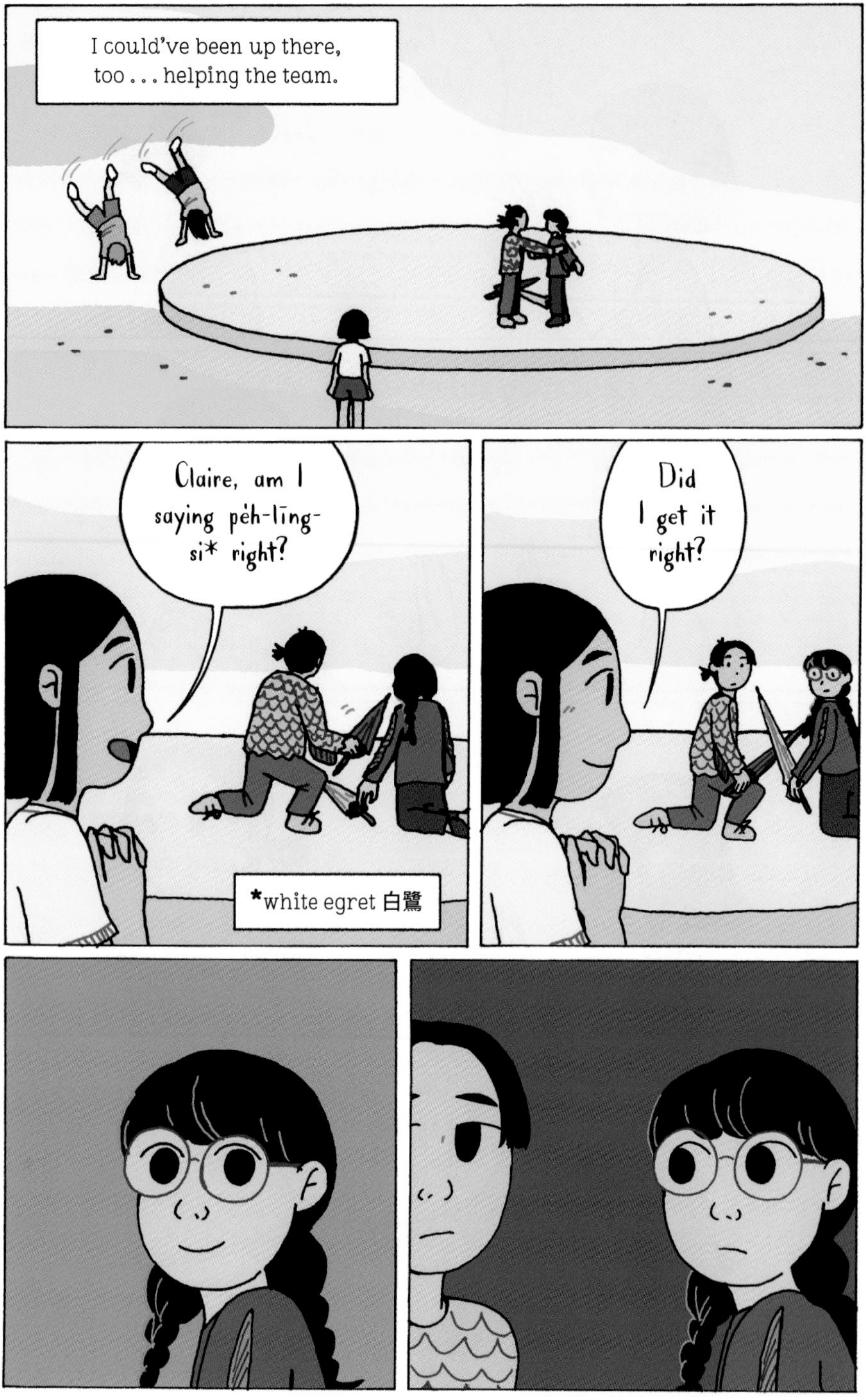

I could've been up there, too . . . helping the team.
Claire, am I saying peh-līng-si* right?
*white egret 白鷺
Did I get it right?

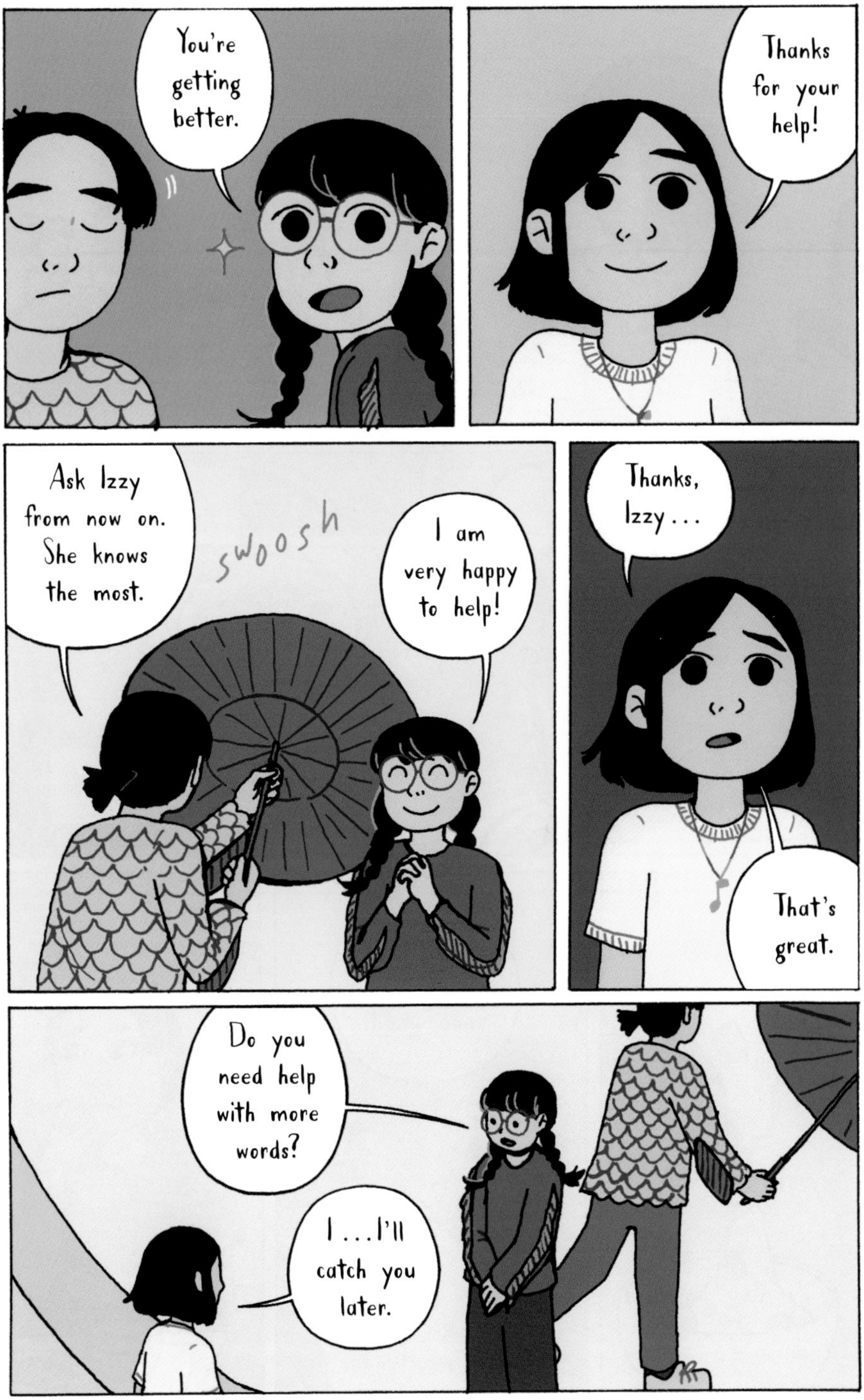
You're getting better.
Thanks for your help!
Ask Izzy from now on. She knows the most.
swoosh
I am very happy to help!
Thanks, Izzy . . .
That's great.
Do you need help with more words?
I . . . I'll catch you later.

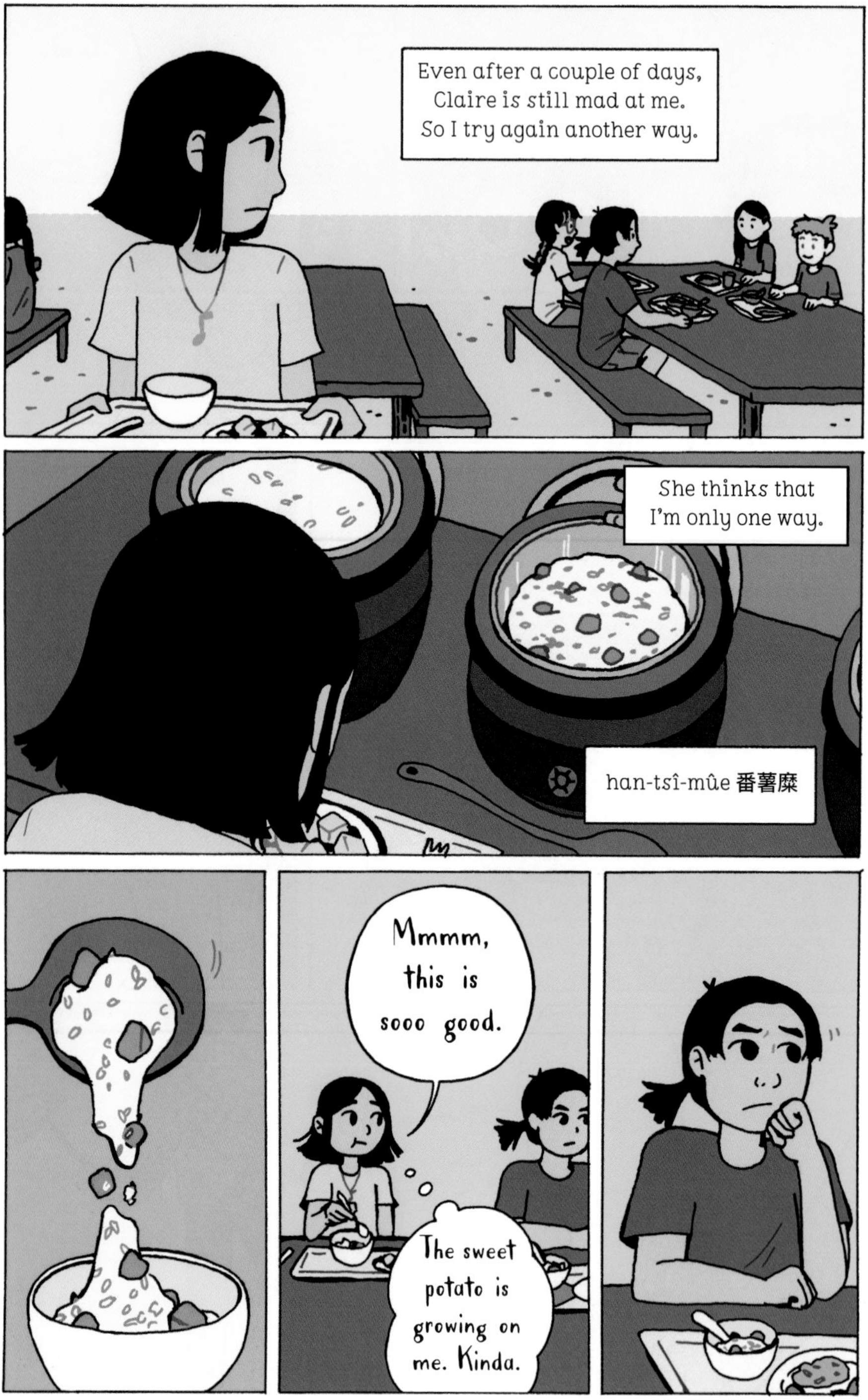
Even after a couple of days, Claire is still mad at me. So I try again another way.
She thinks that I'm only one way.
han-tsî-mûe 番薯糜
Mmmm, this is sooo good.
The sweet potato is growing on me. Kinda.

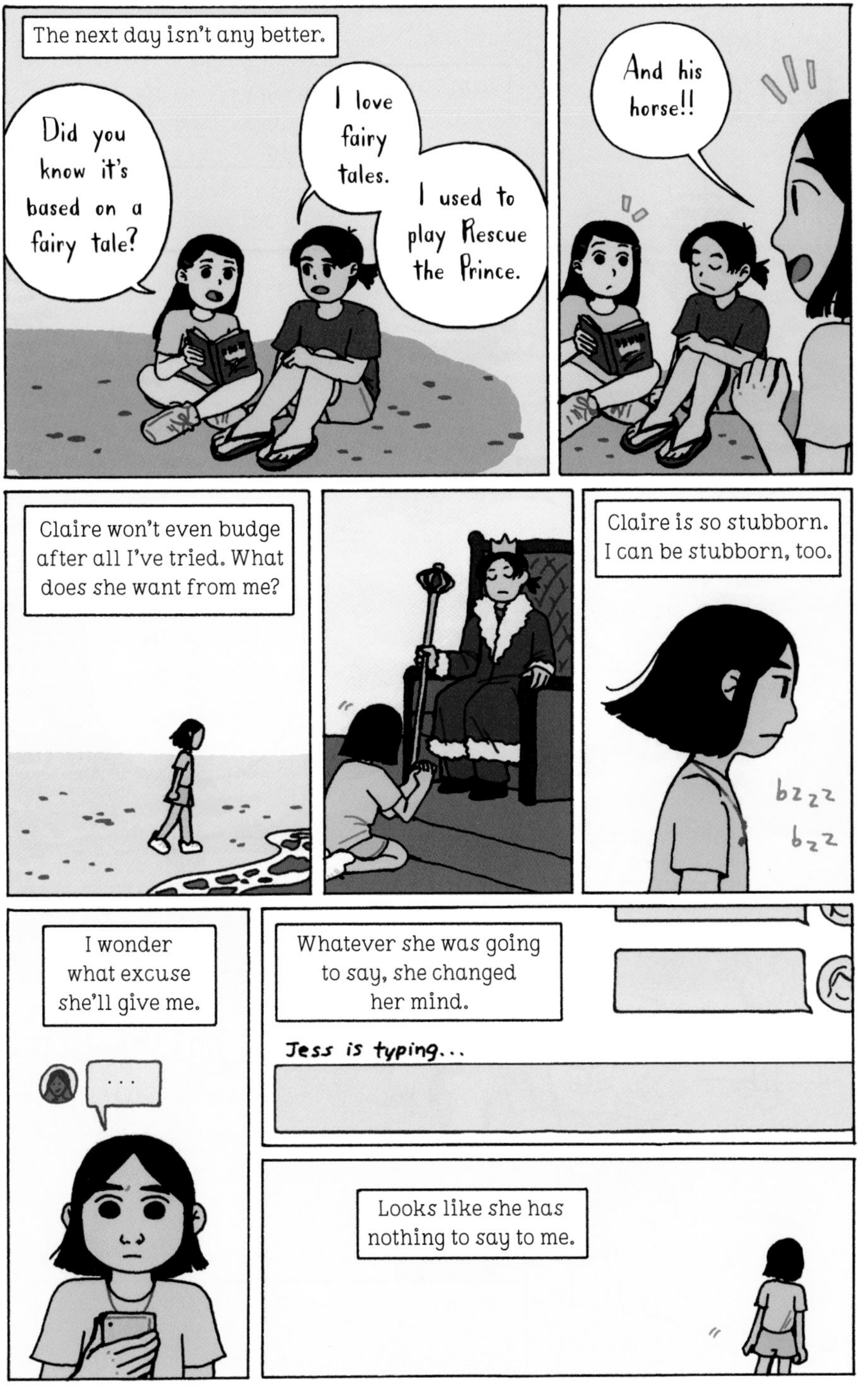

The next day isn't any better.
Did you know it's based on a fairy tale?
I love fairy tales.
I used to play Rescue the Prince.
And his horse!!
Claire won't even budge after all I've tried. What does she want from me?
Claire is so stubborn. I can be stubborn, too.
bzzz
bzz
I wonder what excuse she'll give me.
...
Whatever she was going to say, she changed her mind.
Jess is typing...
Looks like she has nothing to say to me.

chapter FOURTEEN

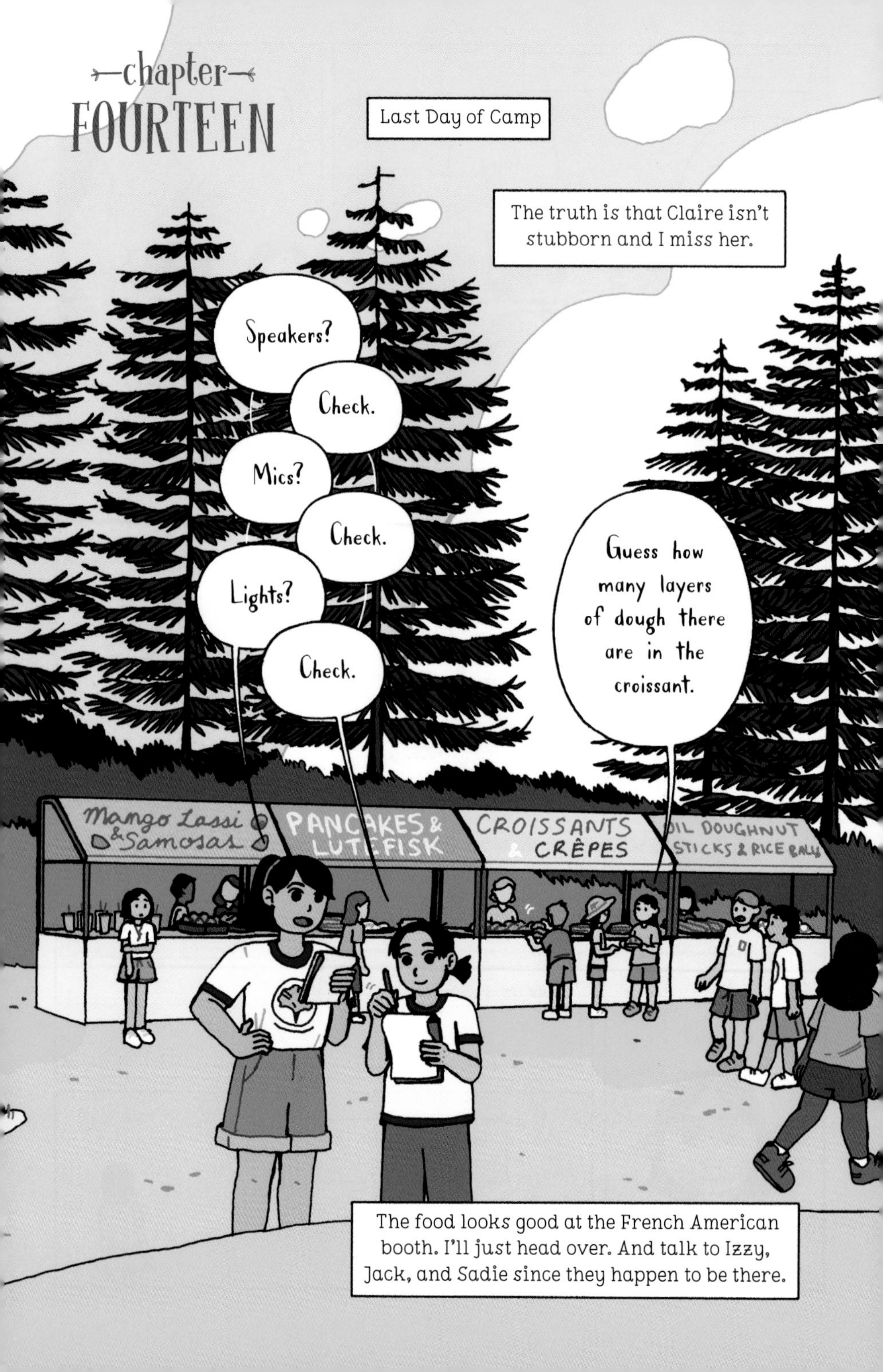
Last Day of Camp
The truth is that Claire isn't stubborn and I miss her.
Speakers?
Check.
Mics?
Check.
Lights?
Check.
Guess how many layers of dough there are in the croissant.
Mango Lassi & Samosas
PANCAKES & LUTEFISK
CROISSANTS & CRÊPES
OIL DOUGHNUT STICKS & RICE BALLS
The food looks good at the French American booth. I'll just head over. And talk to Izzy, Jack, and Sadie since they happen to be there.

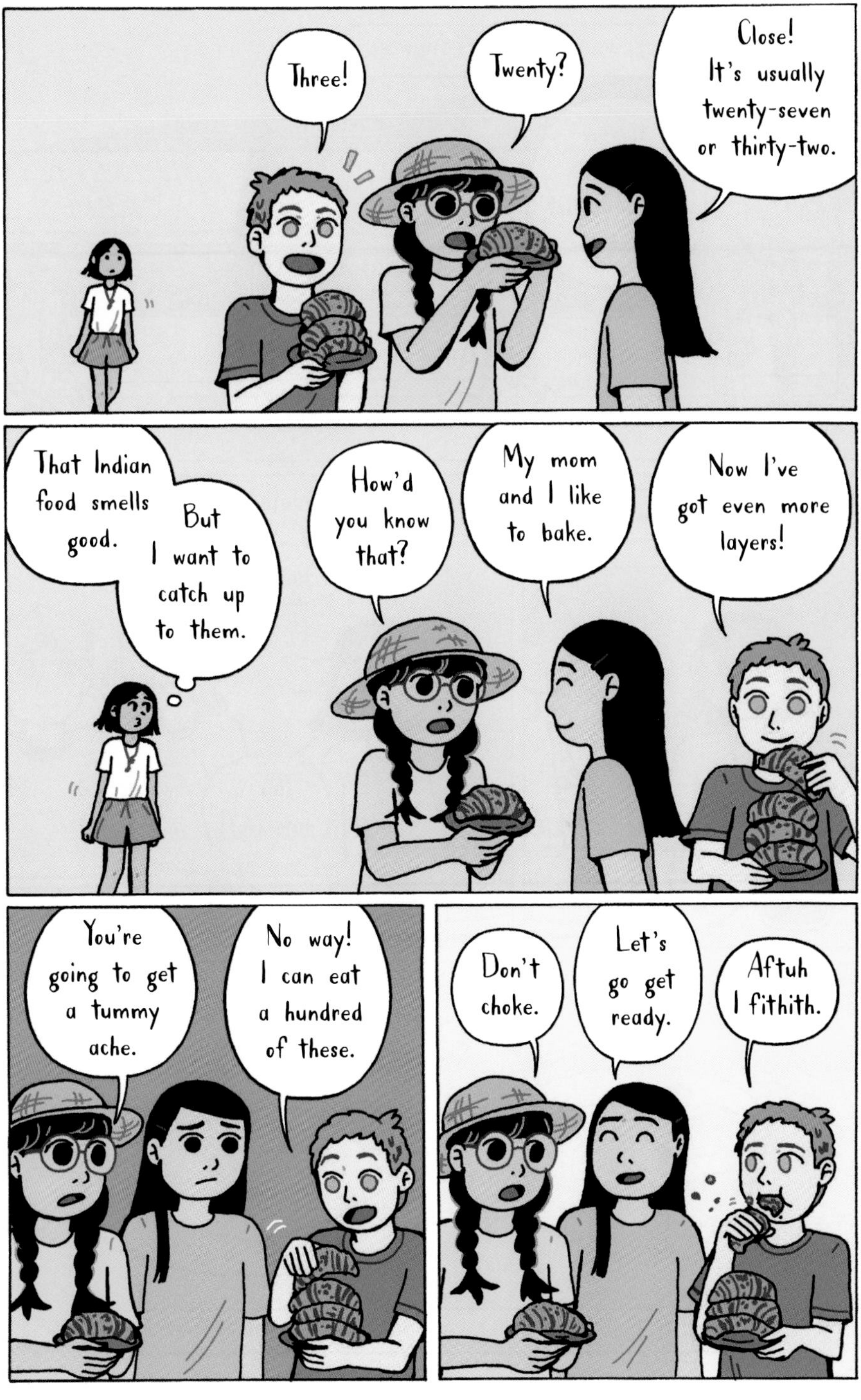
Three!
Twenty?
Close! It's usually twenty-seven or thirty-two.
That Indian food smells good.
But I want to catch up to them.
How'd you know that?
My mom and I like to bake.
Now I've got even more layers!
You're going to get a tummy ache.
No way! I can eat a hundred of these.
Don't choke.
Let's go get ready.
Aftuh I fithith.

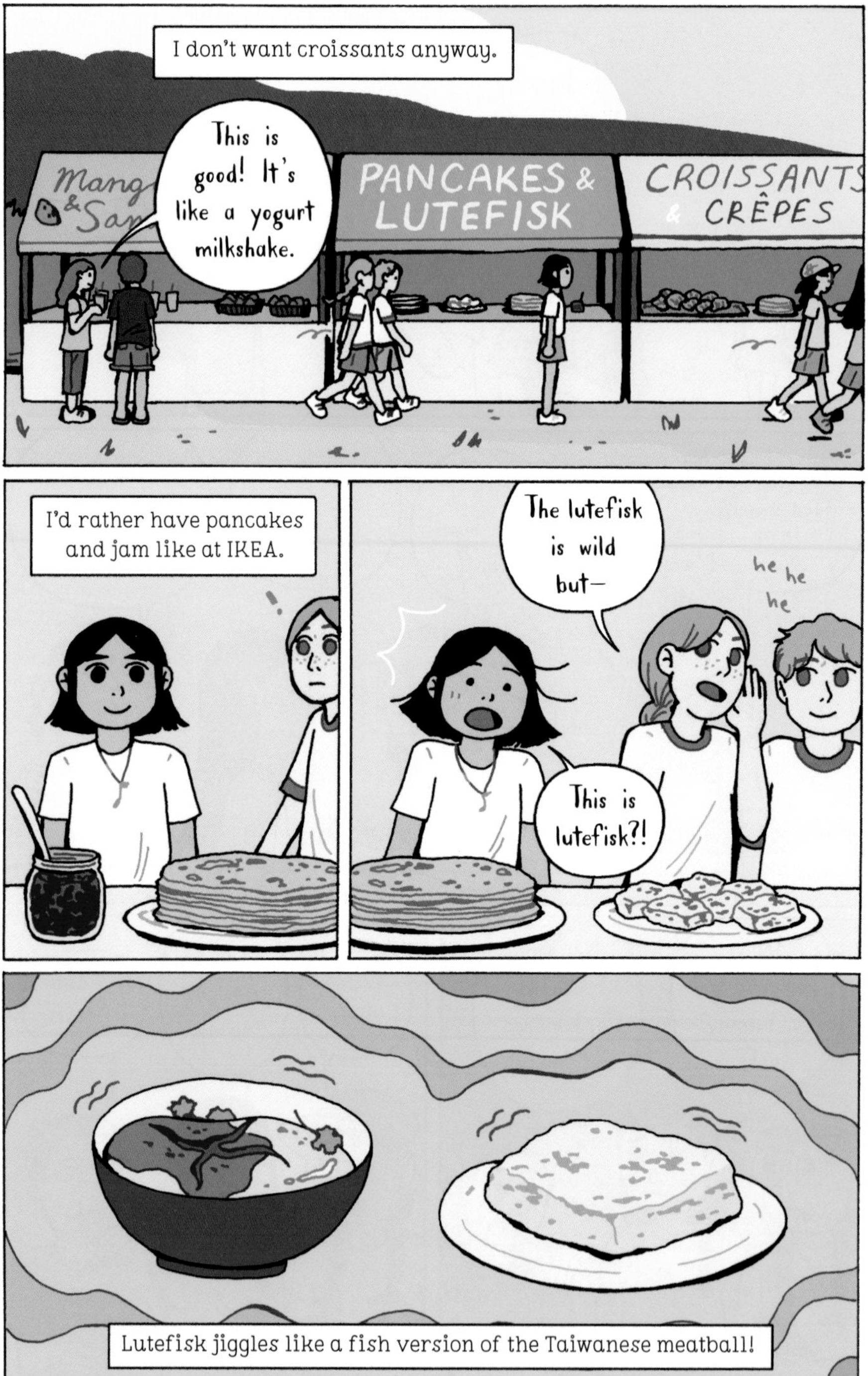

I don't want croissants anyway.
This is good! It's like a yogurt milkshake.
PANCAKES & LUTEFISK
CROISSANTS & CRÊPES
I'd rather have pancakes and jam like at IKEA.
The lutefisk is wild but—
he he he
This is lutefisk?!
Lutefisk jiggles like a fish version of the Taiwanese meatball!

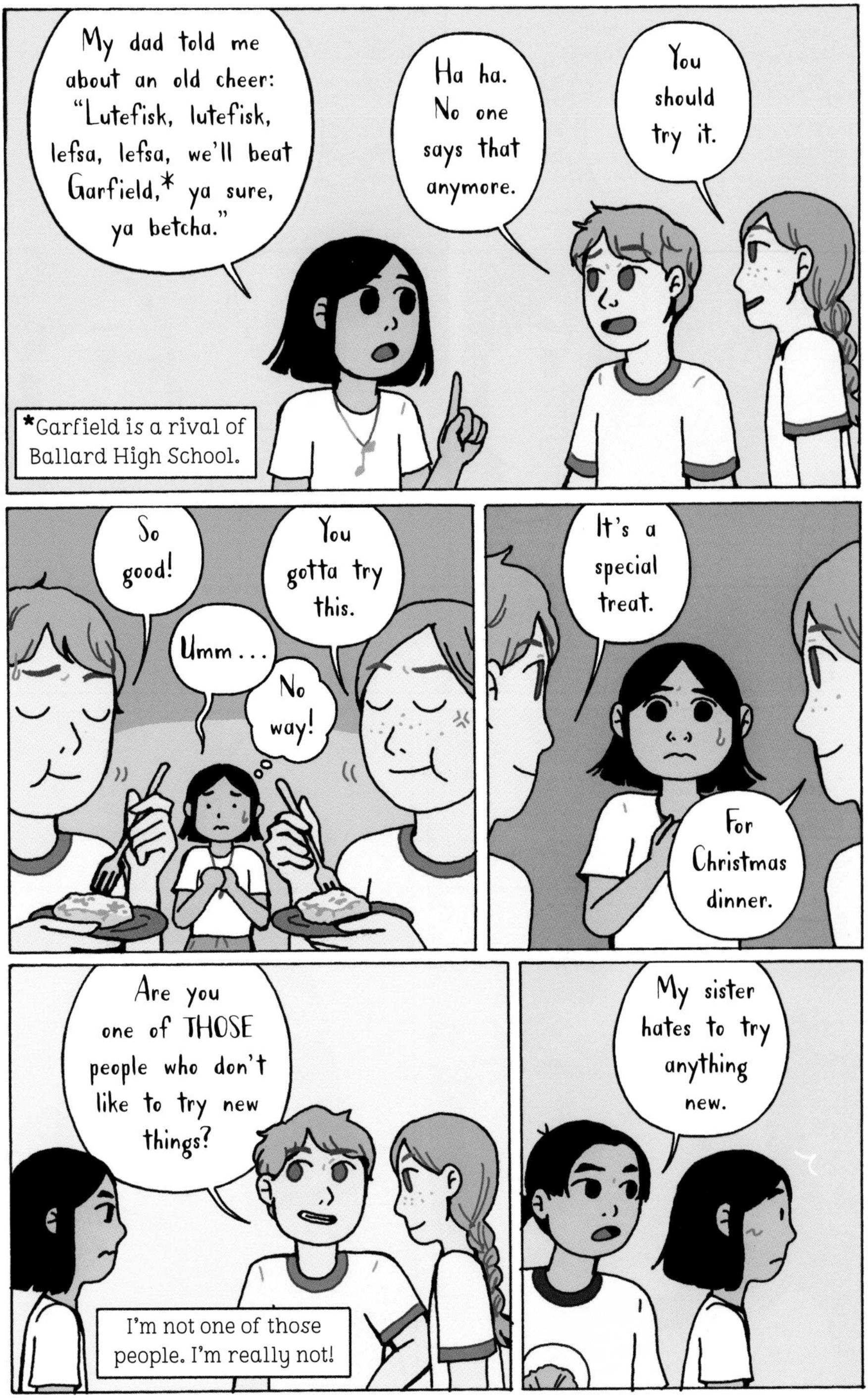

My dad told me about an old cheer: "Lutefisk, lutefisk, lefsa, lefsa, we'll beat Garfield,* ya sure, ya betcha."
Ha ha. No one says that anymore.
You should try it.
*Garfield is a rival of Ballard High School.
So good!
You gotta try this.
Umm...
No way!
It's a special treat.
For Christmas dinner.
Are you one of THOSE people who don't like to try new things?
I'm not one of those people. I'm really not!
My sister hates to try anything new.

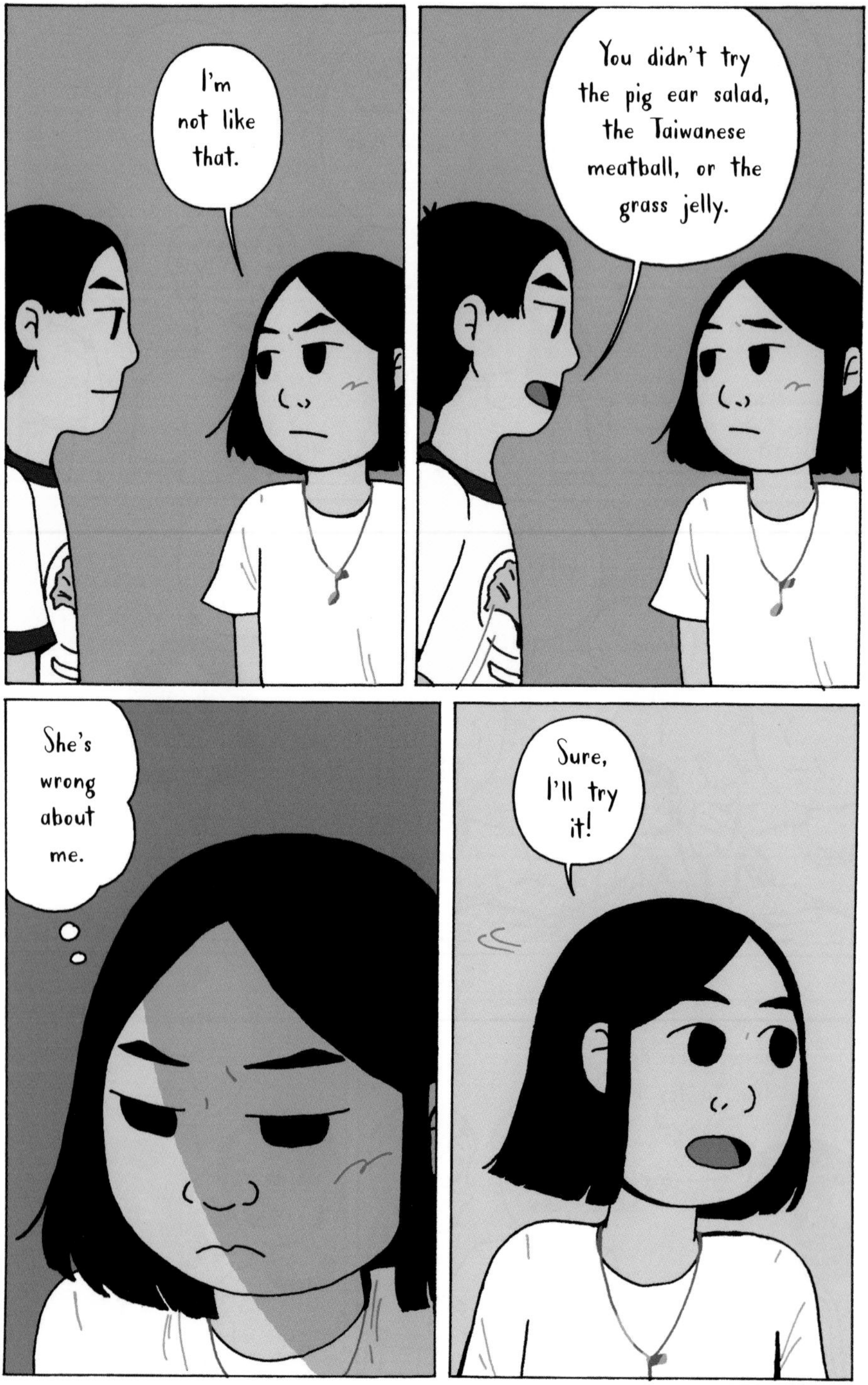
I'm not like that.
You didn't try the pig ear salad, the Taiwanese meatball, or the grass jelly.
She's wrong about me.
Sure, I'll try it!

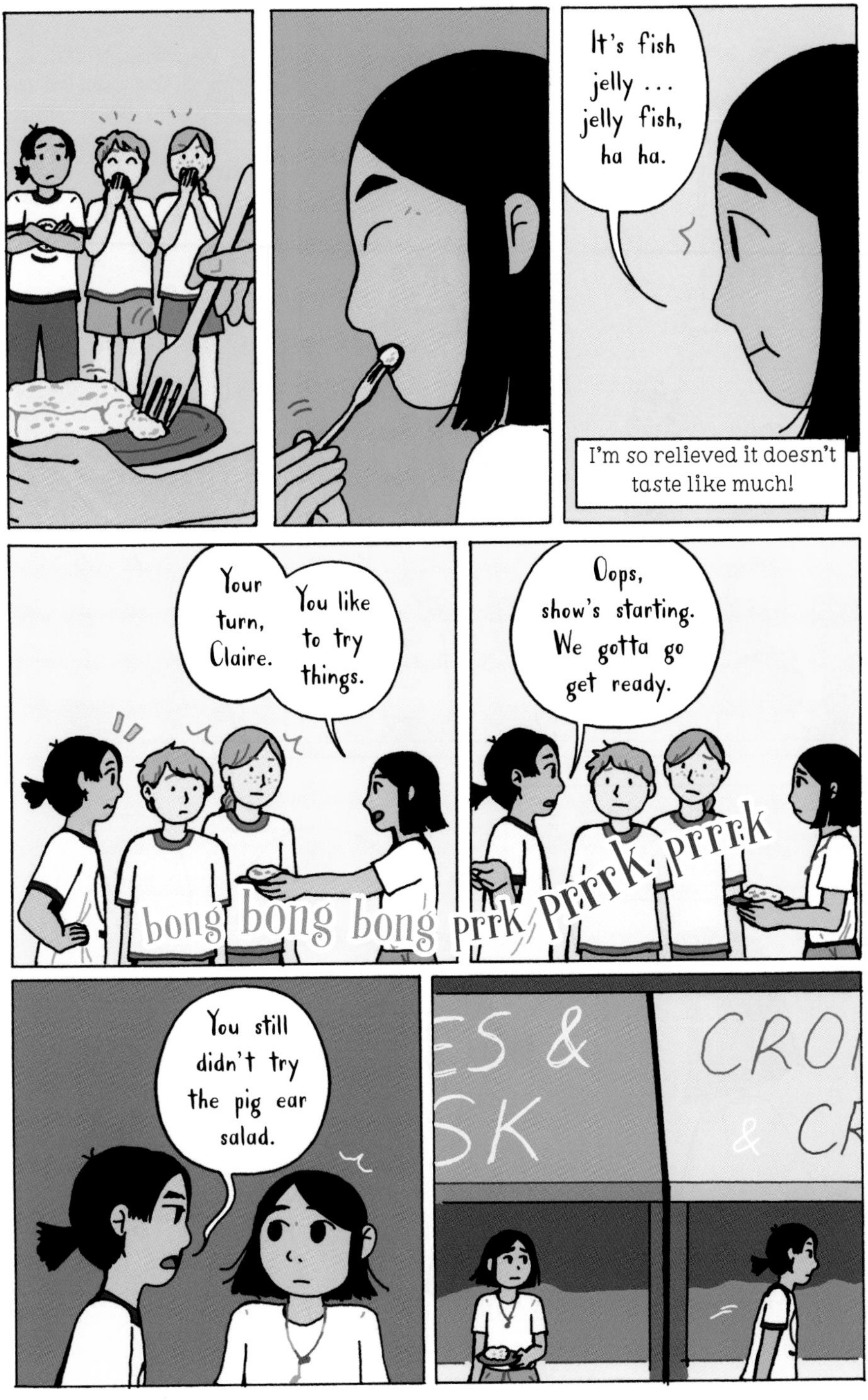
It's fish jelly . . . jelly fish, ha ha.
I'm so relieved it doesn't taste like much!
Your turn, Claire.
You like to try things.
Oops, show's starting. We gotta go get ready.
bong bong bong prrk prrrk prrrk
You still didn't try the pig ear salad.
ES &
SK
CRO
& CR

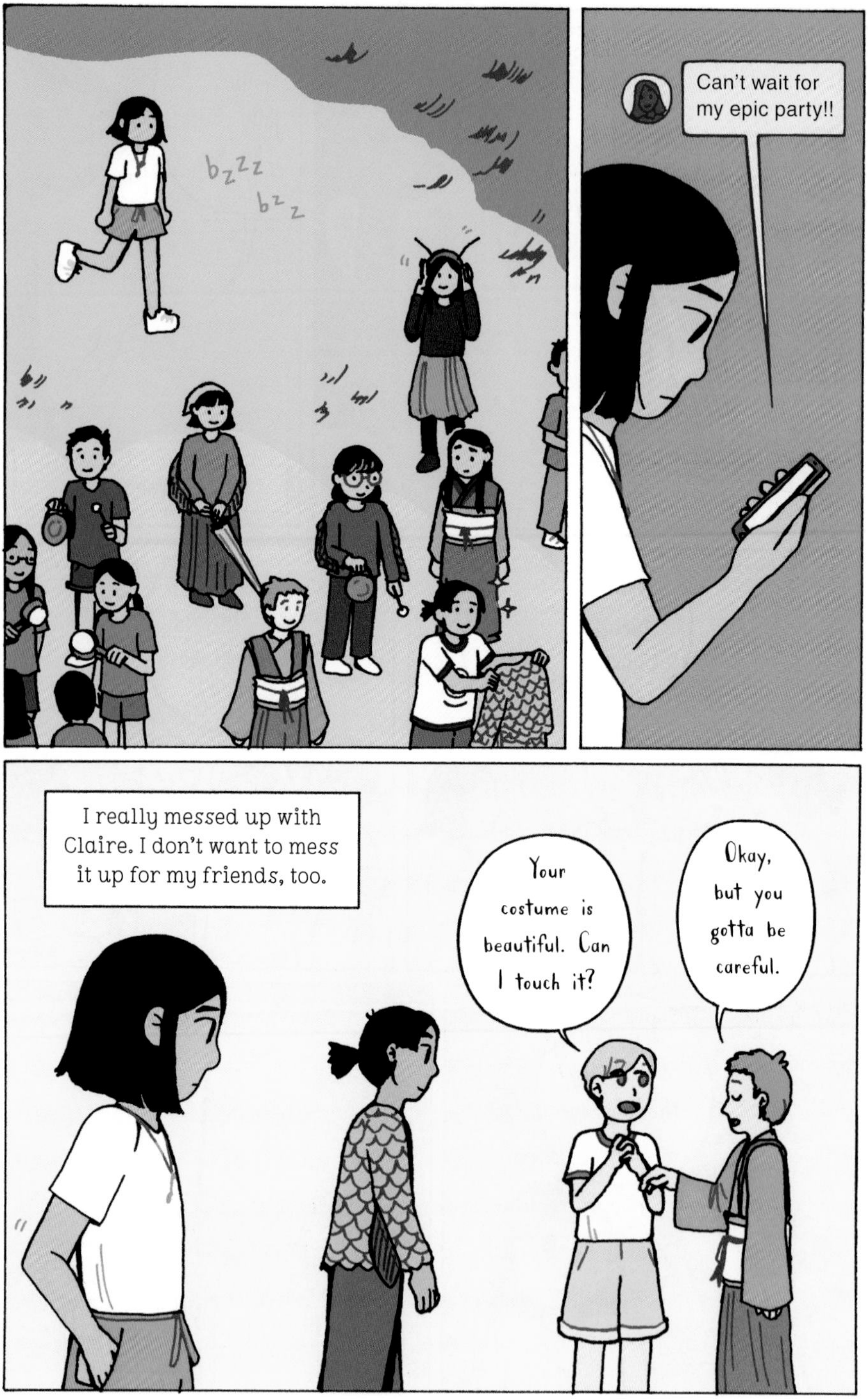
bzzz
bzz
Can't wait for my epic party!!
I really messed up with Claire. I don't want to mess it up for my friends, too.
Your costume is beautiful. Can I touch it?
Okay, but you gotta be careful.

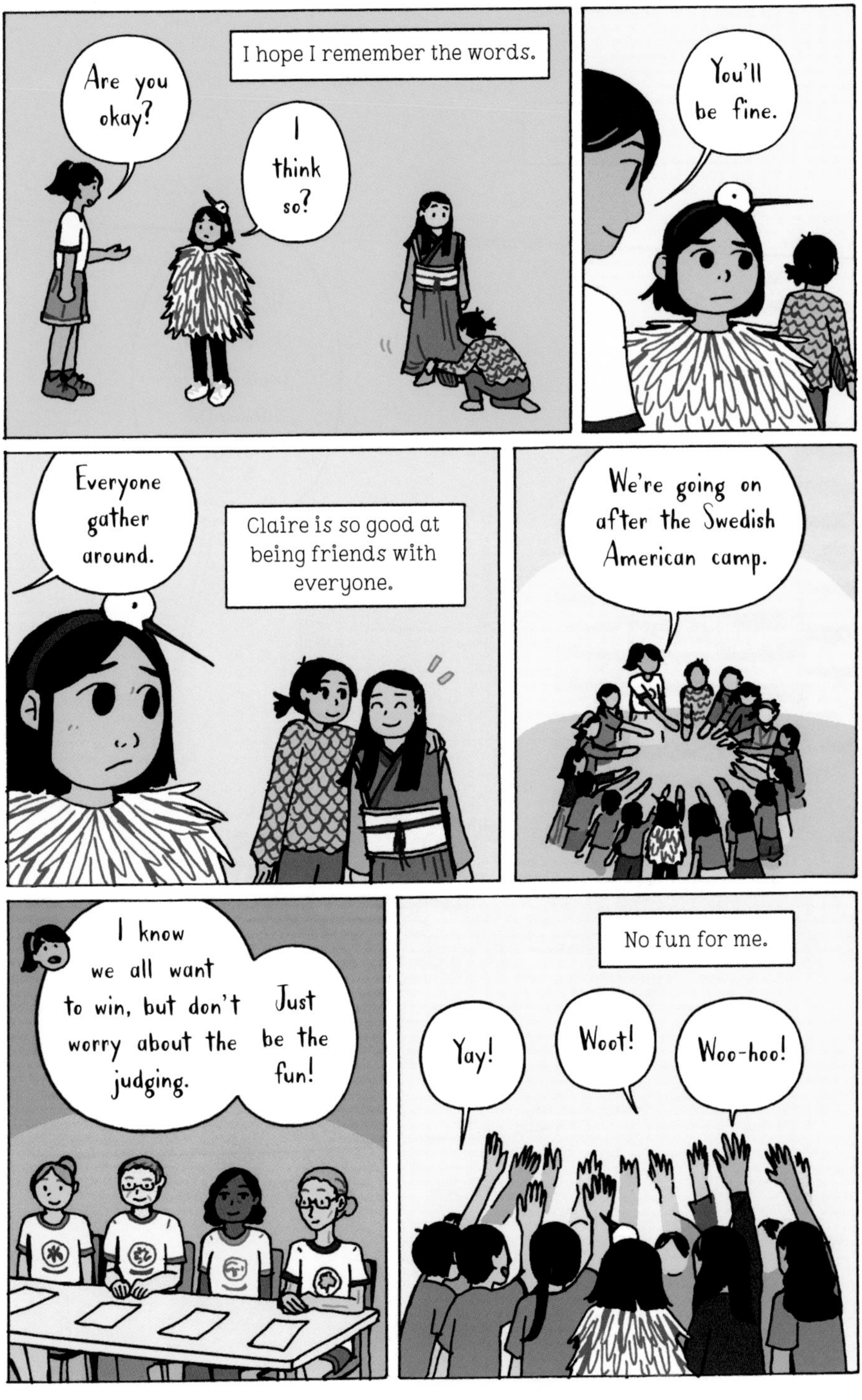
I hope I remember the words.
Are you okay?
I think so?
You'll be fine.
Everyone gather around.
Claire is so good at being friends with everyone.
We're going on after the Swedish American camp.
I know we all want to win, but don't worry about the judging.
Just be the fun!
No fun for me.
Yay!
Woot!
Woo-hoo!

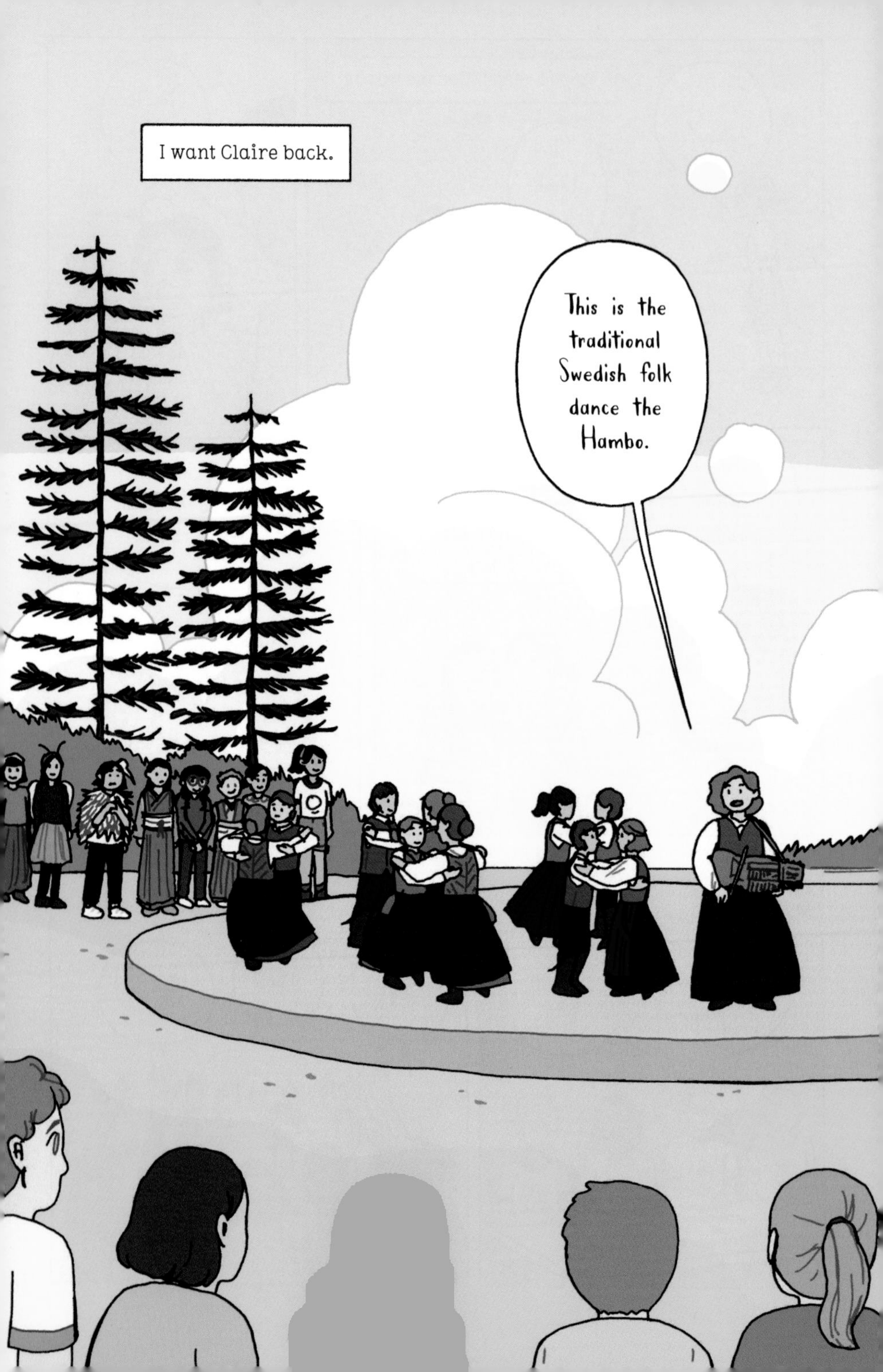
I want Claire back.
This is the traditional Swedish folk dance the Hambo.

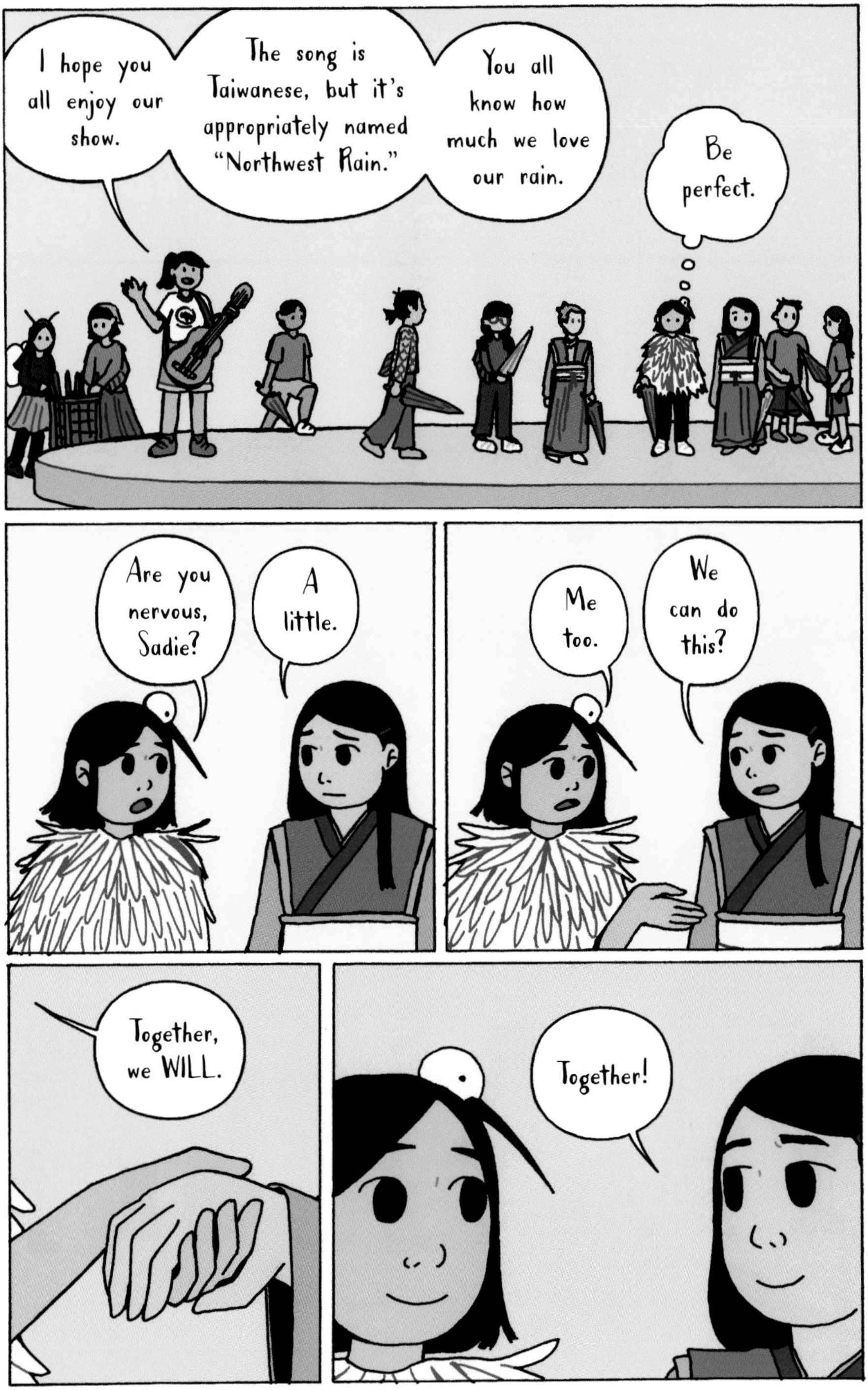
I hope you all enjoy our show.
The song is Taiwanese, but it's appropriately named "Northwest Rain."
You all know how much we love our rain.
Be perfect.
Are you nervous, Sadie?
A little.
Me too.
We can do this?
Together, we WILL.
Together!

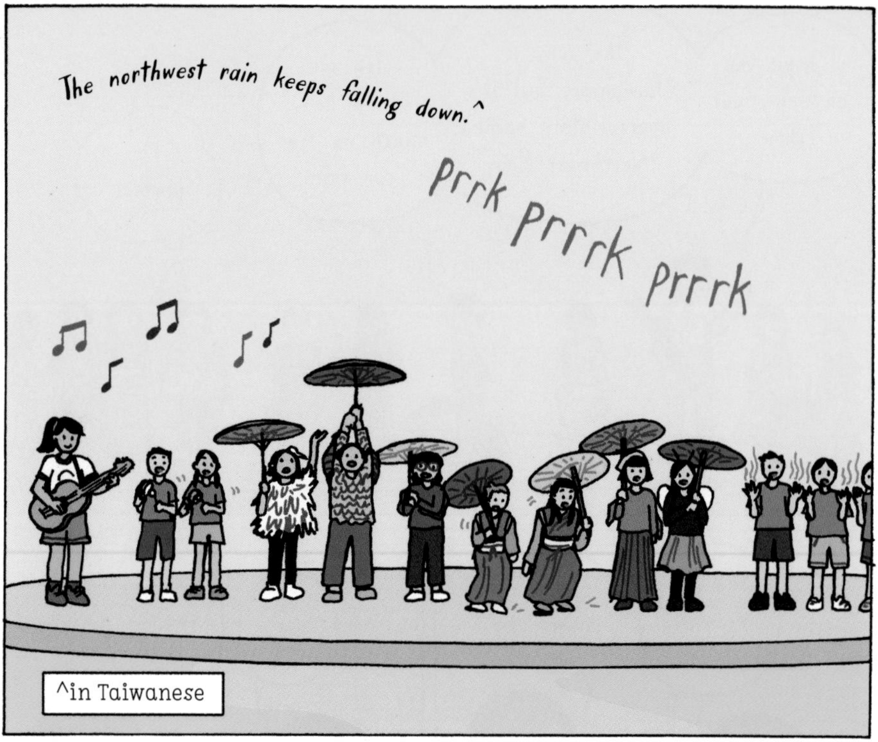
The northwest rain keeps falling down.^
Prrk Prrrk prrrk
^in Taiwanese

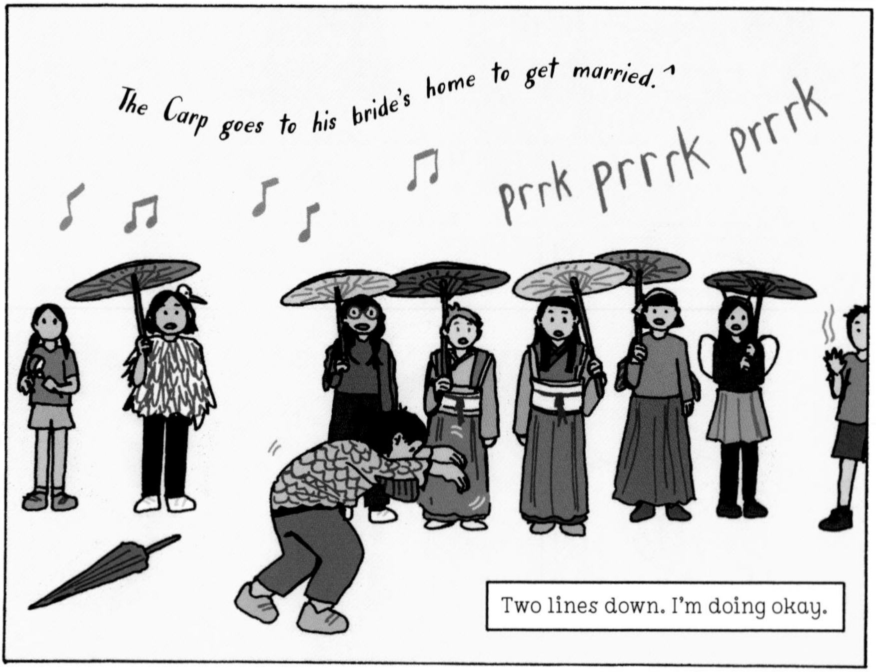
The Carp goes to his bride's home to get married.^
prrk prrrk prrrk
Two lines down. I'm doing okay.

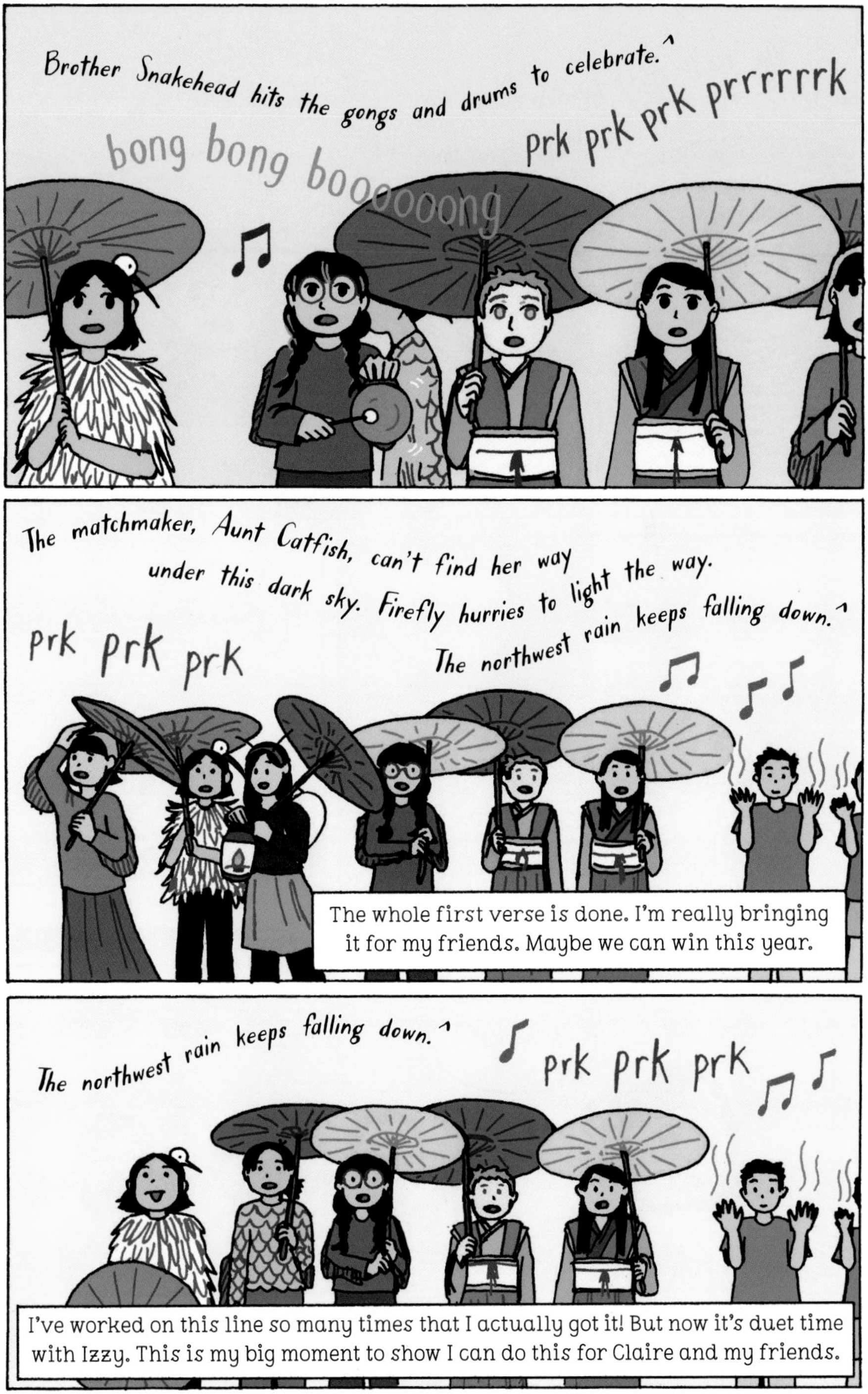

Brother Snakehead hits the gongs and drums to celebrate.^
bong bong boooooong
prk prk prk prrrrrrk
The matchmaker, Aunt Catfish, can't find her way under this dark sky. Firefly hurries to light the way.
prk prk prk
The northwest rain keeps falling down.^
The whole first verse is done. I'm really bringing it for my friends. Maybe we can win this year.
The northwest rain keeps falling down.^
prk prk prk
I've worked on this line so many times that I actually got it! But now it's duet time with Izzy. This is my big moment to show I can do this for Claire and my friends.

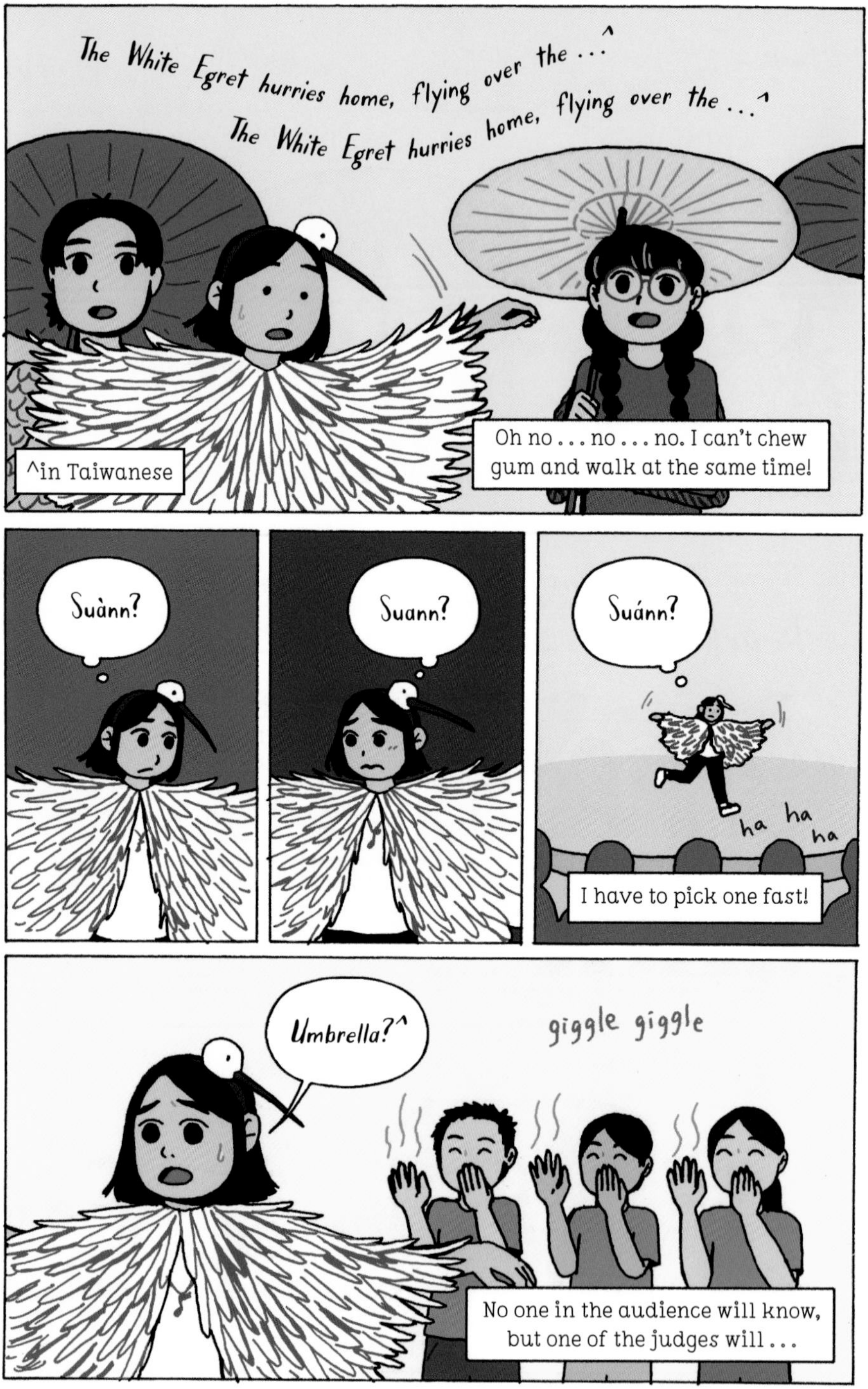
The White Egret hurries home, flying over the . . .^
The White Egret hurries home, flying over the . . .^
^in Taiwanese
Oh no . . . no . . . no. I can't chew gum and walk at the same time!
Suànn?
Suann?
Suánn?
ha ha ha
I have to pick one fast!
Umbrella?^
giggle giggle
No one in the audience will know, but one of the judges will . . .

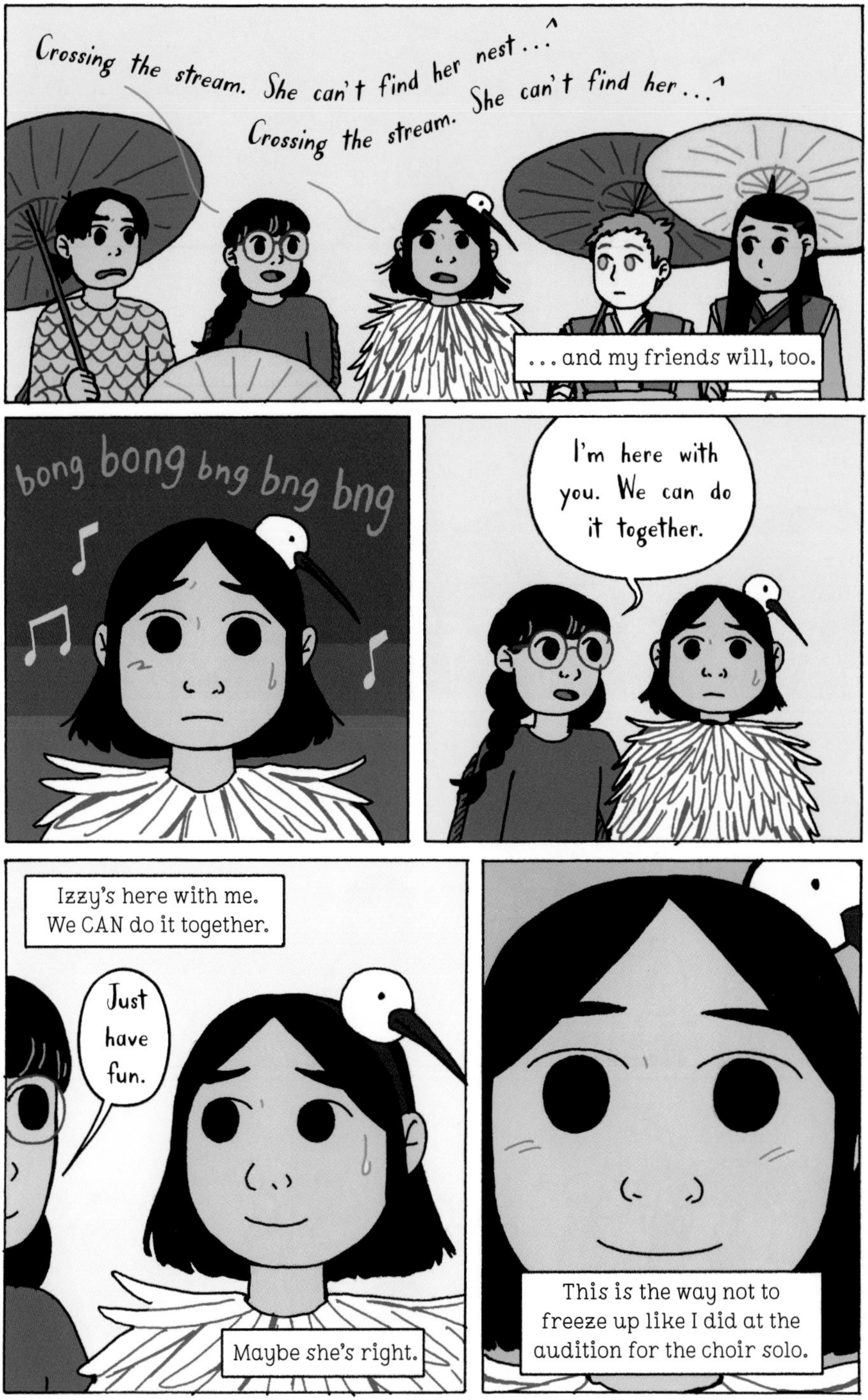
Crossing the stream. She can't find her nest...
Crossing the stream. She can't find her...
...and my friends will, too.
bong bong bng bng bng
I'm here with you. We can do it together.
Izzy's here with me. We CAN do it together.
Just have fun.
Maybe she's right.
This is the way not to freeze up like I did at the audition for the choir solo.

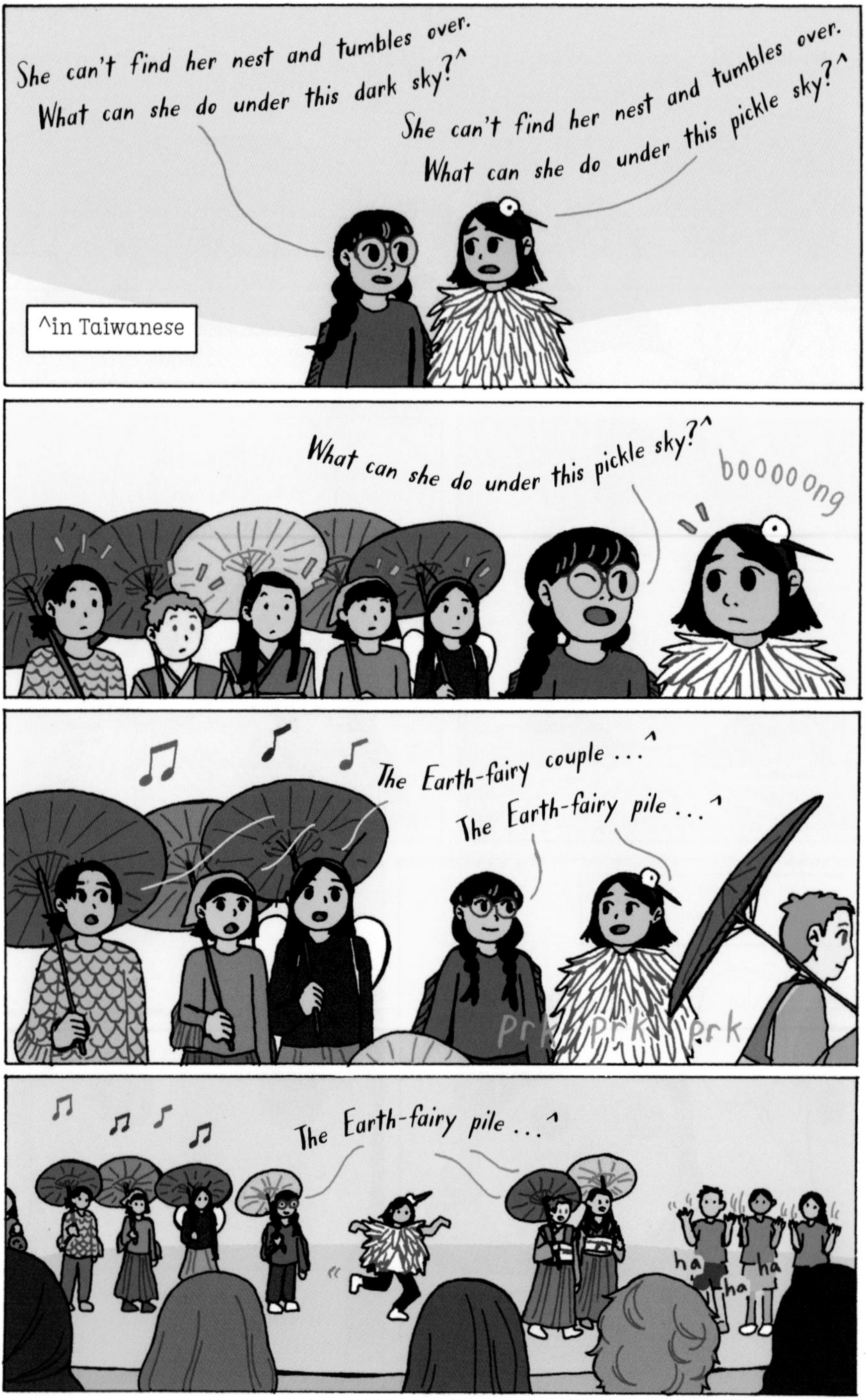

She can't find her nest and tumbles over.
What can she do under this dark sky?^
She can't find her nest and tumbles over.
What can she do under this pickle sky?^
^in Taiwanese
What can she do under this pickle sky?^
boooooong
The Earth-fairy couple ...^
The Earth-fairy pile ...^
prk prk prk
The Earth-fairy pile ...^
ha ha ha

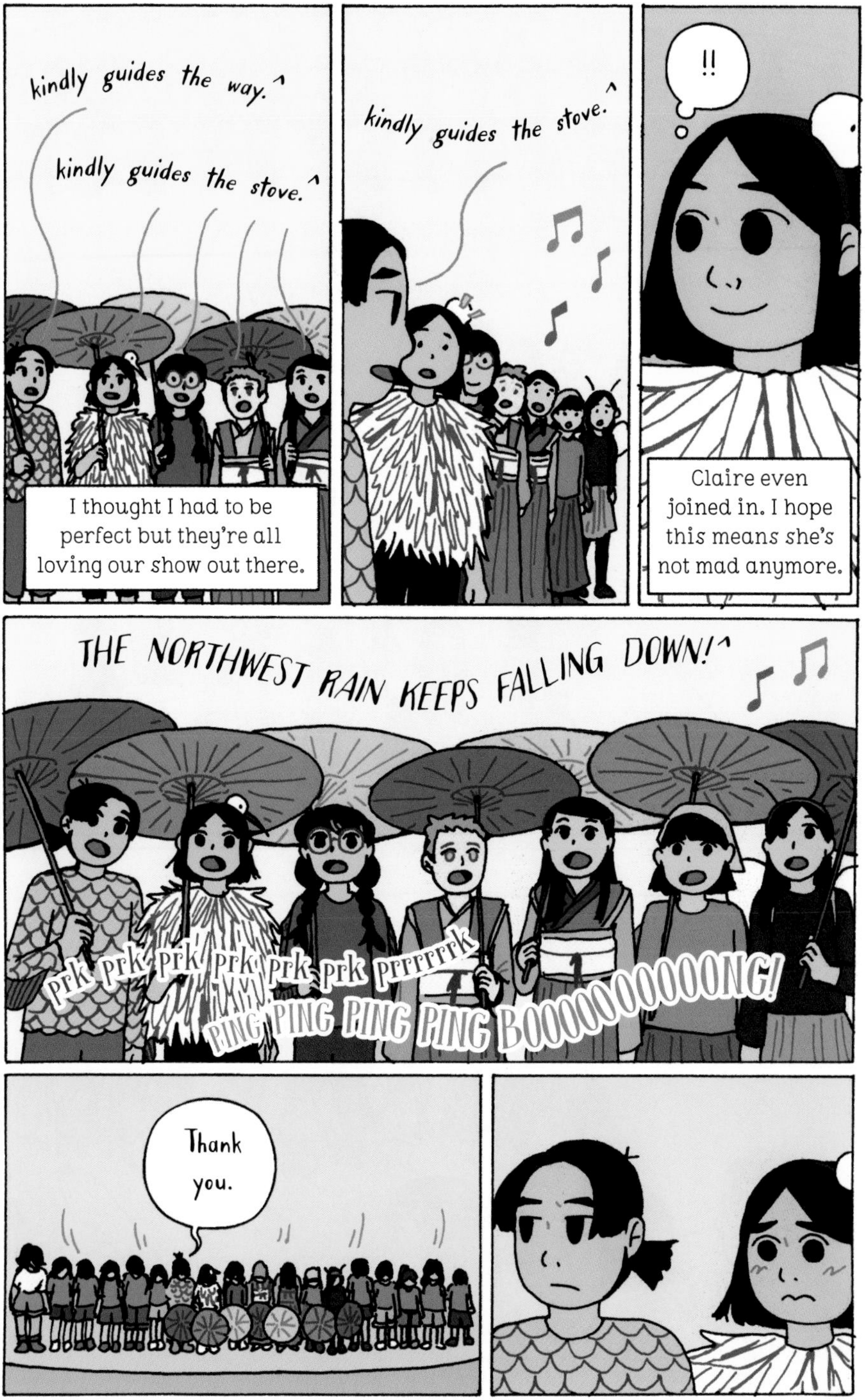

kindly guides the way.^
kindly guides the stove.^
I thought I had to be perfect but they're all loving our show out there.
kindly guides the stove.^
!!
Claire even joined in. I hope this means she's not mad anymore.
THE NORTHWEST RAIN KEEPS FALLING DOWN!^
prk prk prk prk prk prk prrrrrrk
PING PING PING PING BOOOOOOOOOONG!
Thank you.

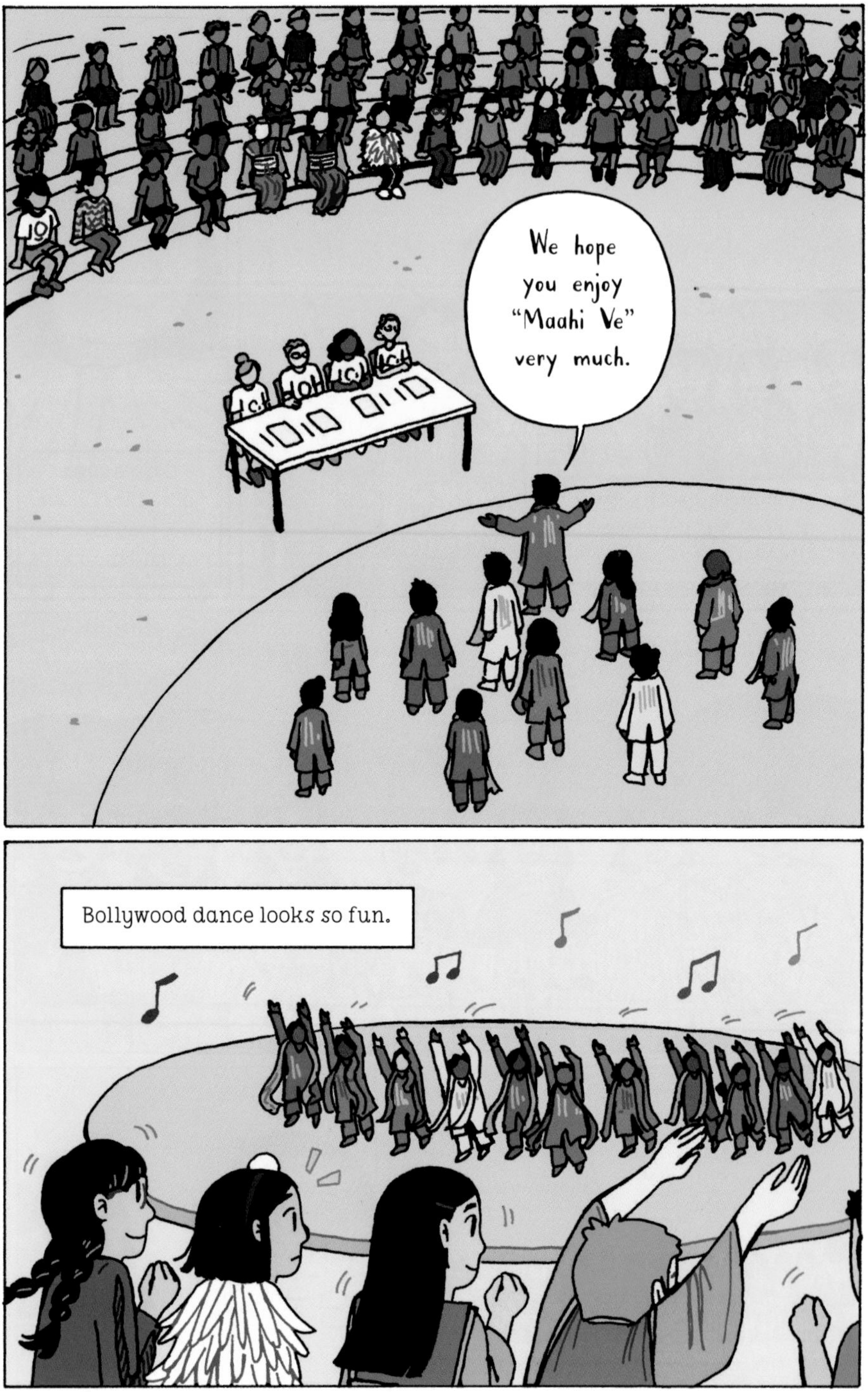
We hope you enjoy "Maahi Ve" very much.
Bollywood dance looks so fun.

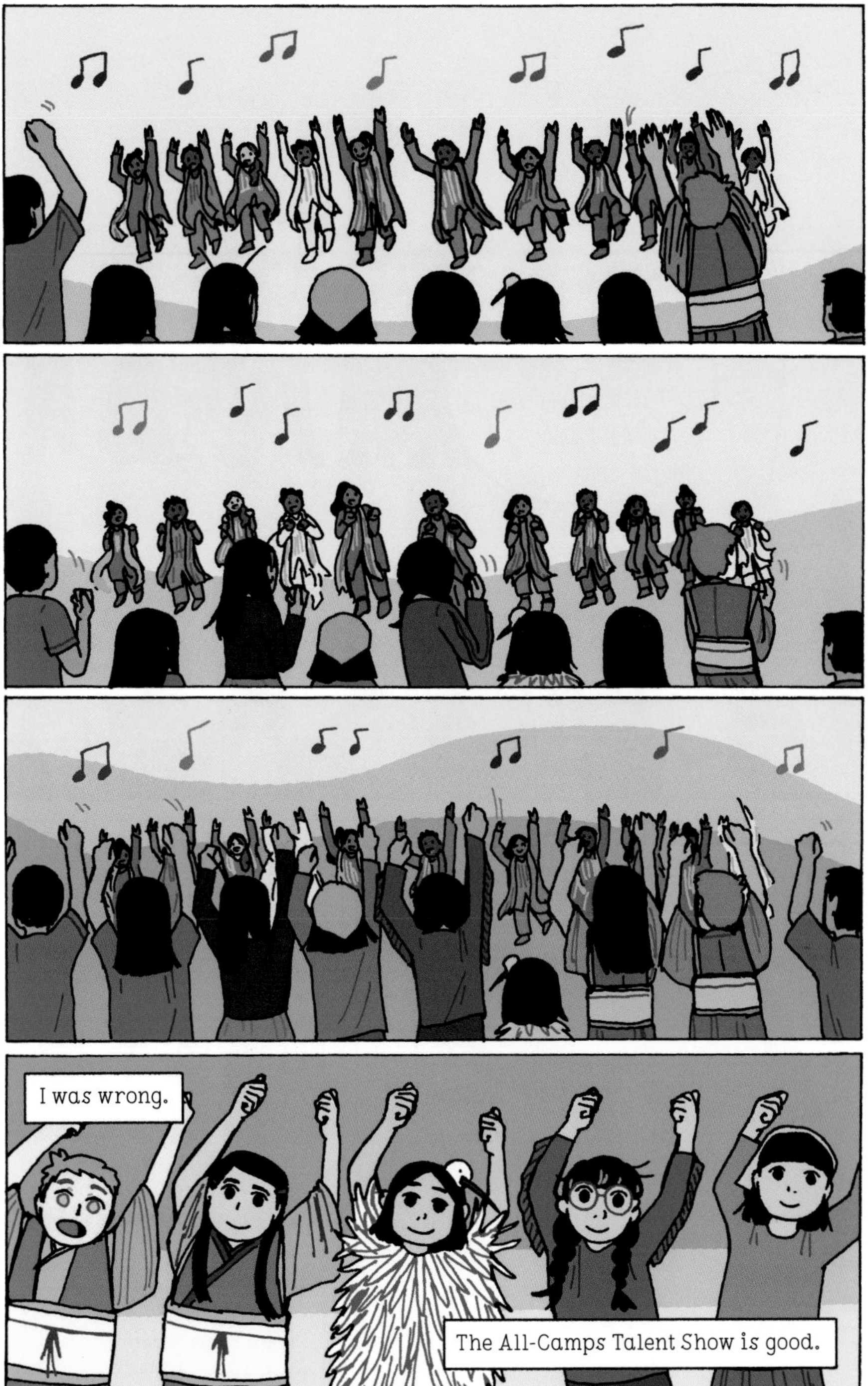
I was wrong.
The All-Camps Talent Show is good.

What are they singing?

Oh! We sang it in choir this year. It's "One Day More" from *Les Misérables*.

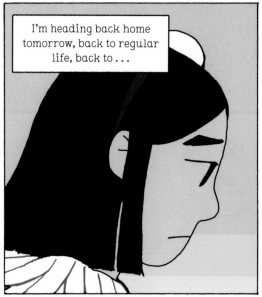

I'm heading back home tomorrow, back to regular life, back to . . .

. . . Jess's party. I don't even want to go, although . . .

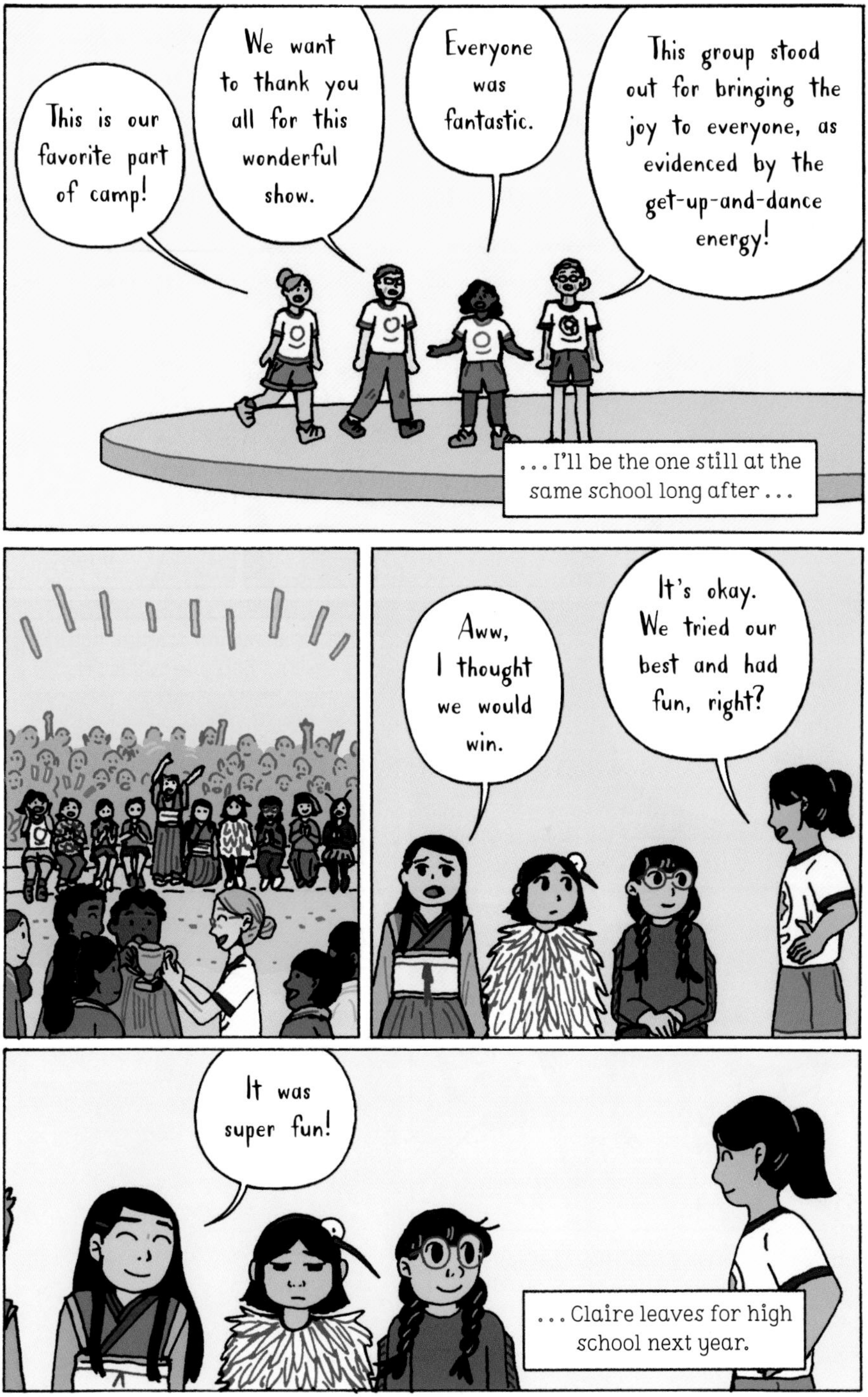
This is our favorite part of camp!
We want to thank you all for this wonderful show.
Everyone was fantastic.
This group stood out for bringing the joy to everyone, as evidenced by the get-up-and-dance energy!
. . . I'll be the one still at the same school long after . . .
Aww, I thought we would win.
It's okay. We tried our best and had fun, right?
It was super fun!
. . . Claire leaves for high school next year.

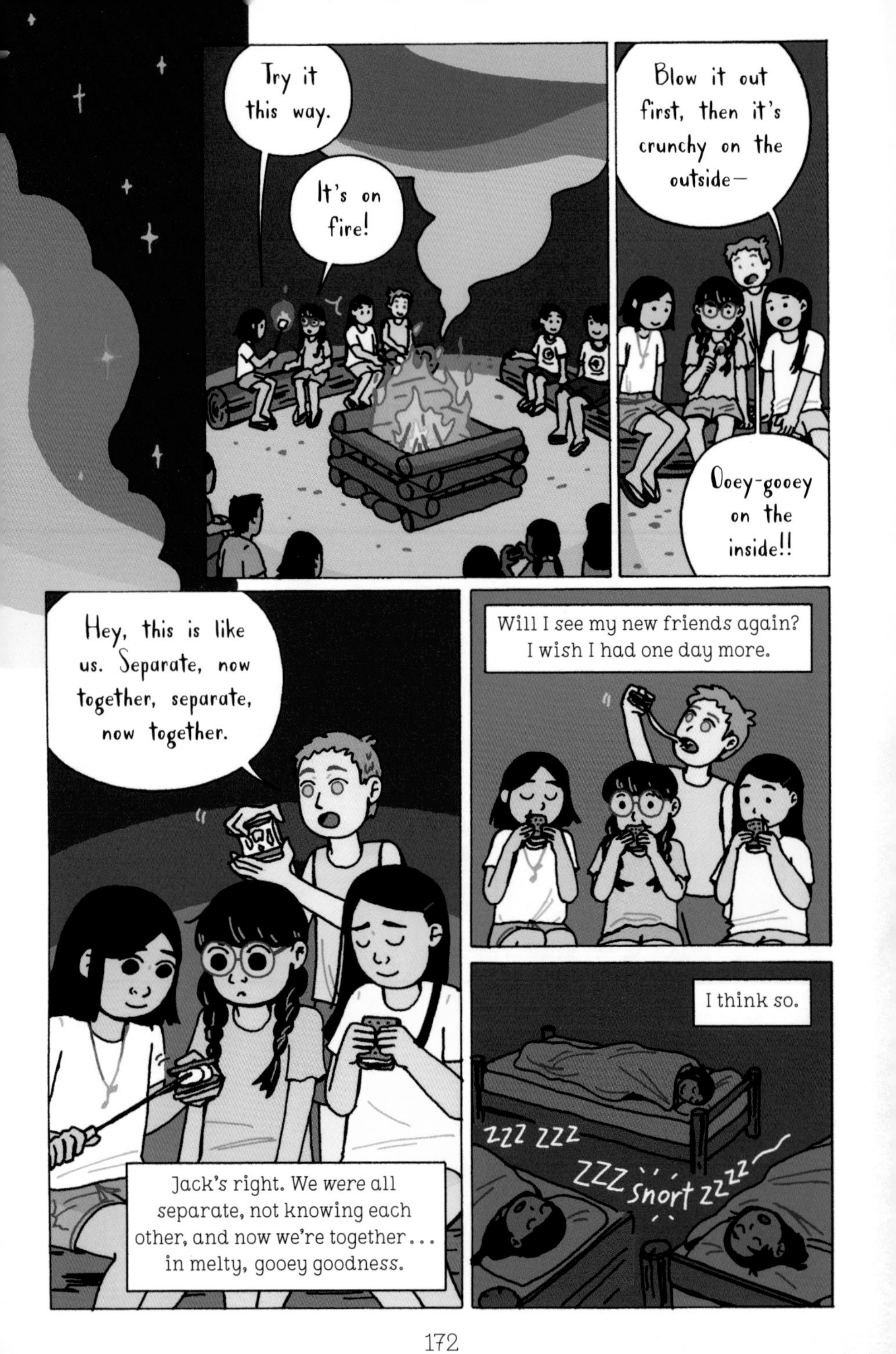
Try it this way.
It's on fire!
Blow it out first, then it's crunchy on the outside—
Ooey-gooey on the inside!!
Hey, this is like us. Separate, now together, separate, now together.
Will I see my new friends again? I wish I had one day more.
Jack's right. We were all separate, not knowing each other, and now we're together . . . in melty, gooey goodness.
I think so.
ZZZ ZZZ
ZZZ
snort
ZZZZ

chapter
FIFTEEN

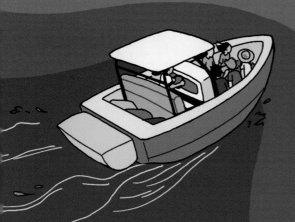

Day Zero

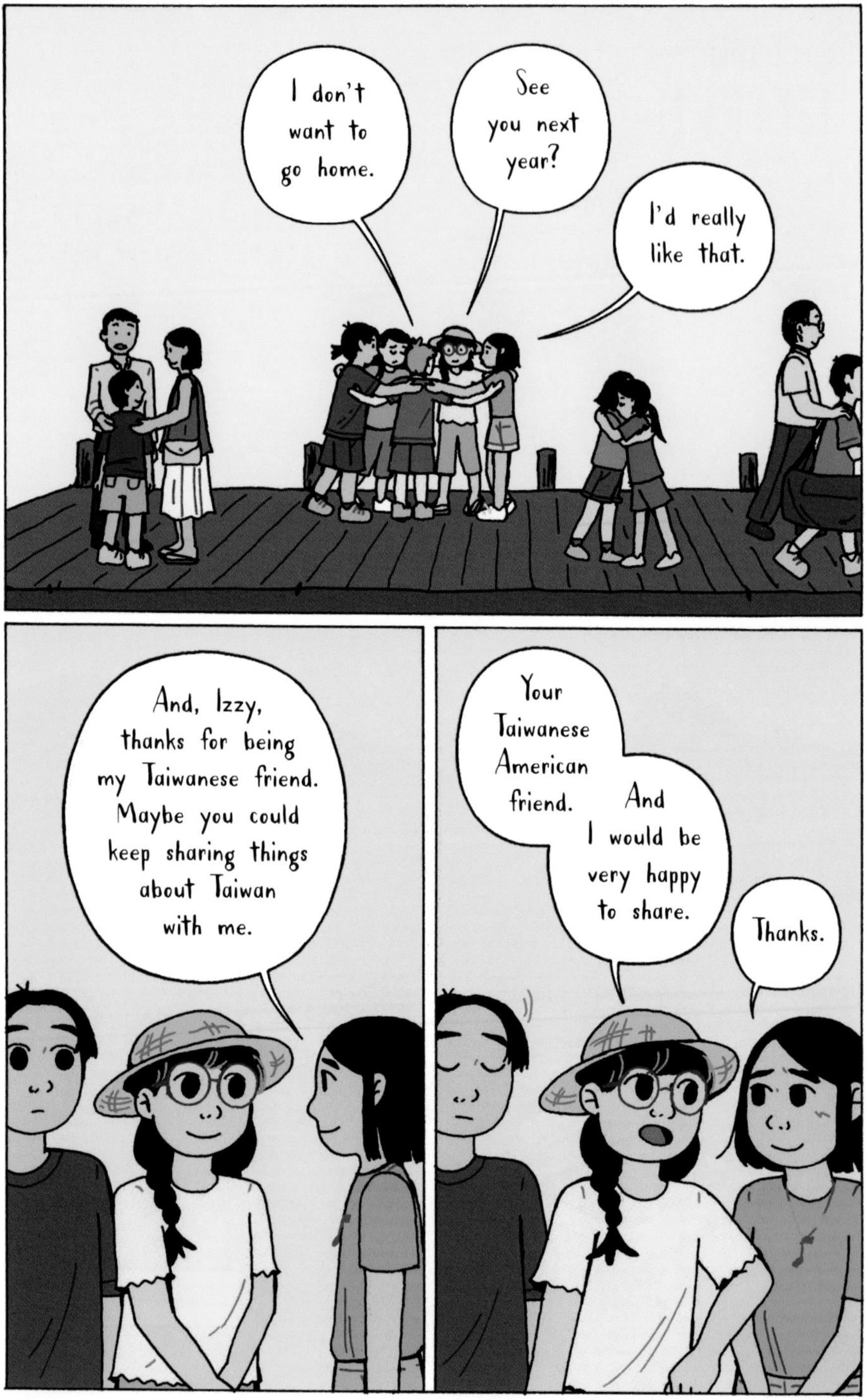

I don't want to go home.
See you next year?
I'd really like that.
And, Izzy, thanks for being my Taiwanese friend. Maybe you could keep sharing things about Taiwan with me.
Your Taiwanese American friend.
And I would be very happy to share.
Thanks.

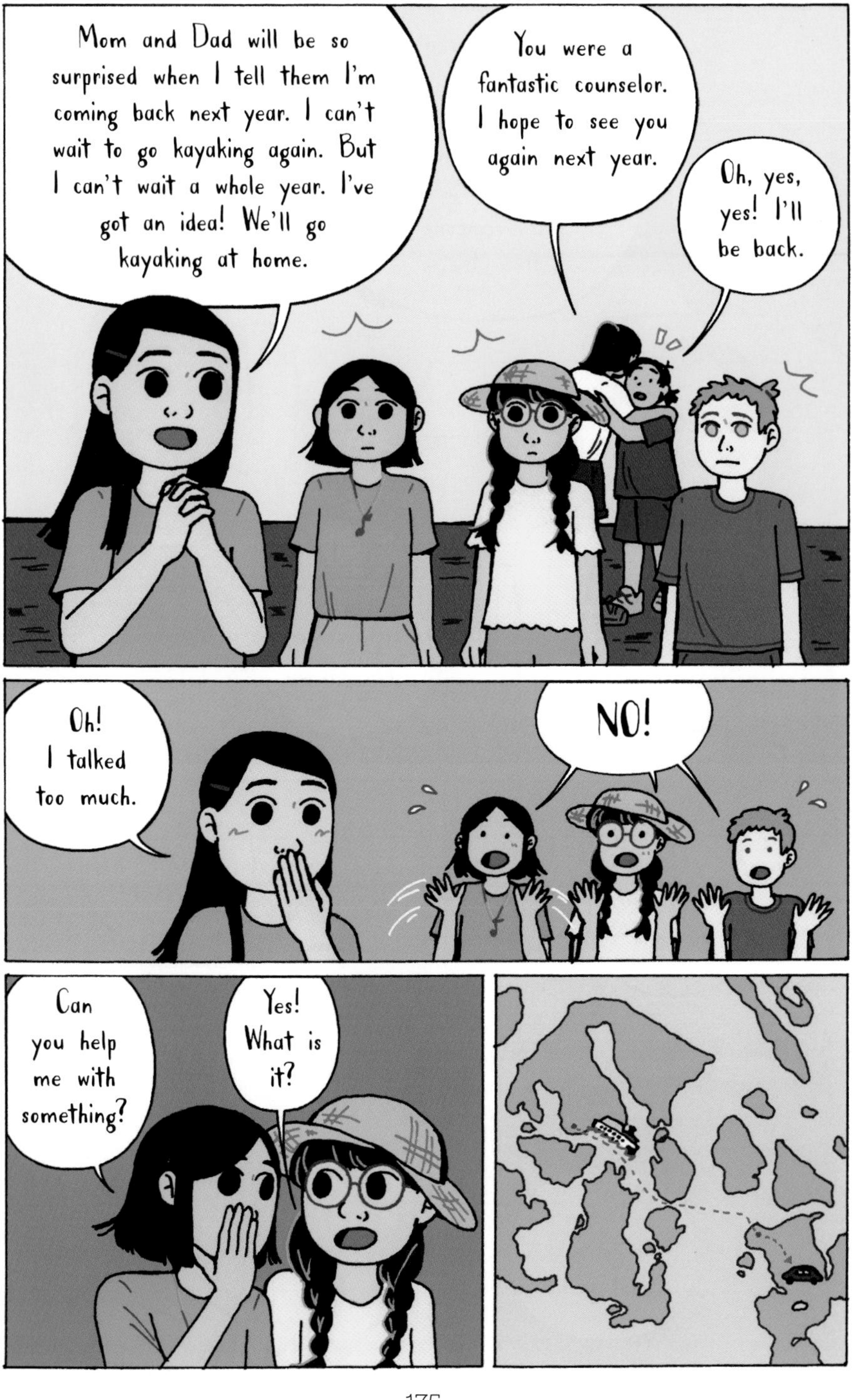
Mom and Dad will be so surprised when I tell them I'm coming back next year. I can't wait to go kayaking again. But I can't wait a whole year. I've got an idea! We'll go kayaking at home.
You were a fantastic counselor. I hope to see you again next year.
Oh, yes, yes! I'll be back.
Oh! I talked too much.
NO!
Can you help me with something?
Yes! What is it?

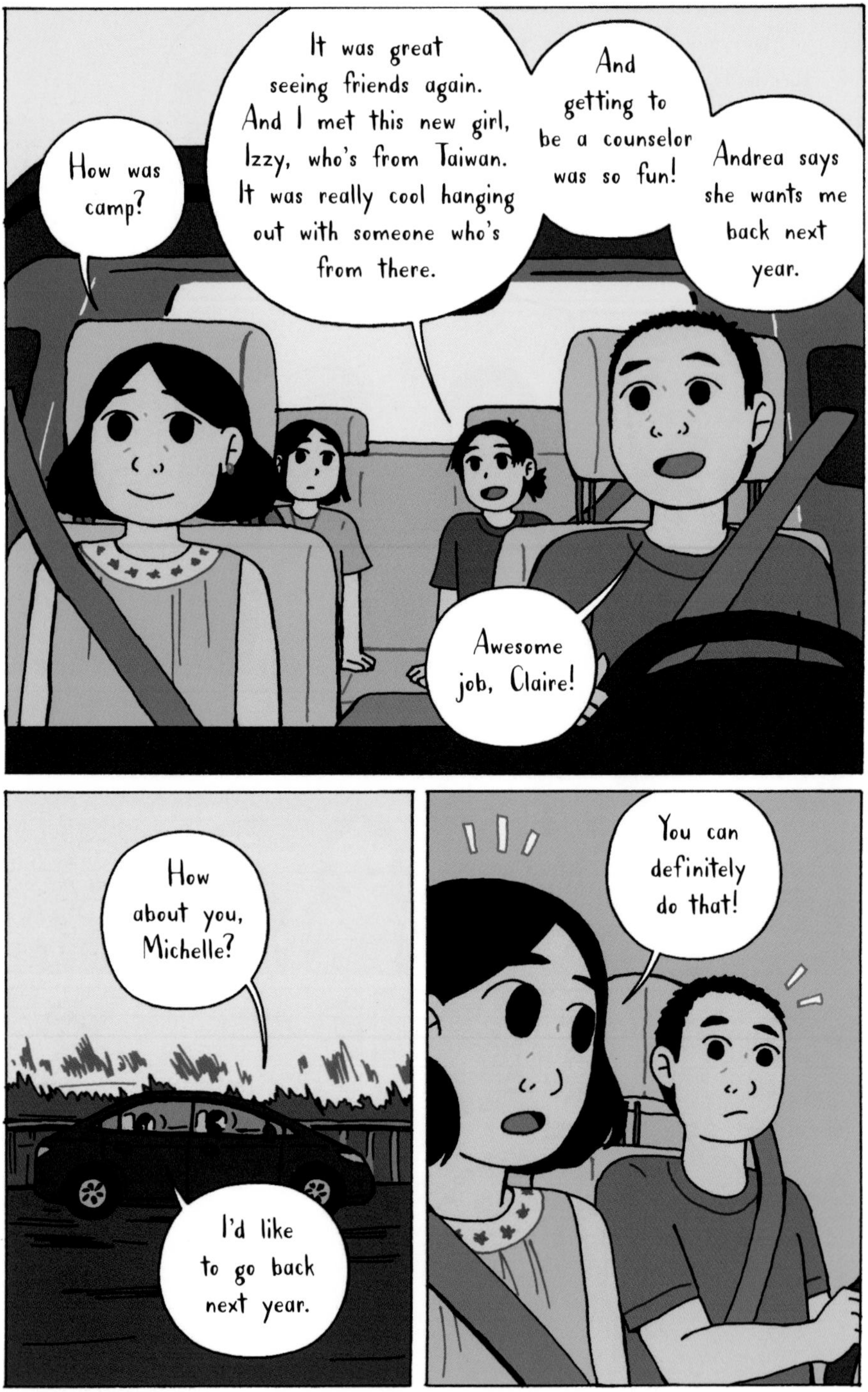
How was camp?
It was great seeing friends again. And I met this new girl, Izzy, who's from Taiwan. It was really cool hanging out with someone who's from there.
And getting to be a counselor was so fun!
Andrea says she wants me back next year.
Awesome job, Claire!
How about you, Michelle?
I'd like to go back next year.
You can definitely do that!

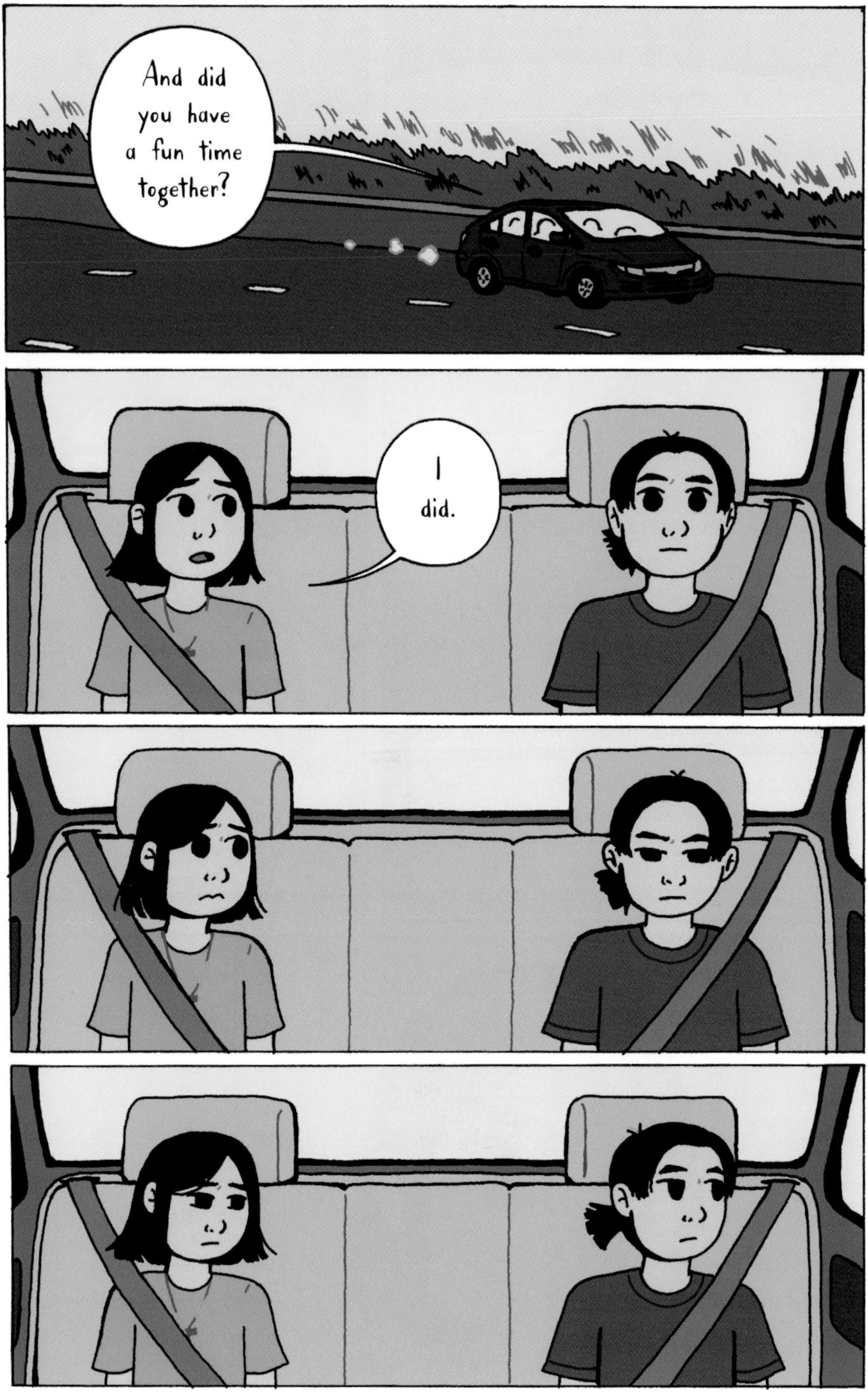
And did you have a fun time together?
I did.

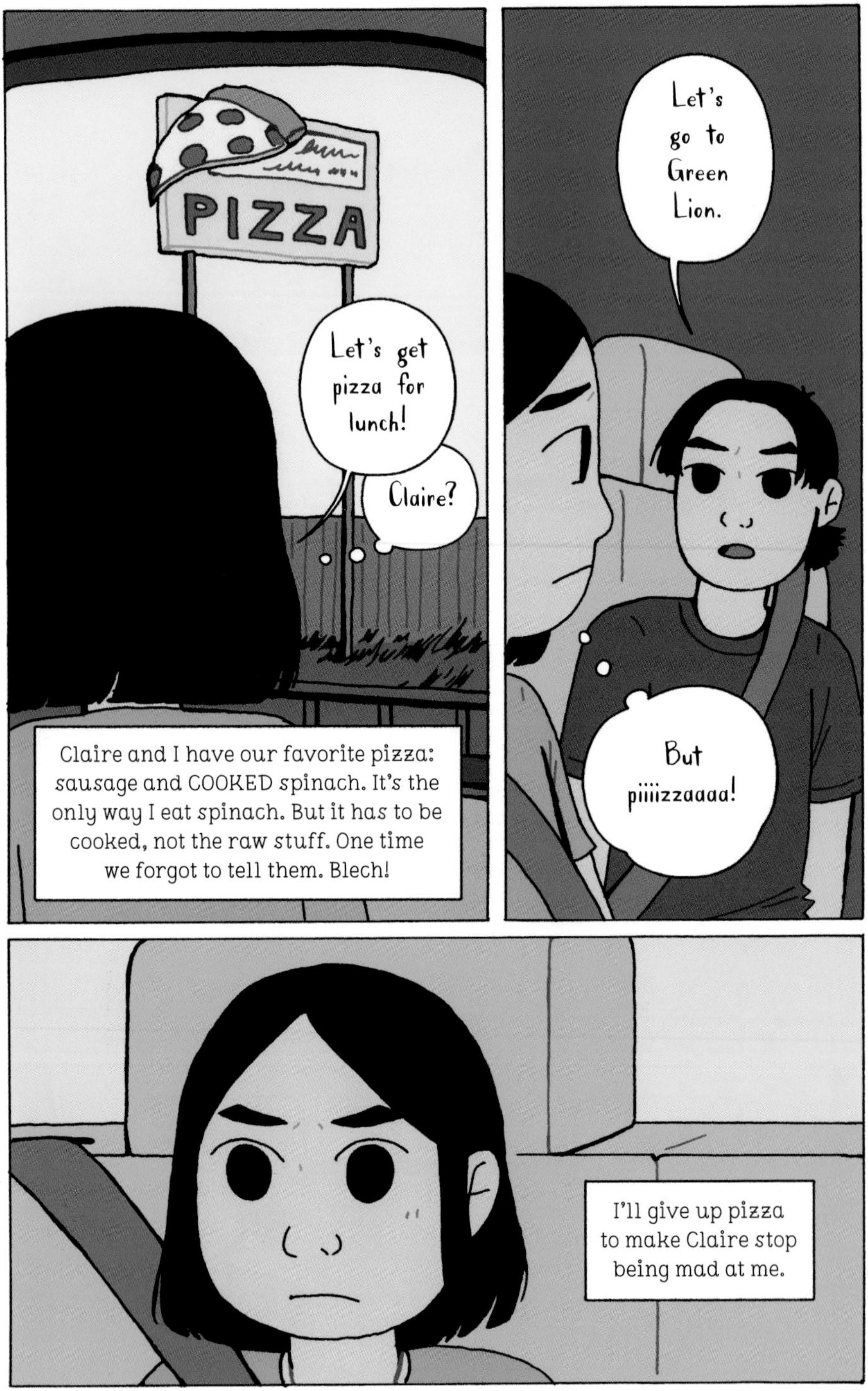
PIZZA
Let's get pizza for lunch!
Claire?
Claire and I have our favorite pizza: sausage and COOKED spinach. It's the only way I eat spinach. But it has to be cooked, not the raw stuff. One time we forgot to tell them. Blech!
Let's go to Green Lion.
But piiiizzaaaa!
I'll give up pizza to make Claire stop being mad at me.

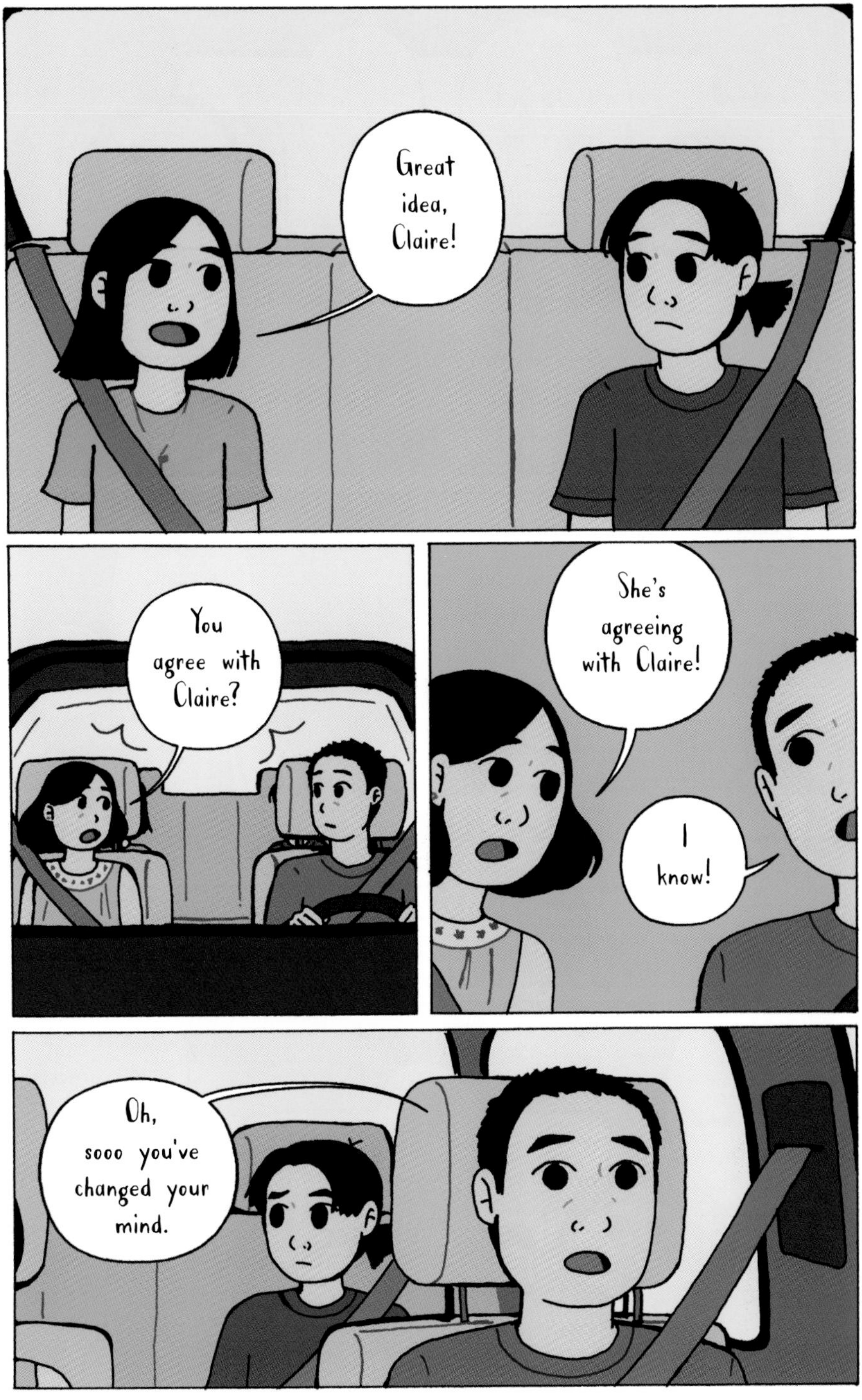
Great idea, Claire!
You agree with Claire?
She's agreeing with Claire!
I know!
Oh, sooo you've changed your mind.

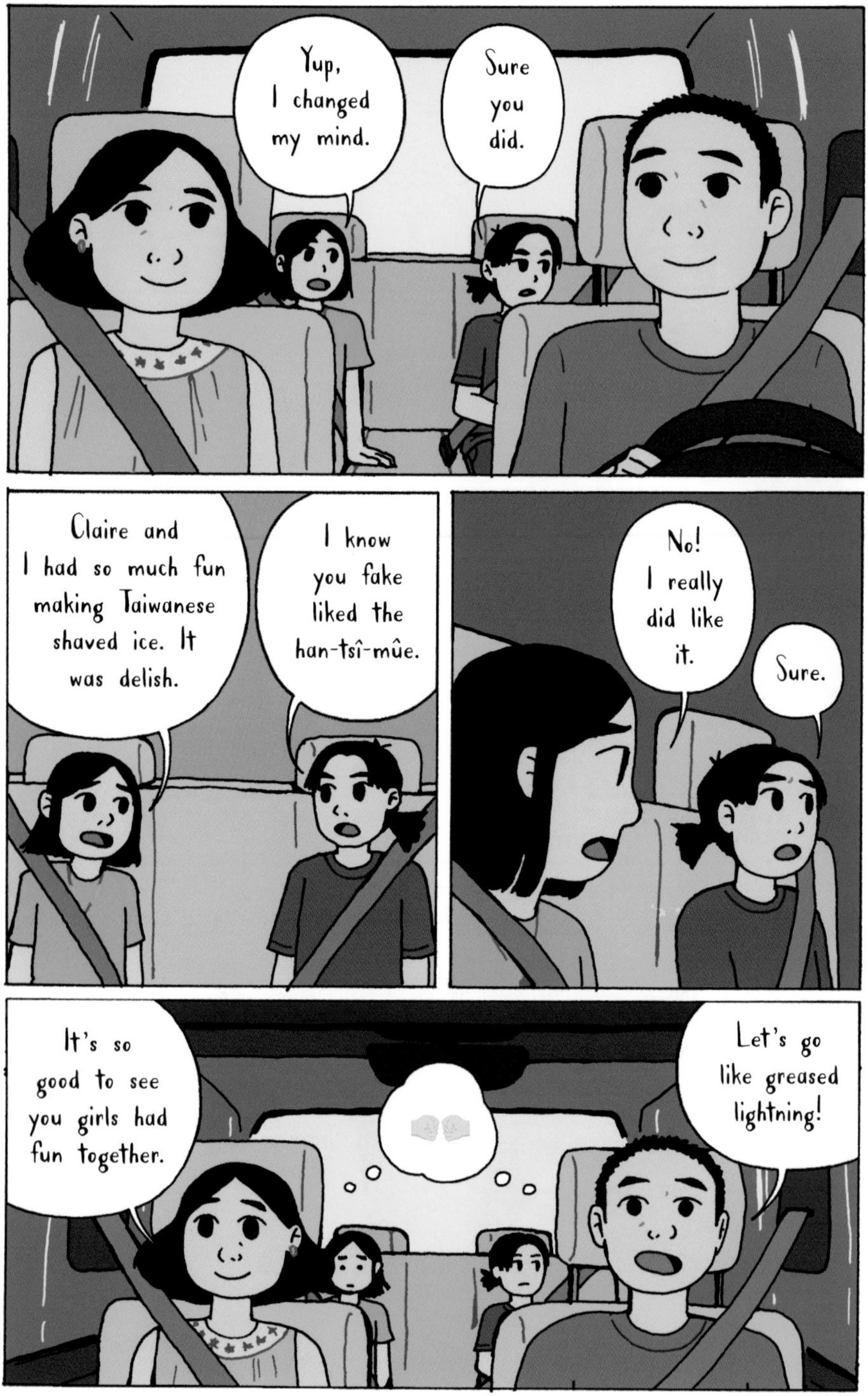
Yup, I changed my mind.
Sure you did.
Claire and I had so much fun making Taiwanese shaved ice. It was delish.
I know you fake liked the han-tsî-mûe.
No! I really did like it.
Sure.
It's so good to see you girls had fun together.
Let's go like greased lightning!

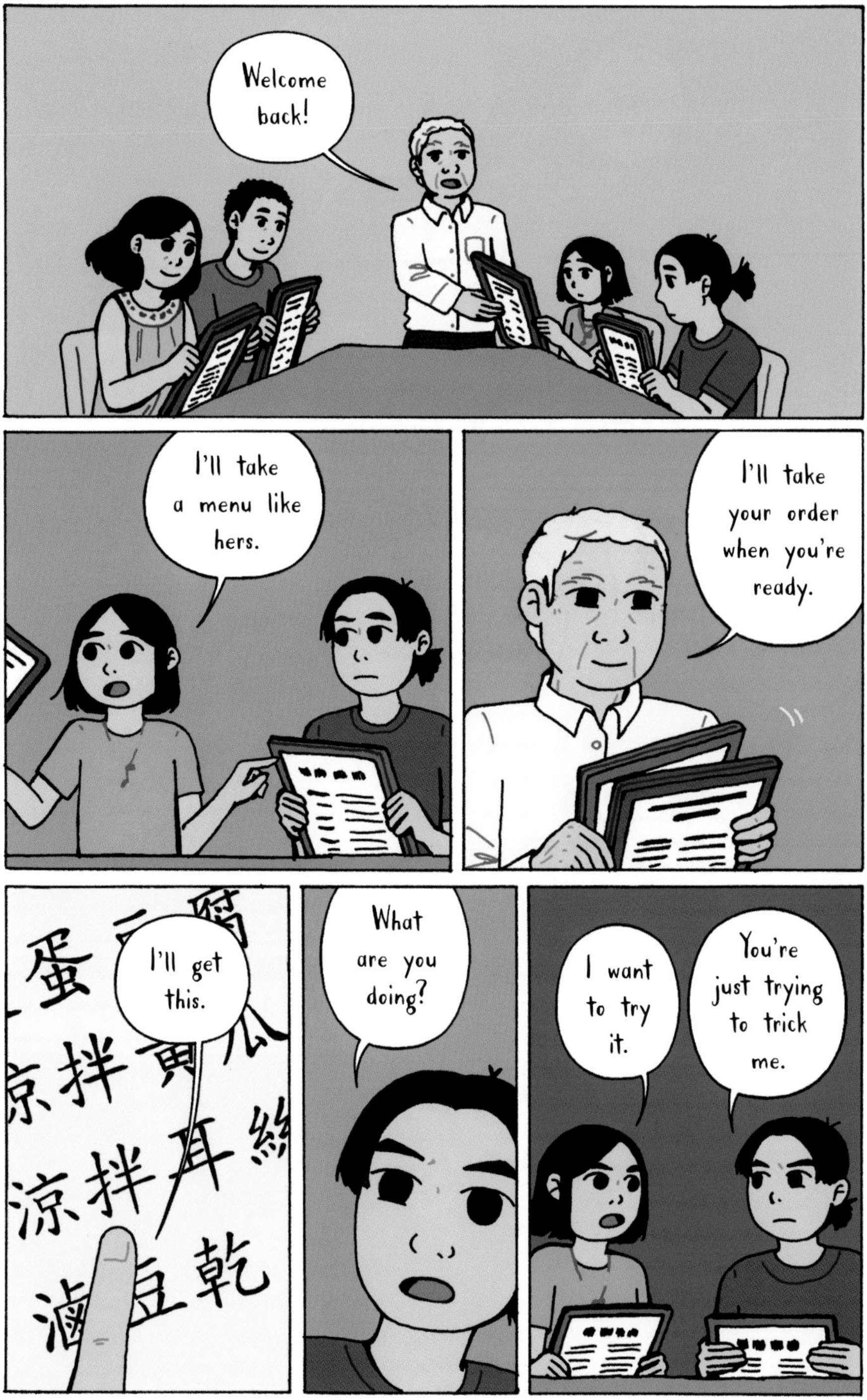
Welcome back!
I'll take a menu like hers.
I'll take your order when you're ready.
I'll get this.
What are you doing?
I want to try it.
You're just trying to trick me.

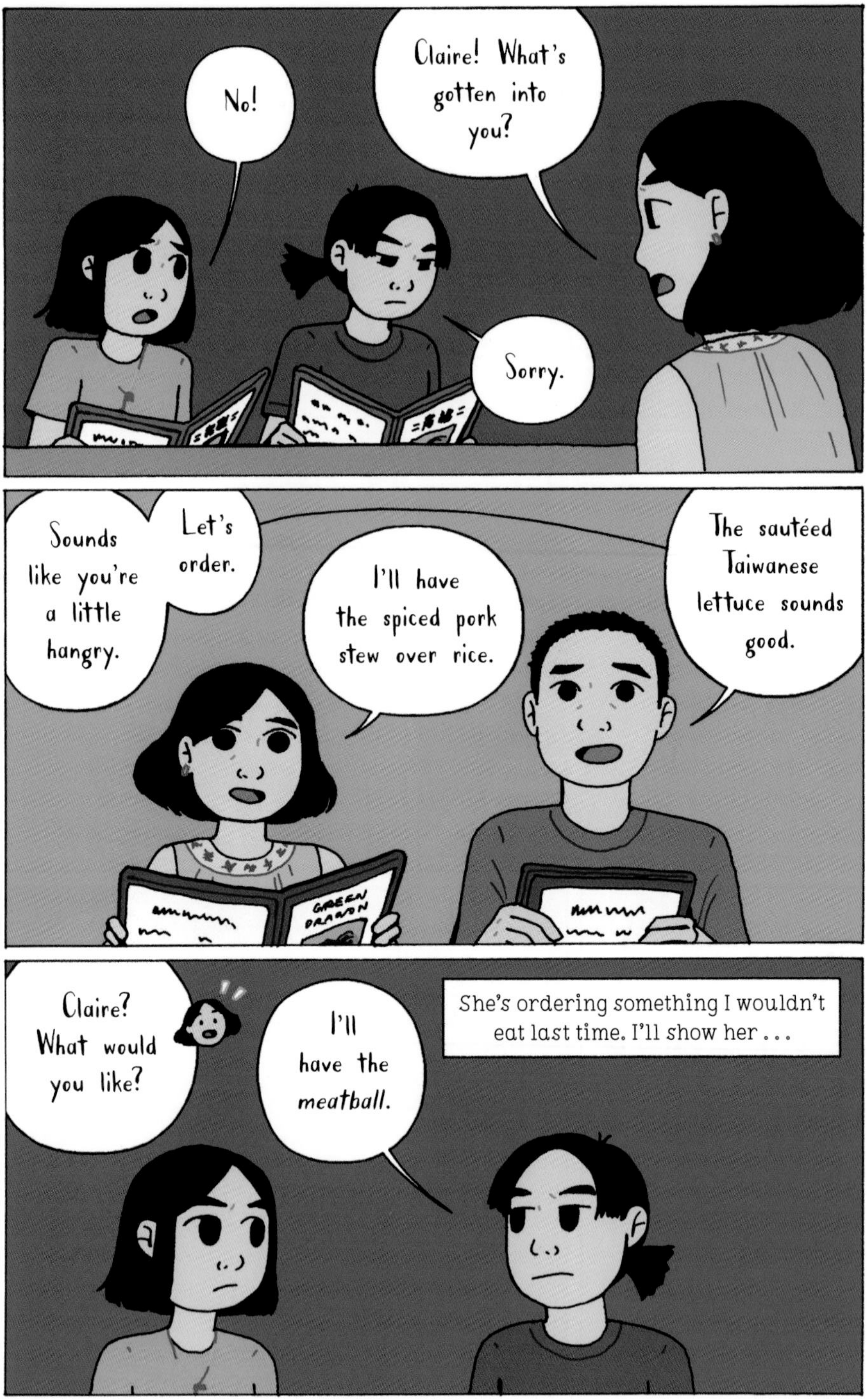
No!
Claire! What's gotten into you?
Sorry.
Sounds like you're a little hangry.
Let's order.
I'll have the spiced pork stew over rice.
The sautéed Taiwanese lettuce sounds good.
GREEN DRAGON
Claire? What would you like?
I'll have the *meatball.*
She's ordering something I wouldn't eat last time. I'll show her . . .

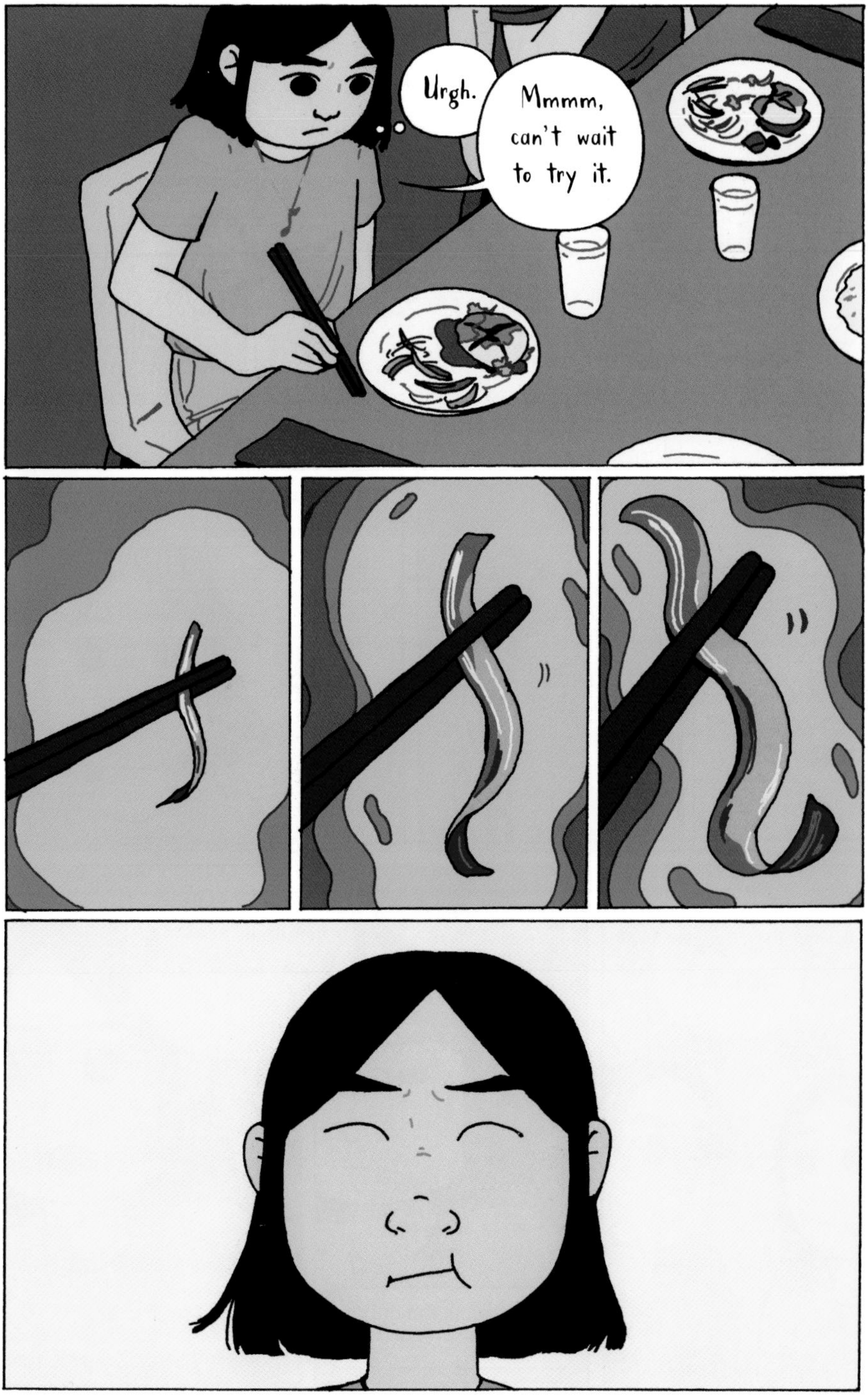
Urgh.
Mmmm, can't wait to try it.

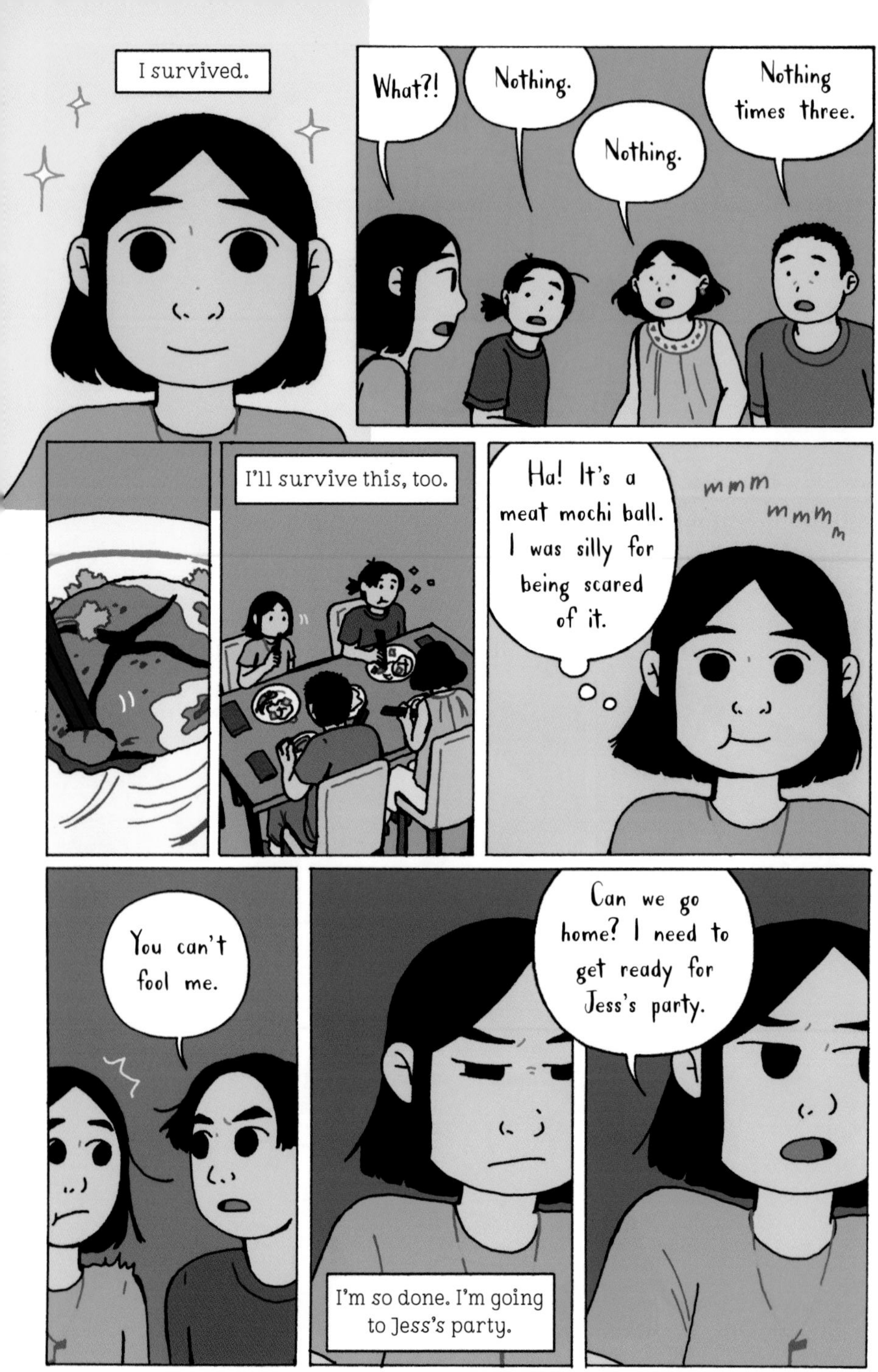
I survived.
What?!
Nothing.
Nothing.
Nothing times three.
I'll survive this, too.
Ha! It's a meat mochi ball. I was silly for being scared of it.
mmm
mmmm
You can't fool me.
Can we go home? I need to get ready for Jess's party.
I'm so done. I'm going to Jess's party.

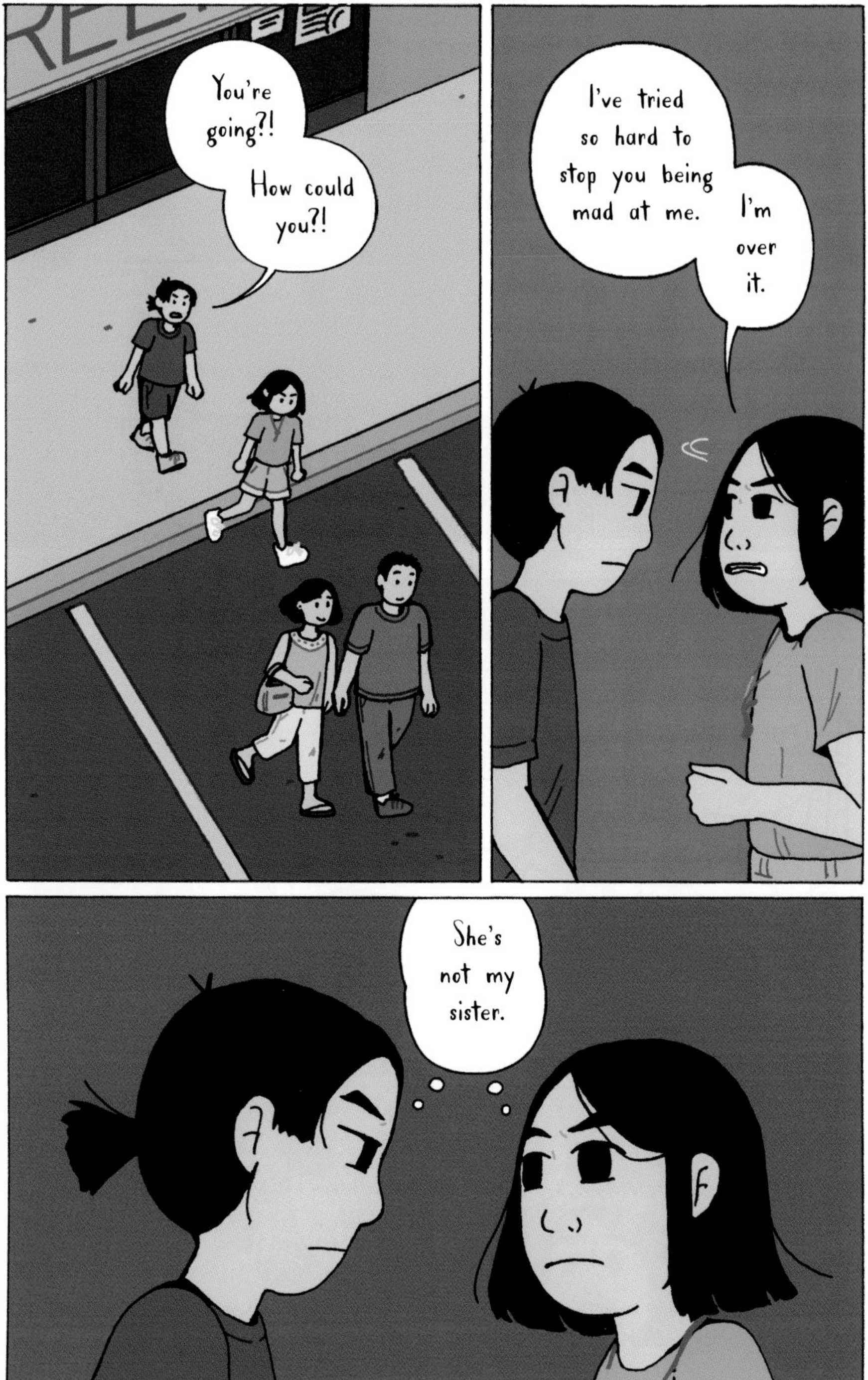
You're going?!
How could you?!
I've tried so hard to stop you being mad at me.
I'm over it.
She's not my sister.

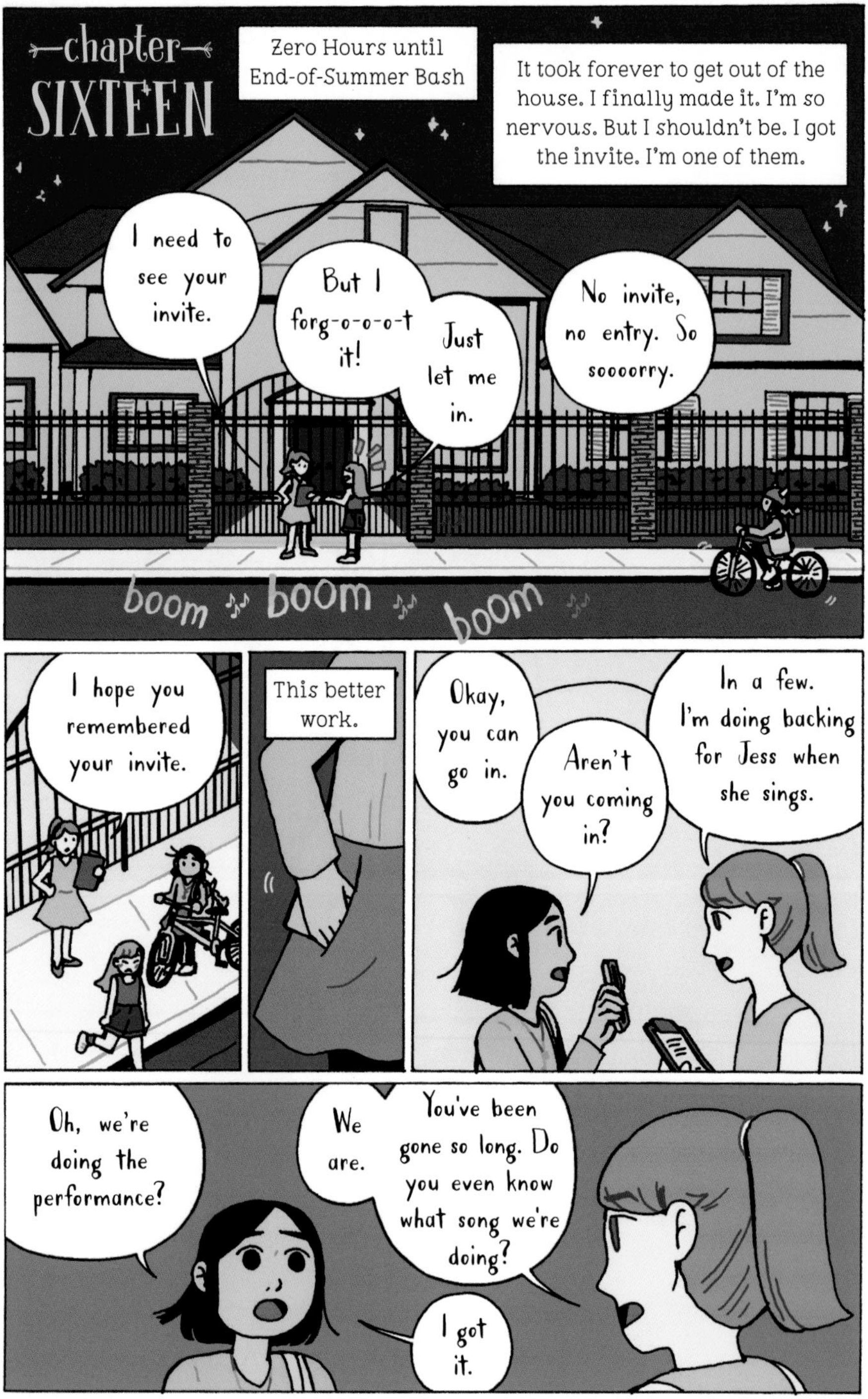

chapter SIXTEEN
Zero Hours until End-of-Summer Bash
It took forever to get out of the house. I finally made it. I'm so nervous. But I shouldn't be. I got the invite. I'm one of them.
I need to see your invite.
But I forg-o-o-o-t it!
Just let me in.
No invite, no entry. So sooooorry.
boom boom boom
I hope you remembered your invite.
This better work.
Okay, you can go in.
Aren't you coming in?
In a few. I'm doing backing for Jess when she sings.
Oh, we're doing the performance?
We are.
You've been gone so long. Do you even know what song we're doing?
I got it.

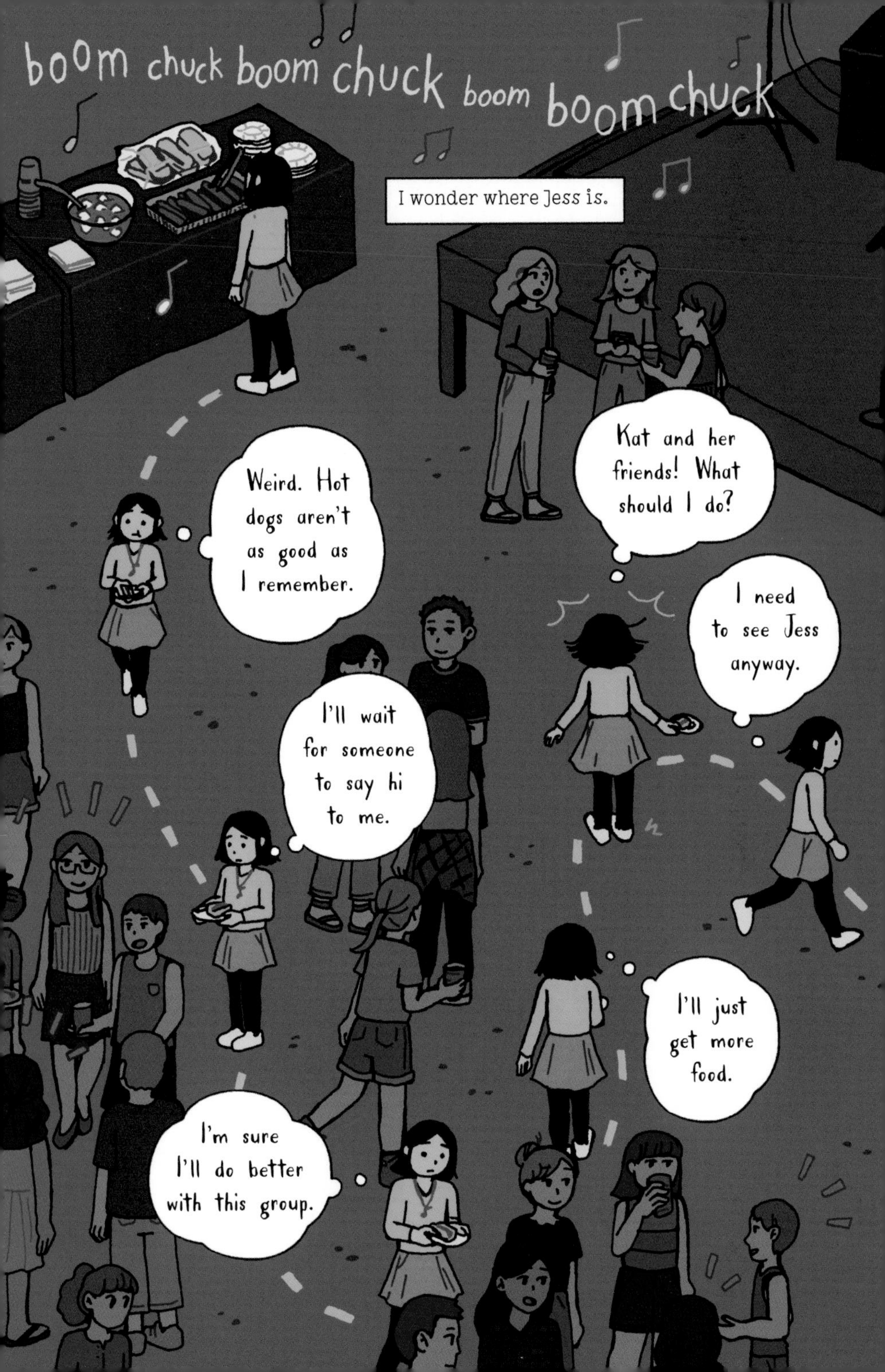
boom chuck boom chuck boom boom chuck
I wonder where Jess is.
Weird. Hot dogs aren't as good as I remember.
Kat and her friends! What should I do?
I need to see Jess anyway.
I'll wait for someone to say hi to me.
I'll just get more food.
I'm sure I'll do better with this group.

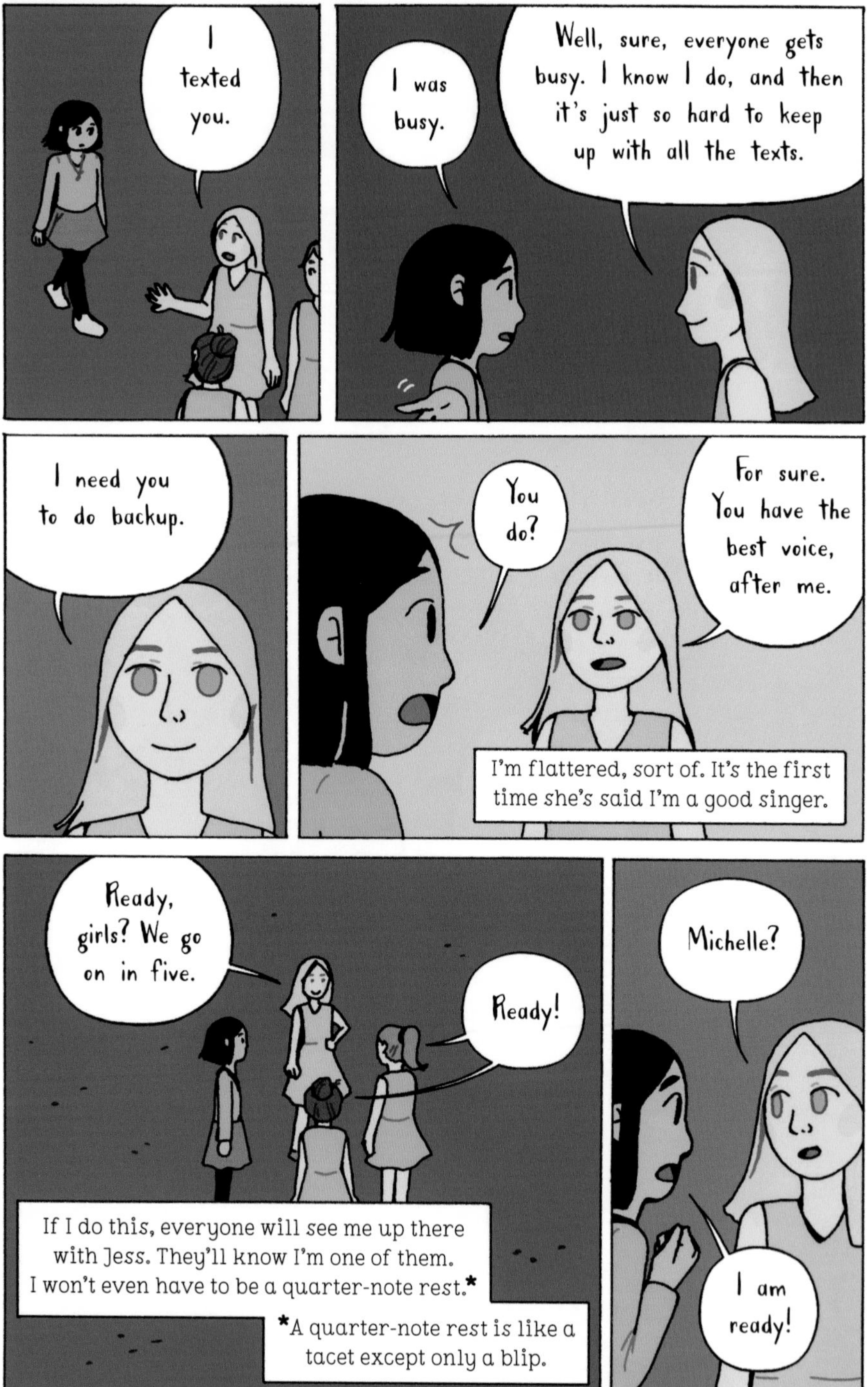
I texted you.
I was busy.
Well, sure, everyone gets busy. I know I do, and then it's just so hard to keep up with all the texts.
I need you to do backup.
You do?
For sure. You have the best voice, after me.
I'm flattered, sort of. It's the first time she's said I'm a good singer.
Ready, girls? We go on in five.
Ready!
If I do this, everyone will see me up there with Jess. They'll know I'm one of them. I won't even have to be a quarter-note rest.*
*A quarter-note rest is like a tacet except only a blip.
Michelle?
I am ready!

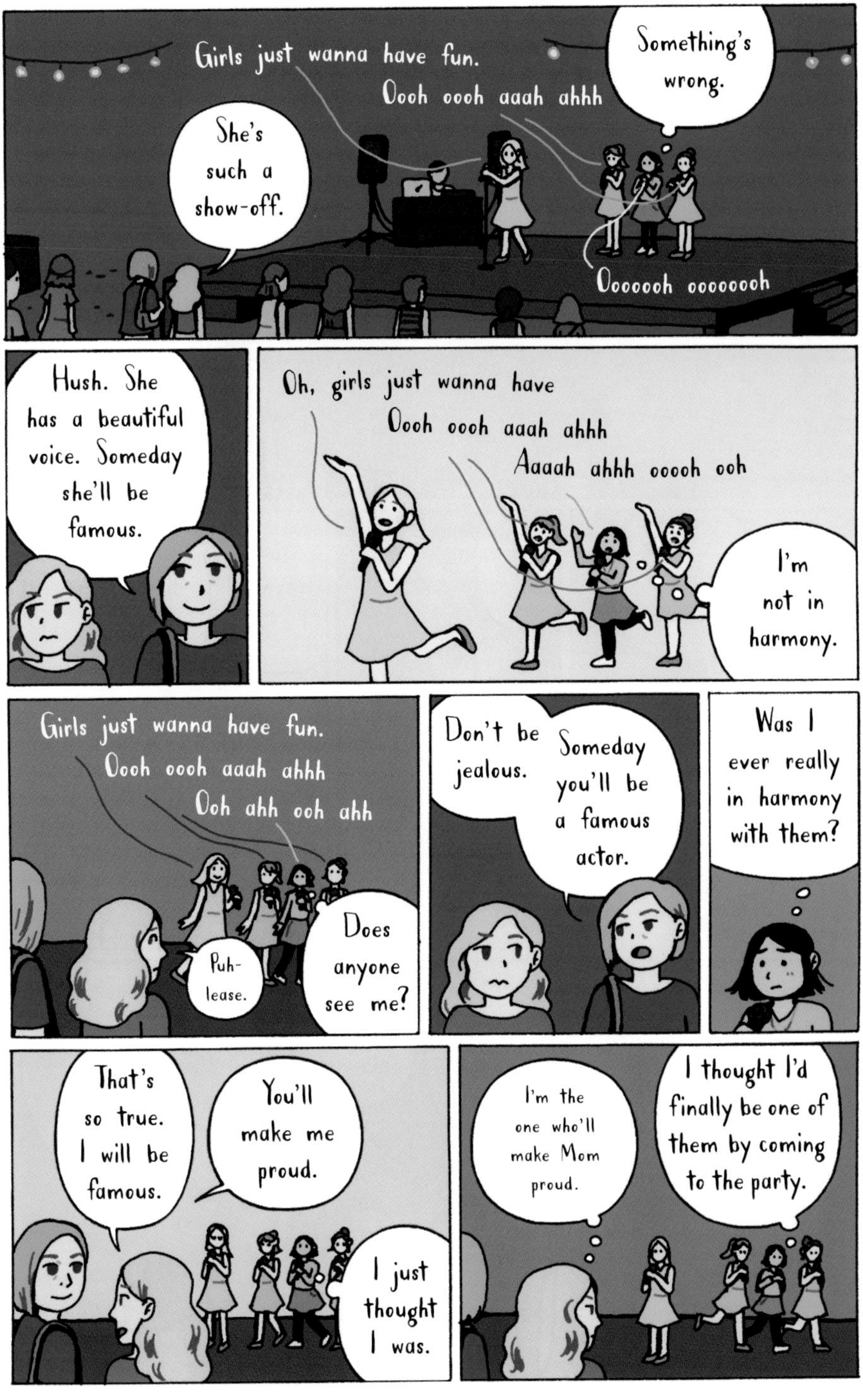
Girls just wanna have fun.
Oooh oooh aaah ahhh
Something's wrong.
She's such a show-off.
Ooooooh ooooooooh
Hush. She has a beautiful voice. Someday she'll be famous.
Oh, girls just wanna have
Oooh oooh aaah ahhh
Aaaah ahhh ooooh ooh
I'm not in harmony.
Girls just wanna have fun.
Oooh oooh aaah ahhh
Ooh ahh ooh ahh
Puh-lease.
Does anyone see me?
Don't be jealous.
Someday you'll be a famous actor.
Was I ever really in harmony with them?
That's so true. I will be famous.
You'll make me proud.
I just thought I was.
I'm the one who'll make Mom proud.
I thought I'd finally be one of them by coming to the party.

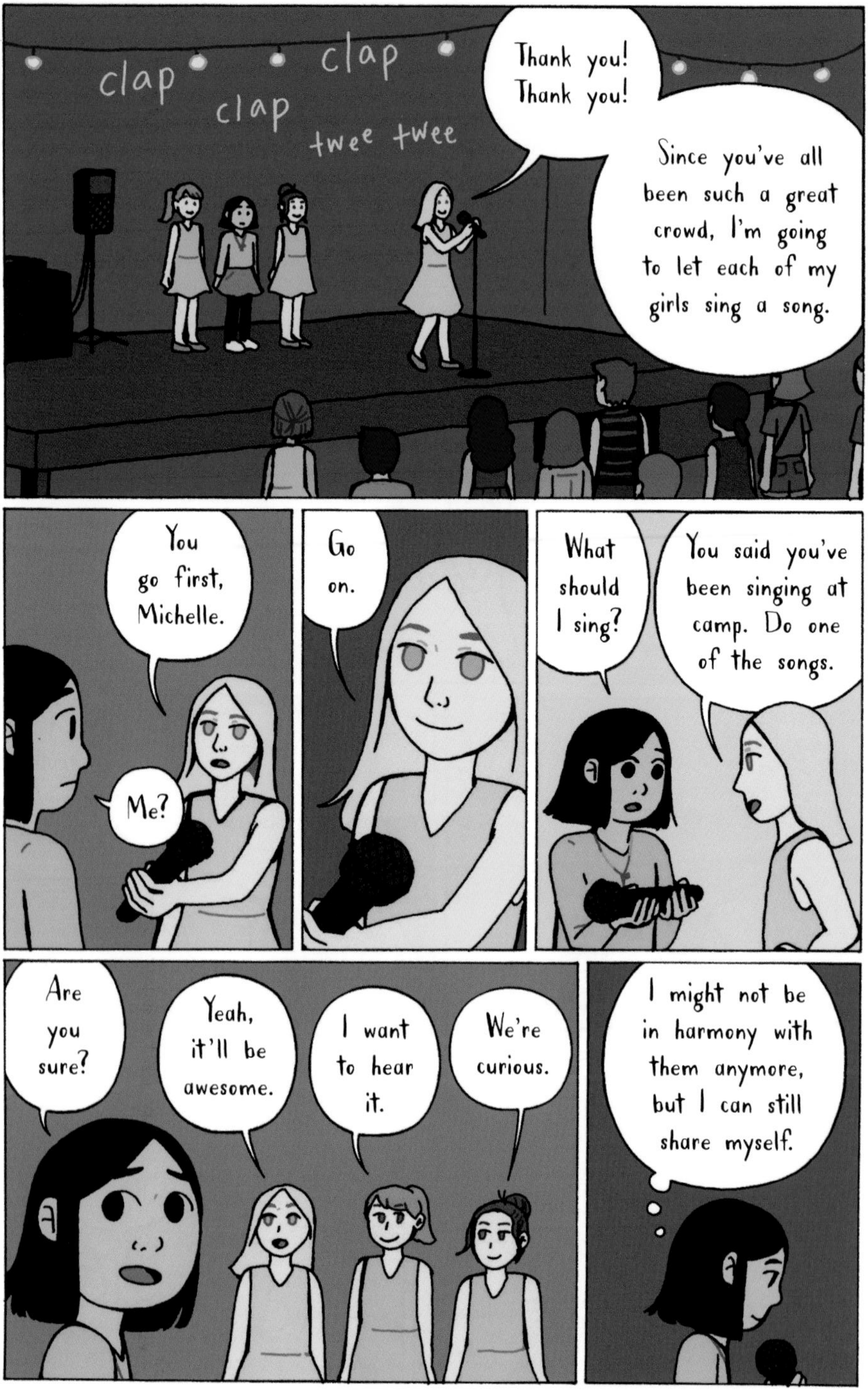
clap
clap
clap
twee twee
Thank you! Thank you!
Since you've all been such a great crowd, I'm going to let each of my girls sing a song.
You go first, Michelle.
Me?
Go on.
What should I sing?
You said you've been singing at camp. Do one of the songs.
Are you sure?
Yeah, it'll be awesome.
I want to hear it.
We're curious.
I might not be in harmony with them anymore, but I can still share myself.

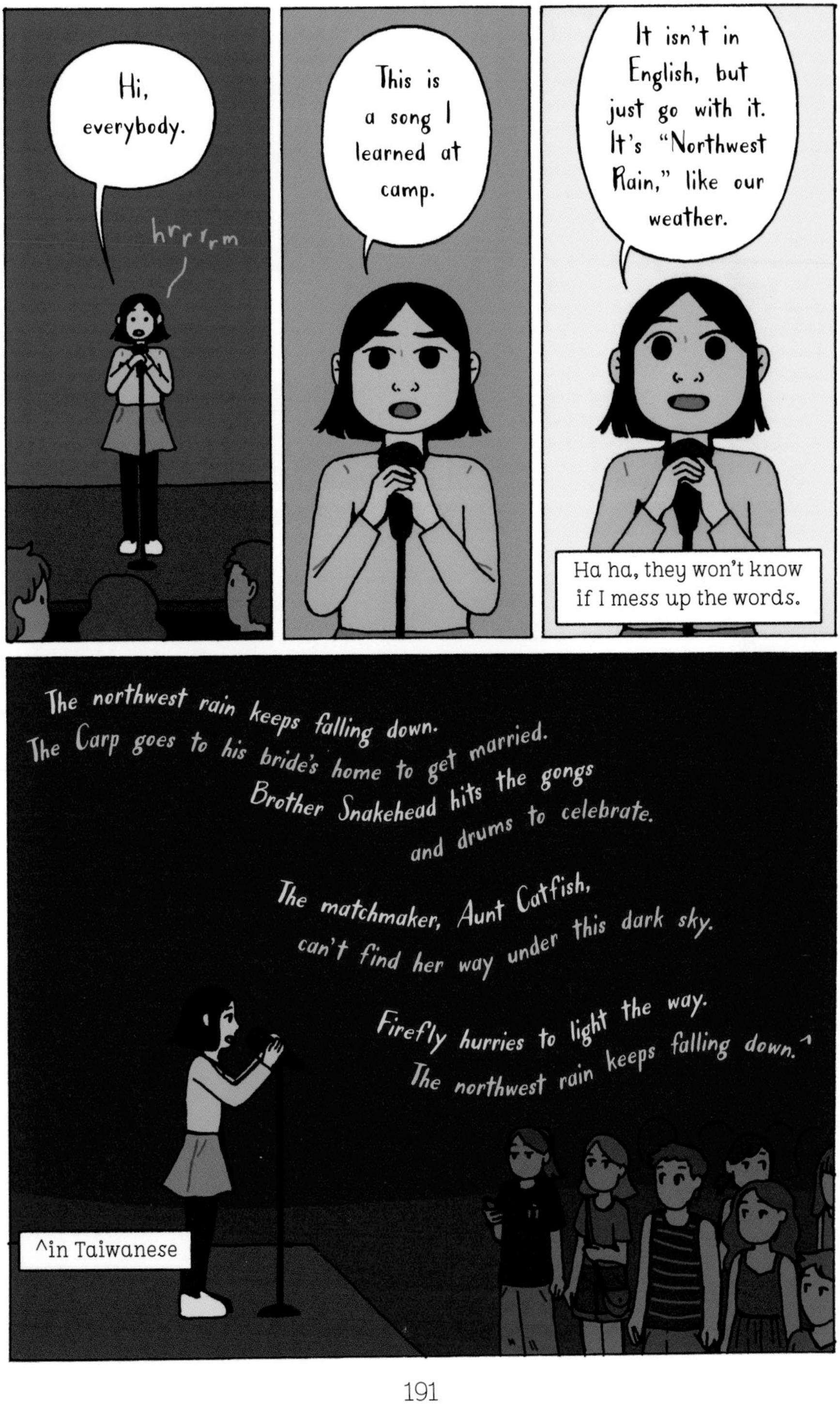
Hi, everybody.
hrrrrm
This is a song I learned at camp.
It isn't in English, but just go with it. It's "Northwest Rain," like our weather.
Ha ha, they won't know if I mess up the words.
The northwest rain keeps falling down.
The Carp goes to his bride's home to get married.
Brother Snakehead hits the gongs and drums to celebrate.
The matchmaker, Aunt Catfish, can't find her way under this dark sky.
Firefly hurries to light the way.
The northwest rain keeps falling down.^
^in Taiwanese

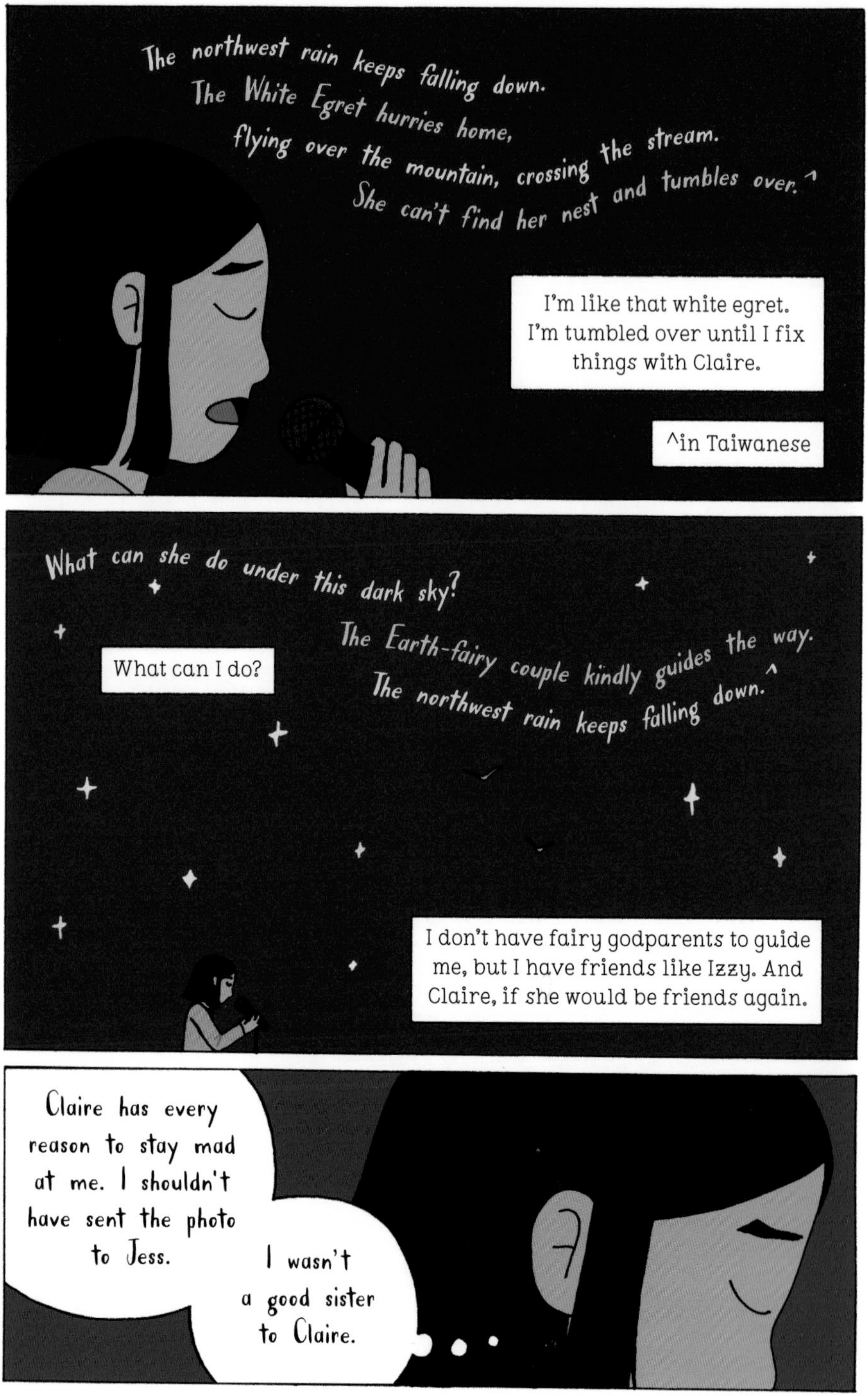
The northwest rain keeps falling down.
The White Egret hurries home,
flying over the mountain, crossing the stream.
She can't find her nest and tumbles over.^
I'm like that white egret. I'm tumbled over until I fix things with Claire.
^in Taiwanese
What can she do under this dark sky?
What can I do?
The Earth-fairy couple kindly guides the way.
The northwest rain keeps falling down.^
I don't have fairy godparents to guide me, but I have friends like Izzy. And Claire, if she would be friends again.
Claire has every reason to stay mad at me. I shouldn't have sent the photo to Jess.
I wasn't a good sister to Claire.

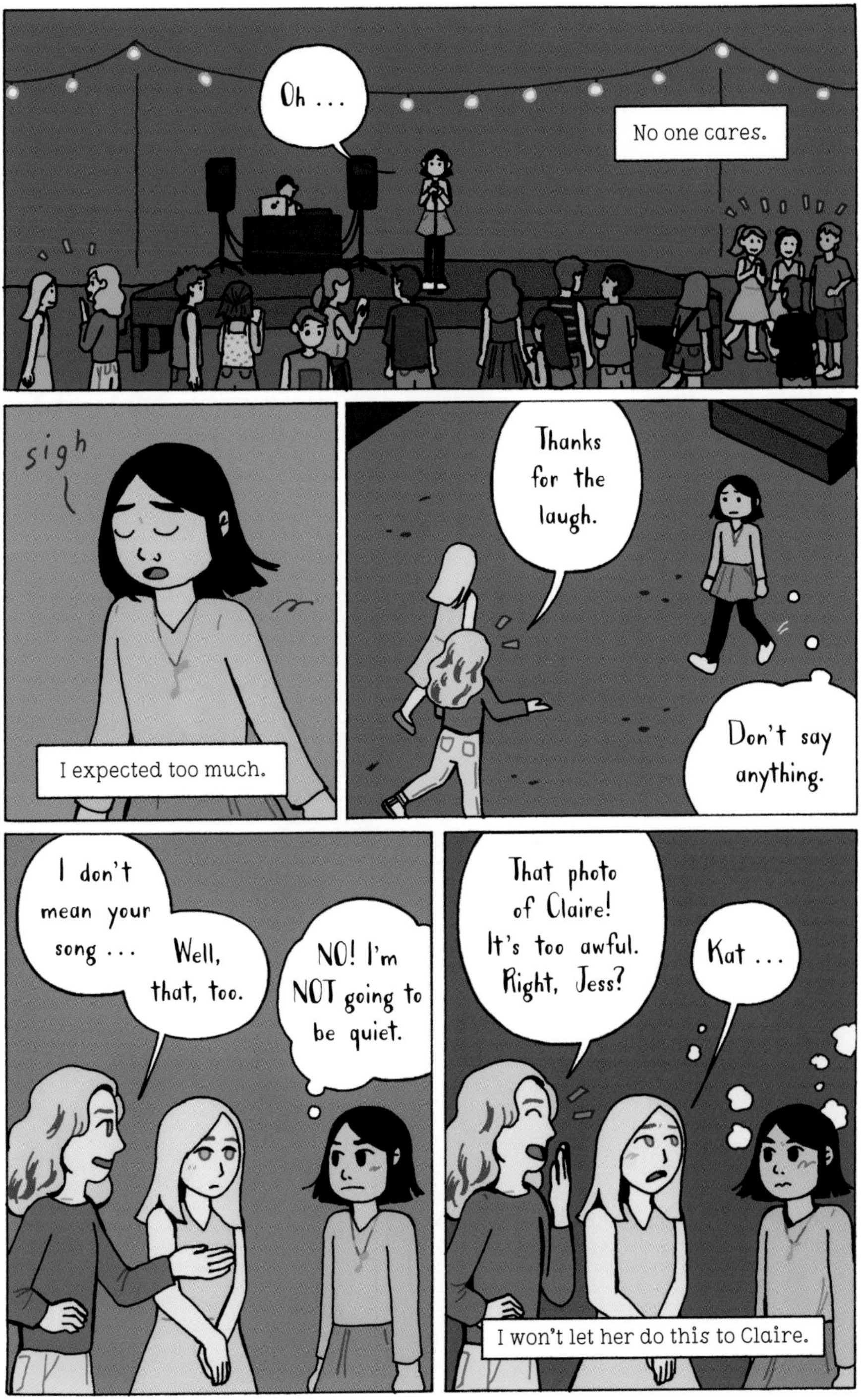
Oh . . .
No one cares.
sigh
I expected too much.
Thanks for the laugh.
Don't say anything.
I don't mean your song . . .
Well, that, too.
NO! I'm NOT going to be quiet.
That photo of Claire! It's too awful. Right, Jess?
Kat . . .
I won't let her do this to Claire.

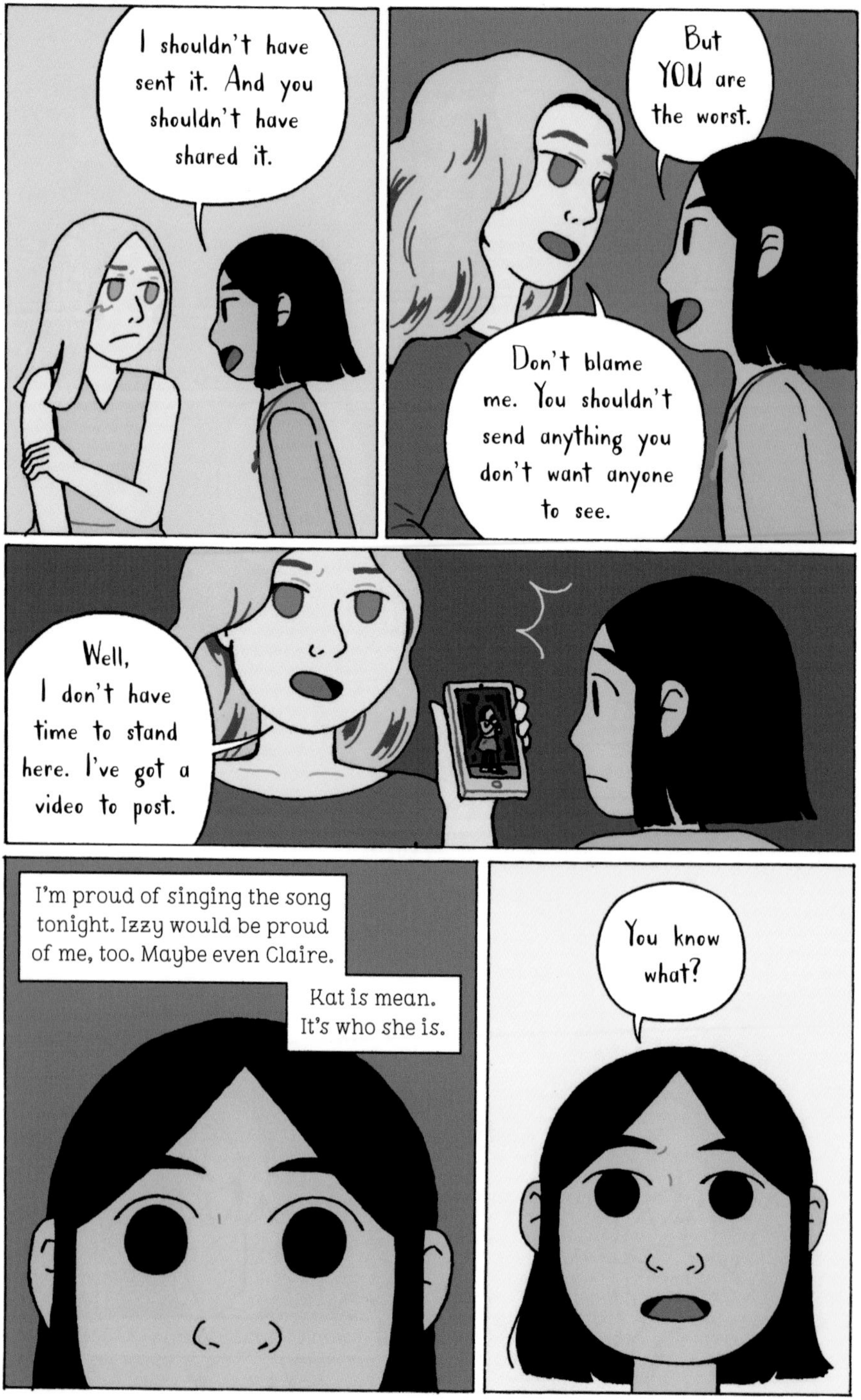

I shouldn't have sent it. And you shouldn't have shared it.
But YOU are the worst.
Don't blame me. You shouldn't send anything you don't want anyone to see.
Well, I don't have time to stand here. I've got a video to post.
I'm proud of singing the song tonight. Izzy would be proud of me, too. Maybe even Claire.
Kat is mean. It's who she is.
You know what?

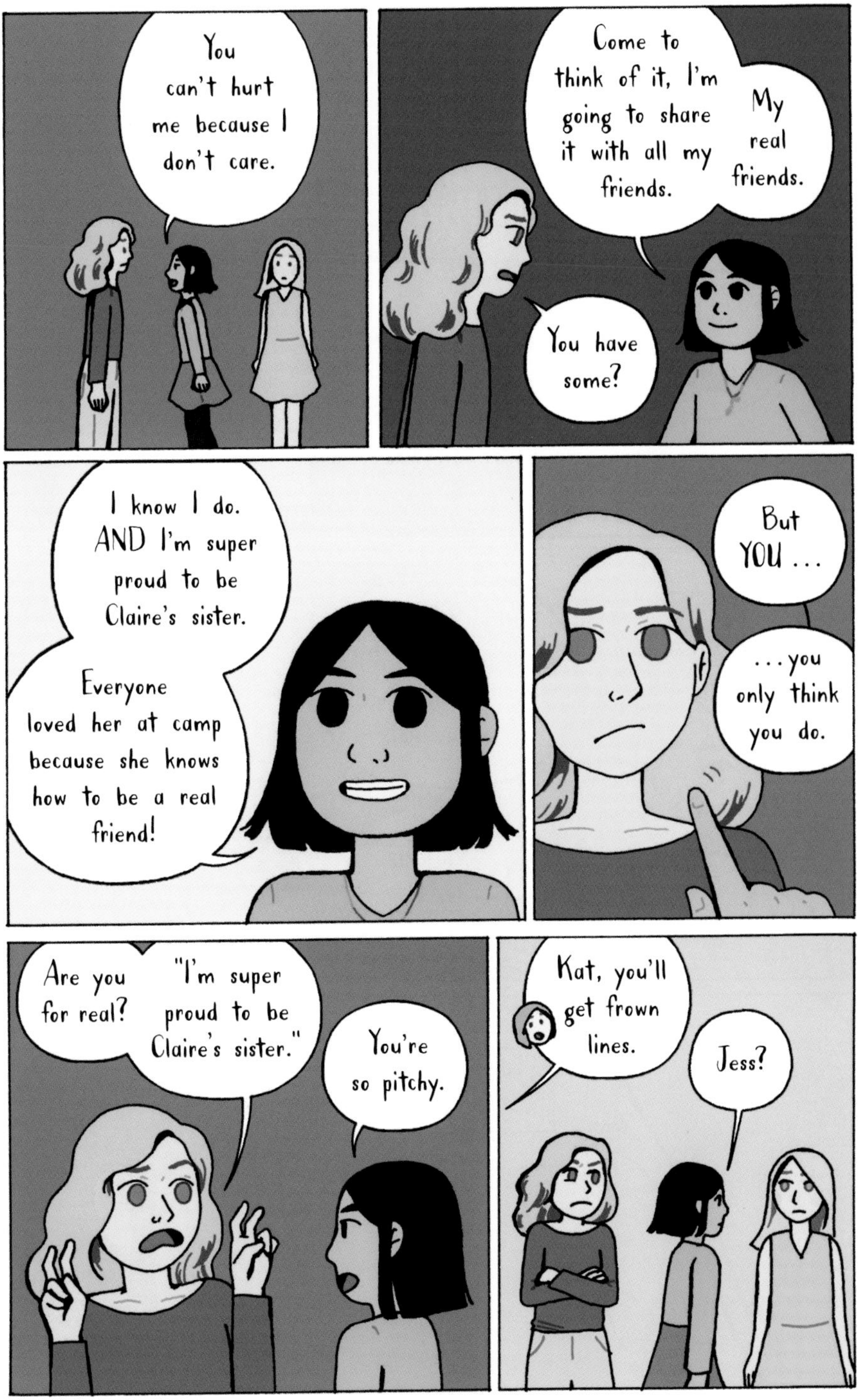
You can't hurt me because I don't care.
Come to think of it, I'm going to share it with all my friends.
My real friends.
You have some?
I know I do. AND I'm super proud to be Claire's sister.
Everyone loved her at camp because she knows how to be a real friend!
But YOU ...
...you only think you do.
Are you for real?
"I'm super proud to be Claire's sister."
You're so pitchy.
Kat, you'll get frown lines.
Jess?

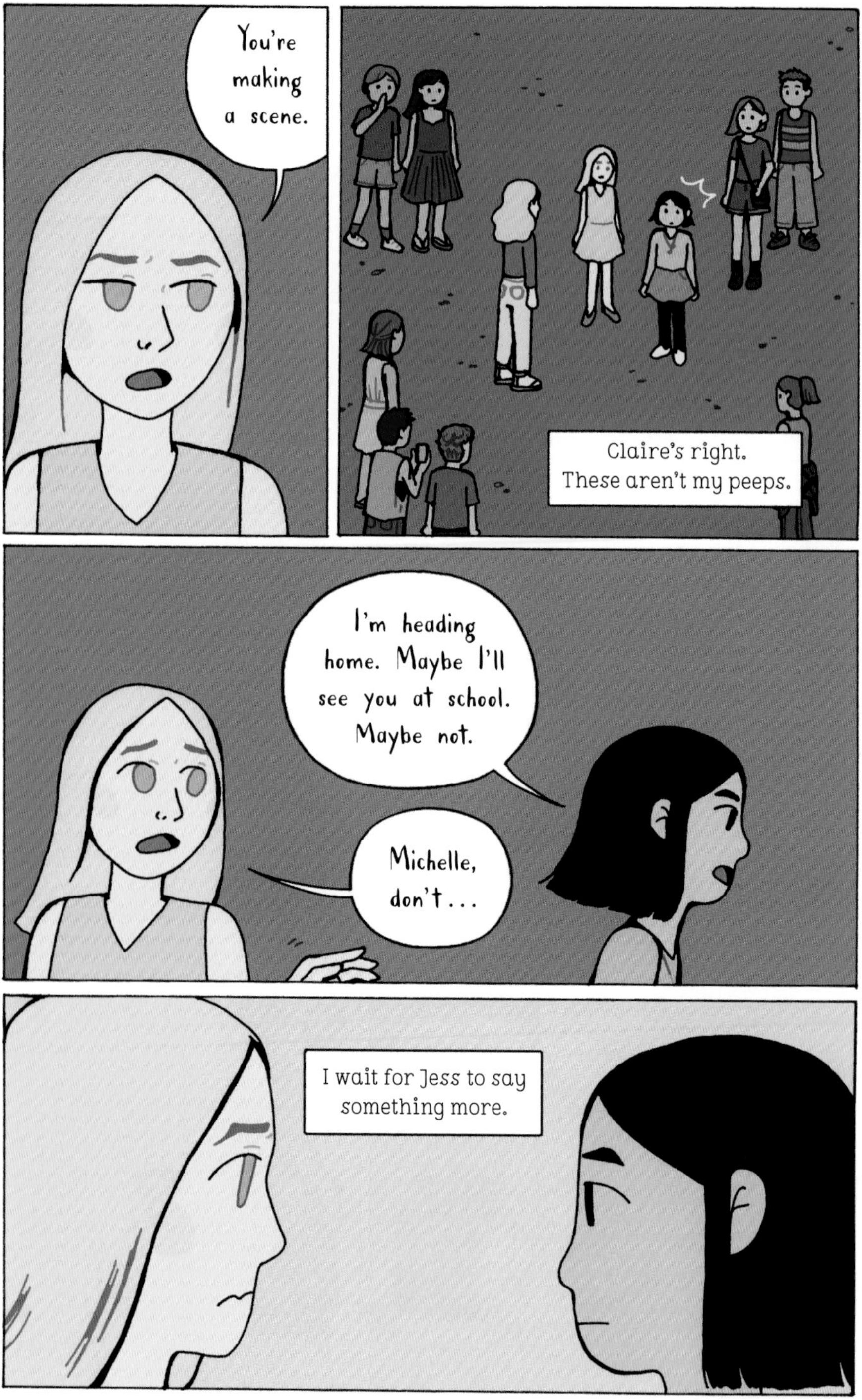
You're making a scene.
Claire's right. These aren't my peeps.
I'm heading home. Maybe I'll see you at school. Maybe not.
Michelle, don't...
I wait for Jess to say something more.

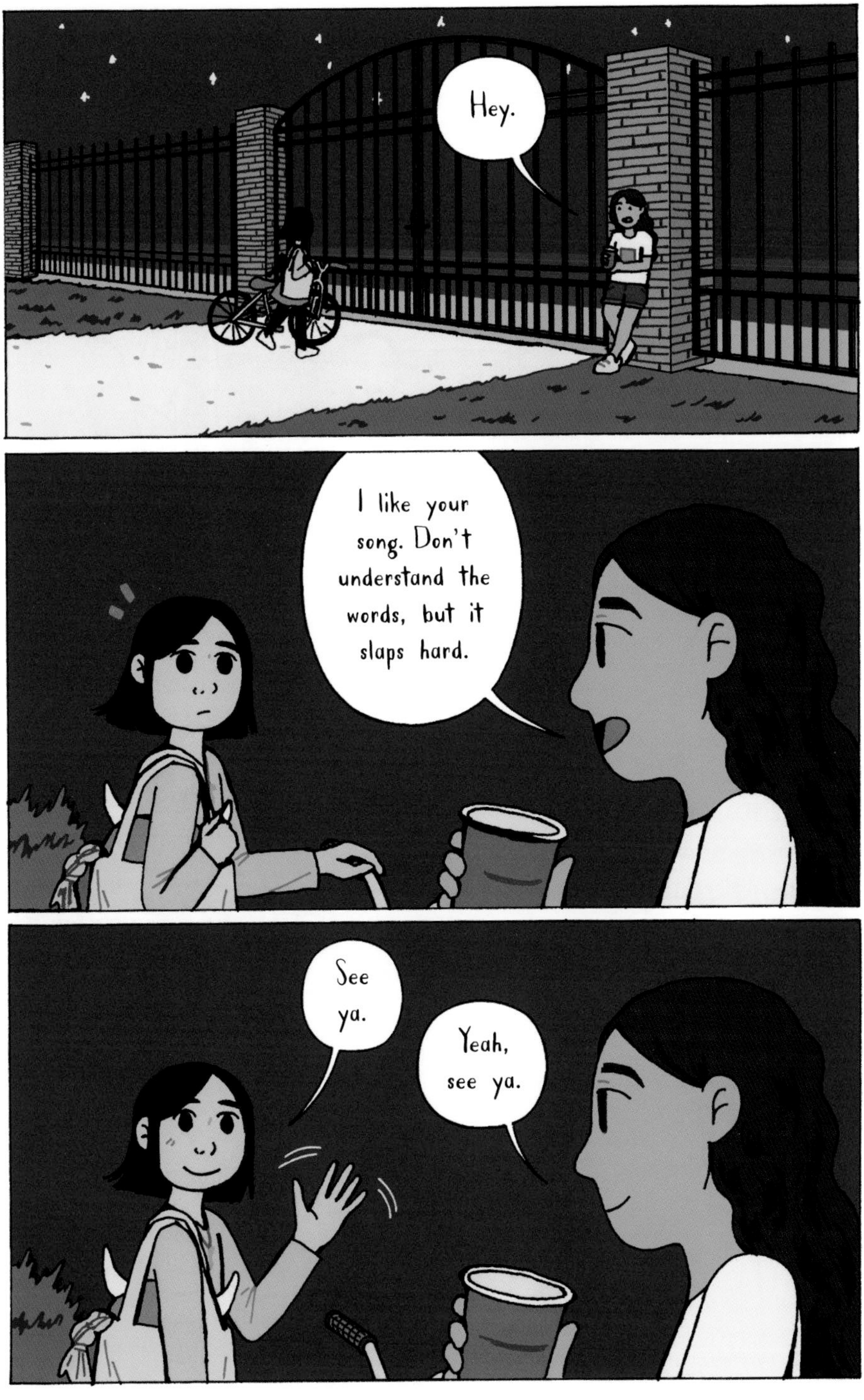
Hey.
I like your song. Don't understand the words, but it slaps hard.
See ya.
Yeah, see ya.

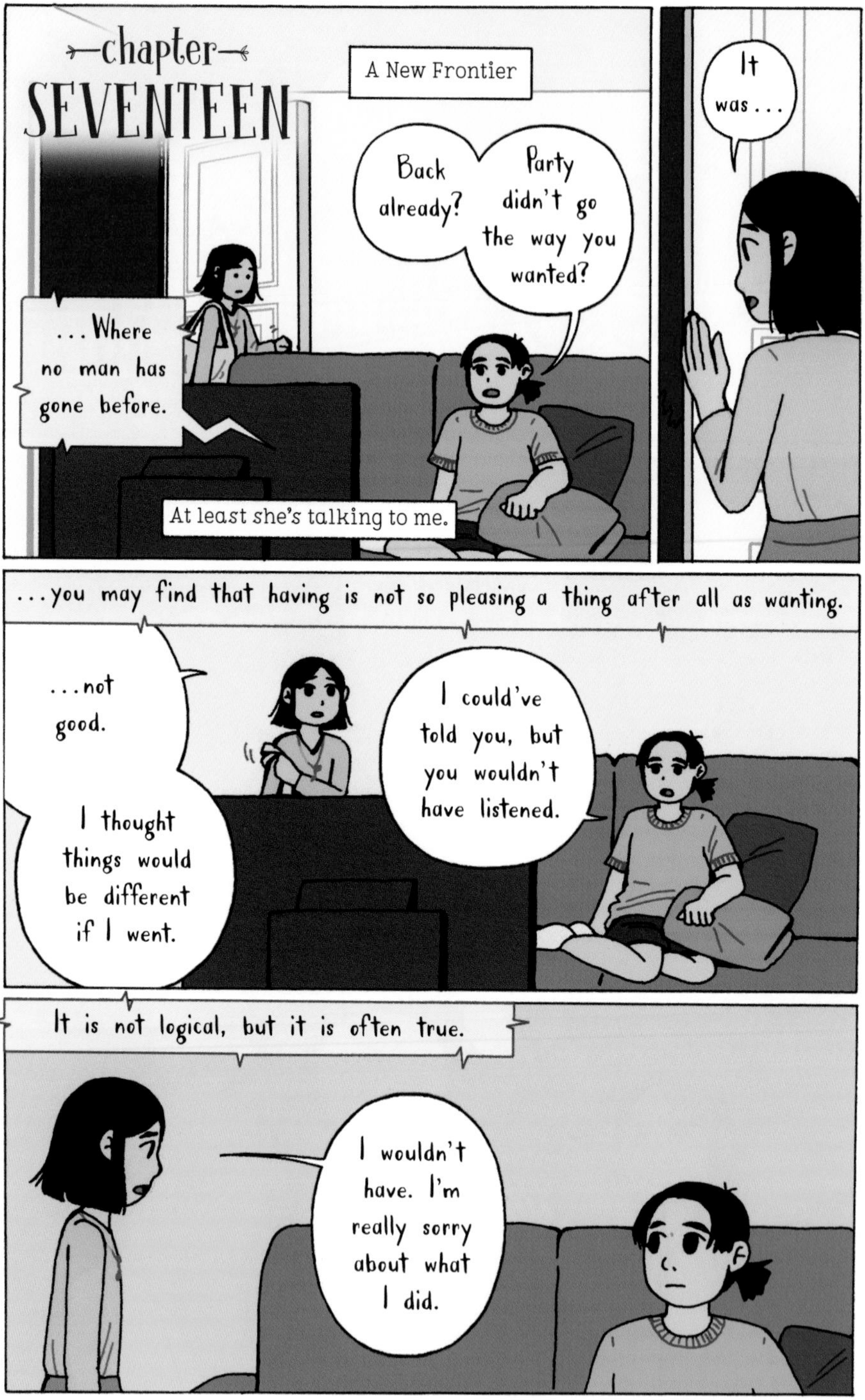
chapter SEVENTEEN
A New Frontier
...Where no man has gone before.
At least she's talking to me.
Back already?
Party didn't go the way you wanted?
It was...
...you may find that having is not so pleasing a thing after all as wanting.
...not good.
I thought things would be different if I went.
I could've told you, but you wouldn't have listened.
It is not logical, but it is often true.
I wouldn't have. I'm really sorry about what I did.

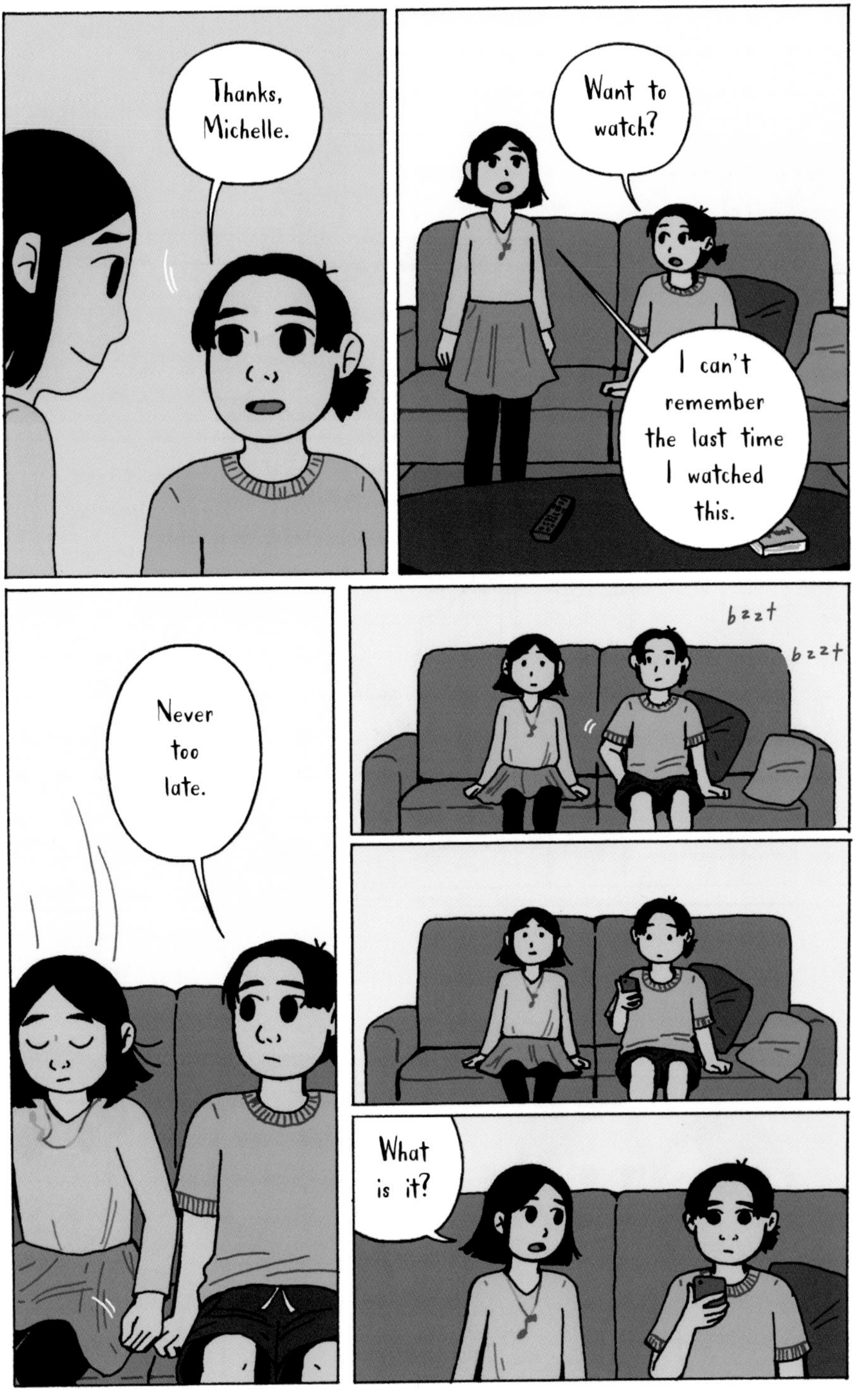
Thanks, Michelle.
Want to watch?
I can't remember the last time I watched this.
Never too late.
bzzt
bzzt
What is it?

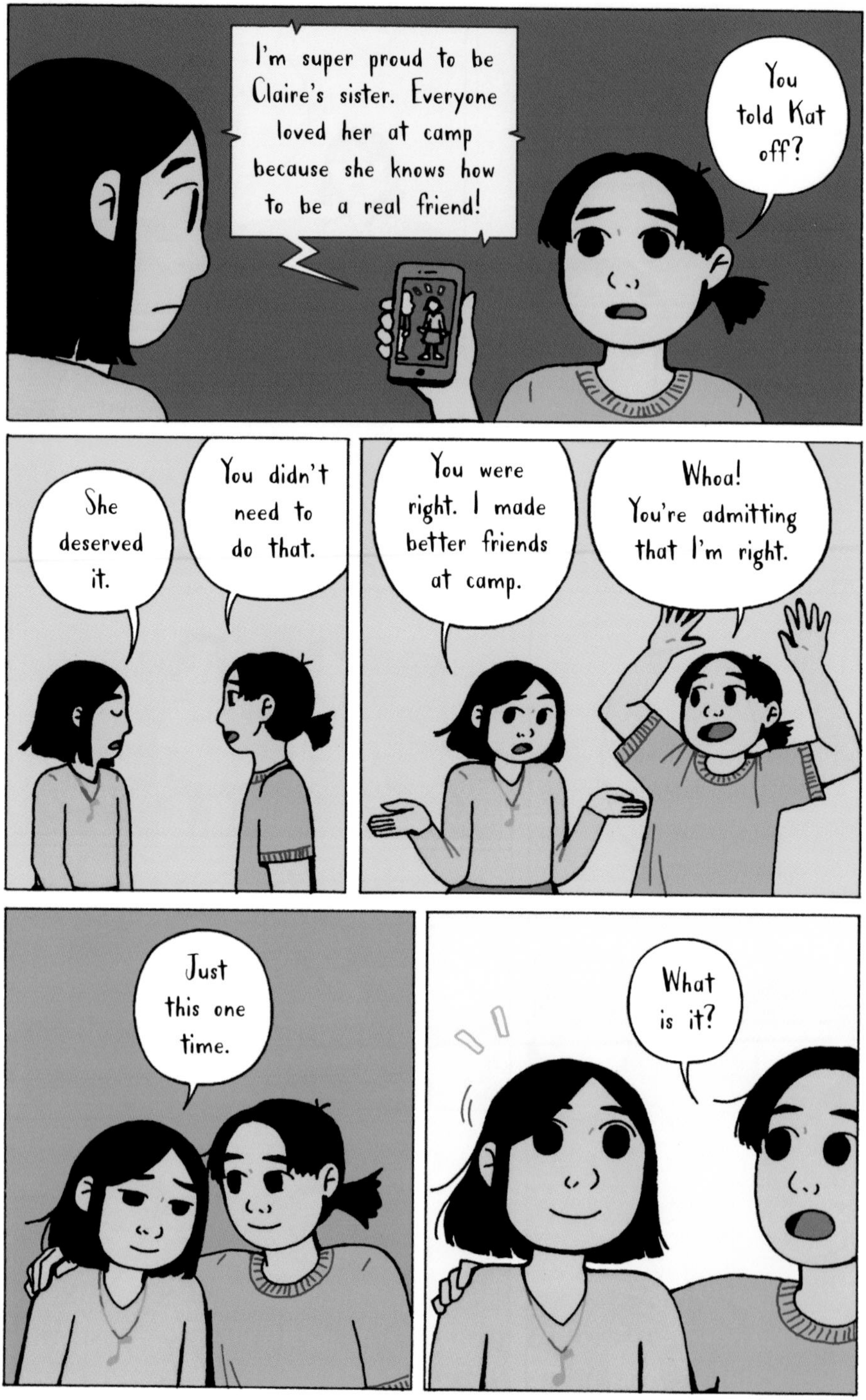
I'm super proud to be Claire's sister. Everyone loved her at camp because she knows how to be a real friend!
You told Kat off?
She deserved it.
You didn't need to do that.
You were right. I made better friends at camp.
Whoa! You're admitting that I'm right.
Just this one time.
What is it?

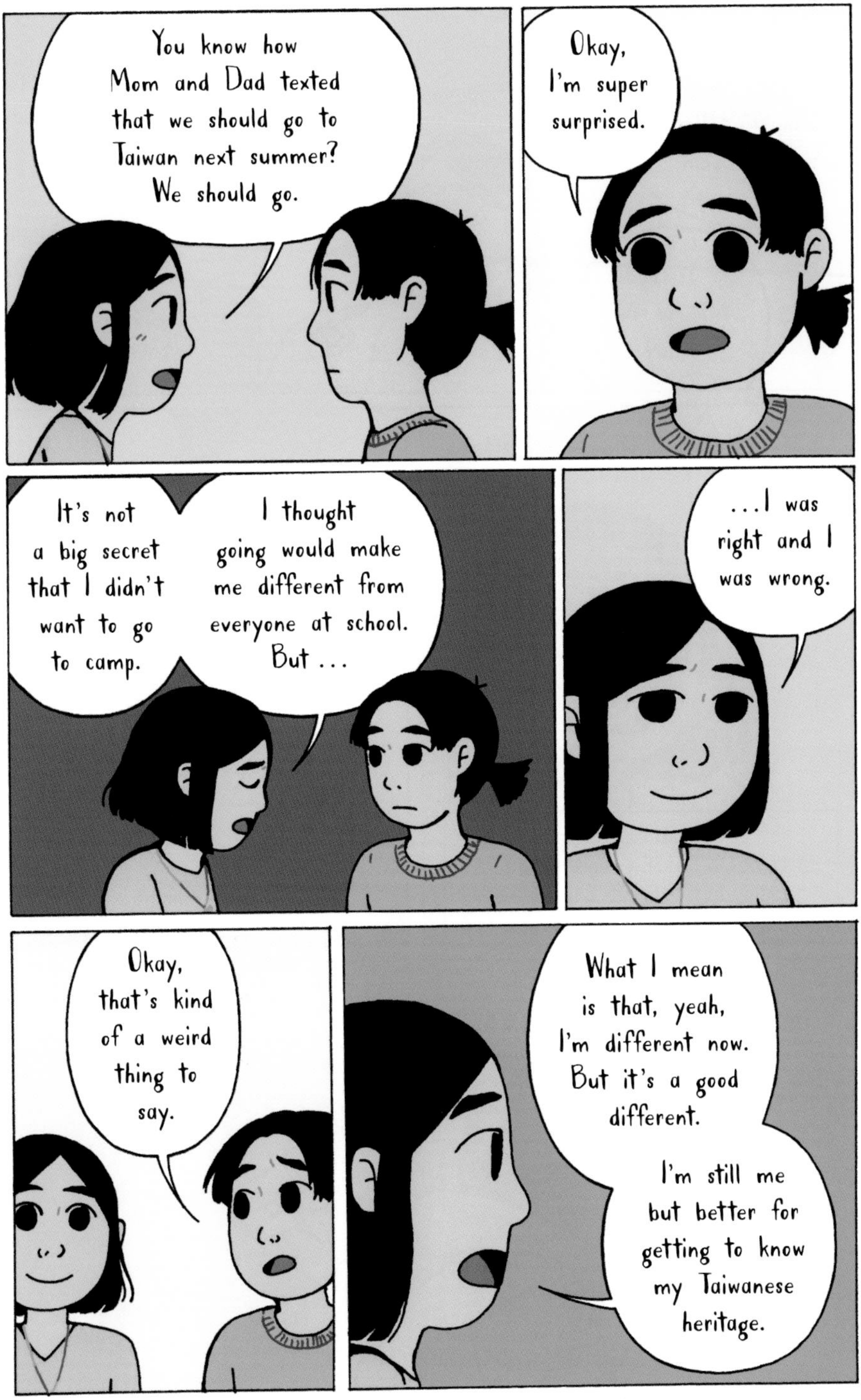
You know how Mom and Dad texted that we should go to Taiwan next summer? We should go.
Okay, I'm super surprised.
It's not a big secret that I didn't want to go to camp.
I thought going would make me different from everyone at school. But ...
...I was right and I was wrong.
Okay, that's kind of a weird thing to say.
What I mean is that, yeah, I'm different now. But it's a good different.
I'm still me but better for getting to know my Taiwanese heritage.

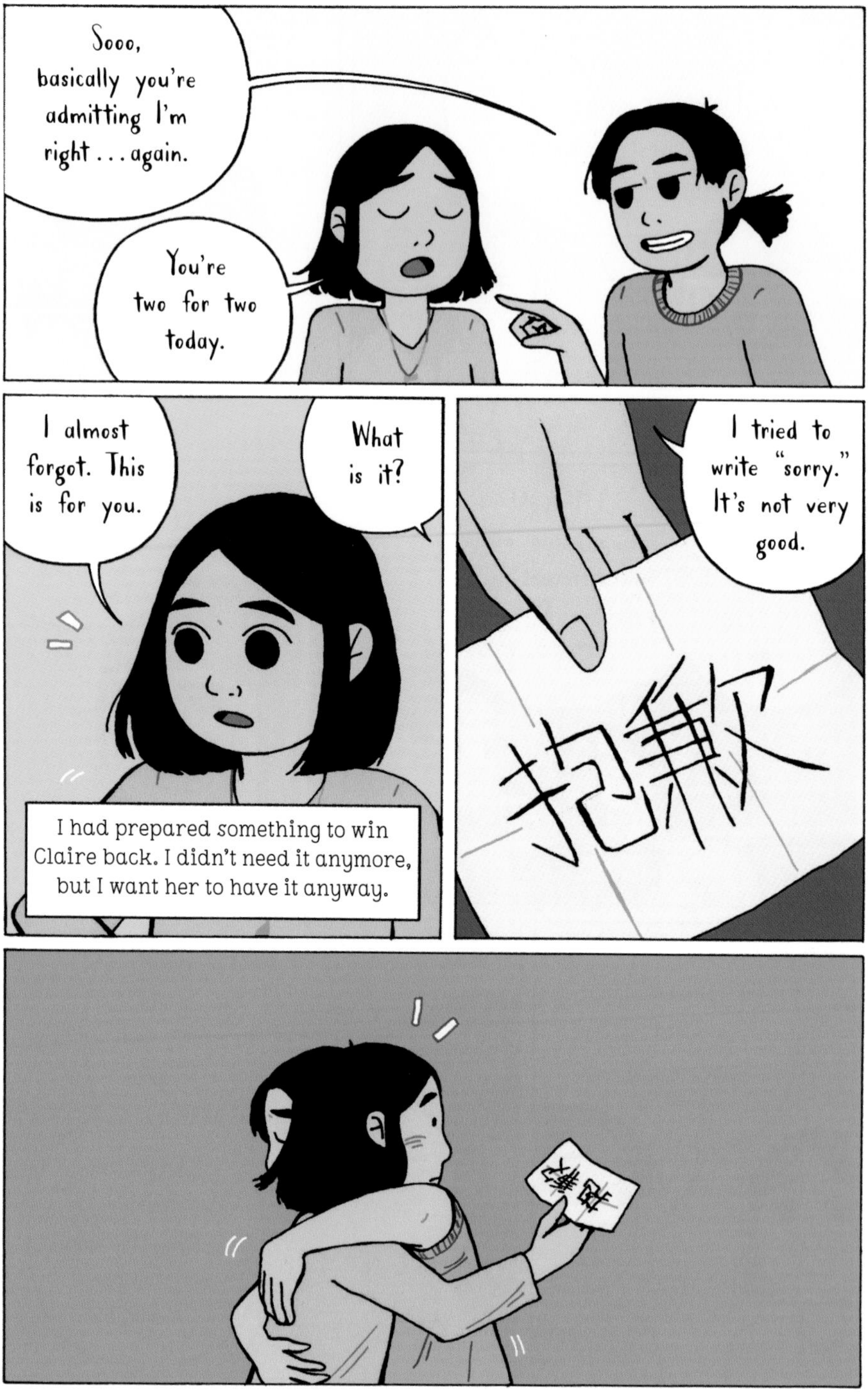
Sooo, basically you're admitting I'm right . . . again.
You're two for two today.
I almost forgot. This is for you.
What is it?
I had prepared something to win Claire back. I didn't need it anymore, but I want her to have it anyway.
I tried to write "sorry." It's not very good.
抱歉

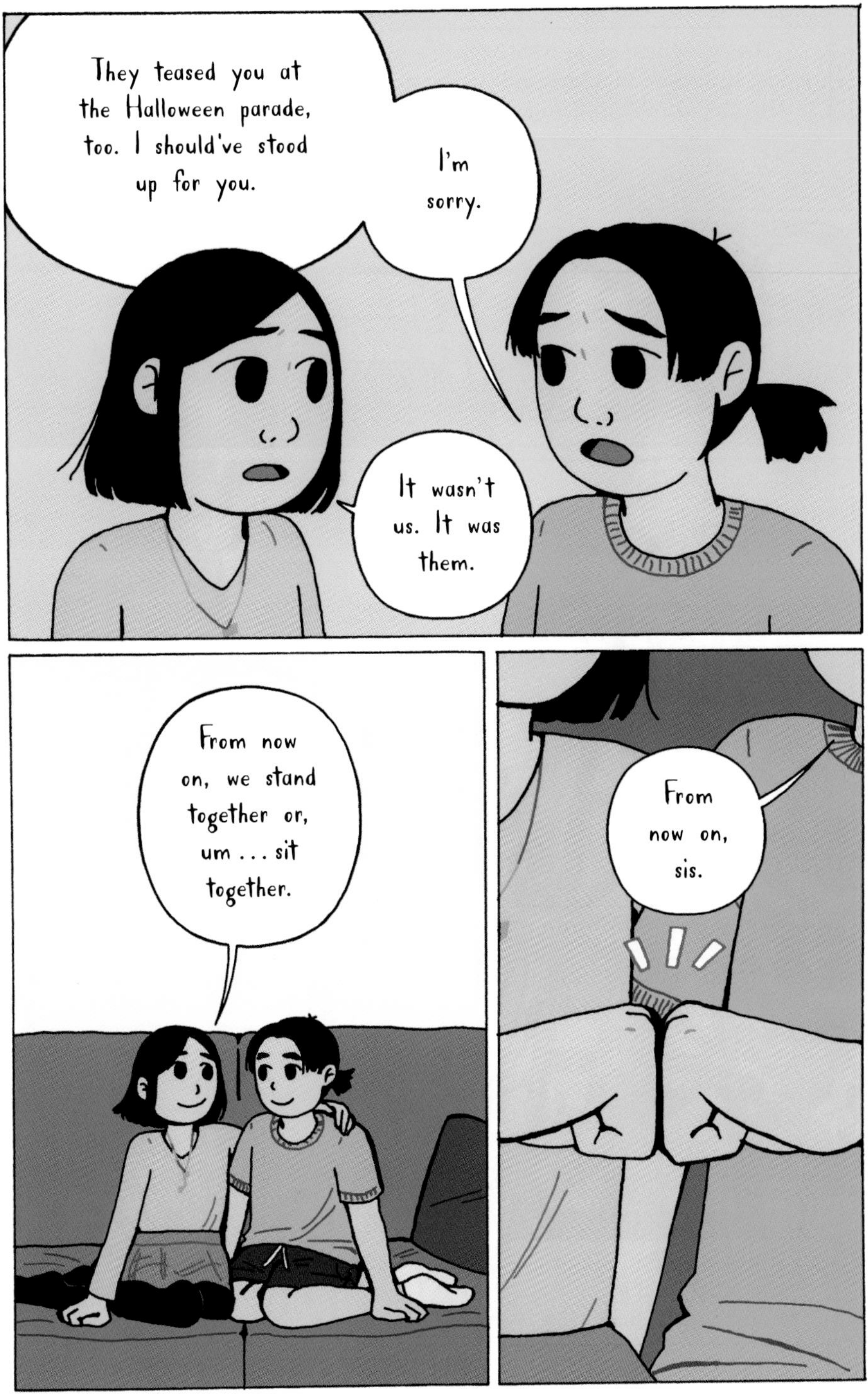
They teased you at the Halloween parade, too. I should've stood up for you.
I'm sorry.
It wasn't us. It was them.
From now on, we stand together or, um . . . sit together.
From now on, sis.

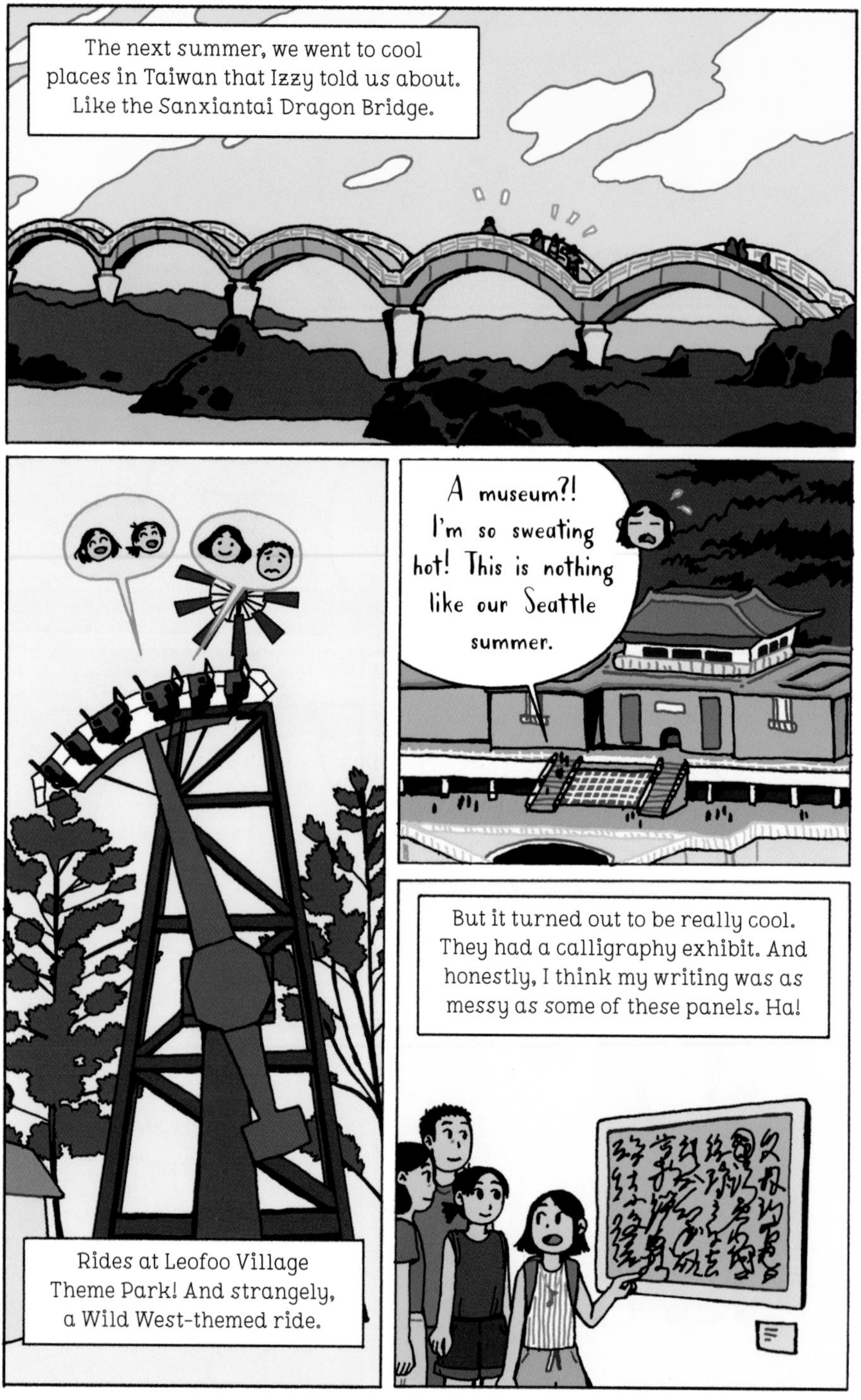
The next summer, we went to cool places in Taiwan that Izzy told us about. Like the Sanxiantai Dragon Bridge.
Rides at Leofoo Village Theme Park! And strangely, a Wild West-themed ride.
A museum?! I'm so sweating hot! This is nothing like our Seattle summer.
But it turned out to be really cool. They had a calligraphy exhibit. And honestly, I think my writing was as messy as some of these panels. Ha!

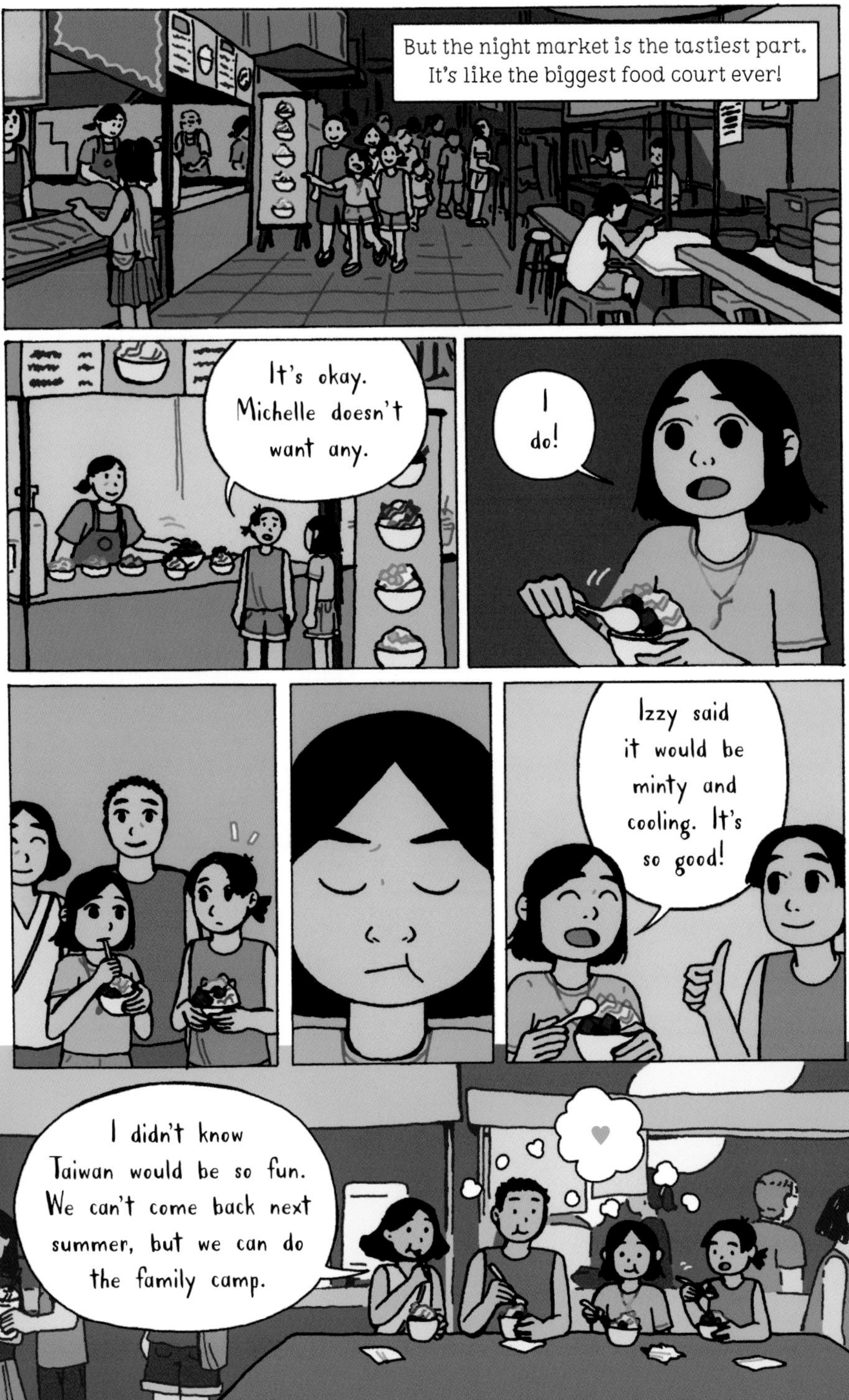

But the night market is the tastiest part. It's like the biggest food court ever!
It's okay. Michelle doesn't want any.
I do!
Izzy said it would be minty and cooling. It's so good!
I didn't know Taiwan would be so fun. We can't come back next summer, but we can do the family camp.

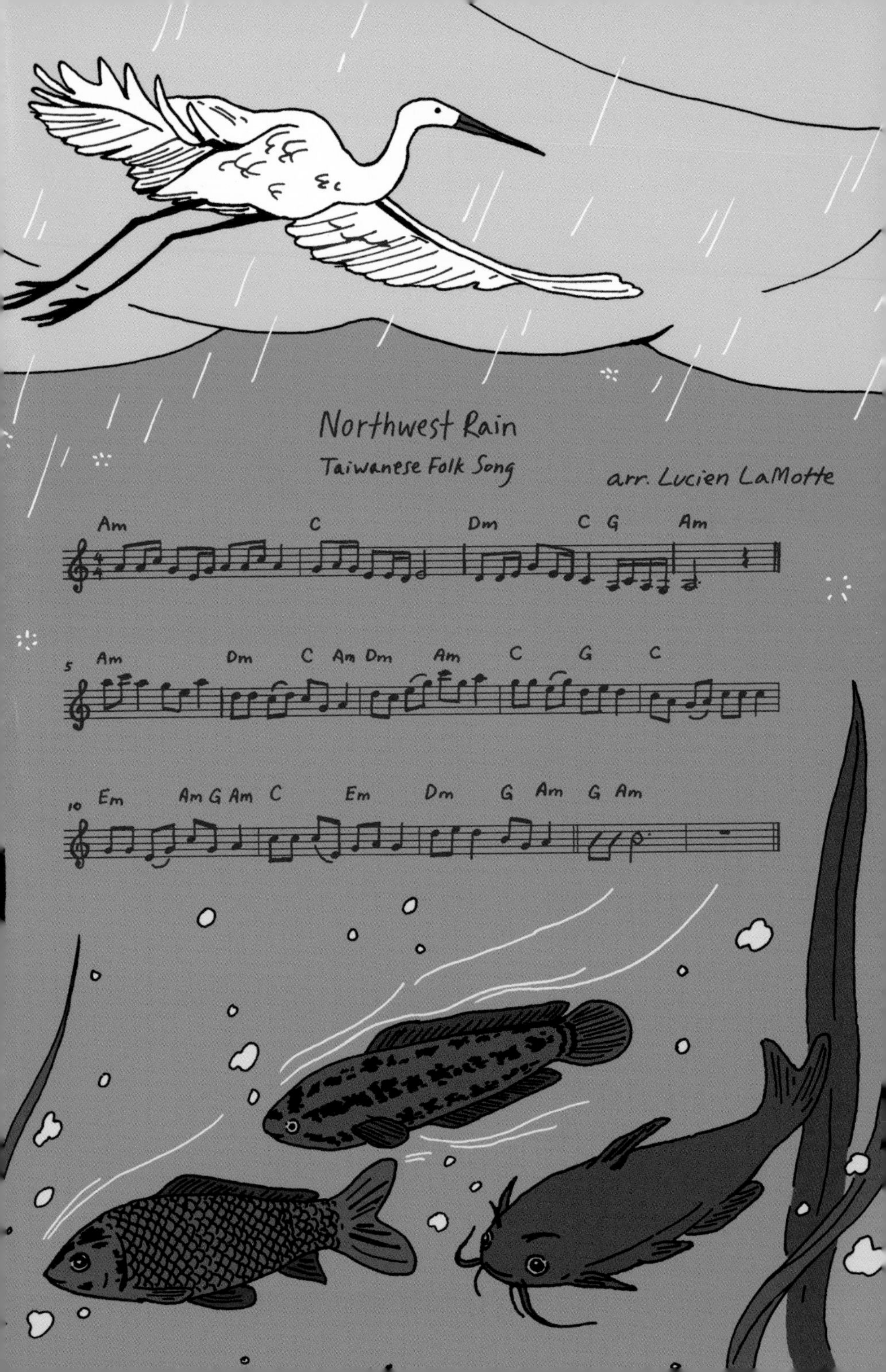

Northwest Rain
Taiwanese Folk Song
arr. Lucien LaMotte
Am C Dm C G Am
5 Am Dm C Am Dm Am C G C
10 Em Am G Am C Em Dm G Am G Am

To Akong for your help on all things Taiwanese.
To my critique partners and beta readers, whose generosity
in time and attention made this book possible.
Thank you, thank you, thank you.
—L. L. M.

For my parents and sister.
—A. X.

HarperAlley is an imprint of HarperCollins Publishers.

Unhappy Camper
Text copyright © 2024 by Lily LaMotte
Illustrations copyright © 2024 by Ann Xu
Colors by Sunmi
For information address HarperCollins Children's Books, a division of
HarperCollins Publishers, 195 Broadway, New York, NY 10007.
www.harperalley.com

Library of Congress Control Number: 2021949283
ISBN 978-0-06-297390-0 — ISBN 978-0-06-297389-4 (pbk.)

The artist used ink on paper and Adobe Photoshop to
create the digital illustrations for this book.
Typography by Erica De Chavez Wong

24 25 26 27 28   GPS   10 9 8 7 6 5 4 3 2 1

First Edition